Penguin Books
Overdraft on Glory

Claud Cockburn was born in Peking, China, in 1904 and educated at the Universities of Oxford, Budapest and Berlin. In 1929, he became a correspondent of *The Times* in New York and Washington. But after four years he resigned from *The Times* in order to found his news-sheet *The Week*, which attained a high degree of notoriety. During the same period he fought for the Republic in Spain and was Diplomatic Correspondent of the *Daily Worker*. Since moving to Ireland in 1947, he has written three novels and three volumes of autobiography, besides innumerable short stories and articles for the *New Statesman*, *Punch*, the *Saturday Evening Post*, *Hibernia*, and *Private Eye*. His novel *Beat the Devil* was filmed under the direction of John Huston. *I Claud . . .*, which is available in Penguins, is taken from the three well-known autobiographical volumes, *In Time of Trouble*, *Crossing the Line*, and *View from the West*, together with a final section bringing his autobiography up to date.

Claud Cockburn

Overdraft on Glory

Penguin Books

Penguin Books Ltd, Harmondsworth,
Middlesex, England
Penguin Books Australia Ltd, Ringwood,
Victoria, Australia

First published by T. V. Boardman & Co. 1955
under the pseudonym of James Helvick
Published, with revisions, in Penguin Books 1971

Made and printed in Great Britain by
Richard Clay (The Chaucer Press) Ltd,
Bungay, Suffolk
Set in Linotype Times

1

It seems to me – not too absurdly I think – significant that my first awareness of Grant Foraker should have taken the form of an intrusive, insistent disturbance: the row, specifically, of a voice, vibrant with urgency, calling out in Anglo-French, '*Ner coupay par!* Operator! *Ner coupay par*, for God's sake!' on the other side of the excessively thin wall of an hotel bedroom.

The hotel, the old Excelsior, was then the newest and reputedly finest in Marseilles. Long years later, some time in the 1930s, I read that the proprietor had been arrested for setting light to it in order to collect the insurance. It had burned like dry shavings. I was not surprised. I knew it was jerry-built within an hour of taking a room there – in 1908.

That was an extravagance, but I was tired and nineteen. And I had been seasick all the way from Barcelona.

I was beginning to feel reposed and drowsy after the sea-tossing when this voice, powerful rather than actually loud, vibrated violently just behind my head, and brought me full awake again. '*Ner coupay par!* Operator! For God's sake!' And then, on a louder note of exasperation – the shout of a person who thinks that an uncomprehending foreigner must be deaf – 'I said *don't* cut me off, Operator!' And then, 'Hell! Hell!' Without being abated, the voice now switched direction, addressing, by the sound of it, someone at the far end of a very big room, or in another room altogether. It abused, in English, the French telephone system.

'Can you imagine it?' it asked. 'First I get *coopay*, and then I get *atawned*. You'd think this was the first telephone in the world. Can't someone tell them this is the year of Our Lord, Nineteen-O-Eight, for the Lord's sake?'

The voice that answered – a woman's, I thought – was only

just audible and its words unintelligible, so that the other's far-carrying tone was obviously unnecessary.

I was dozing again, when the partition wall seemed positively to rattle with a new outburst. My neighbour was now, fiercely, if hopelessly, trying to explain to the operator that he couldn't *atawned* any longer, he had to go out. There was the sound of the receiver being smashed back into place, a renewed, unintelligible murmuring beyond the wall, and, a considerable time later, the welcome banging of a door.

I slept. Judging by the fading of the afternoon light, it would have been about half an hour later that I was jarred awake by the piercing trill of that infernal telephone. It rang over and over again, and nobody answered. In a rage, I lifted my fist and hammered pointlessly on the wall.

Then I felt foolish at acting as though that kind of protest were going to have any effect upon a senseless telephone in an empty room.

And then a woman's voice called to me, clearly though not very loudly, from beyond the wall. 'What is it?' it said in English. 'What d'you want?'

Dumbfounded to find there was somebody in the room after all, then furious to think that the somebody was calmly letting that instrument raise Cain all round it, finally happy to have someone to abuse, I shouted back.

'The telephone,' I shouted. 'Can't you answer it? It's making a horrible row. Please answer it, or something.'

The person was silent. The telephone rang again. 'Listen!' I shouted. 'What's the matter?' Now she sounded dismayed, angry, a little hysterical.

'But I don't know what to say to it,' she called. 'I can't hear them,' her voice had an edge of fury. 'And this one'll be in French, too.' And while I was momentarily silent, considering this, she shouted: 'What d'you suppose I can do?'

There was plainly only one thing to do, and, raising my voice against the nagging of the telephone, I suggested that I come round and deal with it for her, and she called back, 'Oh, all right, if you like,' as though she were indulging some whim of mine, and doing me a favour. The door of the room next to mine had been opened a little way. I knocked, was told, 'Come in,' and had an impression of a room got up to accommodate a meeting of the Cabinet; accommodating, however, at the moment, an angry-eyed girl and the shrieking telephone.

'As it bothers you,' she said, 'I suppose you'd better do something.'

I unhitched the receiver and asked in French who was there? A man who talked as though he had a cigarette in his mouth, and had the accent of the Midi, replied sarcastically that he was delighted that someone had answered the telephone so promptly. He wished to leave a message for M. Foraker, as follows. He began to gabble. I told him to hold on a moment and explained to the girl it was a message. She said, 'Oh! You speak *French*. Now I wonder what best...' She put her hand to her forehead and lowered long eyelashes in a study of a girl thinking. The telephone snarled. I said, 'Shall I just take the message?'

'I suppose so,' she said. 'I suppose he thinks you're the ex. The ex spoke French, too. Of course.'

She sat down at a writing desk suitable for the signing of international treaties, and began a kind of elegant, supple, slow-motion wrestle with the folds of her kimono. Out of one sleeve came ultimately, a notebook. From some other fold came a sharp-pointed pencil. She put them carefully on the desk, sat upright, and said, 'Ready now. Go ahead, please.'

I translated the message, sentence by sentence as it came over the telephone, and she took it down in shorthand.

I noticed that her tongue moved between and round her lips as she wrote. I smiled without knowing it, for the effect of the pink tongue stuck childishly out of a delicately classic profile was somehow comical. She turned suddenly and looked at me. Her eyebrows arched above her large dark eyes in well-regulated *hauteur*.

'Was there something amusing?' she said.

'Not at all,' I said confusedly. But her mouth, now that she faced me, was seen to be a little too large, or too full-lipped, to fit exactly with her other features, and I suppose I went on looking at it, for she said sternly, 'I daresay all shorthand experts acquire certain mannerisms which help them in their work. Thank you for dealing with the telephone.'

She looked at the instrument, and one had the impression of it being in the nature of a mad dog, or a grievous Act of God.

'You don't speak French?'

'Not just at present. No.'

'Well, I'm glad to have been of use, Miss – Foraker?'

'No,' she said, 'I work for Mr Foraker.' It came out as an impressive announcement, and she paused after making it.

She had got up from the ambassadorial chair at the desk and was standing by it, her hand resting on its back, in the attitude of a lady waiting for a gentleman to take his leave. I bowed, very stiff, and moved irritably to the door, wondering whether I could get to sleep now, and what would happen if the telephone rang again. Just as I reached the door, it did. I looked round, and saw her standing staring at it, with one hand to her mouth. Determinedly I went across and unhooked it, and listened.

'It's a message,' I told her, 'for Mr Foraker.'

She pouted, sighed, shrugged, and got ready at the desk again.

The message was from a M. Clos; and, as M. Clos rang off and I lowered the receiver on to its hook, the instrument immediately burst into its noisy appeal.

'Monsieur Foraker is out!' I shouted.

'The party,' said the operator after a moment's colloquy, 'says his message is urgent and he will speak to Monsieur Foraker's secretary. Here is your call.'

I started to say that I was certainly not Monsieur Foraker's secretary, and a voice went off in my ear like the crack of a whip.

'Listen!' it said in staccato French. 'I'm in a hurry. Since you are answering the telephone in Monsieur Foraker's room, I presume you are capable of conveying a message to him? Yes, or no? Or are you a burglar? But in that case why answer the telephone?'

'Look here!' I shouted furiously.

'If you wish,' said the voice sharply, 'to establish your *bona fides*, and that you are not at this moment rifling the effects of Monsieur Foraker, you have only to call to the telephone his lovely amanuensis, that delicious twentieth-century reproduction of an Etruscan terra-cotta, Miss Dukes. I shall not, alas! understand what she says, but the sound of her voice is unforgettable.'

Hypnotized, so to speak, by this glare of verbiage, I signalled to the girl to come to the receiver and she held it nervously. 'Say something!' I told her. In her rather soft, but censorious, tone she said in English, 'Who is it?' There was a crackle of satisfaction from the other end, a stream of words, and then I could hear the man calling for me to take the receiver again. I had scarcely spoken when he cut in.

'Good. You are there with Martha Dukes. For me it is enough. Now listen. I am in a hurry. Point One: The appointment arranged yesterday for Saturday is in order. Point Two: Business prospects seem excellent. *But*' – the whip cracked again—'*but,* Point Three: As the German proverb says, "Firstly things turn out different, secondly from what one thinks." Point Four, which I add solely for the purpose of complicating and distressing the lives of any imbeciles who may be listening in to this telephone call: Please dispatch four hundred and twenty-seven apples to the gardener of my aunt before eleven-fifteen on the third, and inform him that Cousin Emilie is doing well. And a jolly good day to you.'

I gave her the gist of it, so far as I could.

'Apparently some maniac,' I said.

'It was Captain Lenoir,' she said, plying her shorthand. She seemed, however, to feel that the series of telephone calls, climaxing in this absurdity, required some kind of explanation.

'Things around here,' said Miss Dukes, peering about the room as though she were noticing it for the first time, 'are a little . . . aren't quite in order.'

Examining the room for the first time, I concluded that her remark must refer to something other than the physical state of the place. It was totally, almost startlingly, *in* order – in the order, that is to say, in which it had apparently been put when it was rigged up as the sitting-room of probably the Number One suite of the Excelsior. It reminded one of a newspaper photograph of a place where some event of importance is due to happen, but has not happened yet. If people occupied it, they must, it seemed, exist as in a museum, taking care not to touch – let alone, disarrange – the costly exhibits in the shape of tables, sofas, chairs which stood stiffly about. I saw, with actual relief, that, high up under the lofty ceiling, there still hung a faint, flat cloud of cigar-smoke. A moment later, I noticed that, in a far corner, near the window, there stood a child's rocking-horse and an ornate, but solid-looking, upright chair of which the back had been smashed off, as though by a heavy blow.

'It's a good-sized room,' remarked Miss Dukes.

'For an hotel room,' I said, 'it's just not good-sized, it's gigantic.'

'I suppose so,' she said, 'in a way.' She blew an imaginary speck of dust from the desk's surface. 'It's convenient to have plenty of space, isn't it?'

We exchanged a few vapid remarks to the general effect that it is, in principle, and as a general rule, more pleasant to have enough space to turn around in than otherwise, while not forgetting that there is something to be said for cosiness, too. It looked as though this might go on until one or other of us fell stupefied by ennui. There crossed my mind the hazy thought that this was what a pretty, but untrained, actress would look like, waiting for the director to turn up and remind her how the role should be played.

Prodding determinedly, I said that I supposed that the secretary of Mr Foraker, who had been mentioned, normally handled such matters? Was he, I inquired – partly with an eye to the possibility of catching up on my sleep – expected back soon?

'No,' she said, doodling with the pencil.

'Oh,' I said, looking – significantly, I hoped – in the direction of my own room. 'So.'

'He's not the secretary, he's the *ex*-secretary. He is not expected back at all, ever.'

'Awkward,' I said. 'Unless, of course, someone else here,' I gestured vaguely, and noticed I was indicating the child's rocking-horse, 'speaks French?'

'Not at present,' she said, as before. The remark now suggested a really superhuman optimism; a hope that perhaps, by some pentecostal intervention, Miss Dukes would pick up the language before the next call came through. Or were they waiting for the owner of the rocking-horse to push ahead in the linguistic line?

She looked at an ornate clock affixed to the wall.

I said, 'I'm afraid I've taken up a great deal of your time.' To this she was good enough to reply that it was of no consequence. Upon which I told her good-bye and walked, still anonymous so far as she was concerned, out of the room and along the corridor to my own.

Paradoxically, this awareness of being physically obtruded on by other people and their affairs – and people, incidentally, who were quite prepared to suggest that if one didn't care for their proximity one could just take oneself off – caused me to feel lonely for the first time since I had parted from my uncle, primly prophesying woe for me, on the dock at Barcelona.

I had no doubt that my decision to reject his suggestions for my future, and, finally, to shake – as I told him at the time – the dust of his sordid counting-house from off my feet, was a correct and noble one.

But this final decision had been taken rather suddenly. I needed a little time to cherish and consolidate the vision of my New Self, born as I strode – after leaving the said counting-house, which was, in point of fact, the local agency of the London and Liverpool Insurance Company Ltd – through the human uproar of the Rambla de las Rosas, and saw the January moon rising beyond Mount Tibidabo.

A man who visited Marseilles the other day and sat in a café there, reported that an old waiter had told him that the sidewalks of Marseilles were nothing like what they used to be, forty years and more ago, before the first War. I have not been back to see. But I remember that on that afternoon in 1908, the waiter, a hearty, middle-aged man, told me that the animation of the sidewalks – and of this boulevard very much in particular – was pretty small beer compared to what it had been twenty years earlier.

He feared, perhaps, that, reminiscing thus, he had lapsed in his civic duty. 'Not but what,' he said, 'there are still matters of interest. For a stranger like yourself, a man of the world, a keen observer, as is evident, of the human race, for example, one couldn't truthfully say that the special life of this boulevard is entirely lacking in interest.'

I looked out of the window and saw, in the loose, slow-moving crowd, a man with an expression of high resolve who suddenly extended his hand in a quick but firmly controlled movement, and pinched, apparently with energy, the behind of the younger of two women walking together in front of him. Her plump body suffered a small convulsion. She half turned, made a frown, tossed her feathered hat, and walked on; only slightly increasing, however, the pace of herself and her elderly companion.

'Quite a pinch,' said the waiter, in the manner of a connoisseur.

'Quite,' I said.

'Pinching,' he said, 'is quite the rage along the boulevard just now, among the lads, so to speak, of the village.'

It appeared to me that the waiter exaggerated. There was plenty to watch on that boulevard as the lamps were lit, but not, so far as I could notice, much pinching, and what there was, of a routine, conventional character. Indeed, the only excitement of that kind was the appearance on the sidewalk of a well-dressed, rather tall, blonde young woman who, I could see from my vantage point, attracted immediate attention and competition among the promenading men by the fact that she was obviously not a prostitute and yet was alone.

She was walking rather faster and more purposefully than the rest of the crowd, but paused at the sight of the beggar on the kerb. Tucking a fashionably delicate umbrella under her arm, she fumbled in her reticule with gloved fingers. As she bent over, reaching almost down to the kerb to put the coins carefully in the plate, a young man of bold bearing, with a well-oiled moustache, a mauve top-coat, and an air of refinement, lunged forward in the movement of a fencer, shot out his hand, and pinched her behind.

With a gesture of innocent astonishment, she clapped her hand to the place. She straightened herself. Still holding her hand to her behind, she twisted the top part of her body round and, craning her neck, peered backwards and downwards at herself. Standing there, visibly oblivious of the boulevard and of everything except this queer nip that had happened to her, she had exactly the appearance of a young woman alone in a field who thinks she has been stung by a wasp.

At a spectacle so pretty, so naïve, and so unexpected, the faces of the promenaders of Marseilles brimmed with pleasure. Quite leisurely, she completed her investigation. She looked up, puzzled. The faces she saw explained everything. I expected an equally naïve explosion. Indeed, she whipped the umbrella from under her arm as though about to charge with it and belabour the suspected aggressor.

Instinctively, the ring that had formed itself, widened a little.

The blonde young woman, with a sweep of her umbrella that was evidently intended to be final, started to walk again in the direction in which she had been going before seeing the beggar.

The waiter, who had returned to stand beside my table, watched the scene with a critical expression. He formulated, briefly, the view that the affair, though entertaining, had been distinctly unorthodox. The young woman had not reacted quite as might have been expected of a young woman who chose to walk alone on this particular street at this hour of the evening. He took the position that her actions had been fishy, and open to censure.

This led him to some considerations concerning the general unorthodoxy and fishiness of developments in the world of today, easily demonstrable by a study of the newspapers. The crisis in Morocco, for instance, the behaviour of this Mulai Hafid they were writing about. Fishy, and a lot more behind it all than met the eye. The German Kaiser, the English Foreign Secretary, and M. Clemenceau all needed watching.

I said I must read more about it all, and began to study a newspaper. Morocco held that day's headlines. Mulai Hafid, it appeared, was being backed for the sultanate of Morocco. Peace and war turned on the outcome, so they said. But I read without much attention. Happily alone, I permitted myself to sink into a state of comatose contemplation, viewing the future through the fumes of hot rum.

I was disturbed. A page from the hotel stood beside my table. There was a gentleman, he said, in the foyer who wanted to speak to me.

'To me?' I said, astonished. 'Who is he?'

He said the gentleman's name was Monsieur Foraker.

2

Suffocating with annoyance, I said that, of course, if Mr Foraker wished to see me, he was at liberty to come to the café and do so. Then, just as the page was turning away, some instinct – of curiosity, of self-defence – caused me to call him back.

'Who exactly,' I said, '*is* Mr Foraker?'

'Monsieur Foraker,' said the page, 'has the best rooms in the hotel.'

'Well? And? What does he do? He's a businessman, or what?'

'They say,' said the page, ostentatiously lowering his voice, 'that he is arranging some business here on behalf of Mulai Hafid or others. I don't know.' He looked over his shoulder towards the door of the café. 'There,' he said, '*is* Monsieur Foraker.'

A large man, who seemed pent up in his clothes, was standing in the doorway leading from the café to the hotel. The heels of his boots bounced gently up and down on the tessellated floor. His hands quietly mauled the rim of his hat. He was gazing at the ceiling, the light shining on him. The muscles along his jaw moved slightly. His expression was that of one praying; praying, 'O God, let me not be kept waiting, for Thou, O God, knowest what I may do if I am.' The expression was so intense that for the moment it was impossible for me to focus on his face, as such.

I stood up. The page went over to Foraker, gestured, and disappeared behind the suddenly moving figure of Foraker, who reached my table in a few smooth strides, bowed, gave his name, said, 'Please sit down, Mr Hastings,' threw his expensive-looking hat on to a neighbouring chair, seated himself, and put his two hands flat down on the table-top, all, it seemed, in a single, rapidly executed motion. The impression was given that I had been anxiously awaiting his coming, and that he himself had kept his appointment with hair's breadth punctuality. I found myself sitting down.

He was talking almost before I had done so. 'Mr Hastings,' he said, 'I have to thank you for services rendered me this afternoon.'

I recognized the resonant voice which had roused me a couple of hours before. It jarred me now in another way. Its tone seemed to be saying something quite different from the words spoken. I made some banal disclaimer of having rendered any particular service. In fact, I had acted for my own convenience – because of the telephone, I explained.

'Quite,' said Foraker, with a large smile, while his two forefingers drummed fiercely on the table-top.

Now that I could take a good look at him, I found it disconcertingly difficult to judge what age of man I was talking to – a point of importance when one is nineteen years old. I know now, of course, that he was then just thirty-four, but his apparent age kept altering with the expression of his large face, which was extraordinarily mobile, and looked both smooth and jagged; the bones of his nose, cheeks, and chin showing strongly under his high-coloured skin. The hair above his rather high forehead was fine, and as thick as a wig. He might have been anywhere between thirty and a very carefully got-up fifty. His clothes, noticeably good, were just this side of flamboyance.

There seemed to be nothing to be said in answer to that

‘Quite,’ or to the drumming fingers. I just sat there watching him.

Striking a final chord with all his fingers together, he slapped his hands down on the table again, looked carefully from one to other of them as though making some final check-up, and said, talking rapidly to the table, ‘Mr Hastings, since I know that you were in my room, it would be of interest to me to know your real motive for going there. I understand you spent some time listening to my telephone calls.’

The impudence of this remark made me gape. And yet, as I looked at him, there was a curious, almost agonized, earnestness about his downcast face that somehow took the edge off the impudence. For all their mobility, his features, which might have been those of an actor, made an astonishing impression of genuineness, as though they were being twitched and moulded by a series of quite overpowering notions and emotions. It struck me that this personage really did believe that I had had some unavowed reason for going to his room, and believed that for some equally incomprehensible reason I was going to tell him what it was.

I found myself speaking less haughtily than I had intended. I assured him that if his assistant had not, apparently, been incapable of taking a telephone off its hook, I should never have gone into the room at all. And that if she had been capable of taking the messages I certainly should not have taken them myself. ‘And in the circumstances,’ I added, ‘I must say I think your attitude rather absurd.’

He nodded quickly, as if acknowledging a point. He was neither abashed nor enraged; just earnestly and impatiently seeking the facts.

‘You’ll agree, though,’ he said, ‘that the circumstances are curious. For example’ – he looked thoughtfully up at the ceiling, exactly in the manner of a schoolmaster about to face a pupil with a brain-twister – ‘just how did you know that those three calls were going to come through just at that time?’

He smiled widely again, and threw himself back in his chair with a checkmate look. I could hear the chair crack under his weight, and, recalling the smashed chair upstairs, realized that it was Foraker who must have wrought the small piece of havoc in that museum of a room. 'That's stumped you, has it?' he said, as I paused. The situation was too preposterous for annoyance.

'I was just wondering,' I said, 'whether you always break chairs when you're excited.'

He frowned, turned irritably, glared at the back of the chair, and then tested it with his hand, wrenching it powerfully back and forth. For the chair, already enfeebled by the original attack, it was too much. With a rending noise, the back and back legs split away from the seat. Foraker leapt up just as the seat and forelegs tottered to the floor, and stood there, with the back still hanging from his gripped hand. He looked down at the wreck with puzzled interest.

'I don't know why these things have to happen,' he said.

In the couple of seconds it took the waiter to come hustling, Foraker had got hold of another chair, kicked the debris aside, and sat down again. He regarded the waiter with anxious impatience, fearful of some tedious interruption of our business. He made the motion of writing. 'Bill,' he said, 'put it on the bill. *San fairy ann*,' he added magnanimously, waving his hand. With intent gaze, he proceeded to await my answer to his original question.

I felt less capable than ever of being properly insulted by his cross-examination.

'Mr Foraker,' I said, elaborately ironical, 'supposing, which is entirely untrue, I had entered your room for some sinister purpose, would you mind telling me as a matter of purely impersonal interest, just what on earth makes you think that I would explain to you what that purpose was?'

'But don't you see,' he said – the schoolmaster now explaining the obvious to the impercipient – 'that if I don't ask, you won't tell, can't tell, don't have the opportunity. Result nil. No bet. If I *do* ask, there may be some motive for your confessing, spilling – don't you see? – the beans. It gives us both a chance. You might, for instance, want to have me buy you off. You could be wanting to sell out.'

'As it is,' I said, 'I have nothing to tell and nothing to sell.'

He hit the table a rap of exasperation. 'Damn it!' he said, and sighed heavily. I was beginning to feel a trifle light-headed.

'Not to anyone,' I said. 'Not even to an agent of Mulai Hafid, or whatever that Moorish Sultan's name is.'

He looked across at me with interest. 'You have heard,' he said, 'that I am a representative of Mulai Hafid? May I ask you this question: Who told you that?'

'The bellhop,' I said curtly.

I had expected this to annoy him. But he merely nodded, his eyes making a circular survey of the café. 'Is that so?' he said.

' "Mulai Hafid or others" was what he actually said.'

'Ah!' said Foraker, and seemed to be embarking silently on some new train of thought which, however, was more or less violently derailed by a woman's loud cry of 'Grant!' in response to which, Foraker swung round, and then stood up, as the waiters made way for a young woman with flashing eyes and determined tread, whom I immediately recognized as the nipped blonde of the boulevard. She still held the umbrella in one hand, and in the other the hand of a child, who trotted beside her, dodging the table edges, which threatened to bang his ears, and uttering shouts – calling down curses, apparently upon the tables, for obstruction.

The young woman started talking to Foraker from several yards away. '*There* you are!' she said. 'Been looking for you all over.' While he got himself another chair, she explained how she had been refused admittance to the café because in that particular café 'ladies unaccompanied by a gentleman' were not allowed; they did not understand she was coming to join her husband, and she had had to start yelling before they would let her in. This she poured out, not exactly ignoring me, but taking my presence quite amiably for granted. The child, on the other hand, now definable as a small boy about five years old, peered at me sideways, while pretending to be interested in the table-top.

Foraker was unruffled, but still visibly in a hurry. 'What's it all about, Delia?' he asked.

'Why, Grant,' she said, 'it's this Lahmy's Aliment Pure and

Ideal for the Child that Wishes to Grow and Flourish. I just have to have it. It's the only thing Jeph can take.'

'I thought you'd located the store that has it. I thought you'd gone to fetch it.'

'Well, that's just it,' she said, and the child now switched his full attention to her, his eyes shining in anticipation of an epic recital. 'They pinched her behind,' he said in a gruff aside to Foraker, giving him a foretaste.

Mrs Foraker rushed into a description of the scene I had already witnessed on the boulevard.

The child was now looking out of the window at the boulevard and making an incantation. 'If they do it again, I'll beat them, so I will. I'll beat them with a stick, with a big stick, a hundred sticks, a hundred and fifty, and I'll put them in the sea to drown in the sea.' His threats became louder and more vainglorious, he danced up and down and his face glowed with triumph as though, by the power of invocation, he were already routing the enemy.

'Be quiet a minute, Jephthah,' said Foraker. 'Incidentally, Delia,' he added, turning to me, 'this is Mr Edward Hastings, the gentleman who helped Martha with the telephone a while back. They gave me your name at the desk,' he explained to me. 'This is my wife.'

The child reprieved the people on the sidewalks and resumed its scrutiny of myself.

'Why,' cried Mrs Foraker, her eyes blazing wonderfully with admiration and gratitude, 'you're the young man that spoke *French* on the *telephone*. Martha told me. You know,' she said to Foraker, 'the telephone was ringing and ringing, and he came in and talked French on it, back and forth, just as easily ...'

Mrs Foraker was suddenly suffused with the excitement of an idea.

'Listen!' she said to me. 'Would you do something?' And before I could answer, 'Listen!' she said to Foraker. 'I was looking for you to come and take me up to that store where they have this Lahmy's. I was only thinking of how to get along that street unmolested. And how we'd explain it all to them in the store when we got there, I don't know. But, now, if Mr Hastings were to come along? And talk *French* to them, don't you see? Would you do that, Mr Hastings? It's a lot to ask, but it's not far. And I just know that store is going to turn out to be the Frenchest thing you ever saw.'

In a state of confusion, I said that I would be delighted.

'That's wonderful of you,' said Mrs Foraker. 'We'll all go. Come on, Grant, let's hurry or the store'll be closing.'

Foraker looked briefly from one of his hands to the other, sighed at whatever message it was they conveyed to him, and stood up. 'Well . . . if Mr Hastings is agreeable . . .'

The child, fearful evidently of missing something if he took his eyes off me, but speaking to his mother while he stared, said, 'Is that man a spy, Momma? Is he?'

'No, dear,' Mrs Foraker said abstractedly.

'Why not?' said the child, looking swindled. 'Why does he have not to be?'

'Not everybody's a spy, dear,' said Mrs Foraker, standing up. I paid my bill, sent away the fresh hot grog I had been waiting for so happily before Foraker appeared, and, surrounded by the Foraker family, moved to the street door. For the next hour and a half, more or less, I seemed hardly to stop talking – for and on behalf of the Foraker interests.

During the first twenty minutes or so it was just a matter of constantly asking the way to the one and only store in the whole city of Marseilles which stocked Lahmy's Aliment Pure and Ideal for the Child that Wishes to Grow and Flourish. Even the street Mrs Foraker thought it was in was a lot farther off than she had thought, and when we got to it the store was not in that street anyway. When we did find it, it proved to be in the charge of a pioneer, a crusader, a missionary. In his opinion Lahmy was a low purveyor of false doctrine; people were risking infanticide who offered to their children any but the scientifically balanced food of a firm named Paulet and Company, whose product was called Dawn Food – the Nourishment of Tomorrow.

At the name of Lahmy's Aliment Pure and Ideal, he first

shrugged, then jeered, then – as he saw that Mrs Foraker was serious in heresy – howled aloud.

I shrugged back, jeered back, howled back. The noise shocked sleeping cats off the shelves and insects out of the sugar bins. Once there was a still louder noise, a crashing and rolling and bumping, as though God were bowling thunderbolts at the unbelievers. Foraker, watching keenly, and conceiving that our side had scored a point, had thrown himself backwards in a victorious gesture, and knocked down an edifice of sardine cans and stone jars of preserved ginger. Glancing in his direction, I could see his lips moving as the stuff came rattling and thumping down, and I knew that he was wondering aloud why these things had to happen.

Only his son remained absolutely calm. The jeering, the howling, the crashing and bumping brought from him only a wan, tolerant smile. I had the impression that he had not recovered from the disappointment suffered in the café. What he had been all set to do was to see a spy. I could see in his eyes that my unspy-ishness was a blow, like no clowns at the circus.

'Why,' I said innocently to Foraker as, Lahmy's Aliment obtained at last, we started the walk back to the hotel – Mrs Foraker and the child going in front, Foraker and myself forming the necessary rearguard – 'does your child ask whether I am a spy?'

He walked on in silence for several paces.

'I suppose,' he said cagily, 'he thinks it's sort of an interesting thing to see.'

'I see.'

He took one hand out of his coat pocket and examined its knuckles carefully. Then he said. 'He seemed to get interested in the subject a fortnight or so ago when he happened to hear me state that I had just dismissed my secretary because he was a spy. A child's mind works in a mysterious way, Mr Hastings. You know, there's a lot we don't know yet about child psychology. Or so they say.'

'Yes, indeed,' I said, aware of a kind of mental indigestion produced by Foraker's remarks.

'Of course, the child only heard about the fellow being a spy after he had gone; naturally, Jephthah felt he had missed something, so he hopes to see another.'

'You make me feel quite sorry that I don't fill the bill.'

Foraker breathed a half-sentence into the air and left it there unfinished, dangling. 'You said you had nothing to . . .' Once again, the upper part of his face was almost contorted by the earnest intensity of his frown.

'Absolutely nothing,' I said. I found myself sincerely anxious to convince him of the fact, as if it were somehow one's duty to put him on the right lines. Trudging along the street in the footsteps of his small son, sunk in heaven-knows-what complex and, for him, momentous calculation, he had ceased to appear to me preposterous. With the melancholy imagination of youth, I saw the street peopled with individuals frantically attempting, in one form or another, to make adequate, and perhaps, crucial, deductions from insufficient data. My New Self, keen-eyed and undaunted, felt sorry for everybody. I said aloud, '*"Es ist schade um die Menschen!"*'

'What?' Foraker said.

'It's a phrase of a German writer. It means, roughly, "It's a pity about people."'

'Why?' said Foraker.

I walked in silence, vexed.

The silence was broken by his saying, quite suddenly, that, of course, there was no absolute proof that my statement of my reasons for entering his room did not correspond to the exact facts. His tone suggested that in making this statement he was presenting a view of the matter that might prove interestingly novel to myself. He actually stopped on the sidewalk so as to make his point emphatically, face to face.

'You may not have noticed,' he added, as though there were some connection in his mind between this and what he had been saying, 'that a man has been following us. Following me.'

'Indeed,' I said, politely. And really I felt no surprise and not much curiosity. A little while before, such a statement would have been pleasurably startling. After a couple of hours' contact with Foraker, the news that he was being dogged by an unnamed tracker through the darkening streets of Marseilles seemed positively commonplace – just what you'd expect, in fact. From the moment that he mentioned this circumstance, it was as though he would have been somehow incomplete without somebody following him privily in his walks abroad.

Foraker nodded. 'Son of a bitch,' he said gently to himself as he sauntered on towards the hotel entrance, where we rejoined Mrs Foraker and the child, and I started to take my leave of them, it being my intention to husband my money by avoiding the hotel restaurant and dining instead in some reasonably cheap *brasserie*.

I left them with suitable excuses, walked rapidly down the Cannebière, and then stopped to look back. I half expected to see someone lurking at the hotel entrance through which the Forakers had disappeared. I saw no one, crossed the avenue, found in a side-street a *brasserie* of the type I wanted, settled myself on a leather bench near the top of a long almost empty table, and observed, without interest, let alone suspicion, the entry soon after myself of a middle-sized, commonplace-looking man who took his seat almost opposite me and read the newspaper absorbedly throughout his meal.

From the proprietor of this clean and respectable eating-house I obtained the address of a cheap lodging near by, which, he assured me, was clean and respectable, too, and thither, on the following morning, I transferred my baggage.

Safe in my new lodging, I spent considerable time putting the future in order, while awaiting the arrival, at the central Poste Restante, of replies to certain letters I had written from Barcelona. These were concerned with furthering my intention of becoming, among other things, a leading European geologist. It was an intention which I had mentioned to my uncle, as being among the most easily comprehensible and visibly well-founded of my ambitions. I had studied the subject eagerly while supposed to be learning the insurance business, and I had read a paper on certain geological phenomena of the Aragon Plateau to a group of the Geological Society of Barcelona. This had been well received – especially as I was the youngest member ever to have read a paper. On the strength of this, after making my decision to quit the insurance office, I had written outlining my aims to a number of prominent persons in this field of science, requesting their guidance and advice.

Among them was Professor Auguste Michel Lévy, then Director of the Geological Survey of France. I had intimated to him that I was prepared to go to Paris, but stated quite frankly that, in the event of his not being able to offer encouragement, I would probably go to Vienna instead – I had written at the same time to one of the Chiefs of the Austrian Reichsanstalt für Geologie.

During this enforced lull, I walked the streets contemplatively, visited the Poste Restante morning and evening, and, when the flurries of sleet attacked the town, sat in a café reading the preface to *Major Barbara*, which had been out, I believe, several months, but had only reached Barcelona just before my departure. In the evenings I dined at the *brasserie*. On the second evening, the commonplace man with the newspaper was there at my table again. On the third, he asked me, coughing nervously, to pass him a basket of rolls. On the fourth and fifth, he said that it had been a fine day, and that there was very little news in the newspapers.

I and the New Self were at the moment deep in plans and did not at all want to be intruded upon by a possibly garrulous stranger. But, as I replied indifferently to his remark, I looked at him properly for the first time. I have said that his appearance was commonplace. Unfortunately, it was commonplace in a way which rendered him, in my eyes, startling.

3

Everyone, I suppose, carries about with him a more or less grotesque mental picture of such abstract beings as the Statesman, the Artist, the Man of Affairs, which can persist even though he never sees a real-life statesman or businessman who looks in the least like the mental picture.

It happened that the person now addressing me corresponded, almost shockingly, to the picture evoked in my mind by the phrase, the Average Man. It was both uncanny and fascinating.

His face was a pinkish oblong, his eyes between grey and blue, his hair sandy. The features were, so to speak, strikingly – even pathetically – ordinary. Though unlined and rather plump, this face, nevertheless, had in repose a look of general worry and harassment, thus giving the impression that this was a young man prematurely middle-aged – aged, one would have said, by trivial and mean cares.

Two or three evenings later, the Average Man and three companions were there before me, sitting round the top of the table.

The Average Man had evidently finished his dinner, and the group had a pack of cards on a piece of green cloth laid across the table top. It immediately occurred to me that I was the intended victim of a group of card-sharpers who had chosen this slow, but still sufficiently obvious, approach. The clumsiness of their intrigue amused me. I ate my dinner, awaiting the moment when they would seek to inveigle me into a game.

To my surprise, however, I saw that they were not actually playing a game of cards at all. Instead, they seemed to be engaged upon practising some species of card trick, mostly performed by the Average Man.

The other three were: a keen-eyed military-looking person; a stoutish man with a domed forehead and the expression of a philosopher contemplating the nature of the universe; and a swarthy, wiry-haired young fellow whose very red lips twisted up sideways, showing white teeth in a continual sneer, as though disclaiming the extraordinary intentness of interest in his dark eyes.

In turn, so far as I could observe from my place a few feet away from them, each of these three shuffled the pack of cards, handed it to his neighbour to shuffle again. The pack returned to the original shuffler, without, however, being touched by the Average Man, who maintained throughout the proceedings an appearance of polite attention with which a mild boredom mingled.

The man who happened to have the pack before him would then lay a finger on the top card, the Average Man would murmur something – obviously the name of the card which he guessed would appear – and the other would then turn the card and lay it face upwards on the table.

It seemed, at first sight, a childish kind of game for four grown men to be spending their evening at; and yet, glancing covertly from time to time at their faces, I could have believed that something absolutely momentous was going on – that perhaps some enormous wager depended upon the turn of the cards and the 'calls' of the Average Man.

Only one more 'hand' was played before the three got up, shook hands in turn with the Average Man, and took their hats from a rack behind them.

'Then,' said the Philosopher, as he said good-bye, 'we remain in touch.'

'Absolutely,' said the Military Person.

'Good,' said the Average Man.

Left alone at his side of the table, he pushed the pack of cards aside and called for the waiter to bring him a fresh glass of cognac. During the whole of the 'game' he had been sitting sideways to the table, with his back three-quarters turned to me, and, seeming now to notice my presence for the first time, he bowed and smiled slightly, saying that the weather had not been quite so fine today, and that the newspapers seemed to have very little news in them.

'By the way,' he said with his nervous cough. 'I hope I'm not committing an indiscretion by mentioning it. I mean I certainly don't intend any reflection on your, if I may venture to say so, admirable command of the French language. But I was wondering whether you are not, perhaps, an Englishman?'

When I acknowledged that this was the case, he bowed and said with what seemed a painful effort at easy jocosity, 'Always glad of a chat with a fellow-Briton in a foreign land. Amid the alien corn. I happen to be a Scotsman myself.'

With that, he stopped short, raised himself slightly from his chair, and extended his hand to me across the table, looking, in this act of formality, more sensationally commonplace than ever.

'The name,' he said, 'is Robinson.'

I decided on the following evening to take my dinner three-quarters of an hour or so earlier than usual.

Five minutes after I had taken my place at the *brasserie* table, Mr Robinson entered. He was inside a great tent of an ulster which, having struck with difficulty, he draped over the back of his chair. He had the worriedly apologetic look of an unwanted dog following someone in the street. He seemed to feel an explanation necessary and said that he had been sitting in a café across the street, seen me come in, decided to join me 'at the groaning board'.

I learned later that this statement was doubly characteristic of Mr Robinson. It was his habit to employ these worn-out hackneys of verbiage, often faintly facetious in tone, as handy vehicles in which to travel securely through awkward patches of human relationship. Also, anxiously in pursuit of an ulterior objective, he would often proffer explanations of his behaviour which came to pieces the instant they were examined. On this occasion I merely recalled to myself that there was no café across the street.

He looked round the restaurant and made some banal comment upon the sound quality of its food and service.

'Not,' he said, 'that it's quite in the class of the Excelsior Hotel.' He paused, as though expecting me to say something. Since there appeared to be no suitable comment to be made on such a remark, I said nothing.

Then he said, looking down at his plate and suddenly up at me, 'I know the Excelsior very well indeed. You see until a fortnight ago I was the private secretary of the well-known Mr Grant Foraker.'

He was watching for me to jump a little at the name, and I suppose I jumped.

'Just so,' said Mr Robinson, more the worried dog than ever.

I said that the work, no doubt, had been interesting.

'As,' said Mr Robinson, still watchful, 'you probably

gathered from your own association with the gentleman in question.'

I told him I had no 'association' whatever with Mr Foraker, and at that he laid down his knife and fork and stared at me with an expression intended, I surmised, to be stern, sceptical, and judicial. His features, sadly inadequate to express any sentiment very clearly, succeeded in conveying at least an impression of annoyance, uncertainty, and calculation.

He sat up awfully straight and proceeded to make a bewildering pronouncement. What he said was, 'Mr Hastings, I want to make perfectly plain at this juncture that what I am first and foremost is a patriot. This is a point I should like you to have perfectly clear in your mind from the outset.'

I said I didn't understand.

'No,' he said, 'perhaps you don't quite get the bearing of what I have made reference to. Surprising if you did. I was just wondering, though, about that little remark you passed to the effect that you have had nothing to do with Mr Grant Foraker.'

'I said I didn't have any association with him.'

Mr Robinson seemed to relax somewhat. 'But you won't deny that you *are* acquainted with him? That you were with him in the café of the Excelsior a few evenings back? That you strolled with him in the street?'

Was that any business of his, I asked him furiously.

'Well, yes,' he said, coughing and gulping, 'it is. Very much so.'

The events of the past week clicked into a new pattern in my mind, and words of abuse and bitter censure rushed out of me. The very first I had heard of him, I said, was that he had been dismissed from his employment for acting as a spy upon his employer; and now what did I find but that he had been spying on me, too, had obviously tracked me to this eating-place, watched me, scraped acquaintance with me, for, no doubt, some squalid purpose which I did not choose to hear about.

I went on and on, shouting down, I suppose, Mr Robinson's occasional barks of protest.

I must have got to my feet while I was speaking, for I found myself, at the end, looking down on the upturned face of Mr Robinson and seeing it strangely and disconcertingly changed, its dull contours astonishingly pinched, its drab pinkness pumped up into fierce scarlet patches on the cheekbones, the rest of it blazing white, a desperate kind of a clown-face, looking out of a ring where the tiger is loose. His voice was shaking.

'Please, Mr Hastings,' he was saying. 'Please.'

I stared down at him and, at the sight of him, wavered and then simply sat down again, saying lamely that, of course, if he had any explanation to offer, I was prepared to hear it.

He took a deep, gulping breath as though he had been running for a vital train and just caught it. 'Thank you,' he said, 'thank you, Mr Hastings. Just for a moment I was afraid that you . . .'

As though it had been conjured into life by the tap of some appalling menace, now past, the clown-face slowly dematerialized, resolved itself before my eyes into the banal, though still agitated, countenance of Mr Robinson. I began to feel my exasperation flooding back. Before I could say anything, he began to speak.

'Let us,' he said hurriedly, 'nothing common do or mean, upon this memorable scene. I understand, Mr Hastings, that a certain misconstruction could be put upon certain aspects of . . . I mean that when you are cognizant of certain facts you will realize that this is not a matter for petty considerations. Very much, if I may say so, the contrary.'

'Just what,' I said, 'are you trying to tell me, Mr Robinson?'

'Plenty,' said Mr Robinson. 'And, by the way, Mr Hastings,' he had the coolness to add in a fussy, governessy tone, 'if you don't mind my saying so, I'd advise you to take a glass of wine. You don't look quite the thing. Well now . . .'

He assumed, with a visible effort, a maddeningly matter-of-fact manner, as though I were the one in need of a good dose of down-to-earth common sense and straightforward appreciation of the facts. ('What you have to realize . . .' 'The point you probably don't grasp as yet . . .')

He admitted, in a hurried rigmarole, that he had followed

me on that first evening of my encounter with Foraker, that he had come to this *brasserie* with the express purpose of gradually 'making contact' with me. 'But all *for* a purpose, Mr Hastings. So that I should begin by stating quite definitely the following points.' As he made each point, he shot out his short forefinger and folded it up again. 'One, this matter is not a personal one at all. Not strictly. Much wider than *that*.'

Since he was watching me closely, I nodded in a comprehending but non-committal manner.

'Two,' he said, shooting out the finger, 'Mr Foraker is a very dangerous man. Distinctly. An understatement. More than dangerous. Three,' and here he looked at me as impressively as his facial resources permitted, 'I am not alone in this opinion. Am not alone, I should say, in acting on this opinion. By no means. There are others. And four,' he said, leaning across the table so that his finger wagged almost under my chin, 'there is a part here for you to play, Mr Hastings. A role. Of importance. I might say, indispensable.'

I smiled wearily. 'Really, Mr Robinson,' I said, 'you'll have to do a good deal more explaining than that.'

A light of apostolic eagerness leapt in his eyes. 'Explain?' he said. 'Exactly. An explanation is what you are entitled to.'

I find myself unable to remember just how long Mr Robinson's 'explanation' lasted – not, I mean, his explanation that evening over the dinner table, but the further explanation that went on the next day and, as I recall, the day after that. For now there was no way of escaping him except by running away, slinking about the streets of the city looking for another place to eat, and, even so, facing the risk that Mr Robinson was slinking behind, and would pop into the new place and pitch his tent there.

No doubt I should have tried harder to evade him, or shut him up, had it not been for an encounter on the Cannebière with Miss Dukes. To be exact, she was standing in the entrance of the Excelsior Hotel, looking perplexedly at the traffic, and I saw her before she saw me. The sight of her gave me a fillip of pleasure. Feeling tender, big-hearted, and gay, I decided to forgive her for her haughty aloofness of a few days ago during the telephone episode. I was well dressed and had just been to the barber, and I was going to go up and greet her warmly, so that she would be surprised, impressed, relieved, and somewhat excited by the reappearance of the distinguished and rather mysterious young Englishman.

She took my greeting quite coolly, but said that she and Mrs Foraker were just going shopping and I might care to accompany them. I was about to accept the invitation, when she added that Mr Foraker had been too busy to arrange in time for some French-speaking servant from the hotel to go with them. He had, it seemed, been good enough to say that it was a pity that young fellow who had helped the other night was not about any more.

With biting irony I inquired whether they had already run short of Lahmy's Aliment? She said no, but there was a particular laxative without which Jephthah had trouble, and also Mr Foraker was dissatisfied with the coffee supplied in the hotel; he thought there must be something more like what he was used to, if only they could get around among the shops and find it. Naturally, he was too busy to do that sort of thing himself.

I made my excuses and passed on, scowling at the thought of the man Foraker who supposed people had nothing better to do than trot about Marseilles helping his illiterate wife and incompetent staff provide him with coffee and keep his son's bowels open; a man that had a lovely, but evidently foolish, young girl at his beck and call, standing on the steps of hotels looking at young men simply as potential messenger-boys on behalf of himself and his offspring. What I felt then about Mr Grant Foraker was that he was a son of a bitch, and at least it was clear from the outset that Mr Robinson thought he was, too. So far as Mr Robinson was concerned, that was a considerable understatement.

Indeed, as the map of Mr Robinson's feeling towards Foraker unfolded, one found oneself contemplating very elevated country. The British Embassy in Paris was marked on it, and also Almighty God and the Community at Large. For all these interests Mr Robinson held, as it appeared, the agency. He represented them. Against Foraker, absolutely, though as yet undefinedly, the Dangerous Man.

Was I then to understand that he was in the employ of the British Embassy in Paris? Well, yes, and yet in a sense, no. From a rather elaborate but smudgy sketch of his relations with the Paris Embassy – 'certain people in a certain department of the Embassy, if you follow me' – I gathered that the position was that these 'certain people' were deeply, keenly interested, but not to the point where they were prepared to put down cash in advance for information not yet received.

Mr Robinson uncomplainingly accepted this unlucrative relationship; he seemed really to glory in it. As he talked, one could see, behind his humdrum mug, his own picture of a free-lance agent of diplomatic intrigue – working for nothing, and due presently to bring home the quarry; save the country, more or less; an unknown hero, working in the dark, to be ultimately rewarded by a hand-clasp from the Chief: 'It's Robinson we really have to thank.' That, he thought, was approximately what would happen.

Naturally, Mr Robinson said, there had had to be a dossier. Embassy people weren't the sort to take up any matter where there was no dossier. Floundering, I asked whether he meant that the Embassy had a 'dossier' on Mr Foraker. Not at all. That was where 'your humble servant' had come in. 'It took a little doing, you know. Getting things together, with chronological order and exposition and clarification where necessary. However, I think they appreciated it. They get all sorts blundering in there, bothering them and wasting their time. When they see a man that knows enough to bring a dossier with him, they know where they are.'

He referred on several occasions to this dossier.

And then a crisis occurred. He turned up at the restaurant, much excited, with the news that the Forakers were that week leaving Marseilles and returning to Paris. I would appreciate that 'speed is now of the essence'.

It was the moment for me to reiterate, at last, that I had

nothing to do with Mr Foraker, no interest in him, no intention whatever of involving myself.

'But, Mr Hastings,' he said, 'you must see that you have an unrivalled opportunity to act in this matter.'

'Act?' I said. 'How, "act"?'

I had no experience then of Mr Robinson's capacity for, so to speak, skipping an essential beat. It was as though, hours and days before, he had started counting under his breath and was surprised when he shouted out, 'Fifty!' that no one else knew what he was talking about.

He 'explained' – exactly as though he were repeating for my slow comprehension something already fully discussed between us – that now was my chance ('our chance', I think he said), to step into the position just vacated by himself, pick up the rifle of the warrior stricken in the struggle, become Foraker's secretary. That, apparently, was the point of everything Robinson had been up to during the past few days. He had merely forgotten to mention it until now.

'It stands to reason,' he said. 'You can see for yourself how much use Martha Dukes is to him – *as* a secretary,' he added, pursing his lips. 'As you will have noticed for yourself, in other respects she no doubt... Well, I mean to say, a young girl, lively, passionate you know ... a man like Foraker, old enough to be her father, of course, but you know what young girls are like. I must say, it's not very nice, is it?'

He paused, looking at me for confirmation of this judgement. I said it was nothing to me, either way.

'Be that,' he said, 'as it may, the fact remains; the man has to have a secretary. And then you turn up. Speak French fluently. Good appearance. Make yourself useful right away. It stands to reason. All you have to do is to nip around there to the Excelsior before he leaves, and he'll *offer* you the job.' He half closed his eyes and, tapping with the back of a knife on the edge of his plate for emphasis, he said, 'I am certain that when you see Foraker again he will offer you the job. As certain as I am that Signorietta is going to win this year's Derby.'

This preposterous statement, his air of having clinched with this final absurdity the absurdities which had gone before, seemed an opportunity to put a full stop to the whole senseless discussion. I said sharply that, considering the Derby was still several months off, Mr Robinson's 'certainty' did not amount to a great deal, evidently.

He went off finally, looking terribly worried. One could see that he was pondering, and shrinking from, some awfully drastic course of action.

The nature of this transpired the following evening; he was going, he said, to show me the dossier. This pronouncement was made with solemnity. To date, the 'people at the Embassy' were the only ones who had been so favoured. Indeed, Mr Robinson found it necessary to explain to me that he had argued with himself back and forth for quite a while before deciding that he was not committing an indiscretion by so doing. To ensure, I suppose, that I approached the dossier in a seemly spirit of reverence, he gave me a little lecture about its origins. In these, Providence and 'my old man' both appeared to have played prominent roles. At any rate, it seemed now that Providence had been at Old Man Robinson's elbow when, years and years ago in Lanark, and later in Edinburgh – 'my native heath, you know' – he had, from righteous motives, put together certain newspaper clippings, certain letters, and kept them in a tin box by themselves, adding to them from time to time. Providence had nipped in even more – how could one say? – providentially a few years ago, after the Old Man's decease, when Mr Robinson junior, coming across this boxful of documents had been on the point of burning them.

The story from then on was, in a grotesque way, impressive, though by no means quite coherent. Anyway, it did emerge that at a certain point – vaguely defined as 'when I saw what he might be up to over here' – Mr Robinson, his eye on the Embassy and the impropriety of approaching such people without a dossier, had actually gone off – by Channel steamer, and third-class carriage through cold and rain – to that corner of a south Edinburgh storehouse which served as repository for the relics of the Robinson family. He had got out the Old Man's box, bought a suitable file – 'tramped Edinburgh for a good hour before I found just what I wanted' – and started composing the dossier. A loving labour of hate and piety; memories of the Old Man flooding in upon him as he crouched in a granite house on the south side of the Meadows, putting the 'documents in the case' in proper order, penning comment and elucidation where he felt such to be necessary, adding passages – mostly from acid-bitten memory – of history as it had developed since the Old Man had gone to glory. Then back to Paris – via Manchester, where took place what must have been a cross-purposeful interview between Mr Robinson and the firm of textile manufacturers then employing him – and the interview at the Embassy, with the dossier playing its major part. And here, lugged ceremoniously out of the folds of the ulster, it was.

'You'll read it right away – at home tonight, won't you?' said Mr Robinson anxiously.

I picked up the folder, handling it – to such an extent was I now hypnotized by Mr Robinson's fantasies – as though it were some rare or sacred book.

Mr Robinson watched me, nodding with vigorous satisfaction.

'You'll find it very far from lacking in interest,' he said. 'It'll give you a bearing right enough. After all, what can you expect of a man brought up by a father who faked the end of the world?'

'What?' I said, gingerly fingering the bundle of papers.

'That's what he did,' said Mr Robinson. 'Old Man Foraker faked the end of the world. And Grant Foraker aided and abetted. Eight years old at the time, mind you. Can you imagine an eight-year-old child doing a thing like that?'

At this, I reminded myself anew that the simple fact about Mr Robinson was just that he was mentally deranged. It had just happened that during my stop-over in Marseilles I had made the acquaintance of a lunatic. This thought was, in a way, soothing; a relief. It explained everything.

It was with a slight shock that, on returning to my lodging and starting to read the dossier, I found that Mr Robinson's statement was approximately correct. It could justifiably be charged against Mr Grant Foraker's father that, for purposes of his own, he had – in the year 1881, in south-western Indiana – faked the end of the world.

4

A heading, 'The Antonia Swindle' – inked in capital letters, presumably by Mr Robinson – was, in fact, the first thing to catch my eye as I opened the folder. (The cover, as I noticed when I sat down to examine it, had a label neatly pasted on it, bearing the words, 'The Case of Grant Foraker'.)

Under the handwritten heading, were pasted, on the first and a score of succeeding pages, numerous clippings – some running to a couple of columns, some only a few paragraphs in length – from various Middle Western newspapers, each with the date marked in ink beside it. The dates were all between 1880 and the early part of 1883.

Spaces had been left between and on either side of the clippings to permit the insertion of handwritten comments, by Robinson senior or junior, which bristled on the faded pages like patches of thornbush, with words, here and there, underlined in red ink so that they stuck out at one: '*Impudent*'; 'He said *God* told him to'; 'Note early training as *destructive liar*'; 'Truly *amazing* effrontery.'

Though irked by the feeling that I was allowing my time to be filched by the preposterous Robinson, I decided to devote half an hour to the newspaper clippings on 'The Antonia Swindle', since these were at least authentic, although some were contradictory and many repetitive.

I have these, and the other documents in the folder, beside me as I write all these years later; the only material relics of a kind of *grande passion*.

Those assembled under the heading, 'The Antonia Swindle', are concerned with the fortunes and misfortunes of a long-forgotten religious community calling itself 'The Community of the Regenerate Sons and Daughters of the New Word and the Covenant', established at Antonia, Indiana, at the end of

1878 or the beginning of 1879. (The newspaper reports are at variance.)

Founder and leader of the community is a forty-year-old Scottish preacher named Jephthah Foraker. It is agreed that he comes from Lanarkshire; but as to why and how he has appeared in Indiana – at the head of between thirty and forty Regenerate Sons and Daughters of the New Word and Covenant – some of them having followed him from Scotland, others gathered from New England, others again from Tennessee – the newspapers and the penned comments erupt in a boiling turmoil of assertions, contradictions, allegations, and counter-allegations.

One thing, however, emerges clearly from statements made at various times by Jephthah Foraker and his adherents: Whatever else they may have asserted, they assert, repeatedly, passionately, and absolutely, that they and they alone possess the proper combination to open salvation's safe. Those who, for one reason or another, have not had the opportunity to see and love the Foraker way to God are to be, in varying degrees, despised or pitied, and, circumstances permitting, enlightened. Those, on the other hand, who presume actually to oppose, combat or in any way to let or hinder the Sons and Daughters of the New World and Covenant are to be abhorred, denounced and – in Jephthah's phrase – 'pelted with the pitiless stones of righteousness'.

(The phrase is possibly metaphorical, but it is used against him later when he is accused of incitement to riot.)

Jephthah emerges from the newspaper clippings as a man of wide interests and, apparently, ambitions. By the autumn of 1880 the Sons and Daughters are well established on land purchased with funds raised by him, partly in Scotland, partly in the course of a preparatory preaching tour in New England. In November of that year, Jephthah runs for mayor, on the Republican ticket, and is elected.

One of the county newspapers reports, with local pride, that the Reverend Foraker, Mayor-elect of Antonia, is 'not only among the finest preachers in the United States, but was preeminent in his former habitat of Lanark, Scotland, as an authority and practitioner in the field of the Natural Sciences, study of which increasingly reveals the workings of the Divine Will. In his forthcoming lecture "How Isaiah Foretold the Railroad," the Reverend Foraker will,' etc., etc., etc.

And a little later, in a paragraph around which the elder Robinson's exclamation marks cavort like witch-doctors smelling out sin (he has even drawn a hand with an accusing finger, pointing to this paragraph) it is noted, in the same newspaper, that the Reverend Foraker has installed, in the yard of his house at Antonia, an 'observatory' from which he will 'study the movement of the stars in their appointed courses'.

A sermon of Jephthah Foraker's, subsequently unearthed and quoted, shows that in the spring of 1881, the Sons and Daughters were going through some kind of crisis.

Then, in the summer of that year, he makes an announcement: his son, now aged eight, has had a vision of the impending end of the world. 'Out of the mouths of babes and sucklings ...' So, in the Tabernacle of the New Word and Covenant, the child Ezekiel Grant Foraker is put up on the rostrum beside his father, and spouts a terrifying account of not one, but a whole series of visions he has had, which same visions have been accompanied by the Voice of God, explaining things in detail as the dreadful picture unfolds.

What it amounts to is that God, who had given the world a last chance of creating, through the agency of his servant Jephthah, the organization of the New Word and Covenant, is grievously vexed by the failure of the world at large to jump at the opportunity offered. ('God told me,' the boy Foraker is quoted as saying, 'the world didn't seem to have enough plain sense to come in out of the rain of sinfulness on to the porch of salvation.') Disgusted with the whole business, God is going to make an end of the world – probably some time in August.

Jephthah, in a series of sermons and exhortations, expounds the view that the question of saving the world is now fairly and squarely up to the Regenerate Sons and Daughters. It is *their* failure which has put God in His present frame of mind. Only drastic action on their part can now convince God that there is any percentage in keeping the world going at all. They must not only rally in prayer, they must augment their prayer-power by a whirlwind campaign of conversion. Then, when Jephthah gives the word, they and their families, must ascend Mount Harrison and there loose off a broadside of prayer so mighty that it will convince the Lord that the crop in God's Great Cornfield has not failed but been suffering from a temporary drought.

The campaign, according to reports, is a tearing success. Young Ezekiel Grant Foraker has taken to having his visions in public, and sits on the front porch giving, in a piping voice, a round-by-round eyewitness account of what seems to be about to happen. The end of the world, he says, will, according to what he has seen and heard in his latest revelation, start with an awful silence, much like the hush before a hurricane – but more silent. After that will come thunder, but louder than any ordinary thunder; lightning more dazzling than any lightning aforetime seen; and a wind that will make the worst hurricane that the oldest can remember seem like a breeze. And then – the Brimstone, the Abomination of Desolation, and the End.

Crowds gather and listen to the inspired child. Panic spreads. The Regenerate Sons and Daughters come to be widely regarded in the neighbourhood as people who have a megaphone to God; the only one that will carry. If only everyone will gather round and shout into it, He will hear. Some of the local farmers and storekeepers claim later that they got converted as a kind of insurance; if Jephthah were wrong, no great harm would be done. If he were to turn out right, a person would feel a darn fool not having lent a hand to stop the end of the world when he could.

Jephthah seems to have had, right from the outset, the idea that the prosperity of the community of the New Word and Covenant depends on its members occupying and farming a continuous, and continuously expanding, tract of land. Now, he urges that the new converts should move closer to the community in the geographical as well as the spiritual sense. A lot of the new converts sell the land they have elsewhere in the county and join in helping to buy a big acreage west of

Antonia, which approximately doubles the amount of farmland held by the community.

By the beginning of August, the number of Regenerate Sons and Daughters has risen to nearly one hundred. Jephthah divides his time between the Tabernacle and the so-called 'observatory'. Twice he makes a business trip to Evansville, staying away a couple of nights on each occasion. Then, on the afternoon of August 11, he announces that the decisive moment is near. The members of the community trek off towards Mount Harrison, with camping equipment and sporting guns, and cows and poultry and other provisions against the possibility they may have to stay there roaring at the Lord for a week or so. At the head of the trek – for 'a little child shall lead them' – goes Ezekiel Grant.

(Here Mr Robinson senior inevitably scribbles in a story to the effect that Jephthah stayed behind on that first evening, nominally to pray in solitude at the Tabernacle – a sort of rearguard – but that, in reality, he was espied by a non-Regenerate neighbour in the parlour of his own home, embracing the half-naked body of a young non-Regenerate widow named Mrs Kenneally.)

However that may be, all reports are in agreement that by late that night Jephthah was up on Mount Harrison, leading intensive prayer, and that some time in the course of that night people in the camp were actually awakened by the silence, a sudden, empty silence, deep and breathless; as though, according to one of them, God had taken a deep breath and sucked the air away from the world.

During almost all of the next day, there are a series of such breathless times of stillness over Mount Harrison, interrupted by irregular puffs of wind, which are sometimes prolonged into strong breezes, lasting for half an hour or more and suddenly dropping away. In the late afternoon, distant thunder is heard, and a ghastly flicker of lightning, westwards over Illinois, beyond the Wabash River, competes menacingly with the sunset. All evening, a trickle of converts makes its way up Mount Harrison from the valley and the plain.

For an hour before midnight, the Regenerate Sons and

Daughters are caught again in one of those terrible silences. Then, almost exactly at midnight, the wind rushes at them, thunder and lightning crash and blaze and crackle, the place seems to rock under the celestial impact.

Jephthah has set the camp in a wide, treeless hollow before the top of the Mount. Here, protected from the full force of the wind by the sides of the hollow, their carts and wagons lashed together as a barricade, the members of the community kneel in intensive prayer, or rise suddenly to their feet, hurling their arms skywards in desperate supplication, sometimes being thrown violently to the ground by the wind, sometimes actually picked up by it, as though between the finger and thumb of God, and dashed to the ground yards away.

But Jephthah has had himself lashed to the wheel of a great wagon, and beside him, lashed partly to the top of the wheel and partly to the side of the wagon itself, is Ezekiel Grant, white-faced, mostly breathless and silent, but – in lulls of the circling storm – seen to open his mouth and appear to be wildly chanting some hymn, or yelling out a long prayer.

Several eyewitness accounts of the scene are preserved in the records of the subsequent lawsuits.

By those closest to the wagon, the voice of Jephthah can be heard almost continuously. He is throwing into battle against the Divine chaos, the marshalled logic of a Scots sermon. ('And eighthly, O Lord, Thou wilt not be unaware that . . .') His tone is sternly challenging. He makes it clear that in his view the Lord God has failed to make out an indisputable case for adopting His present course of action. If such a case exists, Jephthah is ready and willing to hear it. He sets out various arguments which the Lord might possibly advance in defence of His thesis, in justification of His decision to make an end of the world. He builds them up, brick by brick, and, brick by brick, knocks them down again, proving with hammer-blow after logical hammer-blow that if *that* is what the Lord is relying on, the Lord has not, in effect, got a leg to stand on. So, let the Lord either explain Himself more fully and cogently to His people, or let Him desist.

This continues for the whole of that night and part of the

following morning. Sometimes the wind abates, as though leaving the field clear for thunder, lightning and billows of rain to go into the attack. Sometimes the whole storm seems to circle away from Mount Harrison. Ezekiel Grant is loosed from his place and creeps into the wagon to sleep. But Jephthah, still lashed to the wheel and tearing with hands and teeth at a piece of cold steak, is looking and listening and he tells them that it is not over yet; the Lord is still unconvinced. And, sure enough, the storm comes back and rages for three hours more. (It was in this phase that the far-flung storm lifted a huge coal barge out of the Ohio River and threw it into the streets of Evansville, picked up the southern end of Westphalia township and tossed it right across the new tracks of the Vandalia Railroad, and caused death and havoc at New Harmony, where earlier seekers after God's Truth and the Good Life had once thought to found an earthly Paradise.)

It is almost noon before the storm, beyond a doubt, has gone, and the sun comes out to shine on a world miraculously preserved. There have been casualties, even among the Regenerate Sons and Daughters. Two very young children have perished in the ordeal on the Mount, and of the men one has been killed and another burned and crippled for life by lightning. A woman dies a few days later of pneumonia contracted during that night. And the homes and barns of Antonia itself are grievously damaged.

But the community as a whole rejoices in survival, and also the consciousness that by its own efforts, under the guidance of its tremendous leader, it has saved not only itself but the entire world from destruction. Jephthah is a major prophet in his own country. And when people give Ezekiel Grant candy there is something almost sacramental about the act.

It would seem that Jephthah's position as spiritual and temporal ruler of the community is limitless and impregnable. But, while most people are still thinking thus, there have already come trickling in, from all kinds of sources, rivulets of complaint, doubt, and discontent which are suddenly seen to be eating away the foundations of his place and power.

First, it is a group of the 'summer converts', who attribute any difficulties they encounter at Antonia to a supposed inferiority of the land there to the land they gave up so as to help stop the end of the world. Naturally, they listen with angry belief to the stories of those from outside Antonia who tell them that the whole storm was just an ordinary, violent hurricane. A Democrat lawyer from Evansville is the first to make the suggestion that perhaps the Reverend Jephthah somehow figured out in advance that a hurricane was likely about that time, and acted on that hunch.

The doubt, once created, spreads fast, nourished by every normal grievance or friction existing between Jephthah Foraker and other members of the community. The relatives of those who died on the Mount begin to murmur – declaring that their kin were lured to an unnecessary death.

All these trickles are run together into a flood by the gubernatorial elections. For the first time since 1861, a Decocrat – Albert G. Porter – is elected Governor of Indiana. The struggle is fierce. The case of the Reverend Foraker, Republican Mayor of Antonia, is suddenly transformed into an issue, a scandal, a piece of dynamite. One night, a band of unknown men, probably incited and directed by the Democrat lawyer from Evansville, breaks into the Observatory and removes numerous instruments, books, and papers.

The instruments are reported to include an anemometer, which had been concealed in the roof of the Observatory, a nephoscope, and other meteorological apparatus. Among the books and papers are found the complete works of James Pollard Espy, of Philadelphia, later meteorologist to the War and Navy Departments, with the passages specifically relating to the motive power of thunderstorms and tornadoes underlined; copies of the *American Journal of Science* and Gould's *Astronomical Journal* containing articles by Professor William Ferrell; numerous publications of Kelvin; William C. Redfield's 'Chart of the Hurricane of 1821'; and an almost complete collection of the maps, charts, and predictions of weather published during the previous fifteen months by the United States Government and the Smithsonian Institution.

A confused howl of indignation follows these disclosures,

for the news has been widely published before Jephthah can sue for the recovery of his stolen property.

He is attacked for gross impiety. The 'summer converts' bring actions against him, claiming that in the matter of their lands he has been guilty of vile misrepresentation.

At the outset, Jephthah preaches a hell-fire sermon against the backsliders among the 'summer converts'.

Finally, he sets upon a leading backslider and beats him in the streets, and – despite everything – there are still a score or so of the original Regenerate Sons who rush to follow his example. There is fighting all over Main Street, firearms are used on both sides; the Reverend Foraker is arrested and put on trial for assault and incitement to riot, and it is only with difficulty that the Republican forces get the case dismissed amid new reek of scandal.

In his numerous cross-examinations in the civil courts, he treats judges and counsel with the disdain proper to a Prophet of the Lord in the hands of the ungodly.

He makes no attempt, for instance, to deny that he had for months been studying the meteorological situation with special reference to the incidence of hurricanes or cyclones in the valleys of the Ohio and Wabash.

So far as he can be understood at all, he seems to be maintaining that such studies, leading to the conviction that a hurricane was on its way, are purely irrelevant to the issue: If the Lord chose to utilize the scientific knowledge of His servant Foraker to warn the world of His intention to put an end to it, that was simply the way the Lord wanted things done.

In the end, the charges against him prove too vague to be substantiated in legal terms. The community, as such, falls to pieces. Jephthah remains for some months, apparently, but his function has gone.

According to a letter from Antonia to a friend in Scotland, quoted by Robinson, Ezekiel Grant's plight is indeed unhappy. In the degree to which he was formerly idolized and petted, he is now derided and bullied. Children of his own age, who have no notion of what the whole rumpus was about, humiliate and sneer at him, delighted to find a creature for ill-treatment who apparently, by some act of inconceivably naughty insolence, has forfeited the normal protection of the adults of the community.

Whether on the boy's account, or for some other sufficient reason, towards the autumn of 1882, Jephthah, Janet, and Ezekiel Grant Foraker quit Antonia and, after a year or so during which Jephthah holds some kind of lectureship in New York, return to Scotland.

At this point, the character of the documents in Mr Robinson's folder changes abruptly. In place of long – and though confusing and contradictory, still consequent – newspaper accounts, we have now, so far as the newspapers are concerned, a plethora of more or less disjointed paragraphs, some only a few lines in length, related to one another only by the fact that they all seem to refer in some manner to the doings of the Forakers, and between them pages of notes, extracts from letters, and what appear to be extracts from a diary, all in the handwriting of Mr Robinson senior.

Then, in 1889, the newspaper reports and commentaries blaze up in an action for slander.

Defendant is a Mr Henderson, who admits stating in the presence of witnesses that one of the successful candidates for a scholarship to Edinburgh University from a local grammar school has obtained his scholarship by dishonest means. The boy concerned is sixteen-year-old Ezekiel Grant Foraker. The allegations, confusedly thrown about the Liberal Club by Mr Henderson one evening after dinner, are, roughly, that through 'certain connections' of his father, Jephthah Foraker, the boy had an opportunity to learn in advance the nature of the questions put in the Natural Science section of the scholarship examination paper. (It is not denied that in this section Ezekiel Grant scored a mark of 96 per cent.)

Plaintiff is, of course, Jephthah Foraker, suing on his own behalf and on behalf of his son. Mr Henderson, who at the outset has intimated that he can call unimpeachable evidence of the truth of his allegations, suddenly collapses, is unable to produce any evidence at all, tries at the last moment to change his plea and aver that the words complained of were never spoken, is mulcted in heavy damages, and sharply castigated by the court.

On all this, Mr Robinson's Greek Chorus is venomous but unusually vague. The news seems to shut down again until, in 1896, a few paragraphs in a local south Edinburgh weekly paper record the return from Canada, on a brief visit to the parental home, of Mr Grant Foraker, son of the respected citizen, and leading figure in the scientific instrument business, Mr Jephthah Foraker. Mr Foraker junior, who, after cutting short his University career, served his apprenticeship with a well-known engineering works in Glasgow, has for the past eighteen months held a post as Consultant with the well-known engineering firm of Mathieson and Delavigne of Montreal, whither he is returning at the end of the month.

Silence for nearly a year. But it is the lull before a storm which blackens two pages of the folder.

Mathieson and Delavigne go bankrupt. Angry shareholders, in Canada, Great Britain, and the United States, charge culpable irresponsibility, even criminal recklessness. The investigation shows that, while carrying on its normal business, the firm has pledged its assets to finance a sideline – the production of a new type of self-propelled road vehicle. Expenses had been enormously higher than anticipated, development of the vehicle very much slower. New money had been poured in to keep the enterprise afloat. Finally, the banks had closed in.

The partners, Mathieson and Delavigne, stated that they had first become interested in the possibilities of self-propelled vehicles as a commercial proposition in the year 1895, at the time of the Paris–Bordeaux–Paris race for such vehicles organized by the *Petit Journal*.

Cross-examination discloses that their attention had been drawn to such possibilities in the first place by their Consultant, Mr Grant Foraker. With horrid irony, counsel for the shareholders says he assumes that this Mr Foraker was a person of mature experience? Had devoted long years of study to such matters? The partners, amid outraged uproar in court, are forced to admit that their Consultant was, at the time, just twenty-two years of age.

They had, however – and they retain – a very high opinion of Mr Foraker's ability in this field, and they had seen no reason to turn down a good-looking proposition simply because it was put to them by a man of twenty-two.

And just what was this proposition? In plain language that a layman could understand?

Well, Mr Foraker had demonstrated to their satisfaction that the average speed of fifteen miles per hour maintained by the winner of the Paris–Bordeaux–Paris race was susceptible of being very considerably improved upon. Quite so, counsel for shareholders puts in: To *your* satisfaction, but not, obviously, to anyone else's. Mr Grant Foraker is called, is visibly unrepentant, and makes a speech. It is partly about motors, but chiefly about alloys. 'The motor-power,' says he, 'is only a fraction of the problem. The other part of the problem is to find an alloy that will reduce weight per horsepower. I believe that with continued research it will be possible to find such an alloy.'

Counsel sneers. 'You mean,' he says, 'that the wrapping is more important, in your view, than what is inside the package? I am not surprised, Mr Foraker, to find that you are something of a specialist in *wrapping things up in a pretty packing*.' (Applause in court.)

Mathieson and Delavigne escape a criminal prosecution by the skin of their teeth.

And then the record suddenly and disconcertingly closes up like a squeezed concertina; references to the period from 1896 to 1908 cover only five pages. There are a dozen or so clippings, mostly from small Edinburgh papers, giving such items as the return of Grant Foraker from Kansas City in 1899 to do some unspecified work at Edinburgh University, which an equally unspecified American Foundation is paying for; the deaths, during 1900, first of Jephthah, then of Janet Foraker; Grant Foraker's departure, once again, for the United States; his marriage, in 1902, to Miss Delia Landis, of Canton, Ohio.

5

My overnight interest in Mr Robinson was nearly smothered by the clerk at the Poste Restante who, after so many fruitless visits, handed me a letter from an assistant of Professor Auguste Michel Lévy. This assistant, a Dr Thaypi, thanked me on behalf of Professor Lévy, congratulated me on my interest in the science of geology, would be at my disposal if I should care to call upon him on my arrival in Paris. He hoped that he would be forgiven for reminding me of the fact, doubtless entirely familiar to myself, that the opening of the scientific and industrial Exposition at Lyons was now imminent, a circumstance of which I might care to take advantage, in case I happened to be travelling from Marseilles to Paris at that date.

I had visited the Poste Restante at the moment it opened at eight o'clock, and returned through the bright morning streets in a state of high elation.

I turned the corner by my lodging and almost bumped into Mr Robinson, who was pacing up and down in front of the main door, where the concierge had told him of my movements. With my foot already on the ladder of European fame as a geologist, I felt gay and magnanimous. I greeted him with a smile and a wave of the hand. He clutched me by the arm.

'Just missed you,' he said. 'The concierge wouldn't let me go up and wait in your room. Not even when I told her I was your elder brother. Bureaucratic,' he said aggrievedly.

I remarked that this was a very early call. He looked at me with surprise. 'Well, naturally,' he said. 'About those documents. I wanted to get your impression. Now that you've had a chance to see . . .'

I told him I would get the folder from my room, join him for breakfast at the café across the street.

At the café, he seized the folder eagerly, and fondly looked it through, possibly for the sheer pleasure of it, or because at the last moment he had the idea that I might have abstracted valuable documents.

'So there,' he said at last, 'you have it. The background.'

I pointed out that he had not explained at all how the Forakers and Robinsons happened to be mixed up together in the first place. The Robinsons, it emerged, rather to my disappointment, had had no connection whatever with the Antonia venture, except in the strictly negative sense that Robinson *père*, a corn merchant in Lanark, had from the outset declared that the whole thing was doomed to disaster. The people who followed the Reverend Jephthah would lose their money and probably their lives. The whole idea was rank communism, and would lead to polygamy, orgies, and ruin.

Humility was the least the Lanark citizenry had a right to expect of the Forakers. Instead, they had shown themselves mulishly unrepentant, with no hint of sackcloth and ashes about Jephthah. Deeming such a situation unseemly, the elder Robinson had conducted a private campaign – ultimately successful – to hound the Forakers out of town. During this campaign, Robinson junior, a year or so older than young Foraker, had been given to understand by his father that young Foraker was a lad who in America had had the gall to pretend he was John the Baptist, or something of the kind, and everyone had petted him and given him anything he asked for – sacksful of sugar-plums and such.

To punish such impious presumption, young Robinson had formed a band of Avengers. They used to catch young Foraker after school and beat and pummel him. On favourable occasions they would drag him off to the desolate links and form a ring round him, kicking and spitting on him. Then they would tear his trousers and drawers off and make him run the gauntlet half naked, while they lashed him with leather taws.

And then came the scholarship examination. What was disgusting was that Foraker should have won it at all, living as he did in the very next street to the Robinsons, so that the beastly pride of himself and family in his achievement was rubbed right under the Robinsons' noses. To anyone knowing the Forakers, it was evident that there had been hanky-panky somewhere, but, unfortunately, before Robinson senior had had a chance to secure the proofs which he had promised Mr

Henderson, the latter 'made a bit of a fool of himself – one over the eight in the Liberal Club' and the slander action followed, with victory for the Forakers.

Breaking up fast, Robinson senior had by now, apparently, got round to the position that the respected and successful Forakers were somehow a model of what to aim at in life, a yardstick by which to measure success. There was young Grant – 'dropped the Ezekiel when he crossed the millpond; might have reminded some Yank of certain events in Indiana' – already a consultant to this big firm in Montreal. And what was young Tom Robinson doing? Still clerking in Edinburgh. And Grant, younger than him by a year or more, earning good money, best of everything.

With some idea of drawing level with Grant Foraker, Tom Robinson had sought him out when he was home on leave and questioned him about Canada and its possibilities. Foraker had hinted at something absolutely tremendous that Mathieson and Delavigne were up to, hinted also that people with money, the sort of people that could afford to get hold of a nice parcel of Mathieson and Delavigne shares and lock them away for a year or two, would make a tremendous killing.

Impelled partly by an honest lust for money, partly – as he admitted through the pulp of his second coffee-soaked *croissant* – by a desire to 'wipe that smug sorry-you're-too-poor-to-get-in-on-this look off Grant Foraker's face', young Robinson had taken a last advantage of his parent's decrepit fantasies, and got him to hand over his life's savings, plus the sum realized by mortgaging his life insurance policy, for investment by Tom in the shares of Mathieson and Delavigne.

'Well,' said Mr Robinson, 'you've read what happened about that.'

I said it must have been exceedingly embittering to lose all that money in that way.

Mr Robinson became excited and blew his coffee into stormy waves. 'But that's not the point,' he said. 'You don't appreciate the quintessential fact.'

According to him this was that Grant Foraker really had known what he was doing when he advised Mathieson and

Delavigne to put their money into the attempt to develop a new type of self-propelled road vehicle. ('He was *smart*, don't you see?' Robinson kept saying.)

Eighteen-ninety-five he had started 'cutting that little caper'. And look what had happened in that line since. Look at Ford, at Daimler and Renault. Winner in that Paris–Bordeaux race did fifteen miles per hour and now they have a speed *limit* in England of twenty miles per hour because a motor could do sixty, easy.

'And it's the work on the alloys that's done it,' said Robinson. 'The way *he* said it would. That's where England has the edge on everyone just for the present moment of time. Because they know more about steel alloys than the rest. Less weight, more power, more speed. Ratio of weight to power. Just the way Mr Grant Foraker had it worked out.'

I said that, in the circumstances, Mr Foraker seemed to have been very unlucky. The brown waves leaped over the edge of Mr Robinson's cup and splashed into the saucer.

'*Unlucky?*' he burst out, and developed the opinion – 'crystal clear . . . stands to reason' – that Foraker had not only sold Mathieson and Delavigne shares short and made a packet out of the collapse, but all along had been simply using the money of the Mathieson and Delavigne shareholders to get research work done for him on a grand scale which he could never have undertaken on his own.

He was back, now, on the patriotic track – patriotism the sole motive force of his activities; and this quite brazenly, without any reference to what he had just been telling me of his long-term relations with Foraker. It was, I supposed, the way he had felt when he was belting young Foraker on the links – protecting John the Baptist from sacrilegious impersonations.

His idea, propped up by a huge ramshackle scaffolding of news items, ascertained facts, bits of gossip, pieces of observation, was that here was this Grant Foraker – his dangerous and unscrupulous nature sufficiently attested by the record – loose in Europe with a kegful of explosive knowledge under his hat, and undoubtedly going right ahead exploiting that knowledge in his characteristically Foraker-ish way, regardless of the interests of humanity in general and his native land in particular, climbing up the ladder of riches and power to a position where pretty soon he would be laughing, simply laughing, at ordinary decent folk like Robinson.

What was he actually up to? That was what it 'very definitely behooved' us to find out, in detail. Was there any reason to suppose it so very important? Well, was it likely that Mathieson and Delavigne could have spent all that money – a million or more – on that plant and those experiments without Foraker, in charge of the whole thing, acquiring some tremendous knowledge of possibilities in that line?

His eyes swivelled round towards the waiter and back again, and his breath ruffled the hair at my temple. 'I'll give you just a hint,' he said. 'I'll tell you this: When he was showing me the door, talking about spies and all that order of thing, he said – I'll tell you what he said – he said, "I suppose it's Wilbur Wright that's paying you, you . . ." and called me some really filthy names. You get the angle of reference? Wilbur Wright.'

I had read, of course, in the Spanish papers, of the intention of Wilbur Wright to transfer his aeronautical experiments from the United States to France, because of lack of financial backing in his home country.

He was back at his plan for me to take on the job with Foraker. With the tips of his fingers just touching my sleeve, he reasoned and pleaded with me in tones of passionate sincerity – a man speaking in the name of the Motherland, the Human Race, Common Justice, and the Almighty.

'But you see,' I said, 'in a few days I shall be leaving for Lyons, and then go on to Paris to put myself at this Dr Thaypi's disposal. I'm afraid I can't alter my plans.'

He sat silent for a long minute, then he said gravely, 'Do you want to be rich?'

'Of course,' I said, laughing.

'Naturally,' he said, and brooded.

That evening he was not in his place at the *brasserie*. But on returning home immediately after dinner I was met, in the main doorway of the house, by the concierge, looking agitated, shame-faced, and defiant.

What could she do? she asked. The gentlemen had been insistent; matter of greatest urgency; afraid of missing me; a nasty night; no harm in their waiting in my room.

'What gentlemen, for heaven's sake?'

'Your two uncles, your cousin, and your brother – who was here this morning.'

I dashed up to the third floor, stopped to listen in the dark for a moment outside the door of my tiny apartment. There was a yellow streak of light from the big keyhole, and silence. I opened, and the little room seemed to bulge with silent figures, as though someone had left them there on their way to the waxworks. The Philosopher bulked in the only armchair. At the other side of the table sat the Military Person and the Hairy Sneerer. Mr Robinson, leaning his back against the wall by the window, twitched to attention as I came in, advanced, bowed, and in a moment was introducing and 'explaining'.

A simple ruse ... I would forgive them in the circumstances ... matter of urgency ... much at stake ... permit me to introduce ... 'Monsieur Paca!' (the Philosopher shifted his buttocks slightly in the chair and inclined his domed forehead towards me) ... 'Monsieur Perrin!' (the Military Person stood up and bowed from the hips ... 'Monsieur Bally!' (the Hairy Sneerer did the same).

Trembling with annoyance, confusion, and some alarm – they might, by the look of them, have been the chosen executioners of some unheard-of secret society – I passed through the next few minutes in a dazed condition. Particularly upsetting was the fact that, so far from the intruders, on their side, displaying any kind of confusion or unease, they had rather the gravely assured air of police officials or magistrates dealing with a tiresome delinquent; someone, say, who has failed to fill up a necessary form, and may have done so through either bad citizenship or carelessness; may thus, perhaps, be given the benefit of the doubt.

Before the end of ten minutes they were all nodding or muttering confirmation of an elaborate statement by Mr Robinson to the effect that 'as I told you, these gentlemen are interested in the matter, and in the event of your reconsidering your attitude to my suggestion that you apply for the position as secretary to Mr Foraker, they are prepared not only to supplement on a generous scale whatever emoluments you may receive from him, but also to guarantee you support in case of anything premature happening, if you follow me, in connection with that position'.

I suppose it was at this point that my exasperated bewilderment exploded in a burst of angry words. I was aware of M. Paca whispering something to Mr Robinson, actually raising his eyebrows and shaking his dome in contemplation of a difficult case. And, presently, Mr Robinson was saying that he thought it would be best in the interests of all concerned if he and the other two were to leave myself and M. Paca alone, so that M. Paca might have a few words with me.

Stupefied, I saw them file out of the room, and found myself confronting the grave bulk of M. Paca, whose expression was one of stern, but comprehending, benevolence. Before I could put even one of my angry questions, he raised his podgy hand in a gesture requesting silence and declared he could fully understand that I might be in some doubt about the position.

'The fact is,' said M. Paca, 'that Monsieur Robinson has a gift.'

He left this statement – solemn and incomprehensible – hanging in the air. It was as though, having hung it there, he were now examining it with detached interest. Then he hung another one up beside it.

'You must understand, Monsieur Hastings,' he said, 'that we're not interested in Monsieur Robinson's ideas – as such. We're not interested in this Foraker either – as such.'

I made a disbelieving face at him and he repeated, more emphatically, that he and his friends did not give a damn for Mr Foraker. 'We are simply businessmen and we want to buy something. We want to buy the use of this gift that Monsieur Robinson has.'

'But what is it, this gift?'

'Well, you see,' said M. Paca, 'he can foretell the future.'

He set about lighting a cigar, the picture of a serious, practical, prosperous man of business, his head bulging with brains, too. From such a source this declaration seemed monstrous. If this 'gift' of Mr Robinson's had been mentioned to me in the 1950s, I should not have been startled. Scientists have been at work, thousands of experiments have been made, and the faculty of 'pre-cognition' is, I suppose, an established fact. But in 1908 this kind of talk was associated with magical rigmaroles, spookery, gipsy women with crystal balls. Highland ancients keening in mists, planchettes, ectoplasm and every kind of mumbo jumbo. I was aghast at the idea of anyone trying to take in anyone else with such hocus-pocus.

'Just what,' M. Paca said, 'at a rough estimate, would you reckon the chances would be against a man calling the order of cards in a new, shuffled pack and getting six out of the first ten right?'

I said I had no idea – millions to one against, anyway.

'Just so,' said M. Paca.

'And you mean that Robinson ...'

'Over and over again,' said M. Paca.

'Some trick,' I said, wondering whether M. Paca was himself deceived or just hoping to deceive me, and despising him either way.

'The point is,' he said, 'it works. Horses, too. He sees winners.'

'All the winners?'

'Enough of them,' said M. Paca.

I laughed. 'In that case,' I said, putting my finger firmly on the flaw, and pressing it, 'isn't it a little surprising that Mr Robinson needs to raise funds from you? Isn't it odd he isn't a millionaire by now? Or,' I inquired with sarcasm, 'did he only get this gift last week?'

M. Paca was unperturbed. This, he explained, was where Mr Robinson's funny ideas came in; also his mother, now deceased. She had had this gift, too. And she had told the youthful Robinson that this gift was from God and must never be used for purposes of personal gain. So used, it could bring disaster, or at the best shrivel up.

At first, M. Paca revealed, he had been sceptical of this story, supposing it a feeble excuse to cover the fact that Mr Robinson had no such gift. But then an acquaintance in the theatrical business had told him that this notion or superstition was quite common among entertainers in the thought-reading line. What they did on the stage was just trickery, but a lot of them believed they really did have powers of second sight, but that it was dangerous or unlucky to use them for profit.

'When,' M. Paca said, 'friend Robinson first let fall a little remark about this gift of his – back in Paris, months ago – my friends and I didn't believe him, naturally not. I told him he couldn't tell us the first three winners at Longchamps the coming Sunday. He says, "Yes, I can." I say, "Go ahead, then." And he says, "Only if you'll swear not to bet on them," says he.'

'And?'

'One odds-on favourite,' said M. Paca, 'one at fives, and a damned outsider at around a hundred to eight. The pity was, we didn't believe Robinson's story hard enough to put our shirts on the treble. Cleaned up a nice bit of money all the same. And, of course, we couldn't split with the poor fellow because of having sworn like that not to have any money on.'

Unhurriedly, M. Paca sketched for me scenes from the subsequent relations of himself and friends with Mr Robinson. The philosophical M. Paca, it emerges, is part-proprietor of a *boite*, or perhaps it is a brothel, somewhere behind the Madeleine. M. Perrin is less military than he looks, he is a journalist. M. Bally works in some capacity for a firm of stockbrokers.

After the first episode at Longchamps, M. Paca and his friends have spots before their eyes, followed by golden visions. They cultivate Mr Robinson. Mr Robinson hugs his bewildering gift closely to him, consents only to give little demonstrations with cards. Their six eyes bulge, tears are near at the thought of such possibilities unused. Upon sadness, follows anger. They have never met anyone like Mr Robinson before, and they do not believe he is true. They think that in some way he is holding out on them, or bidding them up. They rise from their supplicant knees and threaten him. But Mr Robinson is less afraid of them than of something awful happening to him if he misuses his gift; his dear mother, no less, had told him never to use it for gain. And others have told him the same. Besides, apart from having this screw loose, he is shrewd; he knows that they dare not risk quarrelling with him. They are tied to him like competitors in an eight-legged race.

'Then something happens to Mr Robinson; this Foraker turns up in Paris. Mr Robinson, the slavering trio note, is preoccupied with Mr Foraker. He shoots off to Scotland, leaving them in agonies of longing for the might-have-been. Just as they think he has given them the slip, taking his gift with him, he returns, resigns his job, takes on another as secretary to Foraker.

Foraker and Robinson go off on a trip to the provinces. Then Paca, in Paris, gets a letter. It apprises him that Robinson has been fired. But also that Robinson now perceives a way by which it may be possible for him, after all, to put his gift at the disposal of the trio. They rush to Marseilles. Robinson reveals his plan. He tells them, evidently, nothing about the dossier or the Embassy people; finds it not necessary to disclose his real attitude to Foraker. He simply tells them that if they are prepared to assist him – in the form of financial guarantees – to induce me to apply for a job as Foraker's secretary, he will be agreeable to placing his gift at their disposal.

M. Paca and his friends were of course entirely uninterested in Mr Robinson's motives. To me, the workings of his mind were vaguely apparent. Providence, which had sent me across Foraker's path, would not wish Mr Robinson to foozle the shot at this stage; if his gift was ever to be used for practical purposes, now was the time. It would be used not for gain, but as a weapon in the struggle of righteousness and patriotism against Foraker.

'And so you see,' concluded M. Paca, 'how deeply interested we are in having you do whatever it is Monsieur Robinson wants you to do. You can see why we are prepared to make you a very handsome offer indeed.'

My angry refusal to involve myself in schemes which

seemed certainly grotesque and probably criminal, came as a total surprise to M. Paca. To his friends, too, when he reported it. During the last four days at Marseilles I seemed never to be free of them.

At the news that I was actually leaving for Lyons, they became frenzied. They declared they would come to see me off, and I knew that they planned an eleventh hour appeal at the station itself. Exhausted by their maddening importunities I made inquiries, discovered that there was a slow train for Lyons leaving half an hour before the early morning express.

I boarded it, and had hardly settled myself in the compartment when I saw, across two intervening railway tracks, the three of them and Mr Robinson hurrying along, peering into the windows of the express, already waiting. Their faces glowed with excitement and determination. They had the dedicated, purposeful air of men in pursuit of the Holy Grail. Finding that I was not yet aboard the express, they waited, staring along the train in taut and silent expectancy.

Already as the slow train joggled northwards up the Rhône valley, the Forakers, Mr Robinson, M. Paca, and associates, seemed to lose substance and reality; reality was Paris and Dr Thaypi, preceded by the Industrial Exposition at Lyons which the New Self would visit and study with intelligent diligence, preparing for its career.

Determined to waste no time, I went, that afternoon, straight from the train to the Exposition and set out on a preliminary survey of the whole, before concentrating on the geological section. In the industrial machinery section, people were streaming away from the bay where a new electric hammer had been showing off – hurtling its steel mass towards the anvil and then just cracking an eggshell or watch-glass or something of the kind. Its attendant operator left it and followed the crowd. I walked along the railing, examining the now-deserted monster. Turning so as to pass behind it and return on its other side, I saw, in the far corner of the bay, hidden by the machine from the main corridor of the hall, Mrs Foraker and an elegantly dressed man who was either just about to kiss her or had just stopped doing so. Whichever it was, she was happy about it; radiant, leaning a little backwards, her hands on a glass-topped case containing some minor electrical exhibits. The man looked exactly like a foreign caricature of a French 'lady-killer', and he sparkled with happiness, too.

I paused, embarrassed.

They had not heard me.

Loud footsteps of a heavy man in a hurry rang on the floor behind me. I half turned, and Foraker, his coat flying out behind his marching legs, his face looking as though some powerful charge of pent impatience or fury were about to explode from it, stormed into view. The strange man had stepped back, Mrs Foraker straightened herself. Presumably they were trying to look innocent, and they looked as guilty as though they had been discovered writhing in one another's arms. If Foraker had rushed at them and beaten the unknown man with his stick I should not have been surprised. All he actually did was shout out, 'Ah, there you are. Look here, what I need . . .' and at that point he saw me for the first time.

He stared, he let out a kind of roar, and the strain went from his face.

'Good God!' he shouted. 'Mr Hastings. You're just the man I want.'

He gripped my hand and shook it as he spoke, and before I could say anything, he said, 'Listen, for God's sake come along quickly. Need you. Interpreter. Vital.' His hand was on my shoulder, and I could feel it trembling with impatience as he talked, turning back the way he had come and impelling me to turn with him. Half over his shoulder, he shouted at the others.

'Can you imagine it? Rosen's there and Halm and the damn fool they brought to translate got lost or something. Mark Crane's busy. All tied up. Thought I'd go crazy. Thought you might help, Delia. But here's Hastings. Bit of luck. See you later. Hotel.' This last word he shouted back at them just as he turned the corner and, with his hand still on my shoulder, went steaming towards the main corridor.

6

'Ce qu'on peut appeler "le principe Foraker" . . .'

'Aber das Foraker-Prinzip . . .'

'The Foraker Principle,' I translated mechanically; using whatever piece of my mind was not being punched to and fro in three languages to think about what a bear-garden I had got myself into the middle of. And why? And how? It was as though Foraker, at that first moment beside the electric hammer, had attached me to his person by some invisible tow-rope. And the impression was somehow given that the attachment of this tow-rope was natural and inevitable, had happened virtually by appointment.

Grunting, and marching at top speed, his big head moving constantly from side to side in mainly contemptuous observations of the exhibits past which we hastened, he had led me into a section of the buildings evidently set aside for use as conference or committee rooms by exhibitors and potential buyers.

I managed to make an inquiry. This Halm, who was he? Foraker repeated that he was a fool, added that he was 'rich as . . .' and waved an arm. As he seemed to think this all that need be said about M. Halm, I tried again, asking who was this Rosen that he spoke of.

Foraker not only slowed his pace but actually stopped and stood stock-still, peering down at me in astonishment. 'Rosen?' he said. 'But you've heard of him. Of course you have. Must have. Biggest man in his line.' He looked at me as though, for some dishonest reason, I were merely pretending not to have heard of M. Rosen. I told him that, nevertheless, I never had. Foraker gave me a long glare of searching suspicion, finally shrugged, and said it seemed a damned extraordinary thing. Two minutes and three corridors later, he was barging ahead of me into a small conference room with two men in it, and violently pushing chairs about while he made impatient introductions.

In the intervening years, the face of the man who then was

called Rosen became, at one period, so familiar to newspaper readers – so much a feature, as it were, of the background landscape of the later Twenties and early Thirties – that I find it hard now to reconstruct a picture of him as he looked at the time of that first meeting.

There was a period when, from almost any article dealing with industrial science, in the illustrated weeklies, or the Sunday supplements of the New York papers, you were liable to see that face looking out at you with a kind of intimidating aloofness. To many people in those years it symbolized, I think, everything that they dimly apprehended about the scientific back-rooms of the world; it suggested that you, the ordinary man, knew very little about anything important that was going on and were lucky at that, because what was really going on would probably scare you into fits.

Later, of course, as the expert, following the austerely perilous logic of his path, moved further and further into back-room after back-room, his picture was seen less and less often in the papers, and finally disappeared from them altogether. Even the name is hardly mentioned nowadays, as though merely to print it, or allude to the fact of his existence somewhere in Chicago, or, perhaps, New Mexico, hidden away behind vast entanglements of 'security', would in itself be a breach of 'security' and not in the public interest.

At that time in Lyons he must have been in his very early thirties, but he had, as I recall, already that look of a somewhat disillusioned Major Prophet, who knows what the wandering tribesmen are going to find on the other side of the mountain, knows how to lead them to it, and knows that they will not much like it when they get there.

It was difficult to grasp, at first, that, as a matter of cold fact, Foraker was evidently here to seek from M. Halm urgently needed aid of a kind which M. Halm could perfectly well either grant or withhold in a manner disastrous for Foraker. Foraker treated him rather as an ignorant, ill-conditioned, and practically feeble-minded hanger-on, whose presence and agreement had become, for some nonsensical reason, temporarily essential. And Halm, on his side, seemed to fall helplessly into the role thus assigned to him. He was a big, rather paunchy, olive-faced man in young middle-age, with brown spaniel eyes swivelling about in his head, as though he expected that at any moment someone would jump out from a corner of the room and poke him with a stick, or detect and snatch away a bone which he hoped to conceal.

It was the look on Halm's face which told me, a fraction of a minute before it happened, that the deal was concluded, the conference over. He looked like a man who has just agreed to have his teeth pulled out and is immediately wondering whether he is not being swindled by the dentist. Foraker jumped up, knocking his chair backwards on to the floor. He spoke with the air of someone whose time has been intolerably wasted in reaching an agreement that was a foregone conclusion anyway. He and Halm put their initials to a document. Foraker shook hands (haughtily with Halm, respectfully with Rosen), announced grandly that he would 'send Mark Crane to talk about the details' and, with his hand on my shoulder, hustled me from the room, and there I was marching again, a little in front of him, down the corridor.

'You'll come back to the hotel, of course,' he said. 'Have dinner with us. That went off all right in the end, didn't it?' he added. 'We got that fool Halm where we wanted him.' By this time I had become used to this kind of assumption by Foraker; for instance, that wherever he wanted Halm, I wanted him, too.

On this return journey he seemed in just as great a hurry as before. It crossed my mind that this might in some way be connected with the scene briefly witnessed by both of us behind that electric hammer. I thought perhaps the episode had suddenly come back to him and was causing him anxiety.

Then he said, casually, 'Had you already met Captain Lenoir?'

'Lenoir?'

'Weren't you talking to him and my wife? When I met up with you over there by that hammer exhibit? I thought you were with them.'

Foraker did not even bother to wait for my answer.

'Nice fellow, Captain Lenoir,' he said. 'A fine technician. Offered to show Delia around some of the exhibits while I did that business with Halm. Then there was all that damn fool business with the interpreter, and I thought I'd have to get hold of Delia and have her translate for me. Good thing I ran into you at the same time.'

He bundled me into one of the two-horse fiacres which plied between the Exposition and the centre of the city. The light vehicle rocked like a dinghy as he jumped into it and hurled himself back against the cushions.

'Of course,' he said, 'Lenoir's in love with Delia. Hardly keep his hands off her. Probably it stimulates him mentally, at that. You know,' he said, as though we were discussing the care of bees or dogs, 'some men absolutely need an extra stimulus of that kind. Ever noticed it? I have. It's natural. It's simply a phenomenon. Patriotism,' he added, 'isn't enough.'

With the air of simply continuing a discussion of the same topic, he said, raising his voice against the wind, 'You did a good job up there this afternoon. There's a place open as my secretary. A position. You can have it.' He started to yell at the driver, who thought he was shouting at him to drive faster, and did so.

'For pity's sake,' Foraker said to me, 'tell that lunatic to stop a minute. How can I light a cigar properly?'

We got the cab stopped and the cigar alight, and were off again.

'You don't,' Foraker said, 'need to worry about that business down in Marseilles. I have to be careful. Last secretary I had . . .'

He broke off, and looked thoughtfully, reminiscently one might have said, at the bouncing façades of the houses. Then, as though I had asked him for information, he shook his head, and said, 'Well, no. Not right now. It's a long story. Point is, in my opinion he probably was working for Wilbur Wright. Well, he might have been. Or someone else. Nothing to prove that he wasn't. A man that . . .' He was examining the houses again.

'Spies everywhere, of course,' he said after a pause, in a tone that seemed somehow to mitigate the offence of any particular spy. 'But as for your story, I checked up.'

I said I hadn't told him any story.

'Did you not?' he said. 'Well, I thought you might be just the kind of fellow I'd like to have working with me. So I had them look up your registration at the hotel – arrived from Barcelona it said on that thing they make you fill up for the police.'

'But why,' I said, 'should I have said I came from Barcelona if I hadn't? Anyway, I don't see that told you much.'

'Lots of people,' said Foraker reasonably, 'say they've come from somewhere they haven't. You might have come from Genoa – been the white-haired boy of that Fraschini lot down there. So I just went to the police – took the hotel porter along, of course, to do the talking – and when I told them I had good reason to suppose you were an accomplice of a pretty well-known American con-man they got busy. Checked up with Barcelona and everything.'

I suppose I looked at him speechlessly.

He gave my knee a pat, apparently of congratulation.

'It was absolutely all right,' he said. 'The fellows down there in Barcelona checked up, had you taped in no time. They went to see that uncle of yours and pretty well got the story of your life. He was pretty excited, I understand. Said he'd expected you to get in trouble but not so soon. Still, he gave them everything I wanted. The police gave me a full note of it. That way I got quite a comprehensive picture of your life, education and business career to date.'

'But –' I said.

'No, no,' said Foraker, the pat this time being of the reassuring kind, 'it was perfectly satisfactory to me. It all fits fine. Now what you'll want to know is the nature of the work.'

The wind and the bouncing increased.

'I'd like,' I shouted, as if Foraker were making an old-fashioned proposal of marriage, 'time. Time to think it over.'

'No need for that,' he shouted back, his cigar-smoke streaming between us. 'You'll be all right. I know you will. Damn cab. Tell you all about it.'

He leaned forwards suddenly and hit the driver in the small of the back with the flat of his hand. The driver turned round to swear at him, at the same time pulling up the horses with a violence which nearly threw us out of the vehicle. Foraker gave him a shout of approval and bounded on to the road, where he stood fumbling for coins. As I joined him, he was passing a small handful over to the driver and beaming at him.

'*Voulons marcher,*' he explained. '*Trop* noise. *Voulons parler quietement. Beaucoup importantes choses. San fairy ann.* Only another ten minutes' walk to the hotel,' he added to me. 'Tell you all about it as we go along.'

He looked up and down the wintry boulevard, deserted under the street-lamps. I thought he was possibly scanning it for eavesdroppers.

'Quiet here,' he said, and started walking.

'Now,' he said, his face shining in the lamplight underneath the tossing branches of a plane-tree, 'the question you ask yourself is: What is the nature and purpose of the work I shall be doing with Mr Grant Foraker? A fair question. But,' he glared at a twig dancing just above his head, 'a question not susceptible of a complete answer . . .'

I said, 'Oh?'

He said, 'You say, "Oh?" A fair comment, Mr Hastings. But I will explain, to your satisfaction. The truth of the matter is that if I were to give you the complete answer to that question you wouldn't understand a word of it. *San fairy ann,* as they say here in France. But you wouldn't, all the same.'

'I gathered,' I said, 'up there at your conference, that you are interested in aviation.'

'That,' he said, peering at a star, 'is so.'

'Interesting,' I said.

He said, 'What?'

'I said it must be rather interesting.'

He jerked his attention free of the star and stopped walking. He looked at me in much the way he had when I had asked him who Rosen was. His face was slightly contorted and he had a little difficulty with his voice. When he found it, it came out in a shout which rang down the boulevard.

'Listen. It's so damned interesting that in five years, ten years it'll be the biggest thing in life. I mean,' he added, speaking in a more reasonable tone, 'in the material life of man upon this planet. As for the rest . . .'

He favoured the 'rest' with an enormous shrug.

This extravagance irked me. A little cold water, I felt, was what was needed. A little moderation.

'I've read about some of the experimental flights,' I said. 'Santos-Dumont, and Farman, wasn't it? And the Wright brothers, of course. It's getting to be quite a craze.'

Foraker tossed his arms skywards in imprecation, throwing his head back and shouting at the stars. The cigar in his right hand hit a trailing branch of the tree and then shattered and fell in sparks to the ground.

'My God!' he said. 'Santos-Dumont . . . Farman . . . The Wrights . . . Christmas night! They don't begin to understand the possibilities. Sure, they *fly*. What's to stop them? Two thousand pounds they paid Farman week before last. And for what? Flew one kilometre. One. At around 25 m.p.h.'

He gripped the lapel of my overcoat.

'There's nothing,' he said, 'to learn from that. We know all that. Of course, they can fly – waddle about in the air. Time goes on, they'll waddle a good bit faster. No problem. Old stuff – just a question of developing it. What they haven't got's a new principle. Something that'll open the way to the real possibilities.'

'Foraker's Principle?' I said.

He lowered his voice reverently. 'Foraker's Principle,' he said. And then added, looking at me with extreme earnestness, 'As you'll have gathered up there at our talk, it's a question of the alloys. Everything else follows.'

He let go of me suddenly, as though realizing the pointlessness of expecting me to understand what he was talking about, and began to walk again, chewing the ruined cigar.

'As for seeing what's to be done, and how – that's my business. And for okaying it when it works – that's Rosen's. Well, and then there's Lenoir and his friends. They don't understand, d'you see, just what it is, but they can see what it might do. Because I tell them so, and they know me. Well, naturally, in case of war.'

I remembered the bellhop at the Excelsior.

'And what,' I said, 'about Mulai Hafid? Are you going to help him fly?'

He looked sideways at me, puzzled.

'Mulai Hafid?'

'I understood you were backing him, or working with people who were backing him or something.'

He threw his head back in sudden comprehension. 'Oh, that! That was something I put about down there in Marseilles. Christmas night! I don't care a red cent about Mulai Hafid, whoever the hell he may be. Who is he, anyway?'

I found myself explaining, more or less patiently, that Mulai Hafid was the new Sultan of Morocco, and there was an international crisis about him, and I would have thought, I said ironically, that nobody could be genuinely quite so ignorant about him – you couldn't open a newspaper without reading of the Moroccan crisis.

'Just so,' Foraker said. 'I became cognizant of just that fact. Well, it stands to reason. A man like me turns up in Marseilles and you can bet your shirt there are going to be plenty of people wanting to know what he's up to. And they snoop.' He pantomimed a crawling, crouching movement. 'Well, so they're all interested up to the eyes and ears in this thing in Morocco or wherever. Situation like that, people want to believe that anything they don't fully understand is something to do with the crisis they're interested in. It's the way people are. I've noticed it. So I send up a couple of little smoke signals to be wafted upon the currents of rumour to watching eyes. I cast' – he tossed an imaginary object into the street – 'bottles with messages in them upon the waters of popular report. But the messages are misleading. And they reach everyone, including the bellhop at the Excelsior. Including you, Mr Hastings. It provides – don't you see? – a diversion.'

He was smiling gently to himself, and suddenly turned on me quite fiercely, replying to some criticism he supposed me to be making mentally.

'And why,' he demanded, 'should I care if people think I'm working for some damn Sultan or other? If it keeps them out of my hair? I've known people who thought I was working for Bill the Kaiser and the Tzar of All the Russias and the Grand Llama of Tibet. What do I care what people think? I get on with my work.'

We walked on in silence until we turned a corner of the boulevard and saw the lighted portico of the Grand Hotel across the street.

He said, obviously treating it as a detail hardly necessary to mention, 'It'll be all right about money, of course. Fix all that with Mark Crane. He takes care of all that. Tell him how much you want.'

We dodged across the street, between trams, and came out at the hotel entrance.

Foraker said, 'There'll be no trouble about that. Especially now that Halm . . .' He stopped, looking at me with a widening grin, as of complicity. He beat his hands gently together, and his grinning look roved mockingly over the façade of the hotel and up and down the street.

I think the realization of what the successful outcome of the tussle with Halm could mean, in terms of Foraker's Principle, had only then exploded in his head, by delayed action. He threw his arms wide, as though to embrace the city of Lyons and France and the material universe. His voice was low, and as vibrantly exultant as a whoop.

'Now,' he said, 'now we can move.'

He walked straight at the swing-doors of the hotel, like a conqueror for whom all doors would be thrown open; which in fact, these were, by two page-boys, who gazed at Foraker with excited admiration. Perhaps, I thought, he had cast some fresh bottle upon the waters of popular report. Perhaps they thought he was the emissary of the Tzar of All the Russias.

A man with a glossy look, thirtyish, who must have been loitering just inside the entrance, came jumping to meet him, his whole body a coiled question-mark. Before he could speak, Foraker, while the page-boys goggled with pleasure, snatched off his hard felt hat and tossed it up hard towards the ceiling, which it hit with a whack, but descending, became caught on the chandelier, spiked.

The glossy man relaxed. To look at him you would have thought the release of tension was such that he would drop on the floor in a heap.

'So it's all right?' he said.

'Truth has prevailed,' said Foraker. 'The man has seen the light. The eyes even of the fool have been opened. Mark, this is Mr Hastings. The providential Mr Hastings. Mr Hastings, this is Mark Crane. A man of importance. Of business. He manages many practical affairs for the poor crack-pot inventor Grant Foraker. My business partner, in fact.'

Mr Crane gave a rather chilly simper.

'He means,' he said, shaking hands with me genially enough, 'that when he breaks things I sometimes sweep up the mess.'

'Mr Hastings,' Foraker said, 'has been invited to become my confidential secretary. For unexplained reasons, he hesitates. We must all bend our efforts to persuade him. He is a man of principle and iron determination. A geologist. Ways must be found.'

It was my turn to feel a little foolish, but by now we were on the stairs behind Foraker, who was surging upwards two at a time, chanting, 'Mr H., I love you, how I love you, Mr H.' Looking down from the landing into the foyer I saw a managerial-looking person in a frock-coat pop out from somewhere and stare in a startled manner at Foraker's hat hanging from the chandelier. He started to shout at the page-boys.

'A ladder. What are you waiting for? That's Mr Foraker's hat. It must be got down and returned to him. He may need it. Hurry!'

Anxious cries of 'Mr Foraker's hat' followed us down the corridor, to the door of a room which Foraker – still chanting – wrenched open, disclosing, seated stiffly on a sofa, Captain Lenoir, and in front of him, dancing up and down in a kind of Indian war dance, Jephthah Foraker, an expression of ecstasy upon his face.

The Captain rose springily to greet us. Jephthah danced round him, shouting and roaring with laughter.

'I'm calling you a muddy toad,' he was shouting, 'and you can't understand. I'm calling you a bit of horse-mess, and you can't do anything because you don't understand. Papa,' he cried to Foraker, 'I called him a yellow horse-mess with blow-flies on it and he didn't know because he's French.' The child rolled about with triumphant peals of laughter, on the verge of hysterics.

'I think,' Captain Lenoir said to me in French, after we had been introduced, 'that the younger Foraker is insulting me. Explain to him, please, that I will now insult him – in French.'

Jephthah glared at him, dashed across the room, and leapt on to the rocking-horse which, as in Marseilles, appeared to be the only inanimate sign of human occupation in this room.

The rockers of the horse made a horrible noise on the floor.

'Silence! To bed!' shouted Captain Lenoir in an English accent as bad as Foraker's French one.

'And now...' Lenoir turned to Foraker, stepped lightly across the room, stood close to him, and said one word: 'Halm?'

For answer, Foraker shot out his big hands and caught Lenoir under the armpits. The Captain was a short man, elegantly lithe, and without noticeable effort Foraker lifted him at arm's length and bounced him gently up and down, tossing him a half-foot into the air and catching him, grinning.

Under these conditions, Lenoir contrived to maintain an easy, even dignified, bearing. His smile as he looked down at Foraker was gay and indulgent.

'Question answered,' he said in English. And then as Foraker dropped him on his feet, he clapped his hands. 'Tip-top?' he asked.

'Tip-goddamn-top,' said Foraker.

'Tip-goddamn-top, enough for goddamn celebrate?'

'Plenty tip-top enough. All signed and sealed,' said Foraker.

'Well then!' shouted Lenoir. 'Champagne!'

Although they could scarcely exchange ten intelligible words, and had to keep turning to me or Crane as interpreters, the two of them managed to create the effect of a hubbub, a near-riot of conversation.

Champagne arrived, brought by not one, or two, but three waiters, who, seemingly affected by the atmosphere, set out the ice-buckets and the wine and glasses as though they were assisting at some occasion of national rejoicing. Or else they had seen smoke signals hinting at the presence of the Emperor of China in disguise. Crane, fussing around among them, succeeded in looking like a handsome, if rather gauche, head-waiter taking a busman's holiday.

As the waiters departed, Lenoir raised his glass and started to make a speech in French: 'To Halm, Ordure-Manipulator in Chief of the principality of Dungania. May his unspeakable crimes be forgiven him. May the good God in His mercy avert His eyes from the vileness of his character. May . . . Ah!'

Both interior doors of the suite, one on each side of the room, had opened simultaneously like the doors of some ingenious Swiss mechanical toy, through which shepherdesses, gnomes, nymphs, goose-girls, or bears emerge with punctual precision. Through the one to the left of the row of windows came Delia Foraker, through the one on the right, Martha Dukes.

'Ah!' said Captain Lenoir again, drawing a breath of unaffected sensual delight which ended in a tiny snoring noise at the back of his throat. It seemed to me that Crane actually blushed slightly, though whether in embarrassment on Lenoir's behalf or because that was what happened to him when he saw beautiful women or girls, I could not determine. He must surely be fairly accustomed to the sight of these two. Or was there, it occurred to me, something unusual about them tonight? Foraker jumped up, his look enfolding them in a comprehensive embrace.

Automatically, as though controlled by the mechanism of the toy, the two young women paused, poised in the two doorways, for the time it took each to draw the door shut behind her. Quick as the flicker of a butterfly's wing, each flashed a look at the other, up and down, from shoes to hair and to the clothes between, in a fast, brutally intensive reconnaissance. Then the pretty figures relaxed, smiled, talked.

'Martha, darling, how pretty you look.'

'Delia, you look just wonderful.'

They came towards us and I thought they looked as though each, on the sly, had entered for a beauty contest. It could have been, partly, the effect of their clothes – a trifle more 'dressed up', possibly, than was entirely correct for a very informal dinner party at a provincial hotel.

Delia Foraker ran across to her husband, almost as Lenoir had done, and put an eager hand on his sleeve, her eyes sparkling back at the champagne in his glass. Nodding at it and laughing, she said, 'You're celebrating, so it's all right, is it? Halm, I mean.'

'It is victory,' said Lenoir, looking attentively on.

'Right down the line,' Foraker said, draining the glass.

Martha Dukes tossed her head and said, 'I knew you'd persuade him.'

'Not without,' said Foraker, 'the able and diligent assistance of Mr Hastings. Much of the burden and heat of the day was borne by him. It was his task to pour the raw material of truth into the moulds of intelligibility.'

At this, Miss Dukes turned to flash her large eyes at me in an abrupt sparkle of approval.

'Mr Hastings,' said Foraker, swallowing another glass, 'is a man of many accomplishments. A fine linguist, a not-inexperienced geologist. As I have told him; as I was saying just now to Mark; it would be my wish that he should join with me in my work. But Mr Hastings, I say it with a heavy heart, thinks otherwise.' He drank with gusto another glass of wine. 'He has his own plans, his own lofty ideals.'

'Oh, Mr Hastings, have you really?' said Mrs Foraker.

'I understand,' said Martha Dukes, 'though it seems a pity.'

Foraker had started shepherding us to dinner in the hotel restaurant which opened out of the foyer where a ladder had now been set up, and one of the page-boys was aloft by the chandelier, angling with a pole for Foraker's hat, which remained obstinately hooped among the lustres. The other page and the man in the frock-coat stood below, calling out directions and exhortations.

'A little minute, Mr Foraker,' cried the frock-coated man. 'One little minute more and your hat will be restored to you.'

Across the round dinner table, where I sat between Delia Foraker and Mark Crane, I was pleased to note that Martha Dukes had very considerably modified her air of aloof uninterest in myself. I caught her eye repeatedly. She had the expression proper to a girl who had, at last, grasped that the strange young man is a person of accomplishment and importance, with interesting aims and lofty ideals. Foraker was apparently giving her and Mark Crane a colourful blow-by-blow account of the conference with Halm. From his voice and gestures it was evident that he saw it in restrospect as something between a championship wrestling contest and St George's encounter with the Dragon.

I had feared that Lenoir's shortage of English would put a brake on conversation at our section of the table. This proved not to be the case. Freely employing me as an interpreter, he talked about Love. Eroticism poured from him in a flow which made him seem more than ever like the caricature of a Frenchman in a farce. He enveloped the three of us in a mauve haze of *amour*, throbbing with electric impulses. Riding on waves of champagne, I was in love with Delia here, Martha over there. Also, I was prepared to share them, magnanimously. I loved Lenoir and Foraker, too.

We were eating a pile of tangerines, cherries, and peaches, drenched in kirsch and maraschino, when there materialized suddenly beside our table a man in an overcoat, with a purplish face looking like a time-bomb which is going to go off now. His voice, apparently strangled by indignation, came out in a savage wheeze. In guttural French he demanded to know which was Mr Foraker. He was told. He tore at a button on his overcoat and stamped.

'Then permit me to say, sir,' he wheezed at Foraker, who regarded him with the calm interest of non-comprehension, 'that you are causing an outrage. You are the creator of an abominable situation.'

Foraker said, '*San fairy ann.* Have a drink.'

The wheeze became a kind of screaming snarl. He let out a sharp kick at the table leg.

'I demand that you act immediately to put an end to an intolerable situation.'

'Something not entirely in order?' asked Lenoir.

The time-bomb burst. Amid the noise of the verbal explosion certain facts were intelligible. The purple-faced man and a friend – a man of importance, a visitor to this exposition – had arrived twenty minutes before to take rooms in this hotel. What did they find? They found the porter missing, the page-boys missing, the receptionist missing. All missing from their proper posts. And what were they doing? They were springing like drunken and degenerate monkeys up and down and round about a ladder in the middle of the foyer, unable to spare a moment to deal with arriving guests, people of importance. And the cause of this disgusting and inadmissible buffoonery? The purple-faced man seemed to grind his teeth and howl like a dog.

He got moving towards the door, the purple man trotting and wheezing just behind him, the rest of us following in disorder. The scene in the foyer was much as described by the purple man, who, indeed, waved a trembling hand at it all, as much as to challenge us to deny the evidence of our eyes.

There was, however, a feature of it he had not mentioned. The tall man who stood twitching nervously by the nakedly vacant desk of the receptionist, peering left and right in evident expectation of stealthy attack, was Mr Halm.

'You see,' purple face was starting to say, 'my friend still waits.'

Foraker, seeing Halm, bounded across the room at him, seized him by the hand and shook it in apparently speechless emotion. Halm, backing up against the wall, quivered with bewilderment and alarm.

'Tell him,' Foraker said to anyone who was listening, 'tell him it's my hat. Tell him not to worry. Not worry at all. *Chapeau de Monsieur Foraker,*' he added solemnly.

Releasing Halm's hand, which dropped to his side like a

dead fish, Foraker swung round and strode across the foyer to the ladder. He peered upwards to where the man in the frock-coat – the receptionist, in fact – was trying his hand at dislodging the hat which seemed to have become, since we had last seen it, more firmly lodged than ever.

'*Desonday*,' shouted Foraker, shaking the ladder.

The receptionist gave a swift downward glance and dropped his pole or fishing-rod. He came rattling down. Foraker gave him just time to clear the last rung before himself springing at the ladder and rushing up it.

'Hold it!' he shouted. 'It's swaying in the gale.'

Lenoir, Crane and myself threw ourselves upon the straddled legs of the ladder and held them. It seemed hard work. They rocked in our embrace. I saw Delia Foraker put a hand to her mouth and Martha Dukes clutch her forehead. From all around came cries of 'Oh, Mr Foraker!' Halm gave a small scream. The ladder seemed to be trying to walk away altogether.

Looking up, I saw Foraker just regaining a sort of balance after, apparently, making a lunge at the hat, trying to unhook it, not with a stick but with his hand. He measured the distance again, a sharp sigh went up from the watchers, and he extended his arm at a gorilla stretch, his hand buffeting and jangling the crystal lustres. As his centre of gravity shifted, his feet seemed to spurn the ladder-top. At the same moment, he got the brim of the hat in his grip, and held on. For a split-second, the tough material of the hat, impaled on its spike, held this enormous pendulum swinging beneath it. A whole branch of the chandelier buckled and gave. In a hailstorm of prismatic glass, Foraker plummeted to the floor. He landed neatly on his feet, bounced, squatted, rose again, hobbling, the hat still clutched in his hand.

Lustres were still tinkling down. Peering upwards at the wreckage of the chandelier, Foraker said, 'Pity that had to happen. Couldn't stand the strain, I'd say. Damage,' he said to the goggling receptionist. '*A moi*. Put it on the bill. *Addition, savez-vous*?'

'And your hat,' said the receptionist. 'Ruined.'

'*San fairy ann.* Halm!' he shouted.

Halm, greener than ever, looked piteously at the glass-piled carpet and the ruins of the chandelier. 'All right?' he said weakly.

'Tell him to come and have a drink when he's fixed up and had dinner,' said Foraker. I did so, but at the suggestion the purple-faced man let out a terrible wheeze, and Halm, fumbling with a registration form, flapped his other hand in a hopeless gesture of self-defence. 'O my God! No!' I heard him mutter to his companion. 'My nerves are all used up. My stomach hurts. I need to go to bed.'

'Little bit of trouble,' Mark Crane said in careful French. 'Just one of those things. All in the day's work.'

Halm shuddered.

Foraker was already hobbling on sore ankles back to the dining-room to finish the liqueur-soaked fruits.

'That man Halm,' he said, 'has ulcers of the stomach. What a fool he is.' And back in the sitting-room he meditated again on the phenomenon of Halm.

'Just think,' he said, 'of all the money that man has, factories all over France. Export and import. Half-interest in the plant in Quebec. Plenty of it in German municipal loans, just in case they come out on top again next time. It makes you think you're going to see a man of intelligence, a powerful thinker. Not so. All the time, he is a damn fool.'

The mocking grin again took possession of his face. At the same moment the door from one of the adjoining rooms burst open, and Jephthah dashed in, wearing pyjamas and a dressing-gown, his face intent as a sprinter's, his eyes rolling. He stood perfectly still in the middle of the room, holding up his pyjama trousers with one hand and fighting for breath. Delia Foraker gave a reproving cry. He rolled his eyes at her censoriously, gasped, and said, 'Fireworks! I heard them. Pop, pop, *bang*.'

Recovering his breath, he jumped in the air and dashed over to one of the french windows, opening evidently on to a balcony. He dragged one of the heavy curtains violently aside. Unable to reach the window catch he jumped, yelling for it to be opened so we could go on the balcony and watch. I recalled posters announcing for this evening a stupendous firework display in celebration of the opening of the Exposition.

Foraker sprang from his chair. Delia started to say it was too cold for Jephthah out there. At the same time came from beyond the window the urgent 'whoosh' of a rocket going off, and a long trail of small explosions.

Jephthah shrieked with excitement and impatience. Foraker looked wildly round the room, seemed not to see what he was looking for, and started to tear off his jacket.

'Jephthah! Here! Hurry!'

Hobbling fast across the room, he dropped the jacket over Jephthah, snuffing him momentarily out under its weight and size.

We crowded on to the little balcony in time to see a great green star soar over the roof-tops half a mile away, hang momentarily in the winter sky, and burst in rivers of starlets streaming down on the city.

Foraker, in his shirt-sleeves, slapped the balustrade with his hand. 'Fine,' he said. 'Fine.' He looked round at us, beaming with pleasure. Lower down, Jephthah gripped the iron railings of the balcony with both hands, hopping in silence from one foot to the other. The starlets went out and the sky remained dark.

Jephthah gave a wail of dismay.

'It's over. We missed it.'

'No!' cried Foraker on a note of anxiety. 'Have we? God-damnit!'

Another rocket came whooshing up consolingly from beyond the roofs. A pack of others chased it to the top of its flight, scattered and exploded together, filling the whole sky with streaming light.

'My God!' Foraker said. 'Just look at that. Isn't that just grand?'

Again there was nothing between the roofs and the stars, and Jephthah wailed aloud that it was over. Again the fireworks whistled upwards, and stars, flares, wheels, and balls of fire of many colours floated, whirled, hovered, and cut zigzags in the dark. Lenoir stepped back into the room, brought out a glass of brandy which he gave to Delia, and walked up and down the balcony with his hands in his pockets, whistling, and watching the fireworks over his shoulder.

Foraker, his eyes on the fireworks, flung out a shirt-sleeved arm and put it round Delia's shoulders. With the other, he gesticulated, displaying to her the fireworks, or the world. His voice rose against the noise of the detonations, fell again in the unlighted intervals, talking about the fireworks, and life, and the Principle, and Halm, and the future. Gusts of it came to me beside him on the balcony, with Jephthah hopping up and down against my legs.

'Look at that!' Foraker would say, pointing at a burst of coloured stars as though he had exploded them there for her. And then, as the sky went dark, 'Look!' He was gesturing at some unseen objective. 'It's a great day. Now I can get right down to it. We'll ...' His voice sank to a kind of purring growl as he talked about the future and what he would do with it, triumphantly displaying that for her, too.

She leaned against him, listening silently. Once she said, 'Grant, it's awfully cold out here.'

His eyes travelled back from far away.

'What?' he said.

'I'm cold.'

'Damn.' He looked about bemusedly for a moment, and with a sudden backward sweep of his arm snatched at the long curtain hanging just inside the window, yanked it savagely through to the balcony, wrapped the dusty folds of it round her.

'There.' His eyes and voice travelled off again. 'I was telling you. Beginning now ... Nobody else, I tell you. The biggest thing ...'

The curtain huddled absurdly round her shoulders, and from there stretched out in an upward- instead of downward-sweeping train towards its rail inside the room. She was shivering.

'Grant,' she said, 'I really am dreadfully cold ... I'm going in.'

I drank some more brandy against the cold, and felt my head again commencing to swim somewhat. Martha sat beside me, looking delicious and talking with animation about Sven Hedin's discoveries in the Gobi Desert. I realized that she was under the impression that the excavation of those ancient cities was a part of geology. Her face and shoulders floated beautifully in front of me. Giving her all possible attention, I hardly noticed Foraker return to the room. When I looked at him, I saw that he had settled himself in his chair and fallen abruptly asleep.

'The President sleeps, the session is closed,' said Lenoir, who kissed Delia's hand, bowed with formality to the rest of us, including the sleeping Foraker, and was gone. Reluctantly, I, too, got to my feet and started to take my leave.

I looked uncertainly at Foraker, and even now I remember thinking, in a vague way, how odd it was that when he was asleep Foraker looked as passive and, as it were, harmless as any other sleeping person.

'I'll say good night to him for you,' Delia said, 'but he'll want to know where to reach you, of course. We had a lot of trouble when you disappeared at Marseilles.'

'Yes, indeed,' Martha said anxiously, hunting paper and pencil at a desk in the corner. 'Aren't you staying here in the hotel?'

I told them my hotel was several blocks away, I was going on to Paris in the morning, and had as yet no address there.

'But *our* Paris address,' Delia and Martha said together. 'You have to take that and the telephone number. You just have to keep in touch,' Delia said. 'You have to talk to Grant about the job – the position.' She gave me the address.

Mark Crane said, 'I'd like a little walk before I go to bed. A digestive, you know. If you'll allow me, I'll stroll a bit of the way with you.'

In the foyer they had swept up most of the glass, but small splinters crunched under our feet as we passed beneath the gaping wreck of the chandelier.

Crane paused and looked at it fixedly.

'All right,' he said, 'but say what you like, it doesn't make things any easier, does it?'

He walked into the street and presently said, 'I hope that

with one consideration and another, due consideration given all round, you'll step into that position. Nobody else will.'

This seemed important, and I remember stopping him and actually holding on to his lapel while I asked him, 'Why not?'

He looked down at my hand and removed it in a dignified manner. 'Don't misunderstand me. Get the facts straight. When I said what I said whatever I said, I simply intended to convey . . . Understand that there are fifty, a hundred, more I daresay, young men, and not young men only, who'd be eager and willing, more than willing to step into this position. A secretarial position as confidential secretary to Grant Foraker. I'll tell the world there are!' he shouted.

'Then why,' I shouted back, 'why don't they? Answer me that!'

The walking and talking seemed to have cleared his head somewhat. 'Because,' he said quite quietly and coherently, 'Foraker won't let them. He's giving the position to you. It's no longer vacant. Can't you see that?'

He stared at me, and added, 'I see your difficulty. You mean you've refused it. You're not taking it. But that doesn't make a damn bit of difference to Grant Foraker. Can't you see that?'

'Not,' I said, 'clearly, in its entirety.'

'It's simple enough,' said Mark Crane. 'It's just that when Grant Foraker thinks he's going to do something he acts like it had already happened. Hold that thought. Well, good-bye, old man. I'll be seeing you.'

'Probably.'

'Again and again and again,' said Mark Crane, moving away down a side-street, waving one hand gently above his head. 'And again and again.'

7

In Paris I moved into a cheap apartment in an aged house off the Rue St Jacques, and wrote asking Dr Thaypi when it would be convenient for him to see me. Life was beginning. The Foraker interlude was over. It was somewhat of a pity that Martha Dukes went with it, but there it was. Our ships had passed in the night.

Dr Thaypi wrote back some days later mentioning Friday week as a suitable date.

At the same time, forwarded by the Marseilles Pose Restante, came a letter from a Dr Gredentheiler, of the Vienna Geological Institute, saying he was at my disposal should I wish to visit him.

Spring began. Walking under the budding trees in the Luxembourg Gardens I saw, a long way off, up the slope, Delia Foraker and Martha Dukes, just leaving the gardens by the gate leading into the Avenue de l'Observatoire. I walked and then ran after them. By the time I reached the avenue they had disappeared. Next day I telephoned Foraker's apartment. Mark Crane answered. Foraker had left that morning for Brussels. Mrs Foraker and Miss Dukes had gone with him.

'He's expecting you to get in touch with him, you know,' Crane said. 'About the position.'

'But I wrote explaining. I am taking up a geological job. Dr Thaypi is arranging it. Didn't Foraker get my letter?'

'Of course he got it. It didn't make any difference to his idea. It wouldn't, you know. Surely you can see that?'

My apartment in the Rue St Jacques was in a house built in the fifteenth century. It was a garret, with enormously thick walls and deep windows looking out on to the garden of some former mansion, its surrounding wall grinning with gargoyles. It was romantic. Suitable for a brilliant young student preparing to conquer Paris. It was also, being at the back of the building, absolutely silent. When you were alone there you were totally alone, and you knew it. I reflected that it was a wonderful place for quiet study, and as the days lengthened, went for longer and longer walks in the Luxembourg Gardens.

I called at the Forakers'.

Martha Dukes was there alone, except for a middle-aged French maid, who was partially deaf, could not understand orders unless shouted directly at her, was unable to hear the doorbell ring, but was thus deemed incapable of espionage.

Foraker? He was at Beauvais, supervising the erection of some kind of factory or workshop. Mark Crane had taken Delia to the Louvre. Captain Lenoir? He was on special work for the Ministry of War, aloft in a military balloon, very busy making calculations that would be used in the impending summer manoeuvres of the French army.

'I thought you'd come,' Martha said. 'I hoped you would.'

In Brussels she had seen a fine performance of *Man and Superman*. I told some lies about Dr Thaypi and my position in connection with the Geological Survey. Then we talked some more about Bernard Shaw; his view, for instance, of women. I stayed and stayed, then suddenly felt I must demonstrate that I was a busy man, and took a rudely abrupt leave. On the threshold she said *au revoir* in a formal manner and, just as I reached the bottom of the first flight of stairs leading down to the entrance of the apartment house, she ran to the banisters above me and leaned over, her hair lolling forward round her face.

'Come back soon!' she called.

I stared up at her. 'Of course,' I said, and ran on down the stairs. I walked straight across the avenue – the apartment house was in the Etoile district – and into a big new café which advertised its telephone. I rang her up.

'It's me again,' I said, and we both laughed. It was delicious to listen to her laughing like that. I felt extraordinarily happy. I told her that, on Thursday, *Major Barbara* was to be given in Paris, for the first time. I invited her to come with me to the theatre.

On Thursday morning they brought out hoses and sprinkled some of the lawns in the Luxembourg. Summer was already in a position to make a raid in force, requiring to be dealt with seriously. The sight reminded me to call on Dr Thaypi.

'You must realize,' he said sadly, 'that the whole thing is simply out of the question. It was hopeless from the start.'

The implications of this interview, its bearing upon my planned career, which, in fact, had just blown up under my feet, were muffled for me by the thought of the evening immediately ahead. I returned to the Rue St Jacques to dress, and found a *pneumatique* awaiting me. It was a hastily composed message to say that Martha would be unable to come to the theatre because Foraker had some urgent letters to dictate and required her to work late that night. She was so very, very sorry, but, of course, I would understand.

The romantic garden looked more like a patch of weedy waste land that somebody ought to cultivate or abolish. Also the gargoyles were merely ugly, without any charm. They were, it occurred to me, just pieces of rotten bad workmanship claiming respect simply on the ground of their age and disgusting decrepitude. On the other hand, she was 'very, very' sorry. I ate alone, drank a bottle of Burgundy, and, after deciding to go to the theatre alone, decided to go immediately to bed, and went for a long walk in the general direction of the Etoile district.

By the time I came in sight of the café with the auspicious telephone I was walking in a trance, moving like a somnambulist. I must have been within thirty yards of its sidewalk terrace before I noticed that the couple sitting at the table nearest to me were Foraker and Martha Dukes. He was drinking beer and talking. She, so far as I could see, was eating melon and laughing.

In a carefully controlled manner I stopped walking along, and stood still where I was. It occurred to me that what might happen next would be that Foraker would suddenly look at his watch, would shout out, loud enough for the whole street to hear, 'My God! Look at the time! We've been here all of ten minutes, and there is that pile of terribly urgent work still left to do. This little break must end at once.' Martha, equally aghast, would gulp the remains of her melon or whatever it was and cry out, 'Considering what I've had to give up this evening, I certainly do think you ought to get that urgent work done.'

Foraker actually did get as far as looking at his watch, and tapping his glass to attract the attention of the waiter. I thought he was going to demand his bill, quickly. I planned, in that case, to intercept them as they crossed the road and say a few pleasant words about how sorry I was that Martha had been unable to come; how well, however, I understood what a rush of work was like. I was as warm-hearted and understanding as the Lord. When the waiter came, Foraker asked Martha some question and she nodded, her hair shaking round her face, and the waiter handed Foraker a menu card. Foraker and Martha spent the next five minutes leisurely looking at it, and equally leisurely Foraker gave some orders to the waiter. Then they just sat there – he talking and she nodding and laughing as before – and then they got up and strolled off to the indoor part of the café, where the restaurant was.

My letter of farewell to Martha Dukes was written and posted before midnight. I remarked simply that I, too, regretted she had been unable to keep our engagement for the theatre, but that I realized, now, that she doubtless had many more interesting and amusing ways of passing the evening. I was sorry, I said, not to have seen her, as I was leaving for Vienna in the morning.

By the same midnight mail, I sent a letter to Dr Gredentheiler in Vienna, stating that I was on my way thither and would communicate with him on my arrival in that city. In the morning, I went to tell the concierge I was shaking the dust of Paris from my feet; going to Vienna, in fact. She reminded me that I had just paid in advance the rent of the apartment for June. I think I gaped at her, astonished that it should be nearly June already. She said the place would be kept vacant in case I wanted to return. This, at the moment, I regarded as tantamount to a sneer.

I took my baggage to the station, but called at the Rue St Jacques later in the day to pick up any mail that might have arrived. It occurred to me that Martha might very well have sent a frantically contrite *pneumatique.* A young lady, the concierge said, had called in person, left a letter which she asked should be forwarded as soon as the concierge got my address.

The letter said Martha was terribly, terribly sorry. She could see I was hurt and offended. She had had no idea it was my last night in Paris. But she had not been able to disengage herself. 'First he was dictating a report, and then, to clear his brain, he needed to talk. We sat for hours in that café across the street, and had supper there. I was very tired, but I like to think it helped him to deal with the problem he was working on. Quite often his sub-conscious works like that.

'Dr Rosen, by the way, is in, or on his way to, Vienna, and I am sure you would like to look him up. I do not know his address, but he is making some inquiries regarding certain ores, and that is part of geology, is it not? So probably you will meet him in the course of your work. I hope you will come back soon and call on us as soon as you get back.'

I travelled in a second-class sleeping car. The other occupant was an Englishman who made a row because the late editions of the evening newspapers were not at the station before we left Paris. Between dawn and sunrise in Bavaria he was up, and making more row, shouting for newspapers at the first station we stopped at.

Trying to sleep, I asked him irritably to desist.

'But I have to get a paper,' he said, 'I have to know what won the Derby.'

'Signorietta,' I said, talking almost in my sleep.

'What?' he shouted. 'How d'you know? You got a wire in Paris?'

'Man told me,' I said. 'In Marseilles . . .

'Four months ago,' I mumbled, dropping off.

I heard him snorting in bewildered disgust and resume his agitation for a newspaper. At Munich he got one and it had no racing news in it at all. He almost missed the train getting another. It contained the news that the filly Signorietta had won the English Derby. The starting price had been 100 to 1.

He looked at me with annoyance and suspicion, under the impression I had played some silly joke upon him. Like myself, he put up in Vienna at the Hotel Bristol. We were both sitting in the lounge a few hours later when two plain-clothes policemen came in, wanting to see me. The Englishman looked as though it were the sort of thing he had expected.

I made out that, as a result of the inquiries made, months ago, by Foraker and by the police in Marseilles, Barcelona, and Paris, my name had got written into some list of people who needed watching, which was circulated to the police of the principal European capitals.

I was not arrested, for fear of complications with the British Consulate. Instead, I was given to understand that I was under strict surveillance, would be arrested at the slightest sign of anything untoward, and might as well give up my game and quit the Empire.

I wrote hurriedly to Dr Gredentheiler, asking for an appointment and mentioning, as casually as possible, that there had been a foolish little misunderstanding with the police, but that the matter was not serious and need cause him no alarm. He fixed a day, and received me, with a muscular young clerk standing at his elbow, evidently alert for action in case I were an armed criminal.

Dr Gredentheiler himself had the face of a nervous bloodhound. He listened, attentively but with apparent apprehension, to the tale of my geological qualifications and ambitions. As soon as I had finished he asked sharply about my trouble with the police.

He explained at length that his Institute was official, part of the apparatus of Austria-Hungary, Imperial-Royal. Not at all the kind of place into which one would care to take the responsibility of introducing dubious elements.

I clutched at a straw. 'Perhaps,' I said, 'you are acquainted with Dr Rosen? Dr Emil Rosen?'

His dewlaps quivered with irritation. Of course, he said, he was familiar with the name and reputation of Dr Rosen. A man of immense ability in many fields. Engineering, metallurgy, even certain aspects of geology. His manner suggested that I had committed an impudence in dragging his name into the conversation.

I inquired for Rosen at all the principal hotels. I went to the Ministry of Industry and Commerce and the Department of Mines. The officials in those branches of the imperial bureaucracy had never heard of Dr Rosen. What, they asked, were they supposed to know about him? I said I had come to them because the business bringing Dr Rosen to Vienna was probably connected with some new kind of metallic ores, perhaps only recently discovered in Austria. I went to the War Office and conveyed that I wanted to get in touch with a man who was interested in the use of new alloys of value in connection with aviation. Two hours later I was visited by the plain-clothes men and informed that I had six hours in which to leave the city and the territory of the Imperial-Royal dominions if I wished to escape serious charges of espionage.

Whither? All Europe seemed shrunken and depressingly full of policemen and spy-mania. In Paris at least I had a roof, paid for. I drove to the West Station and took a ticket and sleeping-car accommodation for Paris, first-class this time, for I had so little money left I felt the extra expense to be unimportant. I should at least have a compartment to myself. Gazing upon the waters of Babylon, from a window of the first-class sleeping car coach, was visible Dr Rosen.

I had a foolish impulse to ask him petulantly what he meant by manifesting himself only now, when he was too late to be of any use? But he bowed gravely and made a slight welcoming motion with his hand, which somehow suggested that we were two tired travellers meeting in the wilderness. It seemed to me that nobody had made any welcoming sign in my direction for a very long time.

He invited me to visit him in his compartment. It looked, even at this outset of the journey, like the inside of a Spanish grocery. Lengths of salami sausage of various types hung from the rack above the berth, together with bottles of wine cased in straw, and a bundle of white muslin, which dropped white gouts on to the patterned upholstery. It was a goat's cream cheese.

On the foot of the bed were baskets, one half full of eggs, the other containing Vienna rolls, wrapped in damp vine-leaves. In the rack itself could be discerned a jar of pickles, a jar of roll-mops, a couple of tins of sardines, and a box of cigars. At the farther end of the compartment a suitcase and an overcoat constituted a sort of fort or buttress, protecting a glass and metal coffee-making machine of unusual design.

I learned later that the design was not merely unusual but unique, being Dr Rosen's own.

This he disclosed after supper as we rumbled across western Austria. He had earlier explained that he did not care for the food served on international express trains, and invited me, in case I shared this distaste, to join him at this meal. In my state of desolate depression, I should have been happy to join him in gnawing an old bone.

'There will be enough, I think,' he said, and so saying dragged from the rack a string bag containing several heads of lettuce, a kilo of butter, some packets of pumpernickel, slabs of chocolate, and some tins of condensed milk. Also, a bottle of red wine. 'This,' he said, 'we drink now. It will not survive the motion of the train. Those,' he nodded at the straw-covered flagons swinging above us, 'will keep.'

I ate and drank, and told all. From Barcelona uncle to Thaypi and Gredentheiler, omitting, only, all reference to Martha Dukes, as being unduly frivolous for the ears of a Minor Phophet of international fame as an engineer, a metallurgist and I didn't know what else besides.

He listened with an air of attention which was at the same time soothingly aloof, almost impersonal. I might have been reading to him from a history book some passage which had struck me as worthy of notice.

He said, 'And the girl, Foraker's stenographer. Pretty as a picture. I should have thought for a young man like you she would have provided some consolation in your frustrations.'

His tone was that of someone remarking that with the wind in the south-west one would have expected rain.

'Very attractive,' I said. 'But the point is . . .'

I talked at length about the 'point'. After all, I had set myself an objective. True, I gathered that Mr Grant Foraker having decided that he wanted me as his confidential secretary, the position was still mine for the asking.

'Certainly,' said Dr Rosen.

All very well; but would it not be a kind of retreat – a betrayal of my aims, an admission of defeat – to go to Foraker now and say I would take the job, after all?

Dr Rosen spread butter and cheese on a slice of pumpernickel and folded the whole in a lettuce leaf.

'I am not at home,' he said, 'with entirely abstract concepts. Especially when they are expressed in metaphors – advance, retreat, betrayal, and so on.'

This remark was not a sneer at me, but – his manner made clear – a statement of fact. He was confessing to what, he felt, some people might consider a defect, though he could not share their opinion. He bit into his leafy parcel.

'Well,' I said, 'apart from that, I don't know anything *about* Grant Foraker.' I paused and perhaps blushed. 'That's to say I know nothing except some things I was told by a man who seemed very much prejudiced against him.'

'Prejudiced?' asked Dr Rosen, screwing up his eyes to peer at something blurred.

'I mean, this man hated Foraker.'

Dr Rosen's expression relaxed. 'Ah!' he said. 'Yes. I understand what you mean. A lot of people do that. That is a fact. As to whether they are prejudiced or not – that is an opinion, I think. Are you speaking of the ex-confidential secretary? His name was Robinson. At least he said it was, and Foraker confirmed it.'

'Yes. He approached me in Marseilles. He took the view that Grant Foraker is a terribly dangerous man.'

This was received with the faintest of shrugs.

'He was a spy of some kind,' Rosen said. 'Foraker thought for Wilbur Wright. There was no evidence of that whatever. But by the questions Robinson asked he obviously was spying for someone. It was so obvious as to be embarrassing. It's a mistake, I think, to let people get on one's nerves, but I do feel – it's simply my personal reaction to certain circumstances – that a spy should be at least unobtrusive . . .'

I spoke of the personal feud, apparently of long-standing, between the Forakers and the Robinsons. I told him the story of the Antonia affair. 'Amusing,' said Rosen briefly, meaning just that and no more. 'Naturally,' he added, 'I had no interest in knowing *why* he hated him. How could such a thing be absolutely ascertained, in any case? It might be what you say, or it might – I state a mere hypothesis – be the case that Robinson has some glandular trouble which causes Foraker to have what for Robinson is a nauseating smell, causing animosity. Most Europeans smell that way to most central and southern Chinese. *That* he hated him seems to be an admitted fact.'

He lifted the edge of the window blind and peered out into the moonlight. 'Good,' he said. 'We are coming just now to a place where the permanent way is exceptionally smooth. It is the moment to make the coffee.'

He busied himself with the machine, and it was then that he divulged that it was his own invention. 'Although,' he said, 'I am not, really, an inventor, like Foraker. What I do is inspect things. I can tell when things will work.'

He lighted a small spirit lamp under the coffee-container of the machine and watched the flame, smiling.

'So far as I recall,' he said, in the manner of someone recalling one rather good picture in an otherwise dull exhibition, 'the only interesting thing about the man Robinson was that he had the faculty of precognition.'

'Of what?'

'Precognition. It is a special form of what is known – vulgarly, loosely, but not absurdly – as "second sight". Under certain conditions, and within limits which it would, of course, require the most exhaustive experiment to determine, he could foretell the future. Quite accurately.'

'But, good God!' I said, '*you* don't really believe that, do you? I thought all that sort of thing was humbug.'

'Why?' said Dr Rosen.

'But isn't it?'

Dr Rosen meditated. 'You may, of course, be right,' he said at length. 'I should be interested to hear your reasons. My own view – and it is simply an opinion, you understand – is that such experiments as have been conducted in this field, and they are admittedly inadequate to provide absolute proof of anything, suggest that the faculty of precognition is a fact.'

'But look here,' I said excitedly, 'that means . . .'

'I have no idea what it means,' said Rosen. He added with his first touch of irritability, 'I don't know what electricity means, either.'

I was dumbfounded. 'He told me,' I said, it being the only thing I could think of to say, 'the winner of the Derby. The big English horse-race, you know. An obsolute outsider. Months ago, in Marseilles.'

'And it won? I suppose so, since you mention it.'

'Yes, it won. About ten days ago the race was run.'

'Interesting,' said Dr Rosen calmly, taking out a small notebook from his pocket and making a note in it. 'By the way, should I congratulate you? Did you have a good bet?'

I admitted that I had not acted on Mr Robinson's information. 'I gathered,' I said, 'that he wouldn't have liked it if I had. One of the things that made me think it was all hocus-pocus was this stuff about his "gift" shrivelling up or turning against him if it was used for profit.'

Dr Rosen poured coffee. 'It is a common phenomenon. You are familiar, of course, with folklore as expressed in fairy tales. You recall the number of such tales in which people are given magical powers to be used for some specific purpose – one deemed noble, of course. Usually there are three brothers. The first two misuse the magic gift for personal gain. They come to grief. The third uses it only for the common good – for the rescue of maidens in distress, for example – and it works.'

Befogged, I drank coffee, praised the unique machine that had made it, and changed the conversation.

'Noble purposes,' I said. 'Would you say that if I were to work with Mr Grant Foraker I should be working for a noble purpose?'

'I said,' Rosen corrected gently, '"purposes deemed noble." I don't know the answer to your question.'

I realized I was back at the query I had been about to formulate before the figure of Mr Robinson, now disturbingly inflated, forced its way into our conversation.

'You see,' I said, 'I don't really know what Foraker does. I understand, of course, that it's to do with flight. But, for instance, is it really genuine? Is it as big as he says it is? I mean . . .'

I hesitated, recalling that Dr Rosen was after all to some extent associated with Foraker.

Rosen said, 'You want to ask: Is he what many people call a charlatan? The answer is: Yes.'

'But then . . .?'

'Obviously it is "Yes" because many people do call him a charlatan. But the answer to the other questions you put is "Yes", too. Yes, it is genuine. Yes, his claims regarding its potentialities are strictly factual. Big? That's a relative term. One could say, perhaps, "as big as the internal combustion engine". But then . . .'

He uncorked a bottle of cognac and poured it into the half-empty glasses out of which we were drinking the coffee. He concentrated attention on the pouring liquid, or an abstruse problem, or a far distant future.

I had the impression that I had committed some error in taste, not by asking questions about Foraker, but by letting the conversation stumble into a tangle-wood of abstractions in which progress was laborious, with factual mile-posts out of sight. Dr Rosen took a deep draught of the coffee-cognac, and said, 'But how "big" ' – his slight pause put the word in faintly derisive inverted commas – 'is the internal combustion engine? Relative to what? Obviously a question that could be answered only out of total knowledge of the totality of time and space. By God, for example,' he said, smiling.

'But Foraker's invention,' I persisted, 'is big in that sort of way? After all, the internal combustion engine has . . . well, it's revolutionized almost everything. We can't begin to see the consequences.'

'Probably,' said Dr Rosen, 'Foraker's thing is just as important. Although,' he said, refilling our glasses, 'when one says "invention" one has to understand what one's talking about. It's not a gadget like my little machine here. It's first,' he peered, frowning, into his glass, 'the recognition of what is lacking. Lacking, I mean, to what is called "progress" in a particular field. Well, of course, hundreds, thousands of people know theoretically the answer to that.

'And then there's the theoretical solution of the problem. There are hundreds of people in Europe and America who could tell you what that is – in India and China, too, I daresay.'

'So,' I said impatiently, 'where does Foraker come in?'

Rosen shrugged. 'Obviously in the recognition *and* the practical realization of a principle. The continuous understanding and exploitation of the possible. Which, of course, up to the moment of the inventor coming upon the scene and doing what he does, is the *im*possible.'

'You mean,' I said, 'people think it's impossible.'

'No,' said Dr Rosen, 'I mean it is impossible. The factors which make it possible are the creation of the inventor. That is, he arranges the factors in the situation so that the impossible becomes the possible. And, of course, all that,' Dr Rosen extended his arms, his glass in one hand, his cigar in the other, 'all that requires, I suppose, some not accurately describable combination of mental powers, characteristics, energies, exertions, states of mind in the operative individual. I daresay it's what primitive-minded people are trying to say when they speak of a "genius".'

The roll and thump of the train carrying us across Europe in a light haze of cigar-smoke had the disembodying effect of certain drugs. I felt myself an outsider, watching Mr Edward Hastings and Dr Rosen on their way to Paris. It seemed important, before leaving Dr Rosen and going to bed, to ask a further question on behalf of this young Hastings.

'It's a big decision,' I said. 'I can't help feeling that getting mixed up with Foraker might be, somehow a risky business.

It's a responsibility. You say yourself most people think him a charlatan.'

'You feel,' said Dr Rosen, 'a sensation of alarm?' His tone was that of an interested and sympathetic physician. While he talked, he was carefully gathering up the fragments and crumbs of our meal and putting them into a paper bag. The unused parts of the salami sausages he attached again to the rack.

In the morning I did not care to disturb him, and had my breakfast alone in the dining-car. We were already banging across the south-eastern suburbs of Paris when he knocked at the door of my compartment and put his head, only, round the door.

He said, 'Apropos of our conversation last night, I would not like to mislead you in any way. You must act with your eyes open. I simply want to make clear that in my opinion – and it is merely an opinion – that to work for Foraker may very well lead you to riches, fame, and the esteem of generations to come.'

People were preparing for the train's arrival at the terminus, and Dr Rosen withdrew his head to swear at someone who had bumped him with a suitcase. He put his head back into my compartment again, and said, 'Equally, I should say, such a course could quite possibly get you ruined, incarcerated, and reviled by children as yet unborn.'

He gave me his tired smile and again withdrew. As the train halted a few minutes later, he stepped off the train just ahead of me, into the wide-flung arms of Mr Grant Foraker, which enfolded him in a bear hug. A little behind Foraker, Martha Dukes hovered, bright-eyed and uncertain, like an amateur guardian angel. Foraker, a peaked motoring-cap aslant on his head, had already gathered Rosen under one arm, about to carry him, almost literally, off, when Martha saw me and ran forwards, both hands outstretched.

'But how wonderful,' she said. 'You've come back after all.'

Her voice and eyes turned my retreat to Paris into the Return of the Victor. Foraker looked over his shoulder at the pair of us. He shouted a greeting at me, said something to

Rosen, and released him. In a moment, our group was rearranged. Martha and Rosen walked ahead of us behind the porter with our baggage. Beside me, Foraker gripped my upper arm and spoke earnestly.

'Listen,' he said, and his tone made it a matter of life and death. 'Come to the train to meet Rosen, and I meet you, too. Maybe that's Providence. Now just tell me in one word: Can you spare me two months?' But before I could say one word, he rushed on. 'I know, I know,' he said. 'It's a lot to ask. You've your career to think of. Geological work in Paris, some new job they've given you down there in Vienna. New horizons. You pursue your ideal. But if you knew what I have been through. The Vale of Tribulation, Mr Hastings.'

'How so, Mr Foraker?'

'When I learned,' said Foraker, 'of your departure for Vienna, I frankly despaired. In my search for a confidential secretary I turned elsewhere. With what result? Two confidential secretaries in a single week. Men with fine recommendations; references as long as your arm. One of them, I believe, was moderately competent when he was not drunk.

'Mr Hastings, I never saw him sober.

'The other was a teetotaller. It may be that under the influence of liquor he might develop average human intelligence. I do not know, I cannot say.

'And in the meantime,' he said, as we emerged on to the station steps, 'I am hampered, hog-tied, frustrated. I knew from the very outset you were the man for the job, the man I could work with. Mr Hastings, won't you help me out?'

'For two months?' I asked, thinking of the helpless Thaypi, the hostile Gredentheiler, my shrivelled funds. I felt fraudulent, just asking such a question.

'Unless,' Foraker said quickly, 'you could make it six? Six would be a lot easier to plan on.'

I stood looking out over the station yard, and it may have been ten seconds or a minute later that I said, 'Yes,' and started to thank him for keeping the job open.

'I hate changing my mind,' Foraker said.

'And when do I start?' I asked. 'Tomorrow?'

He looked astonished. 'Why,' he said, 'right now, right now. I have the automobile out there,' he added, as if this disposed of all obstacles. He led us, and the porter, to a big, brassy, mustard-coloured machine like a motorized galleon. Rosen and Martha climbed to the back seat. While the baggage was being stowed Foraker pulled on an enveloping white dust-coat, and then a pair of goggles. He reported the 'glad tidings' of my agreement to work for him.

After he had cranked the engine to life and we were side by side in the front seat of the machine, he let the engine roar for a while, and shouted to Martha that this would be a big change.

'Now,' he said, turning half round to look at her, 'we'll be able to forget those two fellows I tried out for the job after we heard Hastings was going to Vienna. Remember them, Martha? There was the one called Teebrother, who was a drunk, and the other called Brooklyn who was a damn fool. He had red hair.'

At the time, I was too mentally confused to notice anything odd in the fact of his reminding her thus of two characters who, presumably, had been in his employ during the past week or so. I took their existence for granted. It was only accidentally, and more than two months later, that I discovered, in the course of a conversation with Martha, that there had never been any such people as Teebrother and Brooklyn.

'He always said,' Martha said, 'that you had a kindly and sensitive nature. He probably thought the idea of rescuing him from such horrid experiences would appeal to you. Besides, the moment he saw you on that train he guessed your Vienna plan had come to grief. He was afraid you'd refuse his offer – out of pride, you know – unless you thought you were doing him a favour.'

8

By the time Martha mentioned that drunken Teebrother and dim-witted, red-haired Brooklyn had been figments, weeks of summer heat had blistered the tables outside the Café du Carrefour, a tiny breeze of early September threatened to drop dust into the glasses of iced beer between us, and the moment on the station platform when I had agreed to work for Foraker seemed a long time ago. At Martha's explanation of those characters' brief and imaginary existence I felt no surprise. The incident seemed normal.

It seemed a long time, too, since the evening I first came into this café and telephoned to Martha, asking her to the performance of *Major Barbara*. Just then, laughing with her over a couple of hundred yards of telephone wire, I had felt myself on the edge of a delicious and quite inevitable romantic voyage. And looking back, now, across the summer, it was as though natural motion had been mysteriously arrested; like the movements of actors on Prospero's island, suspended by invisible spells. What appeared within reach had somehow dissolved or eluded one. There had been a rush and tumble of events, but in their jostle we two had moved no closer, no farther apart. We had never even seen *Major Barbara*.

I started to say, 'It's strange,' and she interrupted me. 'But I'm just saying,' she said, 'it isn't strange. It's natural.'

'Oh, that,' I said. 'Yes. I was going to say it's strange that since I started working for Grant, too, I scarcely see you. Alone like this, I mean.'

I sipped my beer and watched a shrivelled leaf drop prematurely from a tree on the terrace and flutter down, looking as though it were too much exhausted by the ardours of summer to wait for autumn. Let's pretend, I said to myself lazily, as though I were a child counting cherry stones, that if the leaf drops on that big straw hat of Martha's – a hat selected as being elegant, bohemian, 'emancipated' at the same time – things are going on very well as they are. If it falls on the ground or the table, it means something else. Before I had time to think just what else it should mean, Martha tilted her head a little forward, and the leaf – which had been going to drop on to the table between us – caught for a moment on the brim of the straw hat. As she tilted her head a little further, to drink beer, the leaf fluttered off again, my hand moved awkwardly to grab it, banged her hat and knocked it a little askew, and she jerked her head back, startled into annoyance.

I was so astonished by my own gesture, that instead of saying I thought I had seen a wasp attacking her, or something of that sort, I started an explanation about the leaf. Suddenly she tugged at her hat and smiled at me with her large mouth and pretended to misunderstand the whole thing.

Probably, she said, I was tired and dissatisfied with my work. I regretted a career in geology. A lot of those conferences I had to attend as interpreter were probably tiresome. But wasn't almost anything about this work interesting and exciting on account of the objective?

'Yes, yes,' I said. 'Naturally I feel that. It's immensely interesting. Exciting even.'

We were back again, talking of the objectives of all this, which were perhaps the more absorbing just because we could not, with our limited technical knowledge, entirely and factually comprehend them. We were like the novitiates of a new Faith.

There had been an hour or two, on the afternoon of the day I returned from Vienna – a relatively quiet pool, it appeared now, before the rapids started and went on endlessly – when Foraker had addressed himself to this problem. He had jumped up abruptly from the table where he and Delia, Martha Dukes, Mark Crane, and myself had been lunching, told everyone he was not to be disturbed for an hour, taken me to his study, told me to sit down, opened his mouth to speak, and then remained broodingly silent for several minutes.

This sudden cutting off of his verbal flow had been as startling as the stoppage of an accustomed noise.

Finally, he had seemed to get his theme under control. 'There are,' he said, 'just a few essentials. First, if you don't have a modicum of belief in this undertaking, you'll be no good at the job, no good to yourself or me. Second, if you can't see the wood without counting all the damned trees in it, you'll never see it. Not for years and years, anyway. In other words, Mr Hastings, until you know about as much about it as I do, or Rosen does, you can't put your hand on your heart and tell yourself you believe Foraker's Principle works because you know just how it works.

'I know,' he said, puffing confidently now at his cigar, 'and Rosen knows, and I daresay a few others around and about are getting nearer knowing it every day. Though I'll beat them to it. Because, I say it in all humility' – he looked as arrogant as the Devil – 'I have a greater share of all those gifts and capacities that are needed in such an enterprise.'

He fell silent again, and to fill the gap I told him the gist of what Rosen had said in the train. He listened carefully and nodded confirmation at intervals.

'And,' he said, 'at the end you weren't a great deal nearer knowing what it's all about than you were at the beginning. Well, naturally Rosen had to be discreet. Now, listen.'

He stared at the back of his hands and seemed to be talking to them.

I suppose a person listening to it today would find more of it obvious, and less of it novel: naturally it was full of matter that was highly debatable even among experts and skilled technicians in 1908, and has been accepted and become part of the common knowledge of today's man in the street.

Foraker could see that I was floundering a good deal. He said again, 'You don't have to understand it all. You can't. Besides, there are quite a number of the things I'm stating now that will turn out to be just not so, as we go along.'

That, I said, struck me as a little disconcerting.

He shrugged. 'Look,' he said. 'As we play along, you'll pick up plenty. All you need right now is to hang on to the central fact. Paste it in your hat. It's not something anyone can argue about. It's not questionable. It's not something I thought up. It's there.'

He got up as he was talking, and walked about the room.

'When the automobile engineers turned out a gasoline engine that you could screw on a glider, and when the Wright brothers did just that thing, five years ago, people said it was a revolution. Conquest of the air and God knows what.

'Well, words are free and anyone can call a thing what they want. But, come right down to it, that only carried a good bit further what Langley did in the Nineties, and Hiram Maxim. All right, so they used steam power and now the fellows can use gasoline. They had a problem of weight in the Nineties that we don't have today. So the fellows'll work away at that, and presently they'll get a gasoline engine that's a little lighter for the power it gives, so they'll get more speed out of the airplane, or they'll be able to push a bigger airplane along.

'And each year they'll go a little faster, or they'll carry a bigger load, and the newspapers are going to clap hands and say, "Glory glory ain't it wonderful?" And progress is marching on. I tell you,' shouted Foraker, 'it's going to march on so goddamn steadily that it'll be a hundred years before anyone bothers to think up anything new. There's nothing like a long stretch of steady progress on sound lines for stopping the mental process of man.'

He glared out of the window upon whatever specimens of man he could see exercising their sluggish mental processes on the boulevard below, and presently swung round to face the room.

'And all the time,' he said, 'I know, and you know and all those fellows know the real problem, the place where the treasure's really buried, the place where X marks the spot – that's somewhere else again.'

He peered around the room, looking for words. 'Nobody that knows anything,' he said after a pause, 'claims the gasoline-driven piston motor is theoretically the best, most powerful, most all-round suitable power for driving an airplane. Anyone can tell you that right now – not some time in the future, but right now – there are ways of developing driving power that could make the piston motor look like a horse and buggy.

'You want to know why they don't get used?' He was marching past me, talking over his shoulder, cigar-smoke trailing. 'Well, partly because the gasoline piston motor works what people call well enough. It'll do. It can get by. It's kind of new, and everyone can see how it'll get a lot better in time, and so people sit around, like I say, on their backsides and think they have the ultimate best. Let alone there's quite a little sum of money invested in it now that has to make a profit. And it will, of course.'

He had reached the window again on his perambulation, and paused there again, his shoulders hunched. He remained like that so long that I broke the silence.

'You said it was only partly because of all that,' I said. 'What else?'

'Now,' he said, straightening up and turning slowly, 'that's the real point. That's the snag. The power exists. But what doesn't exist is' – he groped for a word again – 'a package. A container. Something to carry the power about in. Something to wrap it up in and put it in a flying machine packaged so it won't burn the whole works to damn ashes about fifteen seconds after the take-off.

'It's not power alone that's the problem. You have to think of power, and then you have to think of power-plus-package. Obviously. Take what you can do with the action of, say methyl alcohol and hydrazine hydrate – there are others you could use, naturally – on a concentration of hydrogen peroxide. You know and I know that ...'

'I haven't the faintest idea,' I said.

'Well, that doesn't matter. Like I said, you don't have to know it all. What you could get out of that would be a generation of heat that would develop a power which ... But what's the good of that when you can demonstrate that just as soon as that heat reaches a point where it's going to do some real good in the way of power, anything you've got it contained in is going to frizzle?

'So what they'll all say is – it's what they're saying about Zielkowsky in Russia right now – "Very pretty little notion, old sport, but you can't fly through the air on a mathematical table", and down they settle again to watch that gasoline piston engine that's got such a future.

'Other words,' said Foraker, seating himself abruptly and addressing the ceiling, 'they can see the power, but they can't see a package, so they stop even thinking about the power, and in the end what they get is Nought plus Nought equals Nought.

'But it doesn't, if you just keep thinking of both things at the same time. *If* we had a container that would stand up to a heat strain *x*, we could get *y* power, *z* speed, and so forth.

'So what's the answer? Start looking for the container. And they say to you, "Sure we could build you a container that would stand up to that heat, we could find the metals for it – the alloys – and at the end it'd be as heavy as a torpedo boat and the size of one of those forts they're building up there on the frontier."

'So you say, "Brothers, sooner or later someone's going to start looking for a way of making a container that'll do all that and won't be much bigger than – say for the sake of supposing – a torpedo, so damn hard that he'll find it." Maybe they'll need to have a war before anyone else tries that hard. But me, I don't need a war. I'm doing it *now*!'

The hand with the cigar shook a little.

'That part of it,' he added in a conversational voice, 'is just a question of the alloys. You can see for yourself.'

He had a 'well, there you are, everything simply and satisfactorily explained' expression, and I realized he expected me to go now.

'Of course,' he said, casually, as I got halfway to the door, 'all that – it takes organization, people working, laboratory tests, factory tests, models. All over the place. You'll see all that as we play along. It takes people, lots of people. And pots of money, pots and pots of it.'

That had been the first and last time since I went to work for him that Foraker had talked at all comprehensively of the 'general objective'.

There was not much question of my trying to count the

trees in the wood, as Foraker had put it, and see what they added up to; there were too many of them.

It had appeared to me that something always interrupted my few private conversations with Martha.

We were interrupted now.

The French maid came trotting fussily out of the apartment house and across the street to the café. From a distance of twenty yards or so she directed at me a piercing hiss, rolled her eyes and then her head, and gestured violently with her thumb, jabbing with it over her shoulder in the direction of the Forakers' apartment. It was by this time a familiar signal, a summons from Foraker. I jumped up automatically, calling for the bill.

As I hurried into the apartment, Foraker said, 'We can pass the Rue St Jacques on the way. Plenty of time for you to collect your gear. Train doesn't pull out till seven.'

'Pull out on the way to where?'

'Barcelona,' said Foraker. 'You know, they say the Spaniards are kind of medieval, not modern. Maybe. Maybe it's the Catalans are different. Take this place in Barcelona where they make those precision instruments. It's good, you know. If they can do what I want, and I put them under contract, chances are they can expand a little, move quicker. You could telegraph your uncle. Tell him we'll be at the Ritz.'

We caught the train to Barcelona, with only about twenty-five seconds in hand. This was on account of a prolonged visit to a big chemist's shop over on the Boulevard des Italiens which Foraker insisted on visiting. Here we bought medicaments, patent remedies, essences, compounds, pills, and pastilles designed to prevent or cure a vast range of maladies from the common cold to arthritis, typhoid fever, and nervous debility.

These, Foraker explained, were essential equipment for any expedition or undertaking which involved 'human relationships'.

'Eighty per cent of people,' said Foraker, 'either are sick or imagine they are sick or think they may be going to be sick pretty soon. It's because way at the back of their minds people are deeply religious. They know they've done this and that, and they think God's going to try and pay them out with a jab of sciatica or a nasty little constriction of the bowels.

'Also,' he said, as we dashed from the shop, cluttered with sufficient supplies to start equipping a small field hospital, 'almost everyone thinks people on the other side of the hill have better medicine than he has in his neck of the woods. You come from another country with a box of pills and give them to a man who suffers from spots before the eyes, and he thinks you're his personal saviour. He'll do anything for you.

'It's a way,' he said, 'to get things done.'

We climbed into the back seat of the brass-bound car, and I remembered that the chauffeur – a man Foraker hired for occasions such as this – had once got from Foraker a powder which cured his dog of fits, and had told me that in his opinion *le patron* was the greatest man on earth. He had said he would die for him any day.

'Naturally,' Foraker said as we roared towards the river, 'not everyone wants a pill. In Scotland I guess it's a little different. You know McKechnie?'

I thought for a moment this was going to be another Teebrother or Brooklyn – an opium addict, perhaps, with a white beard. Then I remembered there really was a man called McKechnie who worked in an engineering shop in Glasgow and every two or three weeks sent Foraker long letters full of technical information and speculative suggestions concerning the potential development of various novel processes. I had had to translate two of them into French for the use of Foraker in some abstruse argument with Lenoir.

'Years ago,' Foraker said, 'McKechnie got in an argument, the way people do in Scotland, with an Irishman about the Nicaean Creed. There was a book he'd read once, book of sermons by a very learned minister, that proved this point McKechnie was making, but he didn't have the book and it wasn't in the library or anything. It was quite rare. So when I was in Edinburgh I spent a little time hunting that book through the bookstores, and, of course, I found it and gave it to him. And he triumphed in argument over this Irishman. It was to do with the Trinity, of course. And now he's foreman at that shop there and he writes to me.'

We were sharing a two-berth compartment, and just after I had fallen asleep in the upper bunk Foraker woke me up to say he had been observing me and noted that I was not relaxed properly so as to enjoy the maximum benefit of sleep. He handed me a sleeping pill and a glass of wine.

'You need to get down to relaxing right away,' he said. 'Don't lose time not sleeping properly. Tomorrow in Barcelona we're going to be busy.'

We were. For three days, from mid-morning until near dawn, with myself as interpreter, Foraker was interviewing the two directors of the little precision instrument factory that interested him, interviewing the works manager, sitting with them in their offices, perambulating the factory with them, watching demonstrations of their work, entertaining them or being entertained by them at enormous Spanish meals. On one of our tours of the factory, he detected a couple of English-speaking workers among the score or so of men employed. He immediately made an appointment with the works manager to meet him at our hotel early the following morning, pretended to have made a muddle about the place of meeting, left me to hold the man in conversation at the hotel and himself went off to the factory to 'have a little unofficial talk with those two boys.'

The results surprised even me. It went without saying that he had acquired quite a lot of information about the factory and its product which the directors, for one reason or another, had not seen fit to give him. But when the two directors lunched with us that afternoon he coolly informed them that it had 'come to his knowledge' that there was a strike situation developing in the factory; the men wanted more pay.

The directors shrugged and said that at this time in Barcelona all factories were threatened with strikes all the time. Incited by anarchists and syndicalists and other revolutionary elements, the labour force of Barcelona had become intolerably insolent and greedy. Employers were simply being blackmailed and gouged.

Foraker said it was a pity, because, in view of the urgency and importance of his requirements, he did not feel at all inclined to place a valuable contract with a factory which seemed likely to be paralysed at any moment by strike action. It would be necessary for him to take his business somewhere else.

The directors, exasperated and alarmed, asked what he suggested they could do about it?

'You could announce a pay rise all round, right now. Before any strike gets started,' Foraker said.

Argument rolled back and forth across the *arroz Valenciano* and the bumpers of mauve Spanish wine, and in the end the directors, their stomachs loaded and their nerves screaming out for their delayed siesta, agreed. They said, however, that they reserved the right to revise their estimates of the cost of goods to be supplied.

'What does that matter?' Foraker said to me as the door closed behind them. 'It's Halm's money. He can afford it. And it's nice to think the workers will be happy, happy men, glad to be at work on my contract. Besides, if those fellows at the top try to pull anything at all funny on me, I'll get to hear about it. Those lads in the factory will be pleased to give me any assistance that may be in their power.'

'But was there,' I said suspiciously, 'really going to be a strike on?'

'You heard what those fellows said,' Foraker answered, rather too casually. 'City like this – anarchists about, syndicalists and God knows what all. There's always going to be a strike.'

To my rather impertinent persistence, he replied that possibly the strike situation in this particular little works had not been quite so definite as he had implied, but the point remained that the men were bound to start asking for more money some time, so why should not he, Foraker, turn the situation to his advantage? Do himself and them a good turn?

'I just told them I'd fix for them to get a raise. That made us all feel good. It made for a nice atmosphere.'

I spoke the first thought that came to my mind. It seemed, I said, an elaborate way of going to work. All that ingenuity and trouble expended on such a relatively small objective.

Foraker appeared abruptly tired. 'You think so?' he said, and sighed. We had moved from the dining-room to the sitting-room of the big hotel suite, and he looked lonely, seated in a centrally located armchair in this rented roomful of rugs, chairs, sofas, and tables.

A fierce Mediterranean sunbeam, jabbing through the half-closed lattice of the window-shutters, lit up his jaw and a twist and twitch at the corner of his mouth. He rubbed his face with his hand, looked questingly about the room, and said again, 'You think so?'

9

After a long minute of brooding silence, Foraker shook himself and stretched as if he had settled something to his satisfaction – chained up the dog, perhaps.

'The fact is,' he said simply, 'I do have an infinite capacity for taking pains.'

Having delivered this statement he gave me a long, careful look and fell asleep.

I went out to send the regular evening telegram Foraker liked to have sent to Mark Crane in Paris. These telegrams told Crane the gist of business discussions held, and decisions taken.

I returned to find Foraker refreshed and marching impatiently about the room. He was reading Crane's reply to his telegram of the previous day, and thrust it at me.

'We'll have to get back,' he said. 'I don't like the sound of that at all.'

I read the telegram. It said that there was nothing of importance to report and that everything was going well. Work at Beauvais was proceeding according to schedule. I asked what was wrong with that?

It wasn't probable, Foraker said, that things were going as smoothly as all that. They never did.

'He's just trying to reassure me,' he said.

'And another thing,' Foraker said, censoriously. 'What about your uncle? Why hasn't he called up or sent a message?'

I said truthfully that, foreseeing how busy we should be on our few days' trip to Barcelona, I had thought it simpler just not to inform my uncle that we were going to be in the city at all. I might have added that I had frankly been daunted by the prospect of making clear to my uncle how it had come to pass that I was not a geologist; the task of explaining Foraker to him.

'You did very wrong,' said Foraker sternly. 'You might have deprived that old man of an occasion for pleasure and pride.'

'Well, really!' I said. 'It seems to me to be my business entirely. You know nothing about my uncle.'

'He will rejoice,' said Foraker, shushing me with a commanding gesture, 'in your success. He will take pride in the fact of your important and responsible position, achieved so soon after leaving his protection. He will feel that his care for you has not gone unrewarded.'

'But I don't suppose,' I said anxiously, 'he'll do anything of the sort. You don't understand his sort of person,' I added rashly.

'I understand all sorts of people,' replied Foraker with haughty assurance. 'Now what you'll do, you'll telephone to him right away – there's the telephone – and you'll ask him to dinner. Not here, I think. People of that sort are liable to think this class of hotel ostentatious. Take him to a first-class but small restaurant of modest appearance but top cuisine.'

I hesitated, sighing and fiddling with the telephone. Foraker narrowed his eyes and examined me.

'Ah,' he said, 'I get it. You're afraid he will not believe your story of your new way of life, your success. You think he'll think you're spinning him a yarn. Well, now,' he took a step towards me, beaming benevolently, 'what we'll do is, you'll telephone and ask him to dinner at this restaurant, and I'll come, too.'

More than ever daunted at the prospect ahead, I could only capitulate to this gracious offer. But what about Paris? I asked.

'As you get older, Ned,' he said, 'you get to regret the things you might have done to make old people a little happier, and didn't do. Things you never said, letters you never wrote. It gets to bother you. It bothers me. Besides,' he added, more briskly, 'there aren't any sleepers left on the night train to Paris, I checked up after I got Mark's telegram. We can't travel till morning anyway.'

On the telephone my uncle was expectedly petulant and suspicious. He agreed, however, to meet us, and as we drank sherry before dinner was still suspicious, peering sideways at Foraker out of spectacled, slightly watery eyes, as though on the look-out for some rascally move. Yet by the time we sat down to eat he was quite expansively explaining the difficulties of the business situation in Barcelona to Foraker, who listened with an air of attention bordering on reverence. Before we had finished the chicken *paella* my uncle, in his turn, was listening with respectful attention – a thing I had never seen him do except when he was in the company of people more important in the insurance business than himself.

Of my own attainments and prospects, Foraker spoke with sober enthusiasm, and, to my astonishment, my uncle, instead of ostentatiously doubting his every word, sat there smiling a little smile of shy pleasure.

Seeing that smile, I became aware for the first time, with a singular throb of the heart, that this old man, by whom I had so often and so tiresomely been lectured and thwarted, was actually fond of me and wished me well.

As we ate cheese my uncle was earnestly begging Foraker to tell something about the problems and prospects of flight. He dumbfounded me by hanging on Foraker's words, his papery old face lighted by an inner excitement.

'My goodness, Mr Foraker,' he said, 'you certainly open up some wonderful possibilities. Do you realize,' he said to me, as if fearing lest I fail to appreciate Foraker properly, 'that – if I understand Mr Foraker aright – mankind may, at some not very distant date, be in a position to voyage even into outer space?'

He said repeatedly that he rejoiced at his nephew's good fortune in becoming, to some extent, associated with such a figure of our time as Mr Foraker. And at this, in an equally bizarre transformation, Foraker became modest. He said that probably there were a dozen or a score of men at work in different places in the world who had apprehended the same general idea as he had himself, and – unnoticed and unadvertised – were seeking to express it in terms of practical achievement.

'No great idea, Mr Hastings,' he said, 'is unique in the sense of being conceived only at a single place and time. And before the end of time,' he said, 'all valid ideas come, sooner or later, to fruition. It is just a question of hastening the moment.'

As I said good-bye, my uncle's chief anxiety was evidently that I should prove worthy of the position I had achieved.

Back at the hotel, Foraker looked sadly into a glass of brandy. 'You don't understand, Ned,' he said, 'about the old. They sit there worrying and sorrowing, with death coming on, and there are little things you could do for them that you don't do, and then when you get around to doing them they're gone. It's no good,' he said harshly, 'yelling your damned regrets at a coffin, is it?'

He said he was glad we had had this dinner before our return to Paris. He repeated his doubts about Crane's information.

'Besides,' he said, yawning and loosening his necktie, 'under present conditions his judgement is apt to be a little warped.'

'How do you mean warped? What conditions, exactly?'

'By his feeling about Delia,' Foraker said, easing himself out of his jacket and hanging it over the arm of his chair. 'As you must have seen for yourself, he has a very, very strong feeling about Delia. He wants to impress her, don't you see? Obviously. Very, very natural, feeling the way he does. And, of course, when I'm there, he's in the shade all the time. Playing second fiddle. Cutting no figure at all.' He began to unlace his boots. 'So, the way I see it, he has just a natural bias to be the

Man in Charge as long as he can. That's what I mean his judgement's apt to be warped. Don't you recollect that time he wired me in Marseilles that everything was all right and there was no need for me to get back for a couple of days?'

'Well,' I said, 'but when we got back everything was all right, more or less.'

'Except,' said Foraker, 'that he was wasting a lot of time shopping around trying to see could he find someone that would offer us that steel tubing a couple of cents cheaper than the man that was ready to deliver it right away, and he didn't want me butting in and cutting the corners. D'you call that everything going more or less all right?'

He dragged off one of his boots and pitched it violently through the open door into his bedroom.

'I'd hate to think,' said Foraker earnestly, 'so badly of Mark that I'd believe he'd really and seriously believe in wasting maybe days of time just for the sake of saving that fool Halm a few dollars. No, Ned,' he said, pitching the other boot through the door, 'that's not fair. It's just that he has his judgement a little warped.'

He got up heavily from his chair and made towards his bedroom. 'The fact is,' he said, yawning widely, 'in perfectly simple terms, he's in love with her.'

I asked him whether he wanted me to give the night-porter a telegram to Paris to say we were definitely leaving in the morning.

'No,' he said, 'no, we won't do that.' He smiled to himself.

Just as I was leaving the room, he said, 'It'll be a nice surprise for everyone, us turning up suddenly tomorrow night in Paris.'

This remark horrified me by its implications. In the morning they looked even worse. Rolling up the Costa Brava, and through southern France towards Paris, I was distracted by the crude prospect. I could not doubt that a vulgarly horrifying spectacle was about to be enacted.

The husband, *en voyage,* his suspicions unexpectedly alerted, dashes back to find ... Or perhaps, good heavens, the whole Barcelona trip had been arranged with this sordid denouement in view. A banal trap. The guilty wife, falsely secure, surprised in the very arms of her lover.

An appalling scene. I tried not to picture it, and it obtruded itself upon me with disgusting intensity. Delia tossing in the arms of Mark Crane. Or would it be Lenoir? This uncertainty struck me as really the last straw. No one had the right to misbehave so confusingly. And then what, precisely, did Foraker, sitting opposite me in the restaurant car eating an early lunch, have in mind to do?

With a shock of alarm it occurred to me that he probably had picked up somewhere, in his omnivorous manner, some fatally inaccurate notion of French legal attitudes towards the *crime passionel*. It would be entirely characteristic of him to shoot everyone concerned and expect the police to call round, take a look at the corpses, say, 'Quite right, Monsieur Foraker, that seems to be perfectly in order,' and leave him to get on with his work.

I saw that Foraker was scribbling on a piece of paper. In the circumstances, this action took on a sinister appearance. His face, I thought, wore an expression of particular concentration. He might be going to kill himself, too, in the general holocaust, and was writing a Last Statement. There were only about six hours, now, between us and Paris.

He handed me the paper on which he had been writing.

'It's a telegram,' he said, 'to Delia. Find out from the car attendant where we stop over long enough for you to send it from the station. I know there's a stop-over somewhere about here. I'd like her to have that.'

I took the paper. The telegram said: 'Arriving this evening around ten on Barcelona express stop send machine to meet but tell Jean train may be up to one hour behind schedule so if he has to wait not to go away like that other time love Grant.'

I found out about the stop-over, sent the telegram from there and reported to Foraker that I had done so. I felt I had a grievance. I had been through a small hell, apparently for nothing.

'I did suggest,' I reminded him with dignity, 'that I should have the night-porter send that telegram before we started. Your wife would have had it by now.'

'Well, you see,' said Foraker, 'a thing about Delia is she doesn't like to look forward to a thing too long. Makes her nervous. If she'd had that this morning she'd have been in a state of nervous excitement all day. The time would have seemed so long till I was really there. She told me that once. I sent her a telegram twenty-four hours ahead of time to say I was getting in on a certain train, and looking forward to it all that time made her all nervously upset. So whenever I remember, I don't do it. Just wire a little while before I get in.

'Naturally,' he added, 'there've been a lot of times when I've forgotten about what she told me that time. That was in Canton, Ohio. Nearly seven years ago, not long after we married.'

At the Gare d'Orsay the car was there, so were Delia, Mark Crane, and Captain Lenoir. They had been waiting for an hour and thirty-five minutes, Lenoir said. Delia had suggested they leave the chauffeur out and all come to the station, Mark driving. Both he and Lenoir, it seemed had called at the Forakers' apartment that afternoon, and then the telegram had come, and Delia had made this plan that they should all dine together, Martha too, and then come to greet us. Martha, Delia told me, had dined with them, then excused herself and gone home, saying she had a headache and would go to bed.

Delia looked breathlessly gay. Although the evening was stifling, she reminded me, for some extraordinary reason, of a person at winter-sports; riding a fast toboggan, perhaps.

Foraker was visibly inattentive to the explanation of how they happened all to be there, took it entirely for granted, and equally for granted that, as they did chance to be on hand, they would all come back to the apartment and discuss the situation in Barcelona.

He suggested I return with them, assist their conference; possibly look at some of the correspondence that would have come in while we were away, and stay the night.

At the apartment, Foraker, after pouring drinks for everyone, went across the little passage to the door of Martha's room and called to her, asking how she was. We could hear Martha calling back faintly, and Foraker shouting through the door that he had the very thing that would fix that.

'It's a special mixture they have down there in Barcelona,' he told her through the door. 'I got it from a big chemist down there, and he told me the Queen of Spain uses it all the time. Cured her of feverish headaches.'

He went and got a bottle out of his bag and gave it to Delia to give to Martha.

With me translating most of it for Lenoir, he rattled off a quick-paced account of our trip. Reading, so to speak, between the lines, Mark at once spotted what had happened about the 'strike situation' and was outraged.

'One of these days, Grant,' he said, 'you'll get yourself into jail, or run out of Europe or something.'

Lenoir, on the contrary, was briefly amused and pleased. 'A good stroke, that,' he said. 'Very suitably audacious.' He patted Foraker on the knee and smiled at him. 'If someone like you could take over the Ministry of War, my dear Grant, we might have a chance of being ready for action when the shooting starts.'

But Foraker, running off a few more summary observations on the potentialities of the works in Barcelona, moved over to the sofa where Delia was seated, and put his arm around her while he talked. His hand caressed her shoulder and pulled her against him.

'Well,' he said abruptly, 'I guess that's about all, gentlemen.'

Delia's head was leaning back against his shoulder, and her throat and bare neck shone in the light of the electric lamp. Mark Crane grumbled inaudibly. Captain Lenoir jerked a thin gold watch out of his pocket, glared at it ostentatiously, his expression convicting it of an affront, and pushed it back again. I, too, glanced sideways at a clock which stood on a cabinet at the end of the room. The conference on the situation in Barcelona had lasted a little over twenty minutes.

Foraker stood up, smiling happily, and, with his hand in hers, pulling Delia to her feet, too. She smiled round at us all out of her shining, unrevealing eyes.

'Time for bed,' said Foraker, running his hand over her arm and shoulder. In the circumstances, he might as well have dragged the bed into the room and started getting into it with her.

Lenoir, stiff and elegant as a sword on parade, Mark, awkward as a wooden doll being pulled about by strings, finally said their good-byes and went strutting and shambling off. I said I would take a look at the correspondence in Foraker's study before going to bed.

'If you want a hot drink with your work,' Delia called after me, 'Henriette-Louise-Marie will make it for you. You can ask her as she prowls.'

The Forakers' maid-servant, who came from near Dijon, was called Henriette-Louise-Marie by everyone, all the time, because any two of these names, she had declared, were, by themselves, common, and therefore virtually insulting. Her insistence on the whole trio was an assertion of individuality and dignity. As to her prowling, that was what she did at night. However late the people of the house went to bed, Henriette-Louise-Marie would come briskly out from her room in the kitchen quarters and 'set to rights' the vacated living rooms.

There was a point about her which kept her high in Foraker's esteem: she insisted that she must have a little time every day to go and visit her aunt and drink coffee with her, or an anisette. It cheered her aunt up, she said. Foraker had made up his mind that the aunt was an old lady, and it made him happy to think that by giving Henriette-Louise-Marie time off for this purpose he was contributing, however indirectly, to the consolation of the aged.

He would stand in front of her and, bending down, would shout into her face, '*Visiter les anciens. Bon. Tres bon. Vous êtes bon visiter la tante.*'

And Henriette-Louise-Marie, whose appearance and manner brought to mind a sleek, yet perky, bird, would cock a bright eye at him and reply that he, too, was good, a jewel among men.

Delia said she did not believe there was an aunt at all.

Henriette-Louise-Marie was still a pretty good-looking woman. The 'aunt', she maintained, was a man. There was a pretence in the Foraker household that Henriette-Louise-Marie had a 'weakness' for me. She was supposed to make longing eyes at me behind my back, and once, when I sneezed in the passageway she rushed to the kitchen and made me a special tisane.

She appeared now, a quarter of an hour after I had sat down to work at the correspondence, wearing a gay turban of coloured dusters jauntily tilted sideways on her head, and a cotton dressing gown girdled tightly between her prominent hips and breasts. Although people had to shout at her to make themselves understood, she herself spoke in a hoarse, hissing whisper, which gave a conspiratorial effect to everything she said.

As a sort of compensation for this, she had a strange gift of mimicry, was a natural actress. Delia told Mark, a little to his discomfiture, that when Henriette-Louise-Marie imitated him she actually looked like him – 'but more like you than you are.' And once, working alone in Foraker's study, I had run out into the passage to investigate astonishing noises from the kitchen, a kind of lewd moaning, broken by squeals of passion. I had been met by Delia, flushed and slightly hysterical.

She had taken a moment to get her breath. Then she had explained that for some reason – Delia had no idea how the subject came up – Henriette-Louise-Marie had started to mimic the sexual activities of the cats on the garden walls at the back of the apartment.

'Really,' Delia had said, 'I can't describe it. It was so – well, it was so darn *real*.'

This evening, Henriette-Louise-Marie put her turbaned head into the room, told me that what I wanted was a little coffee and a little brandy, and presently returned with them on a tray, starting to talk before she had even put the tray down on the desk. She seemed in a state of unusual excitement. The least incident, such as a stranger visiting, or people returning from a journey, excited her a good deal.

She now rehearsed such self-evident facts as that I had returned, M. Foraker had returned, to Paris after a long journey and absence of several days.

'Poor Monsieur Hastings,' she wheezed, 'he returns, tired yet excited, no doubt, as one is, by the vibrations of the train – it is the vibrations, Monsieur, against the nerves at the base of the spinal column which make what some call the travel itch, others *l'amour d'après voyage*. The pity of it, when one thinks that just over there, across the passage, is lying in her bed the little Martha Dukes whom Monsieur Hastings would so much like to . . . And she, too, no doubt, excited. What with Monsieur Foraker and Monsieur Hastings both returning. And at such a time she has a stomach-ache and a headache. She lies there tossing.'

Beginning with a sigh that twisted her whole body, Henriette-Louise-Marie gave a slight, disturbing sketch of Martha, tossing about in the neighbouring bed.

She came out of that act and said that, of course, for M. Foraker things were different. With that one, *la belle Madame Foraker*. There came the throaty laugh. Passionate like a cat, *la belle Foraker* was, in her opinion. But more cautious, being Anglo-Saxon. All the same, one could easily see what was on her mind, besides M. Foraker. About M. Crane, for instance, and Captain Lenoir.

She rippled into pantomime. Here was Mark, a little sleeker, a little primmer than in reality, but Mark, all right, in expression and gesture, and then it was Mark turned inside out, as it were, or lit up by some tell-tale beam – slobbering with unsatisfied desire, an absurdly frustrated satyr in a high collar. And Lenoir, perfectly the French officer of the New School and then made ridiculous and somewhat obscene by a series of sensual snorts at the back of his throat.

'Stop! It's enough!' I muttered at her, but to interrupt Henriette-Louise-Marie when she was in mid-act would need a shout that would rouse the house.

She slid from one part to the other, and now Delia was there, too, and they were circling around her, ogling and slobbering, and she was making faint noises, a kind of mewing.

A ludicrous phrase came to my lips. 'Remember where you

are!' I barked at Henriette-Louise-Marie, and this time she heard me, because she suspended herself, as it were, between two impersonations to roll her eyes at me and say, 'I know very well where I am. It is the house of Monsieur Foraker, the great inventor, the superior genius, the great . . .' and strangled the rest of it in her hoarse laughter.

'Good, eh?' she said. 'That's the way it is. And now,' she stepped to the door, 'Monsieur Hastings, so industrious, must get on with his work.'

For the next hour, longer, indeed, than I had intended, I forced myself to concentrate on sorting the correspondence, putting aside some letters to be dealt with by Mark Crane, making summaries, in translation, of two technical reports sent to Foraker from Brussels and Marseilles. It was pleasurable to deal with these aspects of his affairs. It distracted one's attention from those other 'factors in the situation' disagreeably obtruded on my mind by Henriette-Louise-Marie's pantomimic display.

The noble task of making the impossible possible seemed more than ever complex, nagged by ignoble vexations.

In the morning, Delia asked me whether Henriette-Louise-Marie had not been making a lot of noise in the study last night. It had sounded as though she were imitating cats again.

'She was imitating everyone,' I said.

'Oh dear,' Delia said, 'I wish she wouldn't. It quite scares me.' She stood looking out of the window at Paris and said thoughtfully, 'So strange. I never heard of anyone carrying on like that at home.'

This remark, somewhat fatuous in itself, struck me at the time because I had never before heard her refer in just that way to 'home', meaning, evidently, Canton, Ohio. After that, I began to notice how rarely she spoke of 'home' in that sense, or made any comparison between conditions in one place and another. The next occasion on which she did so appeared even less appropriate. It must have been at least two months later, a sad-looking November afternoon, when she had asked me to go with her to the Place des Vosges, which she had heard was an almost perfect specimen of very early seventeenth-century urban architecture.

We had walked round it twice, and she stood still, her boots speckled with mud and yellow leaves, looking over the solid elegance of the arcades, and the lovely brick frontages above. And she said, 'It's all very strange. Not a bit like home.'

I have never been in Canton, Ohio, but I daresay there are not a great many places in the civilized world less like the Place des Vosges in Paris.

I was on the point of rather rudely saying so when I saw that she was crying.

I could have pretended not to notice, only that a tear ran down under her veil and she instinctively put out her tongue to catch it as it passed her mouth, and then, another welled out and hung damply in the mesh of the veil itself and made a little dark patch on her glove when she tried to mop at it.

Mutters of concern, futile, solicitous questions – Was she feeling ill? Anything I could do? – and a flutter of my handkerchief, produced at first only the statement, or it may have been an accusation, that the Place des Vosges was 'so darned old'. To which I replied, soothingly I thought, that it was, in point of fact, only a trifle over three hundred years old.

She actually stamped, and cried out that she was not arguing about just how many hundred years old the place was, what did she care?

At the time, this appeared to me so illogical that I could think of nothing to say, except to suggest that she come into the café under one of the arcades and take a glass of champagne or cognac, and I started to lead the way to it.

As she sipped her drink, and talked in incomplete sentences, becoming animated and a little incoherent, I was once again oddly put in mind of a person on a toboggan – her expression had at times that same mixture of exhilaration and alarm.

It was the first of many conversations with her, much more personal than any we had had before this episode, and I no longer remember exactly just what she said on that day and what she said on other days when I was in the apartment with my work finished and waiting for a new assignment from Foraker.

'And then,' she said once, 'I thought that as I went about and saw all the historic buildings and the great paintings and all that sort of thing, that would do the trick. It's what they lead you to expect about Art and all that,' she added rather petulantly.

I remarked that the view of Art as a moral Baden-Baden, or pick-you-up, was an outmoded conception of the mid-Victorians. I had opinions about Art and I unfolded them for her benefit.

She said, 'It isn't only Art.'

At about this point she usually became vague, but once she said, 'Sometimes I feel the same way about people as I do about all these famous pictures.'

I said I did not quite understand.

She said, 'Oh, I mean you're going to the gallery, and then you're at the gallery, and then ... well, you've been to the gallery. And it'll be the same tomorrow. In a couple of weeks it'll be Christmas, and New Year.'

And one day, when there was January fog in the air, and thick snowy slush underfoot, delaying traffic so that Foraker was late coming back from a talk with Mark Crane in the business office, she said, 'I suppose it's always waiting for something that makes everything that happens sort of unreal. Waiting for Grant.'

I thought she was talking about the fog, and said I expected he would not be long now.

'No, no,' she said, 'I mean the Thing. The Principle. Waiting and waiting for it to come off.'

She was watching the fog beyond the windows, and the blur of the lights coming on, making fuzzy yellow patches in the wet dusk. It was the regular signal for Jephthah to rush into the room from the little room they called the nursery where he played until the street-lights came on.

He brought with him two books, carried importantly like the portfolios of a minister.

One of them had been in his possession ever since I had known the Forakers. It was an English book of stories told entirely in simple pictures, suitable for a child about four years old. All the pictures by now had received additions which, in the course of long months, had become almost indistinguishable from the original drawings. There was a dog with a red crayon beard and a fish with a blotch of ink at its mouth which, because I had been told it so often, I now thought of at once as a cigar.

The other book was carefully wrapped in brown paper. It was large and heavy and grandly bound. It was handsomely, but not lavishly, illustrated by a dozen plates. It was a history of France, in French, intended, as the introduction noted, for students between the ages of ten and twelve, and it had been a Christmas present from Grant Foraker to his son.

At the time, Delia had examined it in astonishment. She had said, hesitantly, that it was a lovely book but after all Jeph, she said, could as yet only spell out a few very simple words even in English. Who would read this book to him? And didn't it seem a little 'old' for him, anyway?

Foraker had appeared perplexed. He had forgotten, momentarily, just what he had had in mind when he bought the book. Later, when he remembered, the purchase appeared as a gesture of impatience. The object, he explained confidently, was to kill three birds with one stone. First, such a book, because it was not told in pictures, but in print, would hasten the process of Jephthah's learning to read. Secondly, since the reading matter was in French, it followed that Jephthah would get to read French at the same time as learning to read. Thirdly, this was a book of history, and a knowledge of history, Foraker said, was of great importance and use.

Delia, who had been still looking doubtfully at the book, had got the sense of the passage in the Introduction about students between ten and twelve. She remarked on it to Foraker.

'After all,' she said, 'Jeph's only five.'

'Well, there you are,' Foraker said. 'He'll be right ahead of the others. He'll have the jump on everyone.'

He had looked intently at Jephthah as he crouched on the floor over the book, as though watching for this mental fertilizer to show immediate results.

Under these circumstances it customarily fell to me, if I were disengaged, to read a few pages of the history to Jephthah at lamplighting time. When Foraker appeared, Jephthah would hurry to him to report progress. 'The identity of the earliest inhabitants of ancient Gaul is veiled in obscurity,' he would state, and march about the room muttering the words 'veiled in obscurity' with pleasure, while Foraker watched him hopefully.

In the light of the lamp in the street, we now saw Foraker and Martha getting out of a cab and coming across to the house. Jephthah hid behind the door. When they came in, he rushed out making a loud screeching sound and shouting, 'I'm a Celt. Hands up, I'm a Celt! Celts are good,' he told Foraker.

'Celts, eh?' Foraker said. 'What else about Celts?' But Jephthah by now had become deeply interested in the darkening fog and paid no attention to him. Foraker jumped out of his chair again like a huge jack-in-the-box and said he would have some 'stuff' for me to work on in half an hour or so, and went off to his study. Martha and I sat alone together, leaving the curtains undrawn so as to enjoy the spectacle of the fog, and the feeling it gave one of a special isolation and security inside the window-panes.

It was the first time I had seen her alone since Christmas, when she had gone to England for three weeks to stay with relatives, some of them old enough to compensate Foraker's annoyance at the interruption of her services. Perhaps because of this, and of the fog enveloping the outside world, I was freshly invaded by sensations and ideas which I had had much earlier in my acquaintance with Martha and I had thought had dried up or petered out.

I felt benign towards one and all, even towards Henriette-Louise-Marie, whom I would sometimes catch peering at me and Martha with disagreeable intentness, gathering material, I made no doubt, for one of her scandalous impersonations. Perhaps, I thought, she entertained her aunt with such performances. Twice, I had actually seen the aunt, sitting with Henriette-Louise-Marie in one of the cafés not far from the Forakers' apartment house. She had a robust figure, set off by an unusually bright, grey costume. She did not, it is true, look old enough, perhaps, to suit Foraker's sentiments, but then she was wearing a big hat with an enormous sweep of pale blue feather at one side of it, and I did not see her face, as she bent forward over a coffee cup while Henriette-Louise-Marie talked to her. A dutiful niece, indeed, reflecting credit on the whole neighbourhood of Dijon.

Mark Crane made no secret of the fact that he regarded my romantic concentration on Martha as somewhat ridiculous. Why? Because it would get me nowhere. And what, might I just ask, about his ridiculous passion for Delia Foraker? Or was that, perhaps, 'getting him' somewhere? If so where? Into the soup, most likely. Him and everyone else.

In lonely moods, he would take me on evening expeditions which would start in many different ways but almost always ended in an expensive *boîte de nuit* in the Madeleine district.

Here we would have supper, drink and watch mediocre cabaret, and on nights when Mark felt the ineluctable sorrows of Humanity pressing upon him especially heavily, he would take one of the girls home with him.

Sometimes Mark's feeling for humanity was not pity, but scorn. One night in early spring, sitting beside me with his arm around a demure-looking dancer from Hungary, he begged me to note the squalor and horror of it all, the greed and stupidity evident on the faces of the customers, the ostentatious waste of time and money at a moment when, if I read the papers, I must realize that Europe was drifting inevitably to war.

He turned to the Hungarian girl and said in a voice husky with pathos, 'You, poor baby, you don't know what it's all about, do you? What are you going to do when they get a war? Bang-bang.'

I expected her to say that she would go to America with him on a great big ship, and that was what she said, but I heard only the beginning of it because at that moment a hand dropped familiarly on my shoulder, I heard a voice I knew wishing me good evening, and looked up into the augustly meditative countenance of M. Paca.

He was so impressive that for a couple of seconds, before I recalled that he was after all merely the proprietor of a neighbouring cabaret or brothel, I felt as if the philosopher Plato had turned up suddenly and asked me whether I found this place Good and Beautiful.

Uninvited, M. Paca sat down.

He looked sideways past my head at the half-turned shoulder of Mark Crane who was engrossed in telling the Hungarian girl about, I think, the completion of the Singer Building in New York.

'I understood,' said M. Paca, as casually as though we had met a few days ago, 'that you and your friend, Monsieur Foraker's partner, are often here. So I dropped round. I would like to discuss the situation that has arisen. In a friendly manner,' he added.

I tried to arrange my ideas and control my reactions. I noticed with a sort of disgust that subconsciously I must have been waiting for this, or something like it, to happen. It was more than a year since I had left Robinson, Paca and the others gesticulating despairingly on the station platform at Marseilles. But I had never quite been able to dismiss the recollection of that obsessed Mr Robinson from my mind.

'The trouble,' M. Paca was saying, 'is that Monsieur Robinson is not quite happy in his work.'

Now as before, the voice and manner of M. Paca had the annoying effect of hypnotizing me into a half-belief that what he was saying was quite natural and matter of fact, whereas I was being a little slow, a little absurd and even abnormal in my bewilderment and hostility.

'Obviously,' M. Paca kept saying as he muttered his story, with a continuously wary eye on Mark's shoulder.

The story, or such part of it as seemed to affect M. Paca's special interests – which was the only part he had bothered to discover or remember – was, in one sense, simple. And while he was telling it I was doing my best to read between its lines, fill in the gaps left by M. Paca's incurious mind.

For example, it was clear that a little while after my defection at Marseilles, Mr Robinson had, nevertheless, consented to a kind of partnership with Paca, Perrin, and Bally. What considerations, I wondered, had overcome his scruples, his memory of maternal warnings, his fear of a lightning blast from the Almighty if he misused the 'gift' for purposes of gain rather than in the clear cause of righteousness?

Paca neither knew nor cared. The practical outcome, from Paca's standpoint, had been satisfactory. There had been some nicely priced winners at Longchamps and Auteuil. Over the Derby, they had made a very considerable killing.

Little as I wanted to enter into any kind of discussion with Paca, I could not help asking him – for it was a point that had interested me from the outset – whether Mr Robinson's gift worked in relation to anything except horses and, as I knew, cards. Again, Paca was uninformative. They had made, I gathered, one or two attempts to get him to foresee the rise or fall of stocks on the Bourse, but with only moderate success.

Mark was saying 'Six hundred and twelve feet high, think of that, baby!' and the Hungarian girl was clucking in her throat to express amazement. Paca eyed them, bent a little closer to me, and said that latterly, within the past ten days, a kind of crisis had arisen. Mr Robinson had become unhappy, agitated, jumpy, altogether an unsatisfactory collaborator for men who had no interest in him or his aims except as they might affect the joint exploitation of his clairvoyant powers.

I made out that, until that moment, Mr Robinson had been content with a modest percentage of the trio's winnings. Was he then supporting himself by these 'earnings'? Paca said no, he had got a job with another textile firm.

'He got married, you know,' Paca said.

I found this piece of intelligence amazing. I had thought of Robinson as, so to speak, an utterly isolated and, I suppose, not entirely human phenomenon – a sort of vehicle for carting about his gift and his obsession with the potential evil and 'dangerousness' of Grant Foraker.

Before I could ask any questions, we were interrupted by Mark who turned to me, bowed slightly to Paca, and said that if it was the same to me, and as I had found a friend, he proposed to go home now. He and the Hungarian left the table, and Paca, without further reference to Mrs Robinson, explained that what had happened now was that Robinson had not only turned moody, but alternated between two extravagantly contradictory moods; in one, he threatened to break off relations with Paca and associates altogether, and spoke darkly of the dread consequences of misusing his powers; in the other, he hinted, in general terms, at the possibility that he might call suddenly upon Paca, Perrin, and Bally to put a very large sum of money at his immediate disposal.

For what purpose? No idea. That was what was worrying. And what the devil had all this to do with me?

Well, the whole thing was essentially simple. What did it all amount to? It amounted just to 'keeping our friend Robinson sweet'. So that he could work his gift happily and properly. After all, Paca said, one didn't want to monkey about with a thing like that. Suppose it 'dried up on him'?

He referred to Mr Robinson's occult or mysterious powers exactly as he would have referred to an unseen oil-well in Texas.

He had said he had no idea of the nature of the crisis that had arisen, but he was sure it related in some way to Foraker. There had been hints, indications. In point of fact he had formed a very definite impression that what Robinson needed to make him 'happy' was 'a little bit of action' in the matter of this Foraker. He had reason to believe that at some not distant date this desire for action would express itself in an approach to myself. That was why he was now giving me a straight tip. With the facts he had now given me, I could put two and two together, realize where a 'little bit of good' might be done. In other words, in the event of such an approach, the thing was to treat it sympathetically, keep Robinson sweet.

M. Paca patted me on the knee, looked superciliously around the establishment, evidently judging it inferior to his own, and took his leave as casually as he had appeared.

'We understand each other,' he said. 'Just a word from a friend. Business is business.'

In the light of day I examined this episode, decided to mention it to Foraker. We were in the car driving to Beauvais when I spoke to him of M. Paca's *démarche*. He listened attentively, with the air of examining quite seriously this flimsy bundle of information.

'Naturally,' he said, 'he'll try to buy you. It would be prudent to show an interest. We must deny ourselves the luxury of too swift a rebuff.'

We had a busy day at Beauvais, and it was not until evening that he referred to the matter again, so much later, in fact, that for a moment I did not grasp what he was talking about.

'Can you imagine that?' he said. 'The little son of a bitch.'

He was standing by the car, the cranking handle in his hand, looking back at the rough open square of buildings making up the workshop, which was in appearance a great deal more like a ramshackle agglomeration of farm buildings, standing in open country three miles out of the town of Beauvais. The place had, in fact, been a broken-down farm before Foraker took it over and converted the cow-barns and hay-barn and the former dwelling for his purposes. Part of the old dwelling house had been turned into an office, and the rest was occupied by the foreman of the works and his family. He and his two sons, a rugged trio from western Normandy, took it in turns to act as night watchman after the little force of other workers had gone home to Beauvais.

'Come right down to it,' he said, later in the hotel restaurant at Beauvais, 'it's on account of the past he carries on this way.'

I said, intending to relieve his mind, that it was not the Forakers who had started this feud, or whatever one liked to call it.

Foraker waved this away with a violent motion of his hand.

'And, anyway,' I said, 'it's all so long ago.'

At that he burst out with a kind of melancholy bitterness that was quite new to me.

'That's the hell of it,' he said, staring down at the backs of his hands. 'It's so goddamn past there's nothing you can lay a hold of. Nothing you can do. You can't get at it, don't you see?'

This thought seemed actually to fill him with despair, and he flexed the muscles of his hands and let them drop inert on the table as if demonstrating their incapacity to take hold of the past and twist it about.

'Trouble was,' Foraker said, 'Father just over-extended his credit somewhat. Say the thing had come off, say there hadn't been a couple of bad harvests or whatever it was right afterwards, and that community we had there had increased and multiplied, prospering mightily. Everybody happy. A great work done for the Almighty and His kingdom upon earth. Who was going to start getting nasty about was there really going to be an end of the world and all that praying stopped it? Or did Father know about the hurricane when he got us all ready to go out on that mountain? What you have to understand,' he said earnestly, 'is Father believed in God.'

'Yes,' I said, 'I can see that.'

'So there it was. Naturally, working for God, he drew a bit more out of the bank, don't you see, than he had in it. I'm not talking about money. I mean he said things and did things that would have been just fine if the future had worked out the way he aimed for it to work out. When it didn't work out that way, he couldn't meet the IOUs he'd floated around. Things kind of closed in on him.'

He looked forlornly into the unmanageable past which, I began to realize, appalled him because there was no way in which you could cajole it with a favour or special service, no means of putting it under an obligation by a present of new patent medicines. And when he talked again of Mr Robinson, it was evident that in his eyes the grave and disquieting thing about Robinson was precisely his connection with the past. He was a bit of it, alive and walking about. A product of the past, embodying its disturbing qualities.

Just then I understood how eagerly Foraker had taken on Robinson as his confidential secretary. It had been a way of doing the past a good turn after all, getting it under control. I tried to imagine the scene when Foraker discovered that so far from being under control, it had nosed its way in for the purpose of biting him.

As his thoughts turned to the immediate situation, Foraker's gloom began to disperse.

'We shall proceed with caution,' he said. 'We shall be vigilant. If the approach they speak of is made, you will use the opportunity to probe their purposes.'

Spring had cut a slice out of the end of winter, and there were days at the beginning of March when, at the café on the corner of the Rue St Jacques where I had my morning coffee, they ventured already to put the tables out on the sidewalk, with a charcoal brazier among them to help the sun.

I used to sit there reading the paper and thinking sometimes, when I saw a girl crossing the boulevard or getting out of a fiacre, how delightful it would be if, as she came nearer, this turned out to be Martha, suddenly moved to race across Paris and join me.

Then I saw a woman get out of a fiacre and, after looking about her uncertainly, start to walk down the farther side of the Rue St Jacques. At a little distance, she stopped, turning away from me to peer at the name above the door of another, even smaller café on that side of the street. As she did so I recognized the figure, the blue-feathered hat and the bright grey costume of Henriette-Louise-Marie's aunt.

She moved on, saw the café where I sat, and at a quicker pace crossed the road. To my astonishment, she came straight to my table and inquired, in English, whether I was Mr Hastings?

As I stood up, bowing confusedly, I supposed that the aunt had somehow been pressed into service to bring a message to me from the Forakers. I had time to notice, as I asked her to sit down, that she was a woman in her early thirties and I wondered if Henriette-Louise-Marie had dared allow Foraker a look at her.

She was slightly flushed, and fiddled with the buttons of one glove as she sat at the table. She started to apologize for approaching me in a manner so unusual, so unconventional. Then she dropped the apology halfway and, catching a deep breath, said, 'You knew my husband in Marseilles. I am Mrs Robinson.'

The 'R' in Robinson burred slightly on her tongue. The cramped living-room of the Robinson residence she spoke of as the 'parlour'. And when she spoke of herself as a 'plain Scots body', I realized that during the first minutes of our conversation at the café, and throughout the drive to their apartment beyond the Invalides, I had been mentally fumbling for some phrase to describe the impression she made, and that this was it.

Not that she was entirely 'plain' in the English sense of the word. She had a face like a fresh apple and the figure of a farmer's wife in a fairy story. She had an aura of healthy simplicity: a plain body, at the moment in a little bit of a pother. And, now, she was brewing tea.

'I always say,' she said, 'a cup of tea's a little bit of home, and as you'll be aware, there is no beverage so beneficial to the nerves and stomach.'

Mr Robinson, she had told me, would be home in 'just a wee while.'

In transit from the Rue St Jacques to this apartment, I had been nearly dumb from bewilderment. Besides, I was concentrating on the memory of Foraker's instructions as to the vigilant and probing attitude to be adopted in the event of an 'approach'.

But the manner of it so confused me that halfway through the drive I had found myself actually asking Mrs Robinson how she, evidently a Scotswoman, happened to be the aunt of Henriette-Louise-Marie from Dijon. To this absurd question she had replied, as though question and answer were both perfectly natural, that, indeed, she was no kin of Henriette-Louise-Marie at all. It had been, in a manner of speaking, a 'wee' deception.

The whole matter would become clear to me; Mr Robinson himself would explain it fully. I would already be aware, though, how very great an interest Mr Robinson took in everything pertaining to Mr Foraker, and the fact was that Henriette-Louise-Marie, as I must guess, had kept him informed of such matters, meeting Mrs Robinson at stated times. How else would it have been known where I took my breakfast?

'I was always high in the French classes at school in Lanark,' Mrs Robinson had said with simple pride, as the fiacre jogged westwards.

Now, after recommending as 'wholesome' a plate of oat-cakes she had brought with the tea, Mrs Robinson seemed prepared to chat freely while we awaited her husband.

As she talked, a rough outline of Mr Robinson's proceedings became discernible.

Married, for instance, in March of last year. Only a few weeks after my encounter with him in Marseilles. A sudden decision? Yes and No. A long engagement. Five and a half years. But Mr Robinson is a man of care and deep consideration, and he does not during that period feel justified in marrying. Things are a wee bit uncertain. Then, in February of 1908, he pays a visit to Scotland. His prospects have enlarged. He is in a position to support a wife in decency.

The future Mrs Robinson hesitates, victim of a momentary faint-heartedness at the thought of Abroad. Mr Robinson implores. His prospects have increased, but so, likewise, have his burdens. He doubts his strength to carry them all alone. Now, as never before, he feels the need of a helpmate. With his dear Peggy as helpmate, he can face anything. She yields, and studies Advanced French Grammar for Higher Students.

After marriage, during the honeymoon at Oban, Mr Robinson speaks at length of Abroad, the World Situation, the Position of Our Country, Dangers Lurking. He has a Mission. In this she rejoices. It is a proper thing for a man to have. Not everyone has a call to the ministry, though it is a grand thing when they have. But any Call or Mission is a fine thing, and elevates a man, bringing out the best and highest in him.

The precise terms of reference in which Mr Robinson envisages his mission are not at this point entirely clear. He frankly admits to his bride, as they face one another in love and confidence across the table of the empty hotel in the Atlantic winter, that he does not himself yet see the full scope. But Mr Foraker is mentioned. Mr Foraker is a focal point. Foraker, arrogant embodiment of the lurking dangers. Perhaps Foraker is not the whole of the mission. But without the pursuit of Foraker the mission itself is not whole.

Mrs Robinson is not ignorant of the 'gift'. It, too, is discussed at Oban. In Mrs Robinson's eyes, evidently, it is simply another of the attributes of her grand man Sandy. The Almighty, whom she sees as a decent, fair-minded body, though given to outbursts of extravagant violence that are not always just quite easy to understand, has seen fit to equip the good man Sandy with this capacity. And why not?

Equally, there are conditions attached. Why not? You would not expect the Lord God to be handing out a thing like that and make no rules about the use of it.

Thus, the question whether the gift is being misused is a serious one, of the greatest practical importance. Somewhere between the beaten shores of Oban and the apartment behind the Invalides the question is decided. Cannily so, in accordance with the newly-wed Mrs Robinson's advice. She is a year or two older than Mr Robinson and makes bold to offer a little guidance in a matter so important, where a mistake could put you on the outs with Providence.

'Ca' canny' is her advice, and the decision is that Mr Robinson will first seek regular employment with a textile firm which is in sharp rivalry, particularly on the Continent, with the firm for which he worked before taking the position with Foraker. They are glad to have him, for he brings with him a little goodwill, and a little confidential information about the trading methods of the rival.

At the same time, Mr Robinson will hire the use of his gift to Paca and associates, for payments which will be devoted to the general prosecution of the mission. And how, more precisely, is this to be carried out? Well, first by the choice of an apartment rather more commodious than the pair would otherwise require, so that Mr Robinson may have the privacy of a small study. Secondly, by the installation of a telephone. Thirdly, by subscribing to a terrible great number of newspapers and periodicals such as will afford a conspectus of the world situation. Fourthly, by small payments to people of goodwill who are in possession of relevant facts.

He had met many people in the course of his business and heard many stories. Things are not at all what they seem. There are conspiracies afoot. The Jews and the Free Masons and the Church of Rome, to name only three conspiratorial forces, are working like beavers to gain their ends. Also the men behind the scenes of High Finance, with Anarchist and Socialist Revolutionary Atheists as their allies and dupes, are scheming to overthrow things for their private profit. As matters stand, ignorance, frivolity, and sloth are all too prevalent in those quarters where countervailing measures should be in process of rapid organization.

And Foraker? Where is he in all this? Has he then been lost sight of? By no manner of means. Indeed, in one sense Foraker may be said to have been providential. One might say that the Lord had chosen to use Foraker for His own purposes. For had it not been for what might be termed the personal relations existing over the years between the Forakers and the Robinsons, Mr Robinson's eyes might never have been opened to the realities of what goes on in the world.

Does he, then, take the view that Mr Foraker is a Jew, a Free Mason, or an agent of the Church of Rome? Not just precisely that, though it remains to be proved that he is not. But, however that may be, Mr Robinson can clearly discern that Mr Foraker is deeply implicated in the general conspiracy of evil forces. And, it is clear, too, that he is among the most dangerous of all the elements involved.

Why so? Because he is a very, very clever man, and as ruthless as a serpent. Also, the resources of Science are at his disposal. Science untrammelled by moral considerations. It is sinister. There is talk in the newspapers of Death Rays that could destroy the British Fleet in half an hour. And if Foraker does not have a Death Ray, he certainly is working at something equally powerful, perhaps devilish, in the aerial line.

Mr Robinson is not moved by any personal considerations, but it is providential that a personal, or family, connection should have led him to see Foraker for what he is.

It is nearly incredible, Mrs Robinson remarks, that Henriette-Louise-Marie should, only three days ago, have had the frivolity to serve notice upon Mr Robinson that she proposed to quit her employment with the Forakers just on account of having been offered a part with some theatrical company in her native town of Dijon.

Is this, then, the crisis which is causing such worry and distress to Mr Robinson? Not entirely. But about that, said Mrs Robinson, her candid blue eyes wide above her teacup, it would be better if Mr Robinson himself were to inform me.

As she spoke, another voice spoke behind and above my head.

'Ah-ha!' it said. 'Tea, I see. The cup that cheers but not inebriates.'

Turning in angry alarm, I saw the head and shoulders of Mr Robinson squeezed out through a door in the wall which could not be fully opened because it was impeded by my chair. I jumped up, Mr Robinson pushed the chair a little aside, and got the door farther open. Through it I could see into a room which appeared to be about the size of a very deep cupboard. It contained, indeed it was filled by, a chair and a small desk like those used in schools. On the farther wall, boards had been fixed as shelves, and these were packed with books.

Evidently I was having a view of Mr Robinson's 'study'. Equally evidently, since there was visibly no other entrance to it except this door, Mr Robinson must have been sitting in it all the time. With his next words he confirmed this.

'I know you'll excuse,' he said, 'a small deception. I formed the opinion' – he was fumbling for my hand to shake it – 'that it would be best for you to gather the background of the situation from my wife. From a Third Party standpoint, you know. And you will have appreciated already that Mrs Robinson has a very practical head on her shoulders. She comes fresh to the matter, and you have the advantage of a practical, unprejudiced opinion.'

This explanation, though ridiculous, was evidently sincere. Mr Robinson looked in grateful admiration at the 'unprejudiced' observer whose views so signally supported his own.

'And now,' she said, 'you men will have great matters to talk of, so I'll just away to my kitchen.'

Viewing the circumstances of our last meeting and of this one, I had expected Mr Robinson to show some embarrassment. He appeared, on the contrary, disconcertingly unembarrassed. As he talked, I understood that this appearance was produced not by any particular state of calm or coolness, but by the current of an overpowering urgency which had simply swept ordinary considerations and hesitations out of his head.

An oatcake snapped suddenly between his fingers, he leaned forward, and I heard him saying in a changed voice, 'And then the Embassy people made this special, very special, inquiry.'

It seemed that since I had last seen him, Mr Robinson had made several calls upon those 'certain people at the Embassy' to whom he had originally taken the 'Foraker dossier'. Their attitude had been non-committal. And this, Mr Robinson opined, was entirely natural and proper. He had not fully opened their eyes to the facts about Foraker. They had, however, treated him with interest and civility. He had no complaint on that score. On the contrary. They had welcomed his visits, and on several occasions had actually asked him for information.

Not, oddly enough, about Mr Foraker, but about the textile business. In such facts as he could supply on this topic they displayed a quite peculiar interest, although the facts themselves were, in Mr Robinson's estimation, relatively unimportant. They would even propound to him a series of oral questions and become quite upset if he forgot them, as being unimportant, or failed to find the answers.

They had wanted to know, for example, the exact quantity of a certain sort of material ordered by a certain firm which held a small Government contract making uniforms, Mr Robinson believed, for some branch or other of the French army. That was the kind of thing that interested them. It had considerably saddened Mr Robinson to see people in their position occupying themselves with such trivialities when, if they had been more receptive, he could have told them of goings-on compared to which that kind of fact was insignificant. However, he had done his best. He had even been able to tell them of a contract for tropical uniforms that had been placed with a new firm they had never even heard of.

And then, three weeks ago, he had gone to the little room in the Embassy annex where he was used to meet the gentleman known to him as Major Jones, and Major Jones had said to him, 'About this fellow Foraker you've mentioned once or twice. We'd like to know a bit more about him.'

Mr Robinson quoted these words as though they had been pronounced from on high through a rift in the firmament.

Know a bit more about him? He had been stupefied with excitement. When he could speak, he had let go a cloudburst of information about Foraker. He knew, he told them, all about Foraker. It had been, in a manner of speaking, his major work. He recalled the dossier, recapitulated the Antonia Swindle, the Mathieson and Delavigne affair in Quebec, suspicious activities ever since.

Major Jones had heard him out. And then had said, 'Quite so, Mr Robinson. But what we might be interested in would be one or two up-to-date facts.'

Robinson then summoned to mind all the reports of Henriette-Louise-Marie. He told them that Mark Crane was in love with Delia, that Foraker was often arrogantly quarrelsome at breakfast and dinner, and that his car was one of the new Renaults.

It had been his big moment. The patient, disregarded witness who had been kept all this time in the ante-room had at last been called to the box. He was the man of the hour.

And, shockingly, Major Jones had been restive, unimpressed.

Quite suddenly Major Jones had asked Mr Robinson whether he had ever heard of Zielkowsky? Mr Robinson could not recall the name, but said that if the man was a Russian Jew he was certainly dangerous. Major Jones – 'Of course they haven't studied the situation as I have' – brushed this aside, and asked whether Foraker had ever mentioned Zielkowsky? Had he seen him when he was in St Petersburg? Did he correspond with him? Had he articles of Zielkowsky in his files?

It was a dreadful moment for Mr Robinson, and he shook when he spoke of it. His supreme moment had come, the long-awaited call for Robinson had been sounded, and Robinson was paralysed by a nightmare ignorance. Even now his eyes had a look of horrified disbelief at the thought that such a thing had happened to him.

Mr Robinson had tottered out into the street, staggered and stricken by a double blow. There was the event in itself – his incapacity to seize the opportunity for which he so long had worked and waited. And worse still, as he told me, was the awful certainty that all this was the coming to pass of something that he had been warned about. For in that moment he did not doubt that he was being punished, perhaps only beginning to be punished, for the evil misuse of his gift.

It had occurred to him that perhaps his gift itself was shrivelling up, too. Or preparing to play some ghastly trick on him. He remembered with abrupt dismay an occasion about three months earlier, about the end of the flat-racing season, when he had 'seen' – as he supposed – the numbers on the race-card of the winners in four out of six of the races at the next day's meeting.

Fortunately, as it turned out, he had been unable to get in touch with M. Paca in time. None of the horses concerned won, and only one of them was even placed. But at another meeting, a few days later, the card-numbers of the winners were exactly those he had foreseen. Fate, without a jog of warning, had summarily altered the 'range' of his pre-cognition. He had 'seen' things that were not twenty-four hours away but nearly a week. He might, as he said, have come a very nasty cropper.

With a view to placating the unseen powers he passed wild notions through his mind. He would hire a gang of Parisian apaches who would beleaguer, invade, and sack the Beauvais workshop, tearing out its secrets at pistol point and presenting them to their commander, Robinson. With this strategic conception in mind he had mooted to Paca the possibility of his requiring at an early date a large sum of ready cash.

It was his awe of Foraker, his conviction of the man's 'smartness' which deterred him. Probably a gang of criminal defenders was concealed somewhere at the Beauvais establishment. The attack would be bungled by the untrustworthy foreign apaches. There would be a pitched battle, frightful publicity. Archangel Jones would be incensed. The affair would not find favour in his eyes. No hand-clasp for Robinson from the moist-eyed representative of a grateful country.

The alternative was clear, Mr Hastings must be apprised of the facts, the noble nature of the objective.

'We needs must love the highest when we see it,' said Mr Robinson, as he laid the matter before me.

Essentially, it was the same proposition he had made in Marseilles. I forbore to say so, partly because it was obvious that in his eyes – their range adjusted by months of studying into ever more complex and expanding conspiracies by the hidden forces – the situation was now incomparably more urgent. And the direct appeal from Major Jones appeared to him as a fact which must instantly compel the co-operation of any right-thinking person.

All he required me to do was: first, to write down everything of importance I knew about Foraker's affairs; secondly, to rifle his private papers and abstract for Robinson's use anything that might appear valuable.

Here, Mr Robinson paused in a piteous dilemma. In his own opinion, the honour and glory of such an enterprise rendered any question of material compensation irrelevant and shocking. Any nice young man, he felt sure, would feel the same. And yet – I could see the puzzle in his eyes – it is known that some people think differently about these things. The younger generation of today, he was evidently recalling, is said to be cynical and materialistic.

He took several minutes to decide whether an offer of cash reward would be alluring or repellent in its effect. He compromised by stating that at any time required, handsome sums for 'expenses' would be at my disposal. What sort of expenses, I asked. He was embarrassed. 'General expenses,' he said.

As he shook me by the hand, his eyes shone with hope and gladness.

That a person such as myself, a nice young Englishman, could actually be in the enemy camp – except by the accident of having a job with Foraker – had obviously not occurred to him at any time. His whole 'approach' had made no provision for such a thing. Indeed, he had hinted once or twice that he half-believed I had really gone to work for Foraker, after all, because I had sensed the possibility that I might be 'needed'.

But he had been uncertain how I would respond to the call of duty. Now he was convinced by my manner that all would be well. The good cause had gained a recruit.

His expression and bearing proclaimed it as he called to Mrs Robinson to tell her I was leaving now. She came out of the kitchen, wiping her hands on a cloth, and her clear blue eyes turned first to her husband. For a moment they were anxious, then the lines of her whole face softened in relief on his behalf, and loving pride in his achievement.

At me, as she shook hands, she looked with simple gratitude. She had known from the first, she said, that I would be 'among the helpers'. At the door of the apartment she said, as though this were the central point, 'You see, Mr Hastings, just of late he's been sleeping so badly.'

For some reason, I mentioned this remark to Foraker as I finished my account of the events that had so unexpectedly occupied my morning. To him I had said nothing of the sensation of pathos with which the Robinsons had disconcertingly affected me. I thought Foraker would regard such a feeling towards them as childish and unseemly. But on my reference to Mrs Robinson's parting words, he said, 'The poor son of a bitch. He has his sorrows.' And after brief meditation, he said, 'How do people get that way? What happened to them? When? What drives?

'However,' he added briskly, 'we must take steps. We must act as the factors in the situation seem to indicate. We must encompass the discomfiture of Major Jones.'

He fell to meditation again, this time, as it transpired, on the subject of Henriette-Louise-Marie. This aspect of the affair seemed to disturb him a great deal less than it did me.

In any case, he noted with satisfaction, she had deserted them. It was true, and Delia Foraker confirmed it, that Henriette-Louise-Marie had given notice the previous day, and departed immediately with her one small piece of luggage.

'And the aunt?' I said maliciously. 'That aged aunt.'

'That,' said Foraker, 'was bad. Really bad. She shouldn't

have done a thing like that – using the aged for personal gain. It's an unfair thing to do to old people.'

'But,' I pointed out, 'in this case there wasn't an old person at all. That's the point.'

'It comes to the same thing,' he said.

I had half-hoped he would after all take up an aloof attitude, a reassuring attitude of indifference, demonstrating that he and his Objective were above interference by such elements as Robinson. In this I was disappointed.

Mrs Robinson had said that it was the accident of a personal and family connection between the Forakers and the Robinsons which had guided Mr Robinson's attention to Grant Foraker. In part, I surmised, it was the same accident which helped determine Foraker's reactions now. Major Jones' interest in him he might or might not have taken seriously. The involvement of Robinson, the man from the past, affected him like the whistle of a long-awaited signal.

I could not help pointing out that he had, after all, been mistaken about Wilbur Wright.

'Don't worry,' he said airily, 'he'll be on the job, too. The thing about these other fellows is, we know where they are. If it wasn't them, it'd be some other lot – some lot we didn't know anything about maybe. And Zielkowsky. He wanted to know about Zielkowsky. Those British Intelligence fellows aren't fools, you see. Except what I'm doing'll make Zielkowsky's stuff look like a quiet afternoon in the nursery.'

Obviously, Foraker said, I must act as though I were accepting Mr Robinson's proposition. I must rifle Foraker's secret files and hand over the results. I asked whether there was not a risk, if we gave them anything, of giving them a line that would lead them to the real secret of Foraker's Principle.

Foraker laughed.

'Listen,' he said. 'You don't understand it, and the way this Robinson talks, he doesn't understand it. This isn't a gadget. It's not a Death Ray hidden in the cellars of Professor Foraker and his Secret Six, and Robinson the Boy Hero sneaks up and takes a picture of it. I could give them ninety per cent, well, say seventy per cent, of the papers in that desk and a couple of weeks later they'd have to come to me and ask what they meant.

'They could offer those fellows at Beauvais ten thousand dollars a head to tell all they know, and they'd still get damn little. It's like looking at something in a language you don't know. You can spell out the letters all right. And you still don't have a notion what the stuff means.'

'Well,' I said, 'then there's nothing to worry about. The secret is as safe as if it weren't there at all.'

But that, it seemed, was not true either. Anyone who had access to some of the results of his laboratory work and some of the results of his metallurgical experiments, *and* some of his purely theoretical studies, might advance their knowledge of the subject by, say, ten years in a week of expert study.

'And then,' he said, looking at me with a mixture of irony and triumph, 'if you think we're going on the way we are now, in this phase of the enterprise, for very much longer, you're wrong. You display a lack of faith. In not a very great while we'll be in a phase where there'll really be something to *see*.'

He paused, tossing his big head in an arrogant movement.

'And before that,' he added, 'it will be useful if we have taken advantage of all these gentlemen's interest in us to lay something of a false trail. To play a little ju-jitsu with them. Tossing them with the weight and impact of their own envy, hatred, and malice.'

Into this exercise he threw himself with enthusiasm. He gave me copies of some of his papers with instructions to copy them out, indicating at the same time where I was to make certain mistakes.

As for me, I became increasingly bothered by a sort of pity for the Robinsons. At the apartment on the following day, I was met by Delia Foraker.

'Henriette-Louise-Marie has returned,' she said. 'She apologizes. She wants her job back. She says she only left because she couldn't bear to spy on such a great and good man.'

I stared at her, with an unspoken question. She nodded, half laughing, half dismayed.

'Yes,' she said. 'He has agreed to her coming back. He says

it's better to have someone we at least know all about. A new one, he says, might be a spy, too.'

'And the aged aunt?' I said furiously, as though this were an immensely important point.

'Well, that's all right too, Grant says,' said Delia. 'It seems there really is an old aunt. But she's in Dijon. It was that gave her the idea. She says she needed the money from the Robinsons to send to her aunt when she was ill.'

'And now the aunt has recovered?'

'Well, yes,' said Delia helplessly. 'That's the way it seems to be. Anyway, Henriette-Louise-Marie will be back on the job tomorrow.'

'And I,' I said dramatically, 'shall probably have quit the job by tomorrow,' and I stalked past her into Foraker's study to tell him so.

He listened silently to my storm of words. At the close of my oration, in which I exposed in full the inadmissible character of the entire situation, I added that I wished to make it clear that I spoke more in sorrow than in anger. I did not, I said, wish to judge, far less condemn him.

Quite suddenly it was as if some unseen piece of time-mechanism that had been ticking away inside him had set off a detonator. His face and voice seemed to explode in a volcano of impatience. His hands trembled. He kept his voice low, and the walls vibrated with it.

I could go or stay, he said, but would I for pity's sake understand he was a busy man? He supposed, he said, that what I really wanted was to keep on with the job, but get his personal guarantee that nothing that would upset my fine feelings would ever happen in it. (I realized with disgust that this did, in a crude manner, sum up what I had had in mind as a desirable compromise.)

'Nobody's going to give you that guarantee.' His voice rasped my ears. 'Nobody can. You want to stay out on the sidelines and keep clean – well, stay there. Or you want to get in the game. The burden and heat of the day. It stinks. Try to do anything big, and not stink.'

He lifted the back of his hand to his nose and gave a kind of snorting sniff at it.

'Christopher Columbus – he stank.' This pronouncement had an air of finality. He let it hang in the air for a long moment.

'By God,' he said at last, 'if I thought you cared so little as that about the big objective, why, I tell you I'd think more highly of that fellow Robinson than of you. Sure he's half-crazy. But he has an objective. He goes all out for it.'

He dropped his hands on the table and his voice changed slightly. He sighed, and said with sternness, 'Trouble with you is, you're cynical. It's a sad, bad thing to be, Ned, in my opinion.'

Dumbfounded by this surprise attack, I said nothing, and his voice boomed on.

He raised his hand, palm outwards. 'Don't apologize for yourself, Ned. Lots of people don't want to scale the mountain. Rather, they would huddle in the featherbed of sordid comfort, selling their birthright for a mess of pottage.'

'Upon my soul!' I cried. 'It's a bit rich to hear you ...' and then, as I watched him sitting ponderously grave behind his desk, like a huge bust dedicated to Righteousness, I was overcome by laughter, and knew that I was lost.

Foraker did not relax his expression of noble gravity and sadness, but continued to gaze at me in statuesque dignity for several seconds as I stumbled into a feeble withdrawal of my ultimatum. It seemed to me that nothing he had said had convinced me of anything, and yet at that moment I was convinced that I was going to go on working for Foraker and Foraker's Principle.

As I finished, a shadowy smile began to flicker over the countenance of the statue, a smile, perhaps, of pure pleasure in his own performance.

'What you need,' he said, 'is a holiday. You have laboured too strenuously in the common cause. What you ought to do is to take the evening off and take Martha Dukes to the theatre.'

'Tonight?' I said.

'Why, yes,' he said. 'Or . . . well, maybe better not tonight. I have a report, just came in from Brussels . . .'

I did not have that evening off, or the next. And then the nature of the report from the metallurgist in Brussels – esteemed especially by Foraker, partly because he had been recommended by Rosen, partly just because he lived and worked in Brussels and thus contributed to what Foraker called 'the desirable dispersal of the relevant facts' – necessitated an immediate trip thither.

Towards the end of our stay in Belgium, Foraker remarked to me that Major Jones would probably be rather interested to get a report from Brussels. Not necessary, of course, if I did not feel it worth the trouble. It had just crossed his mind that if Mr Robinson were to be in a position to pass along such a report, hot from another capital, it would be likely to be treated with special respect.

'Today,' said Foraker, 'would be a good day to send him something really meaty.'

'Why especially today?'

He shrugged, his face beaming with childlike happiness. It was not until nearly three weeks later that I recalled that the date had been 1 April.

During those three weeks, the 'evening off', on which I was to take Martha Dukes to the theatre, had not come to pass. I gathered we were approaching the beginning of the 'second phase' of the practical development of the Principle. Foraker's hours of work became both longer and more uncertain than usual.

Then I saw an announcement that the small, and short-lived Theatre Vingtième Siècle, recently opened on the Boulevard Raspail, was giving a few weeks of repertory devoted entirely to the works of Bernard Shaw. I immediately took tickets for a performance of *Major Barbara*. It was a symbolic act. I intended that Martha should see it in that light.

It was a signal that, despite the brutally persistent interruptions of life, of work, of movement hither and thither which – incredibly, as it seemed, looking back over the speeding months – had kept shouldering their way between us, pushing our relationship about, we were now going to assert ourselves, thrust our way back to the moment when we had first laughed together over the telephone from the Café du Carrefour.

Our romantic voyage was going to begin.

She understood.

In case the voyage now moved swiftly, in compensation for past delays, I bought expensive spring flowers and with them decorated the sitting-room and bedroom of the Rue St Jacques.

As we drove to the theatre, I thought she had a new sort of loveliness. It seemed to me she would not be surprised, hesitant or abashed if this evening ended with the gargoyles on my shabby garden wall watching us in one another's arms.

My thoughts ran on happily in time with the clop of the horses' hooves, and of other hooves trotting behind through the mild spring evening.

We pushed our way into the small crowd which thronged the pavement in front of the narrow entrance to the theatre. We were almost at the door when I was conscious of a disturbance in the little crowd, and then heard my name shouted, almost shrieked, from somewhere behind me, at the edge of the pavement.

With Martha's arm linked through mine, I paused, stood on tip-toe, and looked back. I saw the pale, blotched face of Mr Robinson bobbing at the back of the crowd, his arm and hand stretched stiffly above his head; I could see his fingers snapping in a futile gesture of attracting attention. Seeing me turn, he yelled my name again.

Furious, and with a feeling of panic, I shouted back at him, 'Later!' and tried to push forwards with Martha into the theatre. Almost immediately, a couple of people were buffeted against me as though by sudden and violent pressure from the edge of the crowd. There were cries of protest. The people ahead of us turned to abuse me for jostling them. The buffeting from behind increased. I was swung half round, and saw that the crowd had become a confused and angry mêlée. Robinson, hacking with his elbows, was fighting his way towards me, and now, just behind him, I saw, too, the half-forgotten face of the Hairy Sneerer, whose name I no longer remembered.

Enraged patrons of the theatre were yelling at the pair of them, kicking and bumping with their shoulders. Others turned on me, hissing at me as the cause of the disturbance.

'Get out and join your friends!' one man snarled into my face.

Someone had yelled, 'Help!' and two policemen moved suddenly on the crowd. Fearing an abominable scene; thoughts of arrests, charges and counter-charges, cross-examinations, racing through my head, I started to pull Martha away from the doorway and out of the crowd. Seeing our movement, Robinson and the other ceased trying to battle their way to us and, instead, fell back and moved round the press of people to meet us.

We met, the theatre-goers glaring over their shoulders, the police walking slowly in our direction. Having come thus far to avoid trouble, it seemed inevitable to let ourselves be hustled by the fevered Robinson and the Sneerer a dozen quick paces up the boulevard and into a side-street where, nearly at the corner, was a café, at the moment deserted, into which Robinson made as if to lead us.

With the police out of sight, my patience broke. I halted on the pavement, Martha halting beside me. I addressed Robinson furiously. What was the meaning of this?

He stopped and swung around, no less furiously agitated. He shot one uncertain look at Martha, and then lost control of his emotions. He spat out words, questions, accusations. The Sneerer, whose name I suddenly recalled was Bally, stood by, sneering. Among Robinson's noisy incoherences I caught the improbable words, '. . . room in the *War* Office. In *London*. Burned out, I tell you, man.' I raised my voice, shouting him down, telling him to control himself. Alerted by the fresh outburst of noise, the policemen came round the corner and walked towards us with slow suspicion. Instinctively, the four of us sat down at one of the tables outside the café, looking like peaceful acquaintances meeting for an evening drink. The policemen walked past us, eyeing us, and took themselves slowly off.

Mr Robinson, who had been actually gnawing the sleeve of his coat in his impatience, broke out again in low, bitter speech.

10

Long before Mr Robinson, his face and words alike contorted, had spilled out the whole of the statement that rushed to his mouth, the crude outline of events was shockingly clear. So also was the motive for this pursuit through the streets – they had followed us from Foraker's apartment – and the present ugly intrusion.

Mr Robinson gulped, and spoke with a nervous rapidity that became at times incoherent. It was also uncomfortably intelligible.

Those 'really meaty' bits of information Foraker had transmitted three weeks ago had looked 'meaty' indeed to Major Jones. He had considered them so important that he had taken the documents personally to England. This precaution, it emerged, was not due so much to fear of theft by our country's enemies, but suspicion lest they be 'sat upon' by some faction, as I understood it, of the Intelligence Service, having a vested interest in a policy, or view, opposed to that of Major Jones and his friends.

What it amounted to was that Major Jones and friends believed that aviation had a future, thought it might develop into a serious weapon of war. The opposing faction believed of aviation only what they could see, and not all of that.

As for the notion that the secret funds could profitably be employed investigating some revolutionary form of aerial propulsion as yet not even developed to the stage reached by Santos-Dumont, Farman, and the Wright brothers, that would have driven the non-Jones faction to a frenzy of scorn and savage hostility.

With Foraker's documents in his bag, Jones had mobilized members of his own faction, the believers, broadly speaking, in the future of aviation. The danger that 'the other side' would seek to get these documents pooh-poohed, and rob the Jones faction of prestige and, possibly, even of future funds, was immediately apparent. In some secret annex of the War Office – some house in Fulham Road, Robinson gathered – they had worked, with the aid of 'reliable' scientific experts of their own faction, to elucidate the significance of Major Jones' prize.

Using the formula supplied by Foraker, they experimented, still without reference to higher authority, for fear of reactionary obstructionism. And then one day, as they meticulously followed Foraker's formula, the whole thing literally blew up with a formidable detonation that was heard clear over to Knightsbridge, two of the experimenters were knocked senseless and severely damaged internally by the blast, and the wooden window-frames were torn out of the brick work and hurled into the public street.

The intra-departmental scandal which followed was as violent as the explosion. Concealment was no longer possible. The opposing faction, scenting quarry, rushed into action. In the subsequent investigation, Foraker's documents were subjected to the cold scrutiny of sceptical eyes undimmed by any preformed belief in the existence of secret weapons of aerial war. Harsh and patient analysis revealed the 'formula' as an astoundingly elaborate booby-trap.

Then some investigator, with a sense of humour which perhaps had something in common with Foraker's own, had noted the careful dating of each sheet of the documents – 1 April.

And there, because it had become funny, the affair became really serious. To be blown up, by accident or design, was one thing. The fortune of the 'secret war'. But to be made April Fools of, that was an insult and a challenge.

In one sense, Foraker's schoolboy joke had achieved the purpose of distracting attention from his objectives. The Jones faction, who had seemed unpleasantly close to understanding what he was about, were now discredited. Care had been taken that news of the April Fooling should leak to official circles outside the department.

And this news was received with joy. For, above all, it gave private confirmation to the views of all those who for months, inside the War Office and in Parliament, had been struggling to curb expenditure of public money upon the development of aircraft.

At this point, Robinson, his hands quivering, dragged from his pocket a little bundle of newspaper clippings.

'Look at the background,' he said. 'Look at this first one . . . It'll show you what's been going on.'

He handed me, his fingers shaking so that it dropped on the table before I could take it from him, what proved to be a clipping from a London newspaper, dated 28 January. It said:

'The Report was issued yesterday of the Standing Sub-Committee of the Committee of Imperial Defence appointed in October last to examine problems of military aviation, with particular reference to the balloon factory and school at South Farnborough.

'There has been considerable public uneasiness, expressed several times in Parliament, regarding what is considered, in some informed quarters, a War Office tendency to permit undue expenditure on "wild" experiments, with very little relation to the solid realities of sound military principles.

'Criticism has been directed particularly towards recent experiments at Farnborough in which public money has been expended on attempts to develop the "heavier than air" machine for military purposes.

'The Sub-Committee's Report fully supports the critics.

'While not denying the interest attaching to recent developments of the "heavier than air" machine, the Sub-Committee does not feel that its potentialities as a factor in warfare justify the expenditure of public money upon experiments in connection with it.

'If private individuals choose to finance this type of experiment on civilian lines, that is, of course, their affair. But the Sub-Committee feels strongly that so far as the Army is concerned, work should be concentrated on the development of the balloon which has already – during the war in South Africa and in recent experiments at Gibraltar – proved itself a useful adjunct to the principal military and naval forces.

'The Sub-Committee, therefore, recommends that a small expenditure be authorized for the construction of a rigid airship for the Navy, but that for the Army expenditure should be limited to the development of non-dirigible balloons.

'It definitely advises the discontinuance of all experiments with, and expenditure on, the attempted development of the "heavier than air" machine for military purposes.'

Halfway through my reading, I remembered, with a sudden jab of comprehension, that I had already seen this newspaper report, or rather, this and several other accounts from British newspapers, of the Report of the Sub-Committee of the Committee of Imperial Defence. Foraker had received them and I had placed them in his files.

'But this,' I said guardedly to Robinson, 'is dated at the end of January. It hasn't anything to do with what's happened.'

Other newspaper clippings spilled from his hand on to the table, and he pushed them across to me. They were references to Questions in Parliament, official statements, and a number of protests, including one editorial comment in the *Morning Post* and another in one of the halfpenny newspapers, against the attitude of the Sub-Committee.

'You see? You see?' Robinson said, pushing his face forward, across the table so that the lamplight danced in his blazing eyes. 'People weren't all swallowing that stuff. Their eyes were beginning to be opened to what's going on. Official circles divided among themselves. Not everyone blind. And then,' he gulped, and his fingers scrabbled on the table-top, 'then *this* happens. April Fool. Devilish. A mockery. Major Jones laughed out of London. Foraker planned it.'

There was a long moment of silence. I watched slow-moving vehicles passing on the bright boulevard at the end of the street while I tried to collect my thoughts. I was aware of Mr Robinson's gaze, fixed on me in an agonized mixture of bewilderment and suspicion.

Before I could speak, the question that was torturing him burst out.

'And you?' he said. 'You were his victim? Cat's-paw. I told you he was smart. You know, some of those papers, in the explosion, they got blown right out into Fulham Road, with April Fool as good as written on them.'

And then Martha laughed.

If she had fired a pistol the effect could not have been more startling.

Robinson suffered a kind of convulsion. His face jerked round like a violently tugged puppet's face to look at her. Her head was tilted a little back as she laughed, and all he could see was the soft curve of her throat in the lamplight, her breast quivering under her dress as she leaned back and laughed.

He turned from Martha to me, staring at me with a curious, rapid blinking of his eyelids. He started to say something, which got strangled in his throat. And, without a word coming from him, it was clear that he understood.

The scales, in his own phrase, had fallen from his eyes.

Martha's laugh had suddenly and shockingly told him the truth.

I stood up.

'You ...' Robinson said, and gave a little shudder.

I could not bear to look at him.

'Martha,' I said. 'Please come away now.'

She got to her feet and took my arm.

Robinson said, 'I can't just believe it.'

Before we reached the corner, Bally came after us. I turned to face him. His face was furious and greedy-looking.

'You needn't think it's going to end like this,' he said. 'You needn't think Paca and the rest of us are going to lose ...' He jerked his chin towards where Mr Robinson still sat at the café table with his head on his hand.

I gave M. Bally a haughty look, and prepared to move on. He put the tips of his fingers on my coat sleeve.

'Damned fool!' he said, with a deep throb of intensity. Perhaps he was having a vision of race-tracks, horses running, enormous prizes in peril.

We left him there, turned the corner, and were once again in front of the Theatre of the Twentieth Century.

I hesitated, fumbling to put the broken pattern of the evening together again.

'I could ring Grant up,' I said. 'Just give him an idea of what's happened. And then we could ...'

She peered sadly at the theatre. 'We've missed most of the first act,' she said. 'We've missed it, Ned,' she repeated, with a catch in her voice, as though this were the essence of the misfortune.

I said what did that matter? And knew, as I said it, that somehow it did.

She took a long, careful look at the advertisements of *Major Barbara* outside the theatre, and then she looked at me with some kind of question in her eyes, and smiled rather sadly and said, 'It's no use, Ned. We'd better go and see Grant and tell him.'

She faintly squeezed my arm. 'Dear Ned,' she said. She stared across the boulevard and half to herself said, 'April Fool!' while I mechanically signalled a cab.

Stepping into that cab, we might as well have been stepping on to a conveyor belt at a factory. Once again, the train of events jolted and tugged us along, caught up in the actual movement, it seemed, of Foraker's Principle and all that it implied.

Upon Foraker, the news of his April Fool had a singular effect. His pleasure and arrogant pride in its success appeared to be slightly shocking. He made Martha and me tell him Robinson's story twice over, and later recounted it with enthusiasm to Delia and later still to Mark Crane.

'I don't see,' I said to Mark, 'why he needs to be so proud of it.'

'Don't you?' Mark said. We were alone in his office at the time, and I remember that he fiddled portentously with pens and blotting pads on his large desk. 'Doesn't it just cross your mind that after all this time – not just months, years when you tot it right up – that he's been skating along the Principle he's glad to have something to show for something? Something that came off. God knows he hasn't made much of a bang with anything else yet.'

His tone startled and offended me, but he was too much absorbed by his own ideas to notice.

'He's the hero, see? He has to be the hero. Being a hero to Delia, first of all. He came into her life as a hero and he has to work to stay that way. Glory! Glory! Grant Foraker! Hero to everyone. What did I go into business with him for? What I did, I hitched my wagon to a star. Martha. You. Glory! Glory! But where is it? Man has to work at being a hero, show results here and there. Maybe he felt the credit was wearing a little thin all around.'

And then one day, a pleasantly dry, freshly sunny day at that, Captain Lenoir made a scene. It was about five o'clock in the afternoon, a time when, in summer, anyone at Foraker's apartment who was not busy used to sit with Delia on a small balcony at the back of the apartment, and drink iced coffee or wine or brandy and seltzer water. So far as I knew, it had been nearly a month since Captain Lenoir had called at the house in this way. He would confer with Foraker at a café or restaurant in town. The moment he came on to the balcony, where only Delia and I were seated, the sultry tension set up as he greeted Delia was so strong that, if I had not arrived only a few minutes before, I should have made an excuse to leave. I felt as if I had been pushed abruptly into the position of a Peeping Tom, peering from close range at some passionate intimacy. It was a sensation I had sometimes experienced before, though less sharply than now, when I found myself together with Delia and another man; an atmosphere which she seemed to create automatically.

Delia asked some question about the balloon in which he flew to make observations.

'Listen, Madame Delia,' he said, in the half-intimate, half-mocking form of address he always used to her, 'I am so tired of that balloon. For me, it has become a symbol of futility. I shall apply to join the infantry. At least I'm sure my feet will carry me as far as Berlin. Or, of course, the Pyrenees.'

He went on talking furiously about the balloon. He spoke good English now, with some of Foraker's accent and she said 'But it's closer to what you want, isn't it, Henri? You couldn't join the infantry. You'd be out of touch with' – she fluttered her hand comprehensively, and said – 'technical progress.'

He responded violently. 'Yes, yes, yes,' he said, 'I should be out of touch with all that. With Mr Foraker. With Madame Delia Foraker. Entirely out of touch.'

His eyes flamed at her, and she smiled at him calmly.

'What is it, Henri?' she said. 'What's happened? Has something happened?'

Watching them, I had a wild idea that now he would say, 'I have volunteered for service in Equatorial Africa. Come with me to the banks of the Niger,' and that that was what she was really expecting him to say. She had the air of a person expecting some crucial event, waiting for the toboggan to go over the mountainside.

He deliberately provoked her by sitting down, and slowly drinking his champagne. With a small sigh, she lay back, pretending matronly calm.

From the other end of the apartment came the faint noise of the front door being opened, and then Foraker's voice could be heard raised, telling some story, as he came along the passage with Mark. Lenoir cocked his ear, and spoke into his empty glass.

'My good and admired friend,' he said.

The story Foraker was telling turned out to be some anecdote illustrative of the bumbling folly of 'Intelligence' people, the British or some other. He was finishing it as they came on to the balcony; he waved a glad greeting to Lenoir.

Lenoir's voice cut into the amiable hubbub in a way that made them stop and look at him.

'I am so glad,' he said, 'my dear Grant, that you are aware how infinitely more powerful and clever you are than all these Intelligence people. I have always thought the British Government only paid millions of pounds yearly for its Intelligence Service in order to provide sinecures for idiots who soon would be exposed by a seriously intelligent man. A really great man, like Grant Foraker.'

Nobody pretended it was a joke.

Grant Foraker swung round on him, his cigar as menacing as a weapon, and stared down at him, saying nothing.

'For you,' he said, 'this may be a game. For us – for myself and a certain number of technicians at the Ministry of War whom you know of – it's a matter of life and death.

'I'm not speaking of our personal positions. You know quite well we aren't exactly popular at the Ministry. Our positions are not exactly secure, are they? At the best of times we could be accused of using our special advantages at the Ministry to co-operate with a private person – a foreigner at that. And don't think those British Intelligence people, when they start really knife-fighting, won't be interested in our position. Don't think they won't be glad to give a little information to those on high at our Ministry here. But I am not speaking of that.'

'Oh,' said Foraker nastily, 'I thought you were.'

Lenoir got slowly to his feet. 'I am speaking,' he said, 'of the very simple little fact that soon – next year, the year after that – there is going to be a war here in Europe. Of course the great Mr Foraker will be able to hurry back to his Red Indians and chewing gum across the Atlantic. He doesn't care. To him it's a game.

'But to us, lady and gentlemen' – he raised his hand, so that he looked like a lively monument to a dead patriotic orator – 'to us, it is a matter of importance. It is a matter, in case it may possibly interest you, of life and death for France.

'I and my friends agreed to co-operate with Mr Grant Foraker because, gazing round upon this madhouse of superannuated notions and obsolete techniques, this junkyard of prehistoric military apparatus with which our present leaders propose to face the War of the Twentieth Century, we grasped at a straw. We listened to Mr Grant Foraker, and we said to ourselves, "Perhaps we have here a portent and an ally."

' "Perhaps," we said' – his voice sank to a vibrant whisper – ' "this Mr Foraker, the Great Inventor, has, in this Principle of his, the answer to our need. Perhaps with our co-operation – our ability to put at his disposal the results of years of research conducted by experts of the Ministry of War and pigeon-holed by idiots – Mr Foraker can produce a machine, a weapon which, in a few years, will make bows and arrows of those guns across the Rhine, and assure to France her rightful mastery of Europe."

'And now we find, what? We find that we have been working with an inventor – of booby-traps. A person of such frivolity that one suspects he would, perhaps, publicly jump from the Arc de Triomphe for the sake of getting himself talked about.'

He sank on to a couch at the edge of the balcony, panting like a dog. Looking at him, sitting there scowling and twitching, one could have supposed him simply over-stimulated by his own tirade. But I could see how carefully he avoided looking at Delia, and I was aware again of that tension between them. To me it seemed that his outburst had been touched off by other emotions suddenly released in his moment of disgust and disillusion with Foraker.

Mark Crane, I could observe while Lenoir was orating, thought likewise. His face said as plain as words that this was a damned typical example of a Frenchman making a grandstand play to impress a woman. Mark had kept watching Delia to see how she was taking it. What he saw was the face of a woman watching an enthralling play, absorbedly waiting to see what the denouement will be.

In his rasping voice, the words grinding out under an intolerable pressure of impatience, Foraker counter-attacked savagely.

He implied, without quite saying so, that Lenoir was a play-acting buffoon. He insisted that his 'joke' at the expense of the people in London had been a move carefully considered and brilliantly executed. As for Lenoir, and his associated group of technicians at the Ministry of War – did they have the idea that Foraker was in some way dependent upon them, beholden to them?

He was speaking, he said, with the greatest restraint, and he slowly clenched and unclenched his fist to prove it. He did not wish to hurt anyone's feelings. He simply wanted to point out, as a simple fact, that any contribution the technicians at the Ministry of War might feel disposed to make towards the realization of Foraker's aims was a very, very nice gesture on their part, and so regarded.

But – he hammered one fist softly on his knee, and glared around the balcony with the look of a man menaced by small dogs – that was no ground for anyone getting a swollen head, for anyone trying to make himself important by suggesting that Foraker's Principle owed anything to anyone whatever except Foraker himself. He wished to state as a simple matter of cold fact that, compared to his knowledge and scientific abilities, the sum total of such knowledge and abilities in the entire Ministry of War was a drop in the bucket.

It was, after all, Captain Lenoir who, after a moment of silence and an effort that seemed actually to twist his muscles, exerted himself to put out the fire which appeared about to burn up this conversation and a good deal else besides.

He put on a serio-comic face and shrugged. With a visible strain, he managed to state that he had been carried away; a moment of emotion; the thought of the condition of France in face of impending war; nerves on edge; the weather.

Everyone gazed hopefully at the sky, seeking confirmation. Unfortunately the weather was delicious.

Nevertheless, Captain Lenoir insisted that it got on his nerves, had caused him to make statements which, now he reflected, could reasonably have caused offence. Probably Foraker was right – he, Lenoir, knew nothing, naturally, of the proper methods to be adopted in dealing with the British Intelligence Service. Blowing one or two of them into the streets of London might be the prudent thing to do with them after all.

All this Foraker accepted, at first in a monstrously ungracious silence, then with a patronizing air of accepting no more than what was obviously due to him, which was more exasperating still.

I became conscious all at once of something which presented itself to me as a kind of vulnerability about our situation which I had never noticed before. Instead of faith and confidence, all I could feel at the moment was an irritated pity for all of us. For Foraker, breaking down, evidently, under the strain. A terrible strain, of course, but did that make matters any better?

And Lenoir, was he perhaps a pitiable buffoon, after all? And Delia, going perhaps nowhere on her toboggan. Myself, also going nowhere, as now suddenly appeared. What a crew, I thought, to be engaged, directly or otherwise, in a momentous enterprise – setting up to outstrip the world's most expert technicians, making the impossible possible, just incidentally provoking and challenging the reputedly most powerful secret organization in the world.

Suppose that what Foraker had called the Opposition – now heavily reinforced – were to understand what sort of people we really were, and act on that understanding?

In a sense, it was just what they did do.

It was during the first week in June that M. Paca first approached me with a demand for blackmail money.

11

M. Paca displayed the simple confidence of a man betting on a certainty. He did not hesitate to draw for me a map, as it were, of the situation – so agreeable for himself and his friends, so delicate, he must in all sincerity admit, for Mr Foraker.

I was aware, was I not, of the interest taken in Mr Foraker by certain elements at the British Embassy? An unfriendly interest. Rather dangerous enemies. With such enemies it was worth while for a man to take even expensive precautions against various forms of unpleasantness.

Here was Mr Robinson who, for reasons I understood, had temporarily lost some of the confidence which he formerly had enjoyed on the part of this person who called himself Major Jones. The loss of confidence depressed Mr Robinson. He was unhappier than ever.

Quite frankly, said M. Paca, he bothered his head about Mr Robinson's state of mind for one reason and one reason only. I knew – did I not? – what that reason was.

'Oh,' I said, 'Robinson's gift. Still seeing winners, is he?'

'It's nothing to be laughd at,' he said. 'It is a serious fact. An immense fact. I don't find that you are in a position to sneer at this gift of our friend Robinson. Not at all. Quite on the contrary, you would do a great deal better if you would take it more seriously. At least, you can understand that for us it is serious. We are practical people. Facts are facts.'

In the course of his gravely rebuking lecture on the subject, he disclosed that he had actually given up his *boûte de nuit* or whatever it was.

Instead, he had constituted himself a kind of 'manager' to Robinson, cherishing and nurturing him, playing farmer to that mysterious golden goose.

His functions were necessarily vague and irregular, but they, and the sort of avaricious day-dreaming to which he had become addicted, occupied his time and faculties to the full.

So far as M. Paca was concerned, the gift had swallowed him. He was enslaved by it. It was a drug which paralysed all capacity to busy himself with anything else.

The gift, naturally, did not always work. But it worked often enough to maintain a complete domination over the lives of M. Paca and friends. They had been moderately enriched. They intended to be vastly enriched. Multi-millions were within reach. It was a question of keeping the current in proper order. They intended to do so.

Well then, with that understood, what was the situation? Simple. I knew Robinson, I must, therefore, realize that it was of the utmost importance that he should feel that he was utilizing his gift in the interest of 'this campaign of his. What he calls the good cause. Exposing things, and all that.'

And the surest way to get him feeling that, was to get him some results in the case of the man Foraker.

'Robinson gets this thing of his – call it God, call it electricity – to work for us. We reciprocate. We fix it so the thing isn't just working for money. That shrivels it. No. It's working for us because we are working against Foraker. Fighting all these Jewish conspiracies and the Jesuits and anarchists and all that lot he's heard of. Or whatever he is. Doesn't matter. Reciprocal. We claim we're going to drive Foraker right out of town. Necessary. Essential. We have to show results.'

Having thus impressed upon me the necessities, the essentials of the matter, M. Paca abruptly drew from his pocket a smudgy galley proof, badly printed on newsprint.

'Now,' he said, 'here's a little article about Monsieur Foraker that I don't think he'd be very very pleased to see come out in the paper. The *Echo de la Seine*.'

I had heard of the *Echo de la Seine* as one of the papers which, in that golden age of the simplest kind of newspaper blackmail, made less money out of publishing articles than out of writing – and even setting up in galley proof – articles which someone would pay it not to publish.

I hurriedly read the lines. The articles opened with the traditional expressions of alarm at the doings – 'apparently winked at by a too tolerant Government' – of 'certain foreign elements in Paris'. There were, however, those who went too far. These, whatever powers and resources they might have behind them, whatever the risk involved, the *Echo de la Seine* would courageously and relentlessly expose. For instance: a certain Anglo-Saxon personage.

Barbed questions followed: Was it true that...? What were the true facts about ... ? The questions were obviously framed by someone well acquainted with past episodes of Foraker's financial life, the Mathieson and Delavigne affair to begin with. An 'Alsatian financier' was mentioned. The 'mysterious' workshops at Beauvais were referred to, and also Foraker's frequent trips across the frontiers.

'We can produce proofs,' said the article, 'that in the most serious scientific circles the gentleman in question has either not been heard of, or heard of only as a charlatan more interested in extracting money from the pockets of the incautious than in any other form of research.'

Secondly, it was strongly suggested, 'the gentleman in question' was in reality using his other activities as a cover for espionage, 'an activity unfortunately highly lucrative in these days when certain of the Great Powers', etc., etc., etc.

I handed the galley proofs back to him, in silent perturbation. How much? he wanted to know. How much would Foraker pay to keep that out of the paper? No need for me to answer – he would tell me just how much Mr Foraker would *have* to pay to keep it out of the paper. He named a large sum in francs.

With pretended calm, I said it was ridiculous. Besides, I said, if he believed all he had been telling me about Robinson, and the gift, and the *quid pro quo*, why didn't he go and put the thing straight in the paper? The winners at Longchamps would pay off better than Foraker, I said bitterly.

At such *naïveté,* M. Paca was first astonished, then mistrustful. In the event of Mr Foraker paying, surely it was obvious, this article would not appear, and instead some other article, innocuous, vaguely relating to someone of his type, would appear somewhere else. So far, so good.

Part of the funds received from Foraker could be employed for its insertion.

Such an article would satisfy Robinson that a beginning had been made with the vaunted campaign. Foraker would have prudently saved himself an unpleasantness. The amount was not to be sniffed at, not by normal and reasonable people, Paca said, looking at me with suspicion.

'And what will it be next time?' I said. 'Twice that, I suppose, to prevent another article appearing in *Echo de la Merde*?'

M. Paca shrugged and spread out his hands, refusing responsibility for what the future might bring forth.

I reported to Foraker and he, of course refused to pay.

After a fortnight, a proof of the front page of the *Echo de la Seine*, with the beginning of the article, and of page three, on which it was continued, arrived for Foraker through the mail, with a note saying that it was proposed to publish this in a couple of days, unless he 'wished to make any preliminary comments or corrections.'

Foraker tore up the paper and the note, and we went off to Beauvais.

It was not, in fact, until the eleventh of July that the article appeared.

I had waited for that moment as for the explosion of a long-ticking time-bomb.

I bought that issue of the *Echo de la Seine* at the corner kiosk, and at Foraker's there were Delia, Martha, and Mark Crane, reading bits out of the article to one another in derisive accents, and laughing about it, while Foraker looked on, smiling grandly.

Soon, I was laughing, too. Everything, it seemed to me then, was going to be all right.

The Government was in crisis, on the verge of overthrow. That was what people were talking about, the future of M. Clemenceau, the possibilities of M. Briand. That, and the Tzar. Tzar Nicholas II of All the Russias was about to visit Paris. Such a demonstration of Franco-Russian solidarity would scare the Germans, be a warning to all potential aggressors, perhaps avert war indefinitely.

Such were the topics being discussed, and filling the newspapers. In their light, as it seemed to me, I could see the picayune undertakings of M. Paca and the *Echo de la Seine* in proper perspective. To imagine a wave of public indignation, resulting in some kind of official action, was merely absurd. Nothing of that kind was going to happen.

And, in fact, nothing of that kind did.

What did happen, a few days after we had all been laughing contemptuously over the article, was something quite different, which was that I came unexpectedly into the sitting-room of the Foraker apartment one afternoon and found Delia reading the issue of the *Echo de la Seine* containing the article. She was reading it with an expression of gravity and concentration. The effect was startling. Days ago, the article had been laughed away, thrown away, too, I had supposed.

She put the newspaper on the sofa beside her and hesitated. She sighed, the hesitation and the sigh being evident invitations to me to ask what was the matter. I said I had not known that rag was still lying about the house. She said it had got mixed up with some papers in her *bureau*, and she was just looking at it. Her face said it had not merely got mixed up, but been preserved among her papers, and that she had not been just looking at it, but thinking about it.

I picked it up and glanced through it with an air of boredom and very faint amusement.

'Mark says,' Delia interrupted me; and I realized with astonishment that the article must have been a subject of discussion between her and Mark, serious discussion, it seemed, despite the way we had all laughed about it together a few days ago.

'What does Mark say?' I asked sharply.

'Well, of course he understands about the blackmail and all that, but he says that, of course, in a way there's something in it. About showing results and so on. And about some of these scientists not taking Grant seriously.'

'Rosen takes him seriously,' I burst out. 'What about that?'

'I suppose so,' Delia said. 'Lately nobody but Grant ever seems to see Mr Rosen. And you, of course. How's anyone to know just what Mr Rosen's really thinking? He doesn't say anything, does he? He doesn't talk to Mark at all. Although you'd think the business partner had a right to important information.'

I could nearly hear Mark Crane's voice in the phrase.

She had turned away from me, staring out of the window over the high back of the sofa upon which she drummed with her fists, and she was talking low and furiously, not to me at all, but to the window, to Paris, to roofs under the sky.

I could hardly catch the words.

'It oughtn't to be this way,' I heard her say. And, 'All this *time*. Why doesn't he have anything to show for it? All this *time* that goes by.'

I found myself staring at the shadow of a tree on the boulevard, almost aware of it moving and lengthening with the turning of the earth and the passing of time.

Appalled by the sudden onset of my own doubts and fears, I felt a rush of hatred for Delia and taunted her like a schoolboy.

I didn't see, I said, that she had such a lot to complain of. She had a nice house, didn't she? She had plenty of money, didn't she? She lived here in Paris, didn't she, instead of some forsaken spot like Canton, Ohio? What was all this about time? What was she so impatient about? She had a better time than most women, didn't she? Or didn't she?

She turned around quite slowly on the sofa and faced me with an air of having momentarily forgotten that I was there, or who I was, or what on earth I was talking about.

When she spoke, her voice was entirely calm, an indifferent, colourless voice that might have been talking about someone else at some other time.

'But,' she said, 'don't you see that doesn't have anything to do with it at all? I didn't do anything on account of having money or living in Paris, or anything like that, I'd have loved Grant in a –' she looked about desolately for a word.

'Hovel,' I said.

'I mean garret,' she said. 'I was going to say garret.' She contemplated the word. 'He was going to be a *great* man,' she said. 'He always was. Back in Ohio, and all these years after. There were plenty of people that tried to tell me different. There were a lot of the boys back home in Canton, and some of the old people, too, that wanted to tell me he was some sort of a fake. A swindler. A false alarm.'

She might have been reciting a piece out of a school history book.

'And I didn't believe them at all, Ned,' she said, suddenly looking at me as if I really were a person there in the room, 'I didn't at all. Never. And then time went on and on. And now *that* happens.'

She nodded at the *Echo de la Seine* which I still was holding, half crumpled in my hand.

'This?'

With a gesture I intended to be magnificent, and may have been merely hysterical, I threw the crumpled pages on the floor and stamped one foot violently upon them.

'Just because these blackguards put a thing like that in *print,*' I cried, 'we start, I mean you start, and Mark starts to *believe* it. It's ridiculous. Or rather,' I said, in comforting remembrance of things read, 'it's a very simple, not uncommon, physico-psychological reaction. The printed word, being associated in the inexperienced mind with *authority*, and at the same time, implanting a physical impression on the retina . . .'

Delia stared at me.

'What on earth,' said she, 'are you talking about?'

Very patiently, I explained the matter all over again.

'O Lord,' she said, 'but don't you see if the thing these people say in their filthy paper hadn't been in my head already, it wouldn't have meant anything to me? I wouldn't even have *noticed* it. It's because *I* . . .'

Her mouth contorted in a grimace of disgust at herself, or the *Echo de la Seine*, or the world at large.

'And Henri,' she said, 'it was in his head, too. And Mark.'

So they had all discussed it.

And during the days that followed, I found myself thinking continually of what Delia had said – how the article would have meant nothing to any of us if some such idea about Foraker had not been in our heads already.

Just when it seemed the prickling electric tension of our existence could get no worse, it did.

It was the beginning of the third week in July, the Clemenceau Government had fallen the previous evening, and Mark Crane, Martha, and myself were having a late supper at the Forakers', and discussing the news.

Then Mark Crane said, 'If you ask me, all this political junk's unimportant anyway. Ask me, there's a lot more important stuff in the papers than that.'

What about the news, for instance, of several fresh attempts likely to be made to gain the £10,000 prize offered by the London *Daily Mail* for the first successful crossing of the English Channel by air?

Foraker let out a short laugh. His idea of a damn fool, he said, was a man that would pay ten thousand pounds to have someone prove Christmas was coming. Didn't everyone know an internal combustion engine with wings on it could flop across the English Channel? What was important about that? It was proved the first time anyone flew more than fifty yards in such a machine.

Delia looked at her plate as though, if she looked anywhere else, she would scream.

Mark persisted. He had been reading about the preparations being made by this man Louis Blériot, and he had made some private inquiries from people associated with the aviation business, and it was his opinion that Blériot had a good chance of bringing it off. It would be quite an occasion. And he took the view that it would be a good thing for us all to take a little trip up to Calais and take a look at Blériot's machine, and if the weather was good and he really did make an attempt, why, we should be there to see it.

Foraker put one hand flat on the table and muttered something at it which could not be heard.

'After all,' Mark explained to Delia, 'whoever pulls this off is going to be quite a historic figure. A big man. It'll be something people that saw it will tell their grandchildren about. Pity to miss it.'

'No!' Delia said. And although her voice was quite low, it was as if she really had screamed after all. 'No! I don't want to go. I've no interest in it. It's not so important.'

Everyone stared at her. I saw Martha look from her to Foraker and back again, with a passionate attention and curiosity.

'Of course it's not important,' Foraker said, sneering at Mark. 'Unless you just want to go up there for the bathing or something.'

Mark was still looking at Delia and he put on an air of being just a little puzzled by the whole thing.

'But why not?' he asked. 'I'll admit it's not going to be the biggest thing that ever happened in history. But it's big and this Blériot seems to be a big enough man to do it. I just thought it'd be sort of interesting for you.'

Foraker leaned back in his chair, appeared to control a yawn and was about to speak when Henriette-Louise-Marie came into the room to change our plates and put cheese and a bowl of fruit on the table. Foraker swung around to her, beaming, and she did an imitation of somebody's lowly handmaiden, living for the master's smile.

'Ned,' Foraker said to me, 'I want you to tell Henriette-

Louise-Marie that I very much hope she has not been listening outside the door. Tell her that.'

I shouted this in French at Henriette-Louise-Marie, who listened with downcast eyes in the face of a martyr.

'And now,' said Foraker, 'I want you to tell her why. Explain to her it's because if she had been listening there she would have heard from Mark Crane here a tremendously important piece of information. Mark Crane has revealed, his lips have vouchsafed the intelligence, that within a matter of days a man is going to get into a box with some wings and a little motor-car engine and he is going to fly farther than anyone except a couple of other men last year, only they did it over land and he's going to cross a piece of water all of twenty-two miles wide, probably twenty-five miles an hour faster than he could do it swimming, and maybe twice as fast as people on an ordinary boat. It's a revolution. He's a great man. And if anyone wants an expert judgement on great men, why, he couldn't do better than go to Mr Mark Crane.'

Before he had finished speaking, Henriette-Louise-Marie had understood all that was essential – that the master was making game of Mark Crane, sneering at him, surely for good and sufficient reason: that Mark Crane was a little scared and had bad thoughts about the master: that Delia was eyeing the master with a kind of angry despair: that Martha and I were hestitant and embarrassed, broken reeds. As for Henriette-Louise-Marie she waited only the master's word to go for Mark Crane and bite him, were it at the risk of life itself.

Beaming, Foraker made no pretence of waiting for my translation. He said, 'I advise you all to go and see Mr Berryoh do this very, very fine and remarkable thing. Take some hard-boiled eggs and jam sandwiches. Take some hot cocoa in case you all have to sit up beyond your bedtimes.'

He put a great hunk of cheese on a piece of bread and bit into it, permitting it to occupy his entire attention.

Next day, Mark Crane, taking alarm, went to him and said that he had not really considered the Blériot flight so important, had vaguely thought it might be an opportunity for making those business contacts in a nice, easy way, but felt now that probably the whole thing was a waste of time.

He came out rather more alarmed than he went in. Foraker had been ominously bland. He had said naturally it would be a good thing to make those business contacts. Business was business. Furthermore, he had suggested, there was no reason why I should not go along, too, since Foraker himself was going to be busy in the Beauvais workshop on the 'new phase' – work for which my presence was neither necessary nor desired. And, now he came to think of it, why not take Martha? She might be useful if any business came up for which secretarial aid was needed, and she would enjoy the trip, the sea breezes, the unusual spectacle of this Mr Berryoh in his little machine.

This amicable attitude by its unusualness made Mark nervous. He interpreted it as meaning that Foraker was 'up to' something. I believe at one moment there raced through his overheated mind the notion that on our return we should find the Beauvais and Paris establishments locked up and Foraker fled – having dragged Delia along with him, of course.

'And then,' Mark said to me, 'there's this business about taking Martha. Cool, eh? Typical of him. Sending off a young girl like that with two men. It shows how much he cares about her and her reputation.'

I had to admit that it was, indeed, an odd proposal. In the light of the manners and customs of that time it was explosively unconventional.

I believed, however, that Martha's feelings towards myself were explosively unconventional, too. I said, uneasily, that in the circumstances she would probably refuse to come.

'Don't you believe it,' Mark said. 'She'll come all right.'

I supposed that he, too, was referring to Martha's feelings for me – it struck me that perhaps she had given him some hint which she had been too shy to give me.

'I mean,' Mark said, 'she likes to think she's up to date and emancipated. The Modern Woman. Shaw and all that stuff. If Foraker says she's to go in a professional capacity – secretarial work and so on – she'd think she was behaving like some old-fashioned girl of the nineties if she didn't go along. Matter of prestige. People are so damn modern nowadays they'll do anything.'

I looked at him with annoyance.

'After all,' I said, 'the whole thing was your idea in the first place.'

'Well, I did suggest Delia should come.'

'With you as chaperone, I suppose.'

Disgusted and uneasy, I had an impulse to go to Foraker and say I had no interest in the Blériot flight, no desire to go on this expedition to Calais. But when I tried, in fact, to convey to him something of the kind, he looked at me aloofly across his desk, and asked what the devil I thought I could do that was useful if I stayed in Paris or Beauvais.

It occurred to me, as we waited for the car to be brought from the garage on the day of our expedition, that what Fate had been up to, so far as Martha and I were concerned, was to provide the ideal setting wherein our romantic adventure would burst into flower. Not a commonplace evening at the theatre, followed by a move to the dingily antique décor of the Rue St Jacques. Instead, an exhilarating drive across the fields of France in the blue and gold of a summer's day; a strange old town by the sea; bedroom windows opening to the murmur of surf on the shore or the marine noises of the harbour.

And afterwards, there would be this event, this flight, in case it took place at all.

We should look back on it later as 'the day we went to see Blériot at Calais.'

With an eye to the evening's programme, I had suggested we leave Paris in mid-morning, as soon as possible after breakfast.

Foraker was to accompany us as far as Beauvais. He had insisted – without the least cordiality, but with the air of one giving a necessary order – that we leave him there, and take the car on. If he wished to return to Paris before we passed through Beauvais on our return journey from Calais, he would take the train.

At intervals, Foraker pulled his watch from his waistcoat and looked at it, comparing it with the brass-cased clock on the dashboard of the car, and with the clocks on public buildings in the towns and villages through which we passed. It made Mark nervous, and he drove badly.

'Have a jolly picnic,' were Foraker's parting words to us, as we left him at the entrance to the former farmyard now enclosed by his workshops, and began to bounce back along the track towards the Beauvais road, and the highroad from Beauvais to Calais.

Martha and I looked back at him from the back seat of the car. He was already, so far as we could see, shouting out some order or question to an unseen person inside the main house.

Seeking to avoid a farm cart which appeared unexpectedly from a side-turning off the Beauvais–Amiens road, Mark ran our car over a shallow culvert. As we lurched heavily and stopped as askew as a galleon aground, I heard him shout out, 'God damn that man!'

Thinking he spoke of the man with the cart, I said soothingly that they were not much used to motor-cars in these parts.

Mark glared round at me and said, 'I don't mean him. I mean Grant got me all upset. It wouldn't have happened but for him.'

Mark, believing that some vital part of the machine had probably been cracked or broken, drove gingerly, listening for unusual noises and sometimes cursing aloud at Foraker as responsible for the whole affair. In the village of Conty, a newly painted sign outside a yard advertised it was a place for mechanical repairs – repairs to every type of automobile a speciality.

While we ate sandwiches in a café beside the yard, a brisk young mechanic vetted the car, pronounced it undamaged, beyond scratches and dents. Reassured, Mark agreed that we should push on fast to Amiens, get through the traffic there as expeditiously as we could with safety, and on the road beyond make an effort to recover some of the time lost.

The spires of Amiens looked to me like signposts on a road to some small Paradise.

We were entering the Cathedral square at a careful pace when a police whistle blew somewhere, two gendarmes ran out into the roadway, signalling us to halt; one of them leaping aggressively on to the running board beside Mark, who brought the car to a nervous stop.

The gendarme still on the roadway made a statement. It was to the effect that we were under arrest. We would be good enough to put the car in motion and proceed at a walking pace to the police station.

Why? Why?

Menacing silence was followed by orders to proceed immediately under guidance of the man on the running board.

Two blocks from the square we left the car, entering what appeared to be a combined station of the police and *gendarmerie*. We were informed that we were detained on suspicion of having stolen the car. The grounds for such suspicion? A message telephoned from the neighbourhood of Beauvais by an individual stating that he was speaking on behalf of a Mr Foraker. We would be good enough to remain in the waiting-room, under guard, until communication with Beauvais had been re-established, a report made, identification established.

How long would that take? Five minutes.

It took thirty-five. Mark, his goggles pushed up under the peak of his motoring cap sat on a bench, gulping. It seemed that at any moment chagrin would cause him to vomit or fall in a fit. Martha sat speechless. Every time the telephone rang in the office beside the waiting-room I dashed to the door, ready for action.

When the call came and I was permitted, after the gendarme in charge had talked lengthily, to speak to the person at the other end, it turned out to be M. Léon, the foreman-caretaker at the workshop. He was happy. He congratulated himself on having been able to get in touch with us. M. Foraker wished to speak to M. Crane or M. Hastings on an urgent matter.

Under arrest? Supposed to have stolen the car? That was only because he had told the gendarmes the first thing that came into his head to ensure that they looked out for us in Amiens. Had Mr Foraker told him to say we had stolen the car? Not at all. His own idea entirely. M. Foraker had said his message was urgent, so naturally he had had to be ensured we were stopped. Here was M. Foraker in person.

'Ned? Glad I got in touch with you. Now, listen. Tell Mark...' There followed a long message about an order for some materials: ... had been ordered by Mark ... should have been delivered ... essential Mark telephone to such-and-such people in Calais ... Saturday afternoon? Office closed? ... Find them wherever they were.... Ascertain when materials going to be delivered ... Ring Beauvais again and inform Foraker.... Got that? ... Fine, fine.

'But we're under arrest,' I explained, while beside me Mark pawed at the telephone, trying to get it from me and yell into it.

'Just an idea of Léon here. He knew I was in a hurry, I'll put him on the telephone and he can explain to the police. All's well that ends well. Nothing to worry about. But, for God's sake, have Mark hurry those calls. I have to know about that stuff.'

Whisking the telephone out of Mark's clawing hand I handed it to the gendarme, who listened resentfully, shouted abuse, banged the instrument back on to its hook before Mark could get at it.

Released, we stood by the dusty car in the sunshine, arguing. Mark said he refused to start telephoning from here all over Calais. I thought of Foraker, thought of the diminishing evening in Calais-Paradise, and was suffocated with annoyance and indecision.

Martha said, 'But naturally you have to do it. It's important.'

Mark danced on the roadway. Important? It was another April Fool, a hoax, a spiteful trick to score off us and Blériot all at once. All right, he would telephone, just to show us. It would turn out the materials had been delivered days ago.

We sat in a packed café with a telephone behind its counter. People pushed against us. Beer was spilled in Martha's lap. She mopped at it while I tried to recreate the mood of the car, prepare the mood for the evening. Every ten minutes I was interrupted by a call to the telephone. It was the operator reporting a delay on the trunk line. On account of Saturday afternoon. How long a delay? One hour. At the end of an hour, it was still an hour.

Then the call came through. After the exchange had tried several numbers, Mark got his man, talked at length.

He returned to the table, looking sicker than ever.

'Damn queer thing,' he said. 'It's a fact about that stuff. Some delay. They can't get it delivered till Monday morning.'

The call to Beauvais took another hour to get through. I stood with Mark behind the counter while he talked to Foraker. Mark made his report. Sounding cowed, he made a feeble effort to utter his complaint about our arrest. I could hear Foraker's voice booming at the other end.

'That's all right,' he was saying. 'Everything's fine now. Nothing to worry about.'

As we set off for Calais in the shining sun, the car cast a huge, palpitating shadow which rippled over the house fronts like the shadow of an antique vessel.

12

Shaking and throbbing all over after the terrible vibrations of the car, we sat, at an hour past midnight, in an oasis angrily put at our disposal near the edge of a deserted dining-room – the dining-room of an hotel on the edge of Calais, the only one found, so late, to house us.

After tepid, partially raw, food and good wine, we drank brandy, Mark putting it down fast in the way he did when he began to think about Life and Love. Through the ache in my head, I heard him saying that he thought he would go out and see whether there was any night life in this unenterprising town, and asking me whether I would care to come. I told him no. Then he would just take a look around, he said, and return, to sleep. He had been informed that the Blériot attempt would take place about midday. We could all have a good sleep, and then get out the car and drive out to the cliffs at Baraque where the starting field was.

I had viewed the rooms provided by the hotel. They composed what the manager had termed, without irony or bombast, the Bridal Suite – a double bedroom, a single bedroom, and a circular box got up as a sitting-room, but having a camp-bed in it, besides the table and chairs. I suggested to Martha that it would be more agreeable to move upstairs to our sitting-room. She agreed, her eyes huge in a face drawn with fatigue.

With the courage of near-despair, I ordered the waiter to bring a bottle of champagne, and left the table carrying this and the brandy. Martha looked at these bottles under my arm with weary surprise.

'They'll make us feel better,' I explained, converting these gay little preparations into so many medicine bottles.

She sat wanly on the stiff-backed sofa, and drank off a glass of champagne as though she, too, hoped for talismanic effects. The room smelled of sea mist, and I wandered about nervously shutting windows, at the same time surveying the place with an eye to the moment of Mark's return.

I had no intention that he should intrude, even in the most indirect manner, upon our magical adventure by, for example, returning to find my camp-bed in the sitting-room compromisingly empty, or else himself taking the camp-bed and blocking the exit from Martha's double room towards the single bedroom.

In the end, discovering that the single bedroom had a door of its own opening to the passage, I wrote a notice on a piece of paper, telling Mark that I had given up this room to him, hung it on the passage door, and locked the door between the single room and the sitting-room.

I returned, by way of the passage, with a satisfying sense of achievement, and found Martha keeled over sideways on the sofa, asleep.

On an impulse of loving and chivalric service, I went across and lifted her legs on to the sofa, rather expecting that the movement would disturb her and she would awake to find me in the act of performing this tender gesture. I gently removed her shoes.

She slept on.

Determined that she should see how carefully I had watched over her, I mixed a little champagne and brandy, and drank it at a gulp for the purpose of keeping myself alert. Later, it occurred to me that it would be as well to relax somewhat for a few minutes while waiting for her to finish her doze, so as to be not overstrained when she was awake again.

The next thing that happened was a violent jolt of the sofa, a scurrying in the room, and the bang of a window. As I opened my eyes, I saw Martha from behind, leaning far out of the window, her head twisted round and silhouetted faintly against pale daylight. Then I could hear the noise of feet running in the street below the window, and people shouting.

Martha got her head inside the window long enough to shout, 'He's started!' and leaned out again. I scrambled to her side and looked out on a gap-toothed street, sea half a mile away through the gaps between buildings, windows with other heads craning from them, and, below, upturned faces. A dog barked, somebody shouted, somebody else shouted for quiet, and then everyone was quiet and above us, away to our right, could be heard a small noise, the harsh whirr of an engine up in the air.

The whirr grew fainter, was inaudible.

'Oh, we missed it!' Martha said.

Then we heard the noise in the air again, it went over the roof somewhere, going from our right to our left, and faded. We leaned out together, staring westwards in the direction the sound had taken. On a high building in that direction there was a bright flash in the bluish grey of the morning, and I remembered something. Under the conditions of the competition the flight must not start before sunrise. The sun was only starting to rise now, the first rays catching the tops of buildings.

'It was a trial trip,' I told Martha. 'He didn't go out to sea. He's gone back to Baraque up there.'

I looked into Mark's room from the passage, saw it empty, and the two of us ran down the stairs and out of the hotel. Neither of us could drive the car, which still sprawled in the yard under its moist hood, giving an impression of debauch.

We trotted along the cobbled street side by side, making for higher ground on the way up towards Cap Gris-Nez. To the north, sea and sky mingled in a hazy glitter, but we had long shadows running ahead of us now, and looking back I saw a reddish sun with a little haze hanging below it. We were clear of the town, walking now, passing a small house now and then, with people standing outside it, talking and looking westwards.

A man in a nightcap, staring at the sky, said to someone inside the house, 'All the same, you can't say it's really natural.'

Farther on, a man in a fisherman's jersey, leaning on the little gate of his garden, told us there was going to be nothing to see.

'It's all a hoax,' he said.

'But he just flew over the town, we heard him,' Martha said.

The fisherman shrugged cynically. 'It's a hoax,' he said. 'There are people that like to have their legs pulled. As for me, no.' He put his hands in his pockets and walked back towards the house. When we glanced back at him, he was at the door, watching us with a look of angry annoyance.

Then there was the whirring in the sky again. We stood still. Then the flying-machine was there. Mist drifted between us and it, and then for a moment it was clear in the sun – a long box with wings. Out of the box stuck the head and shoulders of a man. He seemed at that instant not to be a man, but some fitment of the machine. Martha must have had the same sensation. For she said, with a gasp, 'But it's a man. It's Blériot.'

Mist swallowed the apparition, although we could hear the noise a while longer. We stood listening to it, looking over the sea towards England. Then we could hear the bang and clang of an early tram, coming down the road towards the town.

The manager at the hotel had said the night before that, if the crossing were successful, the news would be telegraphed from Dover and posted at the town hall in Calais. As we scrambled on to the tram, I kept saying, 'Hurry, hurry,' as though it were possible the flying-machine would cross the Channel in five minutes.

The tram rocked into town, and we realized there would be more than a half-hour to wait for news. A café, in view of the place where the notice would be posted when it came – if it came – was overfilled. We pushed towards the zinc counter, moving forwards only foot by foot in the crowd, moving in the same direction between the tables, where people were proving that Blériot would fall into the sea, would fly right on to London and terrify the English, would get to the other side and run slap into the cliffs of Dover, in which case would the *Daily Mail* pay the prize to his widow, or what? Legal experts dashed at the question and tore it to pieces.

We stood in the thickening crowd in the weak early sunlight, and the speculations about the result continued all around us.

Then the crowd rippled, stiffened, and then thrust suddenly forward. On the steps of the town hall appeared some municipal official, holding in his hands a big sheet of paper. Other officials dashed out after him, gesticulating, and shouting for silence. Belatedly, another official, in an ornate uniform, ran out and blew an heraldic trumpet.

Then the official with the paper raised one hand, and began to read in a loud, sonorous voice.

'Citizens of Calais! I have the honour to make known to you officially the news just communicated by the electric telegraph from Dover, that in glorious flight, the heroic French aviator, Louis Blériot, has landed on the cliffs near Dover, having in triumph crossed the Channel in his flying-machine BXI in thirty-one minutes.'

Two of the other officials opened a glass-faced case which hung near the main door of the town hall, and the man with the paper, protected by a small cordon of police, fixed it with drawing-pins to a background of green baize.

Through the confusion of cheers, Mark's voice called my name, and his hand tugged sharply at my coat-sleeve. He was gasping after his effort to reach us in the crowd which now surged past us, struggling to read the written words of the notice.

Twenty miles from Calais, where we ate a second breakfast, the news of Blériot's flight was still only a matter of report, although people believed us when we told them about it. Forty miles farther south, it was a rumour. At Abbeville, where we lunched – we had taken the coastal road, as a concession to Mark's hankering for sights of sea and golden sands – it was a traveller's tale, and we the extravagant travellers. One could see by the face of the waiter in the restaurant that he was going to wait for next morning's newspaper before he believed the story. Another man in the restaurant, overhearing us, became indignant. He begged our pardon, insincerely, for contradicting us, but felt bound to point out that a flight of this kind, over the sea, was a scientific impossibility . . .

Beauvais' outskirts were gently alive with people promenading in Sunday afternoon calm.

Then we saw Delia. She was in the garden that stretched along the street at the side of the hotel, protected from the street by a low wall with creeper-covered lattice above it.

It was not until evening that Foraker returned after a day at the workshops, driving up in a car he had hired for the weekend to take him to and fro. He listened with decent attention to Mark's slightly amended version of our expedition, of the misinformation which had prevented us being present at Baraque for the start of the flight, the result of the flight itself.

'Call it fifty-one miles per hour,' Foraker said flatly.

In the later evening we strolled in the square. Instead of the usual concert, a political meeting was in progress, to rally local support for the new Government of M. Briand, likely to be announced the following day. The band played only intermittently, patriotic airs interspersing the speeches.

Successive speakers, and by the time we arrived the whole audience, were in possession of the news of the Blériot flight.

This stirring piece of topical intelligence the speakers seized upon and waved, so to speak, above their heads. It proved everything.

It proved, for instance, that – contrary to what defeatist reactionaries declared – the France of today, progressive, liberal, united, was stronger, more glorious than ever before. It proved also – contrary to declarations by crazy and hate-filled extremists of the Left – that France had no need of violence and revolution to enable her to go forward in the vanguard of human progress and endeavour.

It proved that, at a moment when the flying-machine had for the first time spanned the Channel, when even proud Albion was no longer an island, when science and technical advance were annihilating the historic bastions of the nations, at such a moment it proved that the duty of all true Frenchmen was to abandon sectarian and petty internal strifes and schisms, and rally in unexampled unity behind the new Government.

These attempts at a brisk political kidnapping of M. Blériot were repeatedly interrupted. A knot of oppositionists close to the platform kept up a yelling commentary to the effect, so far as one could gather, that Blériot had succeeded only in the teeth of sabotage by Jews and pro-Germans. A group at the other side of the platform denounced the whole business as a piece of chauvinistic propaganda designed to prepare the minds of Frenchmen for international war.

The name of Blériot bounced to and fro over the heads of the crowd, was batted back and forth between platform speakers and hecklers.

Foraker, at the edge of the crowd, his arms crossed, a big cigar between his fingers, leaned his back against a tree, and seemed to be examining the leaves above him. In reality, he must have been cogitating some problem which had arisen at the workshops during the day, for he twice pulled out a note-book and pencilled a few words or figures in it. It was a gesture which attracted the immediate and suspicious attention of a half-dozen loutish young men, two of them wearing National-ist badges and one the emblem of the Camelots du Roi, who stood near us, occasionally shouting abusive interjections at the speakers. They stared at Foraker with deliberately insolent hostility. It occurred to me that they looked at him in the same way in which the waiter at Calais had looked at the motor-car.

Delia said, 'Let's go back to the hotel. Or go for a walk. All this stuff about Blériot, Blériot, Blériot . . . it's too boring.'

'Just the great man of the moment,' Mark said.

'What?' asked Foraker, coming out of his reverie.

'I said I'm bored with all this shouting about Blériot.'

Foraker, who had not listened to a word that was being said on the platform or around it, ejaculated the word, 'Blériot,' in an explosive manner, and gave one of his loud, short laughs.

The louts turned sharply to stare at him again. Noticing them for the first time, Foraker regarded them with an aloofness which they found, obviously, insulting. Foraker turned to Martha and said something I could not catch, laughing again as he did so.

One of the young men, the well-dressed Camelot du Roi, either overhearing what he had said, or simply hearing that he had spoken in English, came up close to him and in slightly broken English, asked whether he was a foreigner, a guest of France?

'Paying guest,' Foraker said, his smile more insulting than ever. The young man's companions moved a little closer, and one of them abused Foraker in French – a foreign agent, taking notes. Foreign agents were everywhere, paid by the Jews.

Delia said, 'Oh, come on, Grant! I want to go home.'

The young men muttered in French, prompting the one who spoke English, a big fellow with hot blue eyes. This one now said, 'Do we understand you want to laugh at the name of the French aviator, Blériot?'

'Don't want to do anything about him,' Foraker said. 'Doesn't mean a thing to me.'

As he said this, he threw away the stump of his cigar, a contemptuous flick of the hand, a tossing away of the French aviator Blériot. The youths snarled.

Delia said, 'For pity's sake, Grant! Don't get arguing with them.'

The big English-speaking lout, who carried a stout cane, flourished its silver knob under Foraker's chin and said he supposed he was talking to an Englishman, rendered impotently jealous and furious by the French conquest of the Channel.

Foraker shrugged. 'Go away and play marbles,' he said.

On the platform, the speaker was roaring to his peroration. The cheers and yells of protest rose louder and louder. In this corner under the tree, the young men pressed in a little closer round Foraker.

Delia's voice was anxious and angry. 'Grant!' she called to him. 'Will you please stop play-acting and come along? You're not impressing anybody,' she said.

The English-speaker with the cane was dancing on his toes in excited indignation. 'I demand,' he said, 'I and my friends demand, that you raise your hat in token of respect to the French pioneer of aviation, Louis Blériot.'

On Foraker's face I saw the expression he had when he was praying for patience, and almost immediately afterwards the expression he had when he had stopped praying for it.

The young man moved a step forward, close to him.

'Otherwise,' he said with pomposity, 'I shall be under the regrettable necessity of knocking it off for you.'

At this point he turned his head slightly, to assure himself of the admiration and support of his companions.

Foraker shifted his feet, and got out something between a growl and a sigh.

'Hell!' he said, and his left fist and arm lashed across the small space between and I could hear the bones in the angle of the young man's jaw crack as the fist smashed into it. I saw him beginning to fall down. I saw the others stiffened with astonishment for a moment, during which Foraker jumped forwards and punched his right fist, with all his weight behind it, into the face of the one nearest, who went over on his back and his head thudded on the gravelly earth.

Two others closed in on Foraker, I struck out at one of them, and in a second went down half stunned by a violent crack from a heavy cane at the back of the head.

Coming to, crouched on all-fours, I saw Mark wrestling with one of the young men, another holding Foraker's legs, while a third alternately stabbed and lashed at his head with a stick. I heard whistles blow, and shouts of 'Police!' and saw the two leave Foraker and start to run, and the man wrestling with Mark break away and start to run, too.

People were trampling and lurching all about me, and I was aware of the man who had been knocked down first being dragged past me by others, who held him under the shoulders and disappeared with him through the crowd. Foraker, hatless and with his back to me, was swaying on his feet and he and Mark seemed to be explaining to two policemen who looked at them sternly but with relief – relief, as I learned when I got myself to my feet and joined the group, because Mark was saying that Foraker had certainly been threatened, had had to defend himself, but did not want to make a charge against anyone.

I saw Delia looking at Foraker with a kind of alarmed distaste, and, for the first time since the row began, I got a good look at him, too. His appearance was grotesque. He suggested some caricature of a grown man, depicted as a brawling schoolboy. His hat was gone, and there was gravel in his hair. A dirty trickle of blood ran down the side of his nose into his mouth. His face was filthy, and his collar had burst open and was riding up under his ear. When he wiped his face with the back of his hand, blood from his knuckles came off in streaks.

Also, he was grinning. He grinned at Delia in triumph. 'That was showing them,' he said. 'Blériot. They wanted me to take off my hat to him.'

She said, 'For the Lord's sake, don't start swaggering. You look an absolute guy. And, anyway, it's off now.'

He looked briefly around for his hat and it was not to be seen. He put a fresh cigar in his mouth, threw his head back; and started walking, swaggering under the trees with the rest of us trailing unhappily behind him in no triumphal procession: a drum major with no band.

On the way, ideas evidently occurred to him. He sat down in the hotel garden without even washing the blood off his face and started to give everyone instructions. Mark was to go to Paris early in the morning, and do this and do that. He was to go to see Halm. Halm, Foraker disclosed, was currently in Paris. He had written Foraker an idiotic letter, an intrusive, impertinent, cold-footed sort of a letter wanting to know a lot of things that were none of his business. Mark was to go and tell him to stop trying to meddle with things he knew nothing about – mind his own business.

'He thinks it is his business,' Mark said.

'He's a damn fool,' said Foraker.

Martha was to go with Mark to the Paris office, and I was to stay with Foraker at Beauvais. I said something about not knowing that he wanted me around the workshop at this stage.

'Things have moved faster than I expected,' Foraker said. 'Things are going well. I shall need you for a lot of things.'

His manner, or perhaps it was simply the atmosphere, managed to convey a suggestion that this 'going well' had been invented on the spur of the moment, a boast to fit in with his mood.

'And me and Jeph?' Delia said.

Foraker smiled at her through the dirt and blood on his face and waved his arm expansively.

'Do just whatever you like, Delia, my darling. Here – or Paris. Whichever you like best for you and Jephthah. Do just what you feel like doing.'

He put his extended arm around her shoulders and she left it lying there, looking up at the trees against the early stars without moving or seeming to be aware of Foraker and his arm. His face relaxed and he sat looking at her with love. In the light of a lamp on the street it could be seen that one of his eyes was becoming puffy and discoloured.

It was half past six the next morning when the boots-porter wakened me. Mr Foraker's orders. An early start for the workshops, the hired car to be at the door at a quarter after seven. I had hoped to see Martha again before leaving. Perhaps I looked expectant and disappointed.

'They're all having a grand sleep,' Foraker said confidently as we got into the car. A half-hour later the workshop closed around me, shutting me into another world, crackling with urgency, tense with hours of concentration.

13

The world outside that workshop faded and diminished. I had imagined that the 'new phase' would be like the earlier 'phase' in the development of Foraker's Principle, except that it would, in some way, be busier. It was in every way unlike it. I had pictured an increasing rush of anxious telephone calls, excited or furious interviews, train and car journeys, the whole machinery of life with Foraker speeded up and roaring louder than heretofore. Instead, there was a kind of quiet, though by no means any kind of peace.

That first morning, I noticed, standing close to the telephone, that the little clapper which rang the bell of it was whirring and hitting no bell. I was horrified, for by the time I had snatched up the instrument the whirring had ceased, the caller evidently given up in despair.

'That's fine,' Foraker said, not much interested, 'I had the bell taken off. Otherwise people keep calling up, interrupting.'

'But,' I said, accustomed only to the turmoil of conversations by telephone or face to face in which Foraker's life as I knew it was lived, 'I could answer it.'

'How could you?' he said. 'When would you get the time? We're going to be busy.'

I had thought, working a year or so for Foraker, that I knew what being busy meant. I found that I knew nothing about it. I had had, I suppose, some notion of Foraker sitting like an old-fashioned general in a headquarters isolated from the front lines of battle, receiving reports of progress or hitch, sending out orders to subordinates, co-ordinating and ratiocinating from a position above the mêlée. When he had told me that he would, after all, require my services at this stage of the 'new phase' I had seen myself as a kind of aide-de-camp, speeding between the commander-in-chief and the sectors of the workshop front.

The way it turned out, there was apparently no headquarters, no front line: or rather, the front line was everywhere, and the headquarters dashed about from sector to sector.

Also, I had thought that there would be important aspects of the work which Foraker and his aide-de-camp might personally attend to, and unimportant phases which would be dealt with by others. This was not the case, either. Everything, it seemed, was equally important. Nothing could be left to anyone else for long.

The general was one moment a proper general, according to my ideas, and the next was an infantryman manipulating a jammed service rifle. I thought at first that these activities in the front line, at the bench for example, Wing C, were a kind of affectation, at best a display made for the sake of *morale* – the brasshat showing himself at one with the hard-pressed troops.

At the end of the first week of this period I understood that this notion, too, was a mistake. When Foraker worked at the bench in Wing C, or lay on his back fighting with a piece of the undercarriage of the model in Wing A, he did it, I grasped, because, in his opinion at least, the job he was then putting his hands to was the job that had to be done then, and a job that nobody could do quite as well as he could do it himself.

The early start that Monday of July twenty-sixth had been no flash in the pan. Every day we started at that hour, and in the evenings the hotel people kept a cold supper ready for us at ten or eleven o'clock when the hired car brought us back from the workshop. Since Foraker had cut off the telephone at the works, nobody could be sure of catching him at the hotel between the time he returned there and the time he went to sleep, leaving ferocious orders against disturbance. Paris, and indeed all other places, people and events, seemed far away; as good as dead, or part of another life altogether.

Two or three times a week, Foraker rang up Delia, inquired after her and Jephthah, expressed his love, said things were going well. Occasionally there was a message for me from Mark Crane, asking me to get in touch with him. The first time, he wanted me to find out, somehow, from Foraker, details of certain expenditures which had been made without his knowledge, and which he wanted to 'explain' to Halm. I told him I thought it would be impossible to get Foraker to think about anything like that at this time.

The next time, Mark talked as though hostile ears were pressed to points along the line. It was only after several minutes of discreet mumbling back and forth that he became exasperated and said that, to begin with, there had been another article in the *Echo de la Seine,* issue of September ninth. I remember that what startled me was not the news of the article but the realization that we were already in mid-September.

What sort of an article? The same sort of thing as before, underlined.

Mark read bits of the article over to me. Things, he said, were in a thoroughly confusing state. More so than ever. He wanted to do his best; fulfil obligations and so on; at the same time one couldn't go on for ever, kept in the dark, not knowing what was going on, not even knowing whether anything was going on at all.

Outraged, I said there was plenty going on. But how did I *know,* Mark demanded, how did I know what it amounted to? Why had Foraker put himself out of reach of everyone? Why had he 'gone to ground' in this way just after that first article appeared? Did not everything that had happened add up to something pretty disturbing and suspicious?

His voice changed again and he sounded passionately earnest. It wasn't, he said, just the awkwardness of his own position – a false position, he said, if ever there was one. There were others. I must understand that. Others, who had decisions to make. Very important decisions.

Halm?

No, no, not Halm. That was an important factor, too. But didn't I understand that there were other factors involved? Human factors, he whispered over the wire. And after a pause, defying imaginary listeners-in, he said, 'I mean Delia.'

The vulgar, disorderly, exasperating world of Paris, of human relations, of people bothering their heads about all kind of inanities, blazed up briefly in front of me.

'But it's all *right*!' I groaned into the telephone.

'He's been saying that for years,' Mark said. And when I was silent, repeated, 'Don't you understand, he's been behaving like this and talking like this for *years*.'

I doubled back to an earlier bit of the conversation. 'But,' I said, 'he talks to Delia two or three times a week. Everything's all right. They talk on the telephone.'

'Oh, that!' Mark said, and the conversation petered out.

Mark wrote a letter to Foraker, saying he would like to make an appointment to come down and discuss various matters. Foraker had me telegraph a reply saying it was out of the question, he was too busy.

Profoundly agitated, Mark telephoned to me again, getting me out of bed at midnight.

I asked him what he thought he could find out by coming to the works. Was he a technical expert? After all, I said on the spur of the moment, Dr Rosen was coming down in a few days. If he reported favourably on progress, wasn't that going to be enough?

There was quite a long silence while Mark seemed to be thinking it over.

'Well, yes,' he said at last. 'Of course. If Rosie Rosen says everything's all right it's all right. He knows, I admit that. But I haven't heard from him in months.'

'You will,' I said.

I was aghast at what I had said. Then I thought that, after all, it would not be a very difficult matter upon which to approach Foraker. What more natural than that Dr Rosen should be invited to view progress, study the stage now reached in Phase Two?

Tactfully, and after many unsuccessful attempts, I put it to him.

Brusquely, he refused. Not ready. Later on. Some day.

Soon? Impossible to tell.

A letter from my uncle, forwarded from the Rue St Jacques, and received by me a few days before, began to take on an ironic quality. He was passing through Paris on his way to London. Was delighted to hear from my last letter that I was still working for Mr Foraker who had struck him as 'thoroughly sound'. He had formed, during their brief meeting in Barcelona, a very good opinion of Mr Foraker. He liked, particularly, a man who was so ready to explain clearly just what he was doing, not like some of these scientific quacks who wrapped themselves in mystery to impress the layman.

At least, I thought, the letter offered an opportunity to beg leave from Foraker to go to Paris to see my uncle – older and more deserving of attention than ever.

At the Paris terminus, I actually ran from the train, conscious of a mission. No uncle was at the hotel where he had been staying – he had already gone on to London. Mark and Martha, an office boy said, were out: seeing Mr Halm. I telephoned the Forakers' apartment. Line engaged. I drove to the Forakers', and almost ran into Delia at the doorway of the apartment house, on the way out. She looked hardly aware of anything immediately about her, so that I saw her before she noticed me. Her face was excited, intent, a little alarmed, a face for when the toboggan suddenly dips and gathers speed. Her eyes, when she looked at me first, shone with some excitement that had nothing to do with me. Then she recognized me and the light in them clouded.

Was anything the matter? Why hadn't I said I was coming to Paris? She was in a terrible hurry, late for an appointment. What was the matter? Was Grant ill? Was I sure everything was all right at Beauvais?

I said of course it was, gave her Foraker's message. 'Nothing whatever to worry about.'

'O God!' she said, pulling a little at her veil with her fingers and looking down thoughtfully and questioningly at her own toes. Then, making up her mind and looking at me again, she said, 'Well there's no time now, in any case. No time to talk.'

Perhaps, I said I would just go up and say hello to Jephthah? No, because this fall Jephthah went to play, mornings and afternoons, at a kindergarten organized in the neighbourhood by English-speaking parents and French parents who wanted their children to pick up some English early. She must hurry.

I plunged into the dear, familiar Café du Carrefour. There

was more telephoning, without successful result. As I came out, there were sibilant cries above my head. From an upper window, front window, in fact, of the Forakers' drawing-room, leaned Henriette-Louise-Marie, beckoning and calling.

At the doorway, she greeted me with the manners of a conspiratorial dog. She had drinks set out on a tray, and stood over me as I sat and sipped. Questions flowed from her: Foraker's health? His state of mind? Was he happy? Overworked? Eating adequately? Thank God for all that. A prince among men. He ought to be careful.

'You know what I mean,' she said, and bobbed up off her chair to do a hideously thruthful caricature of Delia as she had looked and walked when she left the building a half-hour before. She completed it by a crude pantomime of a woman greeting a lover, falling into his arms.

I managed an indifferent shrug.

'Another thing,' Henriette-Louise-Marie said hoarsely, and put her hand on my sleeve.

What, then?

Simply that Madame Robinson desired to see me, had an urgent message for me.

I uttered a cry of impatient anger. Really, I said, this was entirely too much. Did she not know – but, of course, she knew only too well – that Mr and Mrs Robinson were bitterly and crazily hostile to Mr Foraker? That they had left no stone unturned to do him a mischief?

Too true, all too true, wailed Henriette-Louise-Marie.

'And,' she added, 'they are being punished for it! Just heavens! How that woman suffers!'

'Nonsense! And, in any case, what can she want with me? What is this talk of a message?'

'Monsieur Robinson,' said Henriette-Louise-Marie in a whisper, 'has *seen* something – you understand? *seen* – in connection with Monsieur Foraker. I don't know what. She wants to tell you.'

'Some spying trick,' I said energetically.

More telephoning. Mark was still at Halm's, but in conference, not to be disturbed. An hour before the evening train left for Beauvais, Martha's voice was, at last, at the other end of the telephone. She was at Mark's, picking up some papers, due to return immediately to Halm's. Yes, she would come to the station. Of course.

She came to the meeting place by the central clock at the Gare du Nord, carrying a large dispatch case, a model of an Emancipated Young Woman pursuing a Career. That was how it struck me, and I was annoyed to find myself resenting that dispatch case like an unwanted third for our company of two.

What, I asked, was the reason for Mark's agitation? Why these urgent, mysterious calls to Beauvais? Was it the new article in the *Echo de la Seine*, or Halm, or something else?

Everything taken together.

What did he mean about Delia?

Martha, as she spoke of Delia, looked more emancipated than ever. Excited, but thoughtful, in command of herself and reviewing the situation with cool judgement. Delia, no doubt about it, was behaving oddly. Or perhaps this was behaving naturally – for her. *She*, no doubt, had been affected by the *Echo de la Seine*. By a mood of impatience. By Mark's agitation, too.

'She is that sort of woman,' Martha said.

'But that's terrible,' I said indignantly.

'That's the kind of person she is,' Martha repeated, but her voice did not repeat my indignation. It stated a fact, swiftly and almost, it seemed to me, gaily.

I was suddenly angry with her. 'But it sounds,' I said, 'as though everything were falling to pieces. Don't you care? What's the matter with you?'

'Care?' she said, looking suddenly at me with astonished, wondering eyes. She started to say something more, and I saw the people running towards the gate of the platform where the Beauvais train was standing, and had to run with them.

'My uncle,' I told Foraker when I saw him, gnawing a chicken-bone late in the evening, 'is not at all well. He is in the hands of the doctors. He said that seeing me had given him new life.'

'Let us drink a glass of wine to the health of the good old

man,' Foraker said. I drank with him, and said it was possible I might have to go to Paris to see uncle again.

It was my duty, it appeared to me, to establish this fiction and so open a route for myself to travel to Paris, to keep an eye on the situation.

'You must keep in constant touch,' Foraker agreed. Then he inquired after Delia, Jephthah, Mark, and Martha. Replying cautiously, I was interrupted. He said he was glad to hear everyone was all right. That was fine. As for Halm, the man was a fool. He wasted people's time.

I said I personally believed he was probably worrying about the forthcoming Report of the Military Commission on Aviation. Foraker said it was the sort of thing a man like Halm would worry about. A lot of cavalrymen trying to figure out a plan to put a horse in a balloon. He waved away Halm and the commission and talked of progress at the works.

On succeeding evenings I tried again, approaching the subject of Halm, the desirability of keeping him informed and good-tempered; even the subject of Delia, the possible desirability of going to Paris to see her, to tell her his progress and plans.

Why? Because it would interest her. Possibly, but it involved an unnecessary expenditure of time.

'All the same . . . with women . . .'

'Delia,' Foraker said, 'isn't much like other women. She's fine. She knows me. She knows I know what I'm about. She knows if I say there's nothing to worry about, there's nothing to worry about.'

Gripping my coffee-spoon in both hands, I said boldly, 'You can't after all just sit here expecting the sun and moon to stand still for you.'

A smile of pleasure illuminated Foraker's face. 'Isn't that,' he said, 'a great story?'

He took a sip of brandy and rolled it on his tongue. 'Mind you, Ned,' he said, 'we do not know, we cannot tell, whether that great tale of Joshua be history – as my father naturally believed – or legend, as wise men and scholars tell us today. My father had a sermon he often preached about it. Point about Joshua, the way my father saw it, was he figured out just the miracle he wanted, picked it out of the catalogue, and then ordered it. Many other fine men of his day and age were wont to pray unto the Lord for some miracle or other to happen. Not so Joshua, the son of Nun. He didn't ask the Lord, he told Him.'

The chair cracked sharply under the impact of his shoulders as he threw himself back, turning his face up to the ceiling, searching it for words and presently finding them.

'Tenth book, twelfth verse of Joshua,' he said, talking into space. ' "Thus spake Joshua –" ' His voice filled the dining-room suddenly and made the waiter at the sideboard jump, turn, and gaze at him with affectionate admiration.

' "Thus spake Joshua to the Lord in the day when the Lord delivered up the Amorites before the children of Israel, and he said in the sight of Israel, Sun, stand thou still upon Gibeon" ' – Foraker rolled his head this way and that and a wave of resonant sound rolled through the window and secured attention from two dogs in the street – ' "and thou, Moon, in the valley of Ajalon. And the sun stood still and the moon stayed, until the people had avenged themselves upon their enemies." '

He paused, ruminating and recollecting, and one of the dogs let out a suspicious, questioning bark.

' "So," ' said Foraker, remembering, and intimidating the dog with a new outburst of sound, ' "the sun stood still in the midst of heaven and hasted not to go down about a whole day.

' "And there was no day like that before it or after it, that the Lord hearkened unto the voice of a man: for the Lord," ' shouted Foraker, ' "fought for Israel." '

A few minutes later he swaggered off to bed.

'A great man, Monsieur Foraker,' said the waiter, coming over to clear away the cups and glasses.

'Yes,' I said gulping, 'yes, indeed.'

Then we could both hear the telephone ringing at the back of the hall. Mark Crane, twitching. I hardly had the receiver in my hand before he was calling out, 'Well? Well?'

'I think,' I said in calm tones, 'everything is in order. More,' I added, 'or less.'

Trying to think of something more to say I kept thinking, instead, of Joshua, the son of Nun. In my agitation, I said it aloud.

'What?' shouted Mark. 'Who are you talking about? Listen, you aren't drunk, are you?'

'No, no. Of course not.'

'Well then?'

'Well, taking one thing with another,' I said, trying to make it sound as though it meant something, 'I have the impression that the best thing to do will be just to go on about the way we're going.'

There was a silence which seemed a long one. Then, in a slightly changed voice, Mark said, 'Well, if that's the best you can do, now let *me* tell *you* something. If Grant Foraker has any idea things can just go on going the way they have been, he'd better think again.'

'What d'you mean? You mean Halm? About Rosen not having been called in?'

'That, of course. I've told you that already. But there's a bit more to it. Get this straight.' He paused, and paused between each word, as though he were writing in a state of breathless excitement and pausing to draw a line under each word.

'Delia,' he said, 'is at the end of her tether. She can't stand it any more. She's just about decided to leave him.'

'But look here, Mark . . .'

'That,' said Mark, 'is the situation.'

The line had been bad all along and now got worse. I shouted to Mark that I would come to Paris and see him.

'You'd better hurry,' Mark said.

14

Mark was alone in the Paris office, cutting, I thought, a disturbingly sad figure. His appearance and ideas were disordered.

I reached for the point. 'You said something,' I said, 'about Delia being "at the end of her tether". Something about her going to leave Grant.'

'It's a fact, Ned. A fact. She can't stand the whole situation any longer. Look ...'

I kept seeing, as he talked, Delia's eager face, alive with hope and glory, puckered by bewilderment, sad in disillusion, alarmed but still excited, eager, and questing.

I heard myself asking questions, very proper questions, as it seemed to me, essential to clarification of the situation, and yet sounding to myself a little coarse or ill-judged, giving me the sensation of a dream where you are playing lawn tennis and what you have instead of a racquet is a croquet mallet.

Was it the financial future she was worrying about?

Mark looked at me as though I were a moron. No, no, of course not. 'If he *amounted* to anything she wouldn't care if he hadn't two cents.' And I remembered Delia's assurance that she would have lived with Grant Foraker in a hovel, or garret.

His rush of words rushed on. Nothing to do with money – to do with his not *amounting* to anything, no *greatness* about him, a great big false alarm. 'Obtaining,' Mark said, 'love and admiration – don't you see? – on false pretences. All these years – and never really *doing* anything. And then, after all that time, outsiders begin to talk about it.'

'He rings her up often enough,' I said. 'He asks after her and the boy and tells her he loves her. Has she said anything about how she's feeling? When he's telephoned to her, I mean?'

'Have you,' Mark said, 'ever tried to talk seriously with Grant Foraker over a long distance telephone?'

I had to admit that there would be difficulties, grave difficulties.

'Look here, Mark,' I said, 'when you say "leaving" d'you mean she's leaving *with* someone? My God,' I cried, 'you don't mean to say she's leaving *him* for *you*?'

As I said it, I could sense that my incredulity was insulting. Mark paid no attention to it. He looked at me strangely, went and sat down behind his desk with his hands clasped in front of him and said in a tone of confused wonder, 'I don't know,' and after looking wildly around the room repeated this statement. 'Ned, I just don't know.'

'You don't *know*?' I became frightfully angry and leaned across the desk, hitting it and shouting at him.

'You don't understand,' he said, 'the complexities of everything.'

'How?'

Explaining how, he made another statement, no more coherent, no less compelling than his earlier one. It was as though he were showing me a series of X-ray pictures of his interior life. Embarrassing but serious. Love. The One Woman. Way, way back, a boy and a girl in Canton, Ohio. In the old days, before Foraker. Then parted. But they meet again. She the Great Man's wife, he the Great Man's partner.

Renunciation. She loves the man Foraker, rightly, inevitably. Highest when we see it. Service, able service, by the Faithful Squire, a privilege and pleasure. Restraint and loyalty. The sunshine of her smile, and Glory ahead. Foraker and Crane. The two men whose partnership, union of diverse but complementary capacities, opens New Era, incidentally bringing them wealth beyond dreams. Smooth going, then not so smooth.

Exasperation. Speculation. How great is this Great Man? Quarrels and expostulations. Feet of clay, visible to Mark, not so to Delia. Loyalty maintained but strained. Bursting at the seams. The seed of doubt. Wise counsel increasingly sought from Faithful Squire. Oh, joy! Oh, torture! Oh, hope!

Temptation and aspiration. Results, where are they? Words, words, and other people's money flowing like water. Delia reaching for life, feeling it slipping. More or less Ichabod. The idol fallen, or falling. A little push, it topples. A moment of remorse. Pull it back again, shore it up. But why? It will topple anyway, and that glorious girl with it. Shove it. Save her. Opportunity of a lifetime.

Also, if you don't do it, somebody else will. Forwards. Tell all. No holds barred.

Passion returned? Loyal Squire rewarded? Well, as to that, that's not the main point. Moments of Madness – all very well, but what of the Great Life, the Future, for ever, through sunshine and tempest, hand in hand? Graver, more complex. A heavy sense of responsibility. Now more than ever as Delia glides, twirls, twists in confusion of disappointment, bitterness, and hope towards a moment of decision.

'I can tell you this,' Mark said. 'She's just about made up her mind to go – get away from it all.'

'But not necessarily with you?'

'I haven't asked her. It's so kind of crucial. Whatever she said, it'd be crucial, wouldn't it?'

'And you think, perhaps, Lenoir . . .?'

'Or perhaps she really means to go back home to Ohio – alone. With the boy, of course.'

For some reason, this mention of 'Ohio' and 'the boy' – a geographical destination and a piece of practical family arrangement – dressed the situation for me in a new and dreadful reality.

'But if,' I said, following the same line of thought, 'you go off with her, you'll have to quit Grant.'

'Of course,' Mark said. 'I've thought of all that.'

He then made a remark which, all these years later, I see as one which shone with honesty and human sincerity. At the time, it appeared to me to reveal a revolting spirit of mean calculation.

'It's one of the things that troubles me,' Mark said. 'I mean suppose I did that, and then he turned out to be the real thing after all. Suppose everything he's said, everything I,' Mark drew in his breath and stared out of the window, 'everything I used to think was true, turned out to be so. Where would that leave me? And Delia?'

'You mean, I suppose,' I said with acid bitterness, 'how would you look to her when she thought she'd changed him for you?'

'Exactly,' said poor Mark, again heedless of insult.

'But when?' I shouted at Mark. 'You say she's about made up her mind. *When* does she think she's going to – to do this?'

I had to get Mark to repeat his reply twice, and then it still seemed not to make any sense. What he said was, 'It's to do with the Crusades.' And when I barked at him, he started, irritably, to tell me what the Crusades were.

'History. Knights, and Jerusalem and the Pope and the King who was a saint and so on.'

I was aware of actually shaking my head violently to and fro, as though some pressure on my eardrums were impeding my hearing.

'At the kindergarten Jeph goes to,' Mark said. 'It's a teacher, a Miss Hendricks or some such name. She's telling the children the story of these Crusades. Half an hour each day. They're crazy about it. Delia feels she just can't do anything drastic – anything that would mean she'd have to take Jeph out of this kindergarten – until this Crusade story's finished. She says it would upset him horribly – might affect his whole outlook on life.'

'And how long . . .?'

'I don't know. You know what history's like. Delia tried to find out, tactfully you know, from this teacher. But she didn't seem to get anywhere, nothing definite.'

'But she must have some idea.'

'It won't be more than three weeks,' Mark said. 'She's sure of that.'

'Three weeks?' I cried, and instinctively looked at my watch, ticking off now the first minutes of this hideously small space of time.

'If,' I said to Mark, 'Rosen reported that the thing is going according to plan, if he, so to speak, says it *works*, would you accept that as a final judgement on the Principle?'

'*I* would,' Mark said. 'He's got no axe to grind. And if he says a thing like that works – why, it works. If he said the damned thing would go around the moon I'd believe him.'

'And Halm?'

'It'd help with him. It'd certainly help.' He pulled nervously at his hair. 'But what's the use of all that?' he said. 'If, if, if . . . He hasn't reported, Grant won't let him near the place. It's all so damned shifty.'

Mark gave me a list of telephone numbers which I might ring and inquire if Miss Dukes were there, and then Martha was answering the telephone and saying that she was terribly sorry but she did not see how she could possibly free herself to meet me today, at such short notice. She was furiously busy. I was bemused. But it was a crisis, I said. I had dashed to Paris at a moment's notice. Didn't she realize what was happening? Didn't she understand?

I was so severely stunned by this behaviour that she had said good-bye and rung off before I had fully appreciated it.

'She *is* very busy,' Mark said. 'Work, work, work.'

As I angrily took my leave I told him that, as he had chosen to speak to me of the situation, I felt myself entirely at liberty to inform Foraker of the state of affairs, should I deem it judicious so to do.

'Yes, yes,' Mark said. 'Of course. But I don't think he'll believe it, don't you see? He just wouldn't believe any woman could possibly leave him. For Lenoir or – or anyone else. You know,' he said gravely, 'I really think if you told him there was any question of Delia running off with me, I really think he'd *laugh*.'

And confronting Foraker that same evening at Beauvais I thought to myself that Mark's singularly humble view of the position was about correct.

I had failed to 'mobilize' Rosen, just as I had failed to elaborate a plan with Martha. He was away from Paris, expected back in a week or so. Seven days further forward in the three weeks of grace that seemed to be going to be allowed to us – unless, of course, this unknown and accidentally powerful Miss Hendricks were suddenly to tire of the Crusaders, polish off the whole story in a few days.

For I realized now, with sharper and more menacing clarity than I had at the moment when I was thinking how I was going to discuss it all with Martha, that the future was at stake. That Delia, unless some entirely new element entered, really would leave him as and when she felt that she could do so without excessive damage to Jephthah's 'outlook on life', I could not doubt. The very fact that she was so carefully considering this business of Jephthah and the Crusades seemed to me an indication that so far as Grant Foraker was concerned her mind was made up. And if that were so, and she really did leave, who could doubt that – whatever the personal, emotional effect this might have upon Foraker – the effect upon those I had come to think of as the 'watching enemy', would be immediate and, for Foraker, disastrous?

They would learn, and they would publish abroad, that even the man's wife had perceived him to be a fraud. It would be a weapon which they would know very well how to use for the purpose of destroying him.

And then one morning, as I sat in bitter depression at my morning coffee, Foraker, whom I had heard from afar off shouting into the telephone, came marching into the dining-room and said, 'This morning I want you to ring up Rosen. If he's not back in Paris, find out where he is. It's urgent. You must reach him.'

I suffered a physical spasm of relief. I jumped up from the table as though a spring had been released under me. I wanted to get to the telephone right away, relay instantly the urgent summons to Rosen.

As I started away from the table, Foraker looked at me with surprise.

'But you don't know what message to give him,' he said.

I said I supposed he wanted him to come to Beauvais without delay.

'Come down here?' Foraker said, astonished. 'Not at all. What'd be the point of that? He's to meet us in Paris, of course. Probably won't want to come at first, but he'll certainly enjoy it when he gets there. It'll make a nice change for him. He lives a sedentary life, Ned. I don't suppose he's ever been on a motoring picnic.'

Foraker flicked open his table napkin, and ripped a branch from the large bunch of grapes on the breakfast table.

'Time goes by,' he said. 'It wasn't till yesterday, when I looked in my diary, I realized the day after tomorrow's Jephthah's birthday. Six years old. Imagine that. And months ago he told me what he'd like to do on his birthday would be to go on a picnic, with the motor. So right away this morning I rang up Delia and told her I'd fix it all up. I've told her to get some dry sticks for kindling. We'll need a camp fire, but you can't ever depend on getting dry wood at the place you want to stop and eat at. So we'll take it with us.'

The expression on my face must have been very strange. Foraker evidently felt that more explanation was called for.

'I know, Ned,' he said. 'I know we're busy. But you have to understand a child's birthday's an important thing in his life. Probably more important than you realize. It has to be an occasion, a day that will stand out in later memory as a day of gladness. So what we're going to do is, we'll assign the day to the picnic, we'll be back here in the evening, and then we'll work a long night shift and catch up. It's not a great deal to do when you think it's the boy's sixth birthday.'

I found myself crazily twiddling a fork on the table, 'And Dr Rosen?' I said. 'This message?'

'Why, yes,' said Foraker. 'I want Jephthah to feel this is a big occasion. I want to have all the friends of the family gathered for it. Sort of an honour for him. We'll have Mark and Henri Lenoir and Martha, of course. And Rosen. He's a friend, and he's a pretty distinguished man, too. Jephthah'll be proud to have him along with us.'

He instructed me to remain at the hotel until I had established communication with Rosen; he would send back the car to bring me out to the works later.

'And another thing,' he said. 'I want you to explain to Louis' – Louis was driver of the hired car – 'that he'll be coming on the picnic. I'll take over my motor when we get to Paris, but we'll need this one, too. We'll be a big party. It'll be a nice change for Louis. He'll enjoy it. Everyone will. It's Jephthah's birthday.'

It seemed to be ironic that now, when this was the message I had to give him, Rosen should be there in his office, immediately available. Fearing that he would either be insulted or imagine that Foraker was playing some insane joke, I repeated the invitation flatly – a motoring picnic, everyone to meet at the Forakers' Paris apartment at 11.30 a.m. the day after tomorrow. Rosen said nothing. I thought astonishment and annoyance had probably rendered him speechless. When I had finished, he repeated the invitation and the instructions carefully.

'It means,' he said, 'that we shall motor about, and eat in the open air?'

'Yes, Dr Rosen.'

There was a long pause. Then he said, 'I think that will be delightful. It is something I have never done. Tell Foraker I shall be glad to be there.'

I telephoned to Mark. Yes, Delia had already informed him, as requested by Foraker. And did he suppose Lenoir, too, would be there? No doubt.

'But, good God!' I shouted. 'In the circumstances! I can't imagine why Delia should have agreed to such a thing.'

'What else could she do?' Mark said. 'He didn't give her a chance. I've told you before, you can't argue with Grant long distance. Maybe you can't argue with him at all. See you, day after tomorrow,' he added in a tone of resignation.

'Suppose it rains?'

'What difference will that make?' Mark said.

I saw that it would make none whatever to Foraker, and for that reason was relieved to see, on the morning of the picnic that rain was not actually falling from the low clouds which a fierce easterly wind was hounding across the country. At the hotel door Louis was ready and gravely happy. He was happy, he said, and honoured to be driving M. Foraker and family and friends on such an occasion. He said that M. Foraker was a man of genius, having a most remarkable thoughtfulness and consideration for others. As I approached the car, I saw that the back seat was already partially occupied by a rabbit hutch, with two rabbits in it.

'A present,' said Louis, 'from myself to the young Foraker.'

Beside the hutch, and on the floor of the car, were boxes, presents from Foraker to Jephthah. Others had been ordered and were to be picked up on our way across Paris.

Foraker looked at the rabbits with admiration.

'Animals,' he said, 'are a splendid present for a child. They teach it responsibility, because of the care they require, and at the same time a knowledge of natural history.'

He mounted broodingly beside Louis, while I sat in the back seat with the rabbits, for which Foraker already felt responsibility. He kept peering round at them to see whether they were eating the pieces of green stuff which had been provided. Then he brooded again. At the outskirts of the city he turned around suddenly to tell me to ask Louis to drive to an 'animal shop'. It appeared he could not bear the idea – now that the thought of animals as birthday gifts had been presented to him – of being behindhand in this respect.

'What we want,' he said, 'is a dog.'

'Or,' said Louis, 'in view of the difficulty experienced in keeping a dog in an apartment in the city, a cat might be the answer. A more or less distinguished cat, naturally.'

'There's that,' Foraker said. 'I've heard of people having Blue Persian cats. It's a kind of cat people have in an apartment.'

'Perfect,' said Louis. 'Then there's only the question whether male or female. Some people,' he said, as we reached a big pet shop near the bottom of the Rue Lafayette, 'don't care for the smell and habits of tomcats. Others object to having litter after litter of kittens.'

'Female,' said Foraker, after brief thought. 'It's educative. A boy has a cat and it has kittens and right before his eyes he sees a bit of universal history going on. An unforgettable experience.'

The female Blue Persian kitten, mewing in a wicker basket, was placed on the back seat of the car, soon further crowded with the other presents which Foraker collected on our way. Because of the unscheduled stop at the pet shop we arrived outside the apartment house facing the Café du Carrefour more than quarter of an hour later than the appointed time. At the door, Foraker's mustard-coloured car was already drawn up. It was the central object in a scene of liveliness and movement. Above it, the figure of Henriette-Louise-Marie, shrieking from the open window of the apartment, immediately caught the eye. She shrieked, and with extended arm and finger pointed this way and that. Upright on the back seat of the car stood Jephthah, his face contorted with anxiety, his hands clasped in an attitude of prayer. Around and around the car, as though in some agitated ritual dance, moved Delia, Martha, Mark Crane, Henri Lenoir, and Dr Rosen.

As we leaped from the hired car and ran towards them, Lenoir gave a cry of triumph, followed by an oath. He had scooped something from, so far as could be seen, the underside of the car just behind the near front wheel. As he straightened himself he was seen to be gripping a small monkey, of the type which used, at that time, to accompany organ grinders. Blood was running from one of Lenoir's fingers.

'Extraordinary,' said Dr Rosen. 'The man told me it was absolutely gentle.' He spoke, now, an English that was correct but somewhat slow, and heavily accented.

He was now seen to be carrying a cage, like the cage of a parrot, and, taking the monkey from Lenoir, he thrust the creature into it and closed the door, and stood looking in at the monkey with a grievous and reproving expression, as of a Minor Prophet shocked once again, but not much surprised, by forwardness and backsliding. He handed the cage over to Jephthah.

'It's a monkey,' shouted Jephthah to his father. 'I let it out by mistake. Dr Rosen's given me a monkey.'

'Male or female?' said Foraker sharply, his thoughts evidently still running on education.

'Male,' said Dr Rosen.

'Ah!' said Foraker.

'I thought,' said Dr Rosen, 'that an animal, for example, a monkey – perhaps especially a monkey – would make a nice present. Amusing, you know, and at the same time educative. As regards natural history, no?'

Foraker brooded an instant over the cage, collected himself suddenly, shouted. 'Happy Birthday,' to Jephthah and leaned into the car to kiss his cheek, strode around the car and embraced Delia, enfolding her in his arms for several seconds, kissed Martha lightly, shook hands warmly with Henri Lenoir and Mark Crane, found himself face to face again with Rosen and shook him warmly by the hand, too. From above our heads, Henriette-Louise-Marie shrieked again, and Foraker threw his head back and waved his hat at her in an elaborate gesture. Then he was at the hired car again, calling to Louis and me to help him take out the cat-basket, the hutch, the boxes, and bundles, and carry them into the apartment.

The monkey cage in one hand, Jephthah stood gaping and gulping at the Persian kitten, the rabbits.

'Couldn't we,' Jephthah said, 'just stay here at home and I'd play with these animals?'

'Not now,' said Foraker. 'Of course not. We're going on this picnic. It's all arranged. You'll have a good time on the picnic.'

'When can I play with the animals?'

'After the picnic.'

Dazed by the hurly-burly, I said to myself that, as soon as this uproar ceased, I must take all possible advantage of the situation. I must find occasion for a serious talk with Rosen. I must ascertain from Mark the latest posture of affairs. I must learn whatever I tactfully could from Lenoir; urge, in a general way, discretion and self-sacrifice. I determined that I would also – for it would be a long day – undertake the difficult task of frankly discussing the whole affair with Delia. Above all, I must conduct my postponed heart-to-heart talk with Martha, who, as she flashed about the room, seemed suddenly more lovely, more desirable than I had ever seen her.

Keyed up to comprehensive action on all fronts, I realized that I must, nevertheless, await a moment when nobody was shouting, when the scene was not dominated by rabbits, petrified with fear and being feverishly coaxed to eat; by a kitten, escaped from its basket and swinging high-up, shrieking, on a window curtain; by a monkey, sunk down suddenly in cynical gloom, and looking now so sick with *Weltschmerz* that it was suspected of grave ill-health, of being at death's door, of being not fit to be left unattended.

This trivial confusion, I decided, must be endured with equanimity until it gave place to the calmer, more propitious atmosphere of a long day in the country. It was hours later, mid-afternoon in fact, before I realized that no such calm was going to supervene, however long that long day might be.

I had a mind to hold that monkey responsible for the way in which events were thwarting my most serious purposes. Its fraudulent display of alarming symptoms just before our departure had achieved its objective. Jephthah had pleaded, Foraker had looked intently at the creature and declared that it was best brought with us, fresh air would be good for it, the picnic cheer it up. Hardly had the engines of the motor-cars begun to throb, Foraker and Louis were still at the cranking handles of the respective machines, when the monkey threw off all semblance of *malaise* and began gaily to gibber and gesticulate. Foraker, who at the first had seemed momentarily nonplussed by the fact of someone else having presented the monkey, while he had thought only of a female cat, had now fully taken over, so to speak, the monkey, adopted it as his own discovery. He showed it off, urging everyone to watch it carefully so as not to miss any of its ingenious and instructive antics.

'There's nothing,' he said to Rosen, 'like a monkey.'

The picnic itself, in a field by the Marne, had been a turmoil of fire-making, food distribution, cork-pulling, champagne bubbling on to the grass, and the dry skins of cold roast chickens flapping in the wind. I thought it was now or never. I suggested to Martha that we go down to the river and look at the boats and quaint barges which were beached or moored a few hundred yards from where we sat. She jumped up and started across the field with me, but halfway across started to turn and call out to the others about the quaintness of those barges, on one of which there was a man playing an accordion. In a moment I heard Foraker shouting to the others that the thing to do was to get a boat and go for a sail.

When we had hired a boat, the ones who got into it were the Foraker family, Martha, Dr Rosen, myself, and the monkey, Foraker at the tiller. Mark, Henri Lenoir, and Louis watched us from the boathouse. We got the ragged bit of sail up and bounded out on to the river. Jephthah sat in a kind of ecstasy, looking at the water passing and then with wide eyes of admiration at his father controlling tiller and sheet. Then he tried to hold the monkey cage on the gunwale of the boat so that the monkey could also appreciate our movement through the water.

Delia said, 'Be careful, Jeph!'

Foraker said, 'Don't do that, Jephthah!'

Dr Rosen said, 'The monkey will be seasick, Jeph ... Jephthah ... Which do you like to be called?'

'His name's Jephthah,' Foraker said.

'But he's usually called Jeph,' said Delia.

'I can't think why,' Foraker said.

'Well,' said Delia, 'it's obvious. Jeph sounds like a sensible kind of name that you hear. Jephthah's so queer-sounding.'

'I,' Foraker said, 'wouldn't say it was in the very least queer-sounding. I've said so, over and over. It's a fine name and it means something, it was my father's name.'

Delia turned to look at him, and as she did so I saw Martha looking from one to the other of them with a strange, excited alertness.

'Just because it was your father's name, all that time ago,' Delia said, 'it doesn't mean to say it's the right name to call a boy by all the time, now. I don't see what your father's got to do with it. We're talking about Jeph, now. Not something a long time ago.'

Foraker's face had gone suddenly hard and cold-looking. He stared at Delia. 'You don't seem to understand things,' he said. 'A name like that's something that means something. It links things together. The past and the future. Jephthah's a great name. "Jeph's" nothing. It hasn't any connection with anything. It's just a thing by itself. Jephthah,' he repeated, rolling it out, his voice vibrant, 'is a great name. It has a past.'

'I don't see what difference it makes. It doesn't,' said Delia, her voice suddenly higher and sharper, 'make any difference at all. Not at all, don't you understand?'

'My God,' Foraker leaned forward, shouting, with a violent gesture, 'it's you who don't understand.'

Almost in time with the abrupt movement of his body and arm, the boat lurched, swung, and trembled, the light boom swung inboard making everyone duck, the sail smacked and flapped loudly, and everyone shouted together. In a half-minute lull between two puffs of wind, the boat slid swiftly and silently sideways and forward, making as though by its own decision, for a long mudbank with reeds on it, which shelved away from the more solid shore. In the sudden silence as the sail stopped smacking, everyone sat absolutely silent, too, looking at the mudbank, and then looking at Foraker.

Like a man who still has half his mind on what he was thinking about before he was interrupted, Foraker tugged irritably at the useless sheet, then pushed hard at the tiller, putting his weight behind his arm as though dealing a straight right to someone's body. We were drifting on the current, nothing happened. Everyone watched him: he sat holding the useless tiller and sheet, and then reached for a paddle. Before he could use it, the boat thudded, shaking, into the reeds and its bow pushed firmly into the mud.

The thud threw Jephthah and his cage into the bottom of the boat. He got up and looked at his father with an expression which was both incredulous and hopeful.

'You meant to do that, didn't you?' he said. 'You wanted us to come ashore just here?'

Delia sat looking straight in front of her. Rosen said, 'We have had an accident.' His tone implied that when out on a motoring picnic one had, pleasantly and inevitably, such things as a drive, a meal, a sail, an accident.

It was impossible to push the boat off the bank. I yelled to the people in the boathouse on the farther shore. They fetched us in a rowing-boat. During the transfer from the sailing-boat, everyone was splashed and wetted. At the landing stage, Delia said, 'Well, now, I suppose, we can go home.'

Louis, who, with the others, had greeted our return, said that he had made inquiries from the people at the landing stage and learned that there was a fair in the country town two miles up the river, a fair with steam merry-go-rounds and coconut shies and shooting galleries. It might, he said, be an entertainment for the boy.

'A-ha!' cried Foraker. 'A fine idea.'

'No, no,' Delia said. 'I want to go home.'

'But,' said Foraker, 'it's Jephthah's birthday. We have to take him to this fair. It'll be fun.'

'You're all rather wet,' Mark said nervously, talking to Foraker and looking at Delia. Lenoir looked on, watchfully.

'It'll be all right,' said Foraker. 'Nothing to worry about.'

At the fair I got myself into a 'flying boat' with Martha, one of a dozen boats which were whirled around at the end of chains attached to a central pillar, rotated by an engine which also played a Viennese waltz. Rosen and Foraker whirled around in the boat ahead of us. I spoke to Martha. She shook her head – too much noise, couldn't hear.

'Martha,' I yelled, 'darling.'

I started to put my arm gently, protectively, around her shoulder, and the boat, swinging out higher and higher, keeled farther over and threw me against her, banging our heads sharply together and painfully crushing my arm between us. It was a small, mean fair, saving steam by giving short rides for the money, so, by the time we had made ourselves less uncomfortable, the thing had slowed down and was stopping, and Jephthah ran up beside our boat holding up the cage so that the monkey could laugh at us.

As we started home, the wind, abating all afternoon, dropped altogether and rain fell. For this, Foraker took credit to himself. It had not rained until now. He drove more furiously than ever; as we passed a public clock in the outer suburbs I saw him look at it sharply and then back again at the clock on the dashboard. We were in visible and continuous danger. As we arrived at his home, he immediately shouted to know whether Louis had kept up with him in the other car, and when he saw it drawing up behind us, told me to hurry and change over to it.

'We're late,' he said.

Delia, just out of the car, turned to stare at him. 'You're not coming in?' she said, in a flat tone of voice.

'How can I?' he said. 'The night shift'll be coming on at Beauvais before we can get there, otherwise.'

Delia's voice broke a little. 'You might have left a little more time,' she said, and walked quickly towards the house. The occupants of the other car joined us.

'Of course,' Foraker said, now holding Jephthah in his arms to lift him from the car, and having to bend his head far back to prevent the monkey grabbing at his hat through the bars of the cage. He kissed Jephthah on the cheek, ran with him a little way towards the apartment, put him down, and ran back towards the hired car.

'We have to drive like hell,' he said to Louis. 'Maybe I'd better drive?'

Louis made an agile jump into the driver's seat. The engine was still running, and the car moved almost before either Foraker or I was seated.

As we lurched over the last few hundred yards of track from the public road at Beauvais to the workshops, Foraker took a final look at the time and let out a happy sigh.

'It's been a successful day,' he said. 'Jephthah enjoyed that picnic.'

We had been at work for more than an hour before I happened to hear him remark to the foreman in Wing C that certain operations must be speeded up somewhat because five days from then a Dr Rosen was coming down to inspect and report on the whole project.

He must have seen me start, and gape at him, for he said in a quite casual tone of voice that he had taken the opportunity of today's outing to extend this invitation to Rosen.

'I didn't,' he said, 'want to have everyone else hearing about it and getting excited – Mark Crane gets excited, you know. I waited until I had a chance to speak to him alone, while we were going around and around in one of those swinging boat things. He's coming all right.'

I found the news that this momentous appointment had been fixed up in a two-minute whirl on one of the hurdy-gurdy boats somehow unnerving, and when I had got over that, I remained obsessed and somewhat dazed by the thought that we were almost on the eve of a decisive event – Rosen's Report on Foraker's Principle. I begged Foraker to let me telephone to

Paris and tell at least Mark and Delia that the date for Rosen's inspection had been fixed.

I found myself looking quickly away from him, so sharp was my sudden suspicion that to him the idea of in any way 'reassuring' Delia was intolerable, simply because it implied that she required reassurance. And I realized that, perhaps, I had been incorrect in my estimate of the consequences that would follow the disclosure that the store of Delia's confidence in Grant Foraker had run out. I had seen the chief danger in the signal, as it were, that this would give to his enemies. Now it occurred to me that the direct impact upon Foraker himself might be even more disruptive. In the course of the day, I decided that at the first opportunity – late that night or in the morning – I would disregard all promises just made to Foraker and inform Mark that Rosen was, after all, virtually on his way, urge him that nothing irreparable should be done until the result of this examination was known.

And then I saw that it was too late. For that evening, on our return to the hotel, I saw in the hall letter-rack, a letter for Foraker from Paris addressed in Delia's sprawling handwriting. I knew it well enough – a laborious scrawl – from the occasions in the past when I had taken letters to the post for her. She had often remarked how she hated writing letters, was incapable of putting on to paper what she felt or meant.

'It would take,' she had said once, 'a matter of life and death to make me write more than a few lines.'

This envelope was ominously bulky. I think I was on the verge of snatching it out of the letter-rack. Then Foraker came into the hall behind me. He took the letter and held it a moment in his hand.

'You know,' he said, 'this is the first letter Delia's written to me since I was down here.'

He went on looking at the outside of it, and I – covertly – at him. Then he put it in the inside pocket of his jacket. Forty-eight hours later, when we were out at the workshop with Dr Rosen stalking prophetically beside us, Foraker suddenly saw some piece of machinery which he thought required some immediate minor adjustment. Before snatching at a spanner and squeezing himself between two oily metal casings, he tore off his jacket and tossed it to me. A bunch of papers fell out of the inner pocket to the floor. As I picked them up I saw that Delia's letter was among them, still unopened.

15

'I expect a person like you, Ned,' said Delia, sitting sideways on the sofa and looking out of the apartment window at the Café du Carrefour as though it were the Taj Mahal, and she seeing it for the first time, 'I mean a person that's a little bit of a prig – because you are, Ned, you know – probably thinks I'm really quite – what's the word? – quite despicable. Not that I would mind, the way things are.'

'It seems,' I said, 'quite natural to me. I don't,' I added honestly, 'know why.'

'It's *perfectly* natural,' she said, moving her shoulders and arms in a smooth stretch of contentment. 'I love Grant. And it's grand and lovely.'

The only thing that seemed at all unnatural to me about the situation – so soon as it was (and so long as it seemed) after the day Dr Rosen finally made his report – was that I, too, should find her behaviour natural. Somewhere at the back of my head a squeaky pencil was scrawling on a slate a different map of the situation, showing Positions *A, B,* and *C*. Position *A*: man apparently bound for fame and glory, loved by woman. Position *B*: man apparently bound for failure, about to be deserted by woman. Position *C*: man suddenly bound for glory again reloved by woman.

'You know,' Delia said, talking softly to the window, 'he gave me back my letter. You guessed about the letter, of course?'

'I saw it when it came to the hotel.'

'And then, you see, when Grant came to tell me the news, he said he wanted a change of clothes, and when he was taking papers out of the pocket of the suit he had on there was my letter – not opened, of course. And then he said he supposed any news in it must be stale by this time and there was no point wasting time reading it and just left it there on the table.'

'I never thought of that,' I said, remembering the brisk little pat Foraker had given to his breast pocket the day he got in the car to drive to Paris with Rosen's report in his small leather handbag.

I have no knowledge whether any copy of the Rosen Report on Foraker's Principle and its 'vehicle' is still extant anywhere. But I must say I think there is fairly good indirect evidence indicating that the document must – after whatever wanderings and concealments – have been in the hands of one or other of the state-financed German research institutes, at Berlin or Hamburg, early in the 1920s.

It was a long document – a score of foolscap pages typed in single-space, wth the figures and the complex equations and the formulae marching and counter-marching formidably across and across it. It was, I suppose, because Rosen wrote it, a model of its kind – an historic scientific assessment of a major achievement.

The essence of Foraker's Principle could be described as the 'marriage' of an accepted theoretical possibility with a material partner, to the end that they might produce progeny in the shape of a machine, a tool, a means of direct action upon the material world. The objective of Rosen's inspection had been to determine whether the offspring so to speak, was sound in its limbs and going to be able to do that for which it had been created.

Examination and test of the model, and of the still not fully completed prototype itself, had been a hideously straining and gruelling affair. And what emerged, in language duller than that of a report on the potentialities of a new branch insurance office in the provinces, was news of a revolution as great as Foraker had claimed; of a machine capable – by all applicable tests and principles – of mastering the air in a fashion which, for the present, could render the performance of every existing flying-machine primitive by comparison, and opened, for the future, possibilities which the inventors of existing machines had never dreamed of, possibilities, indeed, which to existing types of flying-machines were, and always would be, closed. And this was not some machine which might accomplish this revolution 'on paper', but a thing growing to completion there in the Beauvais sheds, a thing which in a period calculable in months or even weeks, could take off with its one-man load, rush through the air at a speed which in those days sounded like an impudent lie, and land safely again after a journey that would mark the beginning of an era.

Characteristically, Rosen had refused to disclose his impressions and conclusions until the report had been finally completed. Then he spent a day and a night alone with Foraker at the works going through it with him paragraph by paragraph. When I reached the works early the next morning from Beauvais, Rosen had already left for Paris. I found Foraker sitting by himself in the tiny office, his chair tilted so that he could get as much of himself as possible into the patch of weak winter sunshine which came levelly in from the east. His face was solemn with the serenity of triumph. And for an hour or more he talked to me about the report in a manner more gravely composed than I had ever seen him use before.

Only at the end, as though coming back to trivialities, he suddenly laughed, and when I looked at him questioningly laughed again and said, 'Blériot!' He stopped and stared at the sunrise, tapping the open page of the report. 'Three hundred and fifty m.p.h.,' he said, and broke again into a laugh that shook him all over.

It was just after that that he got abruptly to his feet and said that he must be off to Paris. He lifted his arms in what started as the stretching movement of a tired man, and ended, as we crashed through the mistily chill morning, in a gesture towards the sky that might have been one either of thanksgiving or defiance.

On his return the following evening his expression, however, was serene, and from the outset I noted an oddly unaccustomed gentleness in his manner. His comments on his Paris visit were commonplace. It had been 'fine' to see Delia, he had had a 'couple of good sessions' with Mark and with Henri

Lenoir, everything was 'going along fine'. He had not seen Halm. 'Halm, poor fellow,' he said, 'is suffering with this stomach ulcer he has. He's in bed, has to lie absolutely quiet for a couple of weeks. Can't see anyone.'

The 'poor fellow' took me considerably aback. I waited for some statement to the effect that if Halm had an ulcer, that was because Halm was such a fool. No such statement came. On the contrary, at dinner on the following day, reverting to the subject, he said. 'The trouble with Halm, the reason he has this trouble with his stomach, is just he worries too much.' Then he said, 'You know, Ned, it's been a trying time for all those associated with me, this last few weeks. Because they didn't have, you see, any way of knowing just what was going on. Mark Crane, for instance. And Henri Lenoir. Even Delia. You take,' said Foraker, 'Christopher Columbus. Have you ever given thought, Ned, to what you might call the human circle of Christopher Columbus? His wife, his circle of friends and associates? There he is in Cádiz, and he says he's going off to discover the Indies, and there they are, and they believe him, but they don't have any idea how he's going to do it. And time goes by, months and months go by, and he goes running all over Spain – making plans he says, necessary preparations – and there they are, waiting. And then he disappears down there in the shipyards and docks of Cádiz, and they go on waiting. And everyone around them is telling them "why the man's crazy" – he isn't going to get to the Indies that way, not in those crazy little boats. First, everyone says he's crazy and, then, they say he's fraudulent. Money under false pretences, they say. Some kind of a hoax.

'You have to realize, Ned,' he said, with gentle sternness as he thoughtfully carved up his steak, 'that those associates of Christopher Columbus are up against a big strain. It wouldn't be surprising, nor worthy of our censure, if some of them were to begin to think it was about time to leave Christopher Columbus to his own inexplicable devices and get themselves back into real life in their home towns.

'Naturally, Christopher Columbus knows all along he's on to the biggest thing of his day and age, but he can't fully explain all that to anyone else. And, anyway, he does not have the time. And then one day there come the glad tidings that he really is going to set off across the ocean in those crazy little boats. And, in so and so many weeks after that, he is either going to be at the bottom of the ocean, or he is going to be the greatest man of his day and age. What a day it is when those tidings come! A day of gladness and relief, Ned.'

He ate in silence for a few seconds and then said, 'And remember, Ned, Christopher Columbus' project was a smaller one than mine. In its significance for man in his relations with the material world. Considerably smaller.'

This statement he made quite casually, as though the truth of that enormous claim were so obvious as to be hardly worth stating at all.

Foraker had instructions for me in connection with the report – the report in its physical aspect as a bundle of almost inconceivably explosive documents. I was happy to see that his mood of benevolent understanding did not seem to be relaxing his vigilance in this respect.

One copy had been retained by Rosen. One had been concealed by Foraker in a place, he said, where 'if I were to drop dead tomorrow, it would remain until the Day of Judgement'. The other two he had handed, temporarily, over to Henri Lenoir. They were to be studied, though not copied, by the members of the inner circle of Lenoir's group of oppositional technicians at the Ministry of War. This, it appeared, was in line with a general understanding reached between Foraker and Lenoir at the very beginning of their association.

Tomorrow, I was to go to Paris, receive those two copies from Lenoir's own hands, and, in his presence, destroy them.

I did so. Lenoir was throbbing, could be said to be almost physically vibrating with a scarcely controlled excitement. He was silent until the work of destruction was over, and then burst out with a cry of admiration.

'So the old rascal was right after all.'

He positively danced about the room.

'There were moments – you know as well as I do – when I and my friends were very, very suspicious. We thought him a clown. And, mind you, he did do some clownish things. Perhaps it is indispensable for a man of his type of abilities to act clownishly some of the time.'

'I think,' I said, 'that when he clowns it is a way of expressing his confidence in his superiority to the rest of the world. He would think that other people might ruin themselves by clowning, and he likes to prove that he can clown and not be ruined.'

'Of course,' said Lenoir, 'the degree of superiority he imagines himself to have is an illusion. On the other hand ...' He developed the theory that it is perhaps only by self-delusion that people achieve great objectives. A person with a 'correct' estimate of his own probable capacities and potentialities would achieve very little. He would think himself lucky just to be able to stay alive for seventy years or so in this dangerous world.

'The really great conclusions,' said Lenoir, 'are those drawn from entirely false premises. Victory is always the result of a noble miscalculation.'

As I rose to go, he took my hands as though saying good-bye for a long time. He observed my surprise.

'No,' he said, 'I shall see you again, I hope, soon and often. I am just saying good-bye to a period in our lives which now, I think, is at an end. The period between now and the moment when Grant Foraker really flies will be different. Very exciting, but different.'

I said rather embarrassedly that I supposed it would be.

'You are thinking,' said Lenoir truthfully, 'of my relationship with Delia Foraker. That, too, proves what I have just been saying about miscalculations. I swear to you, Hastings, that when I started to make a little pretence of running after her (that is what I thought I was doing), I did so purely with the idea that to give such an impression to the world at large would be of assistance in our work. It was desirable, evidently, that one of our group should be able to maintain constant contact with Foraker quite openly, without all the delay caused by meetings in holes and corners in case of being spied on. I intended simply to give to watching eyes the impression that if I saw a good deal of Foraker it was merely as a cover for my attentions to his wife. Fortunately, I have the sort of reputation which made it easy for people to believe that.'

He pirouetted slowly on the tips of his toes.

'I was even prepared to pretend to be madly in love with her. I intended her to fall in love with me so that she would not have to act the part, and thus the whole thing would be more convincing to the watching eyes. It was all entirely convincing – but what I had left out of my calculation was the possibility that I might fall madly in love with her.'

At the door he recalled me to speak words of warning. 'All these theories of mine,' he said, 'about the value of illusion and delusion – they are all very well in their way, my dear Hastings, but remember that they are partly illusions, too. Remember that from now on we are up against the most formidable realities. You know as well as I do that there are plenty of people of importance who will do anything – but anything – to encompass the ruin of Grant Foraker. You consider me melodramatic? I mean to be.'

I said that I supposed that if word did get about in the proper quarters that Foraker's Principle really 'worked', could, in actual fact, provide a weapon of war of inestimable power, it might be possible slowly to acquire for Foraker some measure of official protection from the Ministry itself.

Lenoir laughed in my face.

'How innocent you are, my dear Hastings. The Ministry is already committed to a policy of non-encouragement of aviation as a military weapon – a major military weapon, that is. The cavalrymen are opposed to it. No less so are the gunners and – it goes without saying – the infantry. Very soon now, the secret Military Commission will make its report. It will take the same line. Surely you can see that in these circumstances the more evidence there is of the efficacy of some aerial weapon, the more anxious all concerned must be to suppress it? Such evidence is an accusation of their judgement and good sense. To admit it would be to lose prestige.'

On visiting the Forakers' apartment, I was ambushed by Henriette-Louise-Marie, silently conspiratorial. She slid into my hand a letter.

'It is a communication,' she said, 'from Madame Robinson.'

As I made an impatient gesture, as though to push the letter away, Henriette-Louise-Marie folded both her hands over mine and the letter and pressed them together.

'You should read it,' she said, 'it is some kind of warning.'

To avoid a scene, I stuffed the letter, a thick one, into my pocket, opened, and glanced at it in the fiacre as I drove across Paris, saw that it consisted of not less than a dozen pages closely written with pale ink in a copybook hand, read a few lines here and there (references to Free Masons, Jews, and – unintelligibly – coloured pins), and decided that there was neither time nor necessity to read it just then.

I called upon Mark and, once again, an attitude I now recognize as agreeably candid repelled me by what I considered its materialistic vulgarity. The Rosen report had made him merry as a grig.

Mark was quite simply relieved, and said so. He was relieved about the business prospects; he felt sure that, with Rosen's collaboration, he could, as soon as Halm was well enough, convince the financier that his investment had been not only sound, but a brilliant coup.

And, quite unashamedly, he was relieved about Delia. He was just plainly glad, and admitted it, that he was not going to whirl off to Ohio on the magic carpet of a Great Love. He stepped off the Great Love with the pusillanimous satisfaction of a tourist who had the opportunity to shoot the rapids of some mighty river, and at the last moment the canoe has been taken by someone else.

'Things,' said Mark, beaming at me in a manner I found somewhat disgusting, 'are going to be a lot more normal from now on.'

But when I reported to Foraker next day at breakfast, he said, 'What Mark has to explain to poor Halm' – still poor Halm, I noticed – 'is that whatever happens he can't lose; suppose I get up there, and some detail goes wrong. Nothing basic. Nothing basic can go wrong. But some detail. Some little thing that would be adjusted in later models. So the machine hits the earth at' – his voice dropped to a whisper as it always did when he mentioned that terrifying figure – 'three hundred and fifty miles per hour. And Grant Foraker is no longer of our Company. But where, meantime, is Halm? He's in the money. Big money. Because once that machine out there has gone streaking across the sky of Paris, Ned, every Government in the world is going to be bidding for the rights to it. Millions and millions. He can't lose. Halm doesn't have to worry.'

The thought of what would happen if 'some detail' were to go wrong, seemed to have no effect upon the high-charged currents of goodwill which radiated from him. Unless, possibly, the idea of so spectacular an end actually intensified the feelings which had pervaded him since the completion of Rosen's report. And now, when I belatedly remembered, and mentioned to him, that I had in my pocket a communication from Mrs Robinson, the thought of the Robinsons seemed only to sadden him. Mr Robinson, he opined, was an unfortunate man, a victim of the past. He directed me to read the letter immediately. Indeed, he took it from me, sheet by sheet, as I read it, and read it, too, with the concerned air of a man reading from, or about, an old personal friend he has not seen for a long time.

One looks, at the outset, for some immediate explanation of why Mrs Robinson sees fit to write to me at all. None appears. Instead, as if she were a relative passing on interesting family news, an opening statement to the effect that 'Mr Robinson has of late been exceedingly busy and, in my opinion, is overworking.' No mention of how or why this is supposed to be any concern of mine. In place of that, a brief review of Mr Robinson's activities. Things have 'gone as well as can be expected in all the circumstances'. It emerges that despite the 'misunderstanding with the Major,' Mr Robinson has not only pursued but largely extended his campaign to 'get to the bottom of the various conspiracies' and 'set things to rights'. Money, while 'not just exactly plentiful' has been adequate to requirements. (Providence here receives a cool acknowledgement that it has done its duty.) The chosen agents of Providence – Mrs Robinson makes no pretence that they are not somewhat strange agents, but their existence and character show the truth of the lines stating that God works in a mysterious way – are of course M. Paca and his friends. They continue, it seems, to pay to Mr Robinson a percentage of what they make by their exploitation of Mr Robinson's 'Gift'. This is not to say that they are entirely content. Through the coldly disapproving, actually contemptuous eyes of Mrs Robinson, we catch a glimpse of the frantic condition of Paca and Company. Intoxicated by the possibilities of Mr Robinson's gift, they have gradually lost the capacity to deal with reality by more normal means. ('In my opinion they would have been more prudent to have continued their regular business, using these special opportunities only occasionally.') One may deduce from this passage in the letter that what M. Paca and the others of the trio have achieved as a result of their possession of this alchemist's stone is that they work rather harder than they ever did before, that they have a good deal more money than they did before, but are unhappy because they do not have a hundred times as much, and that they are half-crazy from morning to night with nervous excitement, apprehension, and speculative calculation.

So far, so good. But, Mrs Robinson repeats, Mr Robinson is overworking. She, here, in a methodical fashion, lists some of the fields in which he toils, the battle-fronts of his struggle. This is where we come to the coloured pins. Mr Robinson has a map. Pins with various coloured heads denote the advances and retreats upon these varied fronts – the front against the Jews, the front against the Free Masons, etc., etc. When Mr Robinson is not searching the newspapers for information, he is studying this great map which hangs upon the wall of his study – it covers two walls of the study now – and is keeping it up to date in the light of the information so acquired. He sometimes works at it all night, in a condition of the most intense excitement.

'Sometimes, I am of opinion that the task he has undertaken is overtaxing his powers.'

What then is to be done? (I had to read the next page through twice, before I could believe that I was understanding it.)

What is to be done, says Mrs Robinson, is that Mr Robinson should have some reliable assistant, a person with some understanding of the world, but a person very different in type from M. Paca and his friends. A person with a decent, respectable background. Also someone who knows and understands Mr Robinson. And what she suggests is that – again 'despite past misunderstandings' – the proper person, considering the small availability of such persons in Paris, is Mr Edward Hastings.

She can well understand, Mrs Robinson proceeds coolly, that Mr Hastings may have some hesitation in the matter, on account of his very unfortunate association with Mr Foraker. She can understand, too, that a man of the stamp of Mr Foraker – his character and activities all too well known to Mr Robinson – could temporarily exert a powerful influence upon a young man not just too familiar with such character and activities.

In case Mr Hastings should still have any hesitation in the matter, Mrs Robinson wishes to apprise Mr Hastings of a fact until now unknown to him – namely, that Mr Foraker is doomed. His destruction is going to come about at a very early date. To be exact, ninety days from this present writing. Mr Robinson has 'seen this'. Moreover, his vision of this impending destruction has been unusually clear. And this clarity of pre-vision is, doubtless, a reward to Mr Robinson. For at the moment of this particular vision he became aware that, in some way of which the exact nature was not precisely vouchsafed, the doom of the man Foraker is a result of Mr Robinson's own unremitting efforts.

He has had a perfectly clear vision of a field or open space and upon it a machine of strange design, a flying-machine, evidently, for it has a kind of wings, but with no resemblance at all to such flying-machines as Mr Robinson has previously seen in actuality or in photographs or drawings. There are a lot of people about whom Mr Robinson does not recognize. He does, however, recognize the presence of Mr Foraker. Mr

Foraker seems to be approaching the strange machine, and is about to fly in it. Suddenly a kind of blackness comes over the picture – a destructive, explosive blackness. Mr Robinson is aware with absolute clarity that disaster has struck and that Foraker is dead.

These being the facts, concludes Mrs Robinson – writing as though she had just learned that a train I was thinking of taking had been cancelled – it will be apparent to Mr Hastings that to sever his connection with Mr Foraker and co-operate with Mr Robinson is a course which must commend itself alike to idealism and to prudence.

I was annoyed to find myself hesitating for a fraction of a second before passing across the table to Foraker the page containing the account of Mr Robinson's vision. He read it and the succeeding pages with no change in his expression of interested concern.

'Of course,' I said, when I saw that he had finished, 'they are both raving mad. Stark staring crazy.'

Foraker looked at me in sincere surprise. 'You think so?' he said. 'I'd be sorry to think that. Poor Sandy Robinson. You know, Ned, "mad" is an awfully big word. It seems to me that within the limits of their understanding, according to their lights, this is a perfectly sane kind of a letter.

'According to them, I am an evil force in this world. The centre of evil forces, so far as I understand it. You are a good young man, led astray. Robinson, who is good, too, needs you. Or rather, as I interpret this, she is really alarmed about him having too much to do, saving the world single-handed. The way she sees it, the saviour and the world together may go under for want of a competent personal secretary. So why should she not do her best to fill that need?'

'But all this nonsense about his "vision"?'

'Well, first of all,' Foraker said, 'she believes it. And, secondly,' he was getting slowly to his feet, 'what d'you mean "nonsense"? How do we know he didn't have a vision like that?'

He stood up, flicking crumbs from his waistcoat with the table napkin. 'Incidentally,' he said, 'I went over the time-schedule with them out at the works yesterday, and we've provisionally fixed the date for the big take-off. Ninety days from yesterday was how we had it reckoned out.'

I stared straight in front of me, hearing Foraker's boots marching across the floor, and the waiter chinking crockery at the sideboard. I must have jumped up and run after him, saying, I suppose, something incoherent. For we were already in the hall when he turned and looked down at me with an odd smile.

'There's nothing to worry about, Ned,' he said. 'Suppose he saw that? You wouldn't want me to change plans on that account, would you?'

I said stupidly that it was very queer, all the same.

'Looked at in its proper perspective,' said Foraker ponderously, 'I don't see there's anything more strange or wonderful about Robinson having visions of the future than there is about my machine out there.'

The car was at the door, and he pulled on his big motoring coat. He began to laugh.

'You know,' he said, 'what with him foreseeing the future and me making it, it seems to me we two Lanarkshire lads aren't doing badly.'

This thought evidently gave him deep satisfaction. He smiled contentedly to himself all the way out to the works, where I half expected to learn that his time-schedule of ninety days between now and the 'big day' had been invented on the spur of the moment as he read Mrs Robinson's letter. Not so. The decision had, just as he had said, been made yesterday. And once again I found myself caught up and whirled along by the force of a new gale of activity, as Foraker drove towards that ninety-days-distant goal.

My task now was to maintain liaison between Beauvais and Paris. To use the postal or telephone services for communication with Mark Crane, Henri Lenoir, or Dr Rosen was judged imprudent. And it seemed to me that the greater part of my time was spent either on the road or in the train. What with weariness, intense concentration, and a perpetual sense of hurry the days went by in a sort of dream – a nightmarish sort indeed, because almost every day, or so it appeared to me, some minor hitch threatened suddenly to develop into a ruinous tangle, some molehill to grow into an obstructive mountain.

Henri Lenoir said, 'Speed, speed, my friend, and still more speed. There are too many people in this city busy telling Halm nasty things.' He stopped to reflect and added, 'I suppose it may be necessary for us to lend him some of the technicians of our group to help speed things up.'

'Wouldn't that be risky for them? With regard to the Ministry, I mean. In view of the official attitude . . .'

'Certainly it would,' Lenoir agreed gloomily. 'On the other hand, I and my friends are pretty well organized, you know. And pretty well trained in working under cover. And then think of the prize!'

His gloom dropped from him and his eyes blazed. He spoke in a kind of ecstasy. 'Beauvais to beyond the Atlas in a few hours . . .' And it was in this outburst of Lenoir that I heard for the first time of the true scope of the flight to be attempted. I gaped at him.

'Why, yes,' he said, laughing with excitement, 'it has to be sensational, you see. A whizz across the Mediterranean. Europe to Africa. Something that will electrify the world. Foraker,' he said, laughing more, 'wanted to make the objective Timbuktu. He thought from the point of view of creating maximum sensation that would be ideal. Unfortunately, we have not – our group hasn't – suitable contacts with the military there to make proper preparations for the reception, so to speak, of the machine on arrival. But,' he concluded, 'speed, speed, speed!'

All these hitches and hints together rendered me almost sick with anxiety. Two or three times each week I met Martha in Mark's office or at the Forakers' apartment, and once or twice we drank coffee together, but in my exhausted and over-excited nervous condition I met her almost as though she were a stranger, an agreeable stranger whom I met now because she, too, happened to be engaged in the same business as myself. And she, it seemed to me, met me on the same plane.

My conversations with her, like my conversations with the others, revolved only around the Foraker project.

The shops and streets became filled with Christmas, and this, too, seemed to us a strange irrelevance. The festival atmosphere had the effect of increasing our sense of isolation from the everyday world. We felt dedicated and austere. Feeling like that, we stood together – it was 21 December – at the window of Mark's office, looking out at the white blaze of the big store across the street, and the thrust and counter-thrust of the crowds shopping. The telephone rang, and it was Foraker, wanting to speak to me. I took the receiver, and heard him shouting something I could not at first understand. He repeated it.

'Christmas!' he shouted. 'About Christmas!'

As I stammered back at him, he became impatient. Surely I knew Christmas was coming? Well then, naturally, there had to be a Christmas party. It must be organized. In other years, he explained, he always undertook this – it was a sort of present for Delia, so that she had the party without the trouble of arranging it all. But this year it was going to be difficult for him. He was going to find it rather difficult to take time off to see about it.

He explained this as though it were a point I might question. So, instead, would I please apply myself to this small task. For Christmas Eve. Just a party of family and friends. Like the picnic. But it must be properly prepared – drinks of every description, for example, must be ordered. And there had to be a huge cold supper. Jephthah, Foraker said, looked forward to something special in the way of a feast.

Reading, apparently, from a notebook – after telling me to get a pencil and put things down carefully – Foraker listed foods which it was essential to include. They always had those at the Christmas Eve party. Didn't I remember last year's party, he said. I remembered, with a pang, as though I had been guilty of some kind of treachery, that last year I had rejected Foraker's invitation in favour of an evening with one of the girls from Mark's favourite cabaret.

In that case, Foraker said, I must be careful to list everything just as he read it over to me. And this year, he thought it would be a good thing to have music. Nothing was better than an accordion player.

I said, wildly, that I would try to get hold of one.

'But I know the very man,' Foraker said.

'Good,' I said, relieved.

'Don't you remember,' Foraker said, 'the day of our picnic, at that place we took the boat? On the pier at the boathouse there was a man playing the accordion? He was fine. The thing to do is to get hold of him.'

'But, good God,' I said, 'there must be hundreds of them in Paris. Besides, he may not be a professional at all. He may not want to come. He ...'

I gave it up. I knew I should have to get out somehow to that place by the river and find a man who, weeks ago, had played an accordion at the boathouse one afternoon, and persuade him to attend a Christmas Eve party at the home of a Mr Foraker in Paris.

'Nothing to worry about,' Foraker said. 'That man's good. He plays *well.*' He added, after a pause, as though finally demolishing some obstructionism on my part, 'Don't you see, Ned, the accordion will be suitable for the monkey? Probably it will dance to it. Rosen bought that monkey from an organ grinder. And, anyway, it'll be nice to have music this year. After all, Ned, this is a kind of send-off party, too.'

This last casual remark rang in my ears as I went about the preparations, and hummed its exhilarating, menacing tune to us as we gathered under the coloured lights and silver-paper chains and streamers which swung across the apartment above the champagne bottles and turkeys.

As it turned out, there had been no difficulty in securing the attendance of the accordion player from the boathouse up the river. It had cost me a tedious suburban journey, and more than an hour of inquiry before I located him – a M. Marigaud, by profession a market-gardener. After that, everything had been easy. Yes, indeed, M. Marigaud remembered the big Englishman or American or whatever he was who had taken a boat that day. A very fine man, who had told him a most interesting story about an accordion player in New York who was famous. Yes, indeed, he would be more than happy to play at such a party – an honour and a privilege. The question was simply: Could he leave his family on Christmas Eve? His family, I said, would unquestionably be welcome at Mr Foraker's. It was merely a question of how many? So that provision might be made.

In the event there were six of M. Marigaud's party besides himself – his wife, his eldest son, his eldest son's wife, and three relatives of his wife or his son's wife. By the time I arrived, a little late, they, and everyone else, were dancing to the jig of M. Marigaud's accordion. I was late because Dr Rosen had, at the last moment, telephoned to me at Mark's office, saying that he had – after several efforts to see Halm again and re-impress him with the essence of his report – suddenly been asked by Halm to come and see him immediately at the house Halm that had in St Cloud. He needed a file of papers that he had lent to Mark.

The door was opened first by Henriette-Louise-Marie, who, however, was thrust aside by Jephthah, and he, gripping my hand, dragged me to the room which normally was Foraker's study to show me his Christmas presents. Those from his father included a mechanical train and a paid-up advance subscription to the forthcoming Eleventh Edition of the *Encyclopaedia Britannica*. This small document Jephthah caressed with pleasure and pride.

'This you see,' he told me, 'is of permanent value. It will be of use and value through many a long year to come. He told me so. And also it has the whole of the Crusades and everything else. The entire thing is going to be in it. Everything. Highly valuable. And,' said Jephthah, looking at me challengingly, 'enduring. Thus it would not matter, he says, if he were to get knocked on the head tomorrow – I could study everything that's going to be in this book they're going to send me – don't you see? – and it would be all right. I think so.' He held the little paper pulled taut between his two hands and studied it with the expression of a person studying a big cheque. Henriette-Louise-Marie at the doorway bowed nearly double, the feudal retainer in the presence of the adored young master.

From the room across the passage came the lilt and moan of the accordion, and in a moment I found myself taken by the hand by Martha, and we were waltzing in company with Foraker and Delia, with Mark who was dancing with one of the Marigauds, with Lenoir, who was dancing with another, and dancing, too, were still other Marigauds and many members, too, of the family of Louis, the chauffeur from Beauvais, whose wife was there, and his eldest son and his eldest son's wife, and a number of their relatives.

'Darling Martha,' I said.

'Darling Ned,' she said.

Foraker had stopped dancing now and was singing softly to the melody of the accordion. And, looking at him, I kept thinking – and by their faces one could see that it was what Delia and Mark Crane and Henri Lenoir and Martha were thinking too – this is the send-off. In thirty days and nights, we were all naturally thinking, Grant Foraker will either have accomplished something beyond all our imaginations, something beyond the imagination of almost everyone in the world but himself, or he will be dead somewhere, dispersed upon the surface of the sea or the mountains or the sands of the desert.

Delia said to me, 'I suppose it's only what everyone feels when someone goes to war or whatever.'

'I suppose it is,' I said.

'It doesn't make it any better,' she said.

We turned together to look at Foraker, and what he was doing was acting as *compère* to that monkey, which Jephthah now had brought in from the nursery room and let out of its cage. Sure enough, the monkey had leaped upon the shoulder of M. Marigaud with the accordion, and there was performing a dance of a nature at once dignified and gay. And Foraker, looking as though he had invented dancing monkeys and was introducing the species to the world, was beating time for it, drawing to it the attention of the company, and watching its every movement with pride and affection.

Mark, his hands in his pockets, looked on with his eyes popping slightly.

'Say what you will, Ned,' he said to me, 'say what you will.' He pulled his hands out of his pockets and stretched his arms in a gesture of universal admiration and goodwill. He gazed at me and added, 'Nothing anyone can say matters now. It pales, Ned. It absolutely pales.'

It seemed to me that champagne – the party had been going on for nearly two hours now – had caused Mark for once to express, however incoherently, some sort of truth.

'It does, Mark,' I told him earnestly. 'It does.'

'For instance,' Mark said, 'on such a night as this, I could tell Grant all. All. Henri Lenoir could tell all. Delia could tell all. Grant could tell all. And it would pale. Entirely pale. Entirely pale into insignificance compared to those things which are to come. It would, you know, Ned.'

'Yes, Mark,' I said. 'It would.'

'And Martha,' said Mark. 'That beautiful girl. She could tell all. And on such a night as this you'd say, "It's all right," you'd say. "I understand it all." '

'I expect I should, Mark,' I said.

Mark became a shade censorious. 'Don't,' he said, 'say you expect you would, say you *know* you would. You know as well as I do she's been madly in love with Grant Foraker ever since she set eyes on him. What more natural? You know and I know, Ned, because we are old friends and companions in arms, that what happened a few weeks ago was a big blow to that sweet and beautiful girl. What more natural? She was buoyed up by a great hope.'

He paused to gaze thoughtfully at Martha, dancing now in the arms of one of the Marigauds.

'A great hope,' he said solemnly. 'She believed that Delia was going to leave Grant Foraker. I believed it. Delia believed it. Everyone believed it. And what she felt was, Ned – and what more natural? – that this was her moment. This was the moment where she, more worthy, Ned, of a great man's love, would step into that rightful place which so rightfully and naturally was hers.'

They speak of a person's life passing before him in a flash. At this moment it seemed to me that the whole of my own and Martha's life since I had known her whizzed past my eyes – upside down. Or rather, for the first time, right way up. Although this thing Mark had said was strange, and catastrophic, and nearly incredible, I knew the very moment he said it that it was true.

I should have thought that the shock of such a disclosure would have pretty well bowled me over. I actually said to myself, 'This is a shattering blow.' And, at the same time, I was aware of not being shattered. On the contrary. It seemed that Foraker's imminent departure, the grandeur of his enterprise, the enormity of the whole event, had impregnated the atmosphere like an increase in the oxygen content, which, being breathed, gave a sense of immunity to ordinary rules, lets, hindrances, and distresses.

Across the room I watched Martha among the dancers with love and understanding. Very much increased love, I mean, and, naturally, very much increased understanding. With all my heart I wished her well. For a moment I believed I even felt sorrow on her behalf that her plans had gone so awfully awry. But not much sorrow, nor for very long, because I thought to myself that very soon, now that I understood everything, I should cause her to transmute this perfectly intelligible, and as it seemed to me at that moment, really admirable, feeling for Foraker – old enough, I smiled to myself, to be her father – into a different but essentially more realistic feeling for myself, a more suitable object.

There would be difficulties to overcome, obviously. The situation as I saw it was a challenge. I should overcome these difficulties and meet this challenge.

In fact I should start to do it almost immediately. I danced presently with Martha, and presently I drew her aside, isolated her in Foraker's former study among the piles of Jephthah's Christmas presents. There I told her that I knew and understood all. All, I said. I took it for granted that she would understand what I thought I really meant. And she did, immediately. I do not recall after all these years just what she said, but whatever it was it showed that she, too, had breathed in the atmosphere which gave that sense of immunity – a sense, too, of having seven league boots, and ability to roll mountains into molehills.

We were in the middle of a luminous kind of conversation on these matters arising, when it seemed that gradually the study was invaded by other people. Although invasion is hardly the word because, while under other circumstances we should have resented their intrusion, in the circumstances of that evening we felt it to be not an interruption but some kind of continuation. Delia came in and Foraker and Henri Lenoir and Mark Crane, and Mark Crane was making a sort of speech. Looking at Henri Lenoir he said that we Anglo-Saxons were in the unfortunate position of not being able, like other races, to give physical vent to our feelings. We never, he said, showed our emotions. He sobbed. Tears actually ran from his eyes. Henri Lenoir, composed yet electric with excitement, pirouetted as he, too, made a little speech – a perfect little speech such as would have been suitable for almost any occasion upon which one wanted to say that one entertained sentiments of the highest admiration for the departing hero, that heroism of this quality had rarely been equalled, and that France – the true France, the France which throughout history had, etc., etc., etc. – would never forget.

Somewhere just before the end of this Foraker was making a speech, too. Even in that oxygenated atmosphere I felt a little bit surprised at one or two of his observations. He said that he felt that he owed to everyone present an apology. (This phrase which seemed to me in Foraker's mouth a contradiction in terms was the phrase which caused me to pay serious attention.) Yes, he felt, an apology was due to one and all. How often for example, had he, with a minimum knowledge of the workings of business and finance, in his arrogance and haste, overridden, and even derided the thoughtful, prudent, and expert suggestions of Mark Crane. How often had he failed to appreciate just what the work of Henri Lenoir and his friends meant to him, to them, and to France. How grossly had he failed to realize, above all, the loyalty of his long-suffering wife, how extravagantly he had drawn upon it, how little he had done to justify such behaviour.

On an evening when almost anything seemed credible, I was yet almost incredulous as I heard Foraker's great voice declaring that if the events of the past few weeks had taught him nothing else they had taught him humility. But, should he return in glory from his enterprise, this lesson would not be lost upon him and he hoped that one and all would find in the future that when they had to deal with Grant Foraker they had to deal with a man repentant of past errors, and determined that henceforth his ideal would be Humility.

'Like,' he said, 'Christopher Columbus when *he* came back.'

As naturally as they had come into the room they left it, leaving Martha and myself again alone together. It was the moment for a cool absolutely realistic appraisal of our situation. I pointed out and she pointed out that we were not by any means living in the 1890s. She spoke at some length on the subject of the emancipation of Women, I spoke enthusiastically of the position of the new Viennese psychologists. We agreed that the proper thing to do for people so sensitive and enlightened as ourselves was to give ourselves time to examine the entire situation with proper detachment. Almost immediately we were in a fiacre thrusting through a flurry of Christmas Eve snow on the way to the Rue St Jacques.

The snow picked out the gargoyles on the garden wall and they peered at me through the window of the bedroom, reminding me that this was the climax of a dream, that Prospero's wand had waved.

It was morning – but only so to speak, a technical, 3.30 a.m., morning – when from the street came the familiar roar of a particular motor-car and a couple of moments later an insistent uproar at the outer door. Half in a dream and still incredulous that such a thing could really happen, I was aware that Foraker was at the street door, was shouting to the somnolent and hostile concierge, was bounding up the stairs, was hammering on the door of my own apartment. I ran through the outer room and opened the door to him and it was as though this were some scene which, although terrible, had been somehow rehearsed. Whether or not he knew that Martha was there I had no idea and it seemed not to matter. In a thick urgent undertone, addressing himself most of the time to the back of his knuckles which he kept examining with care, he told me he wanted me, I was to come with him at once, we were going to see Halm, at St Cloud. With that same rehearsed feeling I explained to Martha something that to her needed no explanation, bundled into my clothes and before I was rightly aware of leaving the building was joggling beside Foraker westwards across Paris with the snow whipping at me from one side and from the other Foraker's fierce growl telling me a story of bitterness and disaster.

Rosen had telephoned. He had just returned from St Cloud. He had seen Halm and the reason for Halm's sudden summons had been the fact that, that very morning, the morning of Christmas Eve, Halm had at last received from his *homme de confiance* the approximate text of the report of the Military Commission on Aviation which was going to be published just before the meeting of the Chamber in the New Year. Rosen had seen Halm. Halm told him that he now knew for a certainty that the report was not merely going to throw considerable cold water on the whole conception of aviation as a weapon in warfare but was going out of its way – and here one saw the hand of the 'enemy' – to denigrate and asperse those who, it alleged, were seeking to exploit a natural public interest in aviation for grotesque projects which any practitioner of applied science could tell him were, at the best, chimerical and, at the worst, plain swindling. This section of the report, though without mentioning his name, pointed as clearly as possible to Foraker and Foraker's Principle. It went considerably further than the British report published in the previous year.

As a consequence Halm had informed Rosen that he refused to associate himself any longer with Mr Foraker, and, when Rosen protested, he said that on the one hand he did not choose to be swindled and on the other, even supposing that Foraker's Principle were 'some good', it was no good to him because the moment the report was published all possibility of interesting 'bigger money' in such a project would vanish, there would be no possible market for any such product, anybody who attempted to finance further such an undertaking would be regarded as a fool and a dupe, and, therefore, his only course, with an eye to not only his investment in Foraker but to his position in the financial world generally, was to cut his losses, place an immediate embargo on all future activity at the Beauvais works, and hold all physical assets there as some kind of compensation against his certain losses.

It was one of those moments when one does not know whether the awful cold one feels is physical, because of the snow and the racketing pace of the car towards St Cloud, or a cold in the soul because the news is what it is.

'We are going to see Halm,' Foraker said.

'Yes,' I said, with assurance but without hope.

16

Halm wanted to be understood. This was the element in the situation which gave to the episode its peculiarly grotesque quality and has remained through all these years as my dominating memory of the scene at St Cloud. Possibly, too, it provides the reason why the scene remains in my mind as a thing apart, bizarre but almost light-hearted, like the farcical curtain-raiser to a performance of tragedy.

There was our entry – a man servant with a German accent trying to go through the proper formalities of asking our business, having us wait while he informed his master of our presence, and Foraker sailing in past him with an air as overpowering and violent as a blow. He had been to the villa before, and found without hesitation the door of the room where Halm, in scarlet smoking jacket embroidered in gold with Chinese dragon patterns, was already on his feet to meet us, a big quaking figure amid a thick but ordered grove of *chinoiserie* – intricately carved chairs, occasional tables, vases and bric-à-brac – holding in his hand a sheaf of papers.

His first words were, 'I am working late – very late. It is

supposed to be bad for me, but business is business.' Nobody sat down, although, as I recall, Halm's right hand kept up throughout the interview a fluttering, almost suppliant gesture of invitation in the direction sometimes of the sofa, sometimes at one or other of the armchairs, suggesting that at the outset he had said to himself, 'We shall sit down and I'll explain it all,' and could not get out of his head that to get Foraker to sit down was an essential part of the business.

Foraker was as coolly overbearing as some kind of superhuman Inspector General sent from on high to uncover and rebuke transgression. Was this so? Was that so? Had he been correctly informed that Halm had acted thus and thus?

Yes, yes, yes, but, but, but, and Halm's hand fluttered urgently, in its please-to-be-seated-sir gesture.

And then Halm abruptly sat down and said, looking up at us with his spaniel eyes, that he did most earnestly desire to be understood. Foraker blinked as though he had run into some small, unexpected obstruction, and seemed, for the first time, to be actually listening to Halm.

Understood, Halm said, gaining a little confidence, understood as one who fully appreciated the grandeur of an inventor's conception, the historic part played by the inventor, the pioneer, in the progress of humanity. Understood as, in fact, a fellow labourer in the vineyard. No insensitive financier unaware of horizons beyond those of the market place; rather a companion in arms, a man alive as any to the larger issues, the underlying responsibilities. Yes, indeed, the responsibilities. And it was just on account of his realization of a responsibility that he, Halm, felt it his duty to examine all situations arising with a special care, exercising to the full that particular knowledge and experience which he, as a financier, could on his side, contribute to any enterprise in which he and others might find themselves jointly involved. This was what he wanted understood. It was only reasonable that he should ask for such understanding. Otherwise, his decision, the decision he had finally taken with regard to Foraker's Principle could be, well, it could be misunderstood.

His upturned eyes encountered a flame of sheer amazement

in Foraker's. Foraker obviously had, until that moment, no notion of what this tiresome rigmarole, this plea for sympathy, was all about; what it all added up to. He had taken for granted that Halm must, of course, be gassing on like this as a preliminary to reversing his ridiculous decision. And now, for the first time, Foraker grasped the truth that this spate of words really was an explanation by Halm of an act, a decision, which was absolutely final. Nothing on earth could prevent Halm cutting his losses. He merely hoped that he could get understanding as well, a bonus share.

Staring up at Foraker's face, Halm saw there something terribly startling. He started to get up out of his chair, one arm half raised in a sketchy gesture of defence, and his mouth suddenly opened wide, and let out a strange kind of screech, a cry for help. Foraker took a quick step forwards almost on top of him, and Halm, hitting out feebly with his raised arm, at the same time staggered, was caught behind the knees by his chair, and fell heavily into it. Behind us the door crashed open, and, as Foraker and I swung around to it, the man who had let us in and another – Halm's chauffeur as it turned out in court – were coming across the carpet at us.

Of the next ten brawling, punching minutes, I recall no details, beyond a sight of Halm lying flat on the floor with his hands covering his head, and, finally, of Foraker and myself fighting our way down the passage, and the door being slammed violently behind us by the butler, whose head was bleeding.

I remember Foraker going slowly over the sidewalk, with a little light snow settling and immediately melting on the warmth of his shoulders. Feeling as though I were moving in a disagreeable dream, I got up into the car and sat there, shivering slightly, while he swung the starting handle, and presently climbed in beside me. We had been travelling for a considerable time before I realized that we were not moving in the direction of Foraker's home but apparently had driven first to the centre of Paris and now turned northwards.

I knew without asking any questions that we were on the way to Beauvais; in fact, Foraker was heading for Beauvais with the fixity of a maniac. We were actually clear of Paris somewhere in the semi-derelict territory between the city and the country before I heard my own voice suddenly crying out loudly, 'It's no good. I tell you it's no good.' And again, 'There's nothing you can do tonight.' I thought nothing would happen and was appalled. And then something did happen, and I found that somehow more appalling still, it was so strange, so far from normal – Foraker slowed down carefully and stopped the car.

He stared ahead of him, his hands resting on the steering wheel, and presently began to conduct a kind of dialogue with himself, putting forward things he had in mind to do, and answering himself, pointing out their futility. As I had supposed, he had intended a swift dash to Beauvais, a raid of some kind on the works, an attack on whomever it might be that Halm had put in possession.

And then what? What good would it do? He had aimed at some kind of 'rescue'. Rescue what? The model? The nearly completed machine itself? Absolutely futile. Where were the men to carry out the dismantling and removal? Where was the transport? Where could the dismantled parts be taken to?

This one-man dialogue continued for some minutes and then reached a bleak conclusion. 'Nothing at all,' Foraker said. 'Nothing to be done.'

He sat still a while and then put the car in gear and began to drive forwards at an awfully slow rate. We had been joggling along in this listless fashion for perhaps half an hour when I saw just ahead of us the raw light of a place I suddenly recognized from my innumerable journeys to and from Beauvais. It was a desolate kind of café-bar which catered mainly for the drivers of market wagons going to and from the central markets of Paris. It was customarily open all night and seemed to make Christmas Eve night no exception.

Foraker drove gently up to the café, stopped there, got down into the road and walked heavily to the door, which was opened immediately. Inside, the place was empty of customers but the middle-aged man who ran it was there as usual and took our order without any sign of surprise at the sight of us.

When I made some comment on our luck in finding somewhere open on Christmas Eve night he said, 'It gets to be a habit. Customers or no customers, it's a habit.'

For a while we drank and ate sandwiches in silence. Foraker brooded at the table with his head resting heavily on one hand in a slack position I had never seen him in before. Then we began to discuss the various vicissitudes of the fight at Halm's, talking of it in a detached manner, as though it had been a dog fight we had both witnessed. Then I said, 'I suppose when we get back we shall have Halm suing us for assault and battery.'

Foraker nodded, said, 'I suppose so,' and then drew in his breath in a kind of gasp.

'Back,' he said. 'I can't go back.'

I stared at him and he sat up straight and put his hands on the table.

'Go back now,' he said, 'how will I do that?' He talked wildly for a moment to himself more than to me apparently. I heard him say, 'Mark Crane used to say I always overdrew my account. He was right all right. What about last night? You remember that, Ned. All those people, everyone believing I was scheduled for death or glory in next to no time.'

He looked me in the eyes.

'Listen, Ned –' he said. 'Christopher Columbus. What do you suppose would have happened if just when everything was ready and they'd had the last party, the great send-off, for the man who was going out like that to get around the world, and a few hours later he said, "It's all off, folks. Little accident came up and I'm staying here. Just carry on. Like as before." '

He paused, contemplating that scene.

'Mark Crane's right,' he said again. 'I'm not in at all what you could call an ordinary position.'

'That,' I said, 'is true.'

'I'm a man,' Foraker said, 'with a big overdraft – overdraft on glory, Ned. Drawn on everyone. Delia. Everyone.'

Again he paused brooding and contemplating, 'Ned,' he said, lowering his hands and holding on to the table, 'do you realize that last night I solemnly promised that in future I was going to walk the paths of humility? I told them all how I was going to become a humble man. *Humble!* Me!'

He shook his hands in the air again and lolled back with his arms dangling limp by his sides. A sigh shook him and seemed to take the life out of him, leaving him a lolling hulk, horribly spiritless and heavy.

I forced myself to talk, to say something adequate, and felt myself talking to a man who was actually no longer there, who had gone a long way down and away. He answered me, kept up some kind of a conversation, and his flat, utterly uninterested tones made him seem more distant than the silence had, and told me as little of what was boiling, or more likely festering, in his mind. Once a kind of life came into his voice, he spoke loudly and with animation, but in the manner of somebody describing a distant scene or possibly a proclamation stuck up on a wall.

'They say,' he said, 'start all over again. You think it's going to be different but it's going to be just the same, Ned. You see, Ned, nobody's going to let me get away with it. You go on and up and around and you come out at the same place. Same things trip you, same things do you down the whole of the time.'

For a moment, as he relapsed into listlessness, he had the agonized face of a man drowning and after that no expression at all.

Finally I gave up trying to talk to him. It seemed to me that nothing could rouse him now, even perhaps that nothing would ever rouse him. And at the moment the thought crossed my mind, I saw a little twitch in his face and a tautening of his body. Then I heard what he had heard a second before, the sound of a motor-car furiously driven, coming from the direction of Paris. In the night silence of that waste land on the fringe of the city it made a fierce, purposeful noise. At that first sound of it there was no reason at all to suppose that it was any business of ours. Perhaps to Foraker in his bog of despondency it was simply a jolting reminder of the world going on outside. The car came roaring up and, in a couple of seconds, would have passed the café and away. The roar abruptly, startlingly, ended, and was succeeded by the high scream of the brakes. Sitting up straight, his hand slapping gently on the table and a little bit of life in his eye, Foraker looked towards the door.

'Who?' I said.

He shrugged impatiently as though angrily waiting for some enemy, any enemy, to do battle with.

There was the sound of running feet on the paved roadway, the door was thrust violently open, and in a little flurry of snow and wind we saw coming through it Henri Lenoir, slamming it behind him and stepping briskly across the room to us on his springy cavalry legs.

Foraker and I stared in amazement but he greeted us, as he sat down at the table, in a briskly dry manner, taking his own arrival as a matter of course. 'Of course', yes, on getting the news – Rosen had, of course, been in touch with him – he had learned that Foraker was going to see Halm. Got a car, went to Halm's house, no sight of Foraker's car; 'nosed about', of course, saw tracks in the snow, then someone opened the door of the villa, shone a lantern on him and shouted to know was he the police? The man at the door seemed upset.

'Bet your life he was upset,' Foraker said mechanically.

Well, then, what with this episode, and the tracks in the snow, Lenoir had made certain deductions. Assumed there had been some 'little unpleasantness'. Drove back to Paris, used telephone at all-night post office in the Eighth Arrondissement, found Foraker not back at flat, came to 'obvious' conclusion. Where had Foraker gone? Where would he go? Beauvais.

'For you, in the circumstances,' Lenoir said, 'it was an obvious thing to do. Mistaken. Of course. Pointless. Well, of course. But it was what you would do. It became necessary for me to follow you in order to prevent foolishness and consult. On the way outside here, I see your car, fortunately unmistakable. Now I have a drink and a sandwich, we consult and determine the necessary course of action.'

During the first five minutes of this I thought, looking from Lenoir to Foraker, that Lenoir was simply making a fool of himself. During the next quarter of an hour I changed my opinion. It was not until a little while later that I realized the nature of the force which motivated Lenoir. I saw only the result, the performance. It was a great performance. It was, in fact, an oration, but by an almost hypnotic trick of the orator one had the impression that the silent Foraker was actually responding to and answering the various points made by Lenoir.

He made no fatal attempt to minimize the catastrophe, and that alone was enough to engage Foraker's flickering interest. As for Halm, Lenoir visibly exerted himself to produce a villification and denunciation so lurid that it must surpass the resources even of Foraker's imagination and vocabulary.

In his opinion, said Lenoir, Halm was not merely and simply a cowardly financier, but almost without question a German agent, and, if one came to think of it, very probably an agent of the British Intelligence, too. As he talked Halm swelled into an embodiment of vast international forces, forces massing to attempt the discomfiture of Foraker. I saw Foraker nodding a kind of reluctant agreement.

Tacking again on his difficult skilful course against the wind, Lenoir went on from there to state as a matter of evident fact that these forces, however gigantic, were, in the nature of things, blundering and helpless if and when confronted by the intelligence, the tough will to victory, the genius of Grant Foraker. Foraker would – of course – outsmart them all.

By now, incredibly as it seemed to me, Foraker was actually listening, actually throwing in a word here and there and beginning to discuss future plans. 'There is a phrase,' said Lenoir, 'that boxers have. They say you must roll with the punch. And so that is why you must come back, and perhaps, when Halm brings his little action against you, you will get a fine, or even, if they are very vicious, you will get a little time in jail. All that, of course, is nothing. After that we shall see. In the meantime we must make a defensive action. There are all sorts of ways in which lawyers can prevent his destroying or selling the material at Beauvais. We must mobilize the lawyers. Gain time and then act.'

Foraker was almost smiling, slapping the table gently with the palm of his hand. Watching Lenoir, I could see his face relax a little after that immense effort, and just then, sucked back down again by some black undertow of thought, Foraker stopped in the middle of a sentence, stared at his hands and said, 'But it's no good after all. I can't do it all over again here. I shall get out.'

Lenoir allowed a little silence to fall. Then he said softly, 'Where to?'

Foraker made an expansive gesture; it said the world was wide.

'No,' said Lenoir.

'Why not?' said Foraker.

'Because,' said Lenoir, in the same soft voice, 'you are too important to us to be allowed to go anywhere else. For instance, if you tried to cross the frontier I should personally myself denounce you to the police.'

I was awfully startled – partly, I suppose, because I expected some really terrible explosion from Foraker. This did not occur, and one can see by hindsight that, of course, this strange threat from his own associate and companion in arms was, in fact, flattering to Foraker.

But as for me, half attending to the rest of their conversation in the café, and all the way back to Paris, my tired mind was preoccupied by Lenoir's remark. We left Foraker at his apartment, and Lenoir offered to drive me home. As we approached the Rue St Jacques, Lenoir said, 'You're surprised, I think, by what I said to Foraker, there in the café, about the frontier. I could see you were. Why should you be?'

I shrugged wearily.

'Because,' said Lenoir, in his most pedantic manner, watching the whitish road ahead, 'you are obsessed by personal relationships. The good Henri Lenoir who is a friend of the good Grant Foraker, was in love with Madame Delia Foraker, etcetera, etcetera, etcetera. You forget the force which has brought all these relationships into being.'

'That force,' I said with pompous irritation, 'is, I should have said, Foraker's own genius. The Principle.'

Lenoir lifted one hand slightly from the steering wheel and waved it in a negative movement.

'No,' he said. 'It is the history of Europe.'

I found this remark so exasperating that I made no reply, and when the car stopped at my door left it with the briefest word of good-bye.

Martha had left a note behind in my room that Christmas morning. She had gone alone across the city in the snow, back to Foraker's apartment 'in case I can be any help.' I could have imagined that that was merely a natural, dutiful thing for her to do. But she had added the words, 'I'm sorry, Ned darling,' and that seemed a good-bye to our briefest of love affairs.

When we met later on Christmas Day we knew without speaking that the knocking on the door in the night had been not an interruption but an ending, as though someone had seen that the play could not succeed and rung down the curtain in the middle of the first act.

I said that I understood. 'It is the forces of history, I expect,' I said bitterly.

Later, when the luminous February nights – already smelling of the premature spring of 1910 – seemed to push Christmas far away, and it seemed that things had taken, at last, a sharp turn for the better, that they were, in fact, going well, this notion of the forces of European history at work in our affairs appeared almost exhilarating. The frustrations of life, the irritations and disappointments and regrets became dignified by that benign figure of History.

I remember, of those days, chiefly sensations and emotions. At first, the sensation was of sinking hopelessly and helplessly in quicksands. This sense of disaster was so strong in me that I could hardly believe it when Mark's lawyers actually did get some kind of injunction, restraining Halm from destroying or disposing of the material at Beauvais, and then – more astonishingly still – the assault proceedings against Foraker developed along more or less farcical lines, and culminated in nothing worse than a fairly heavy fine accompanied by some sneers from the judge.

There came a day when Mark, tilted complacently in his

office chair, said, 'There's no reason, no reason at all, you know, why in a few months, a year at the outside, we won't have made up all this lost ground, launched the Principle after all.'

'I suppose so,' I said. 'No reason at all.'

He outlined, reasonably, the new road forward. Number One consideration, naturally: money. Halm wasn't the only possible source, was he? There was the report of the Military Committee that – naturally, would be a handicap. On the other hand, there was the Rosen report: not, for obvious reasons, a document that could be very freely employed as a kind of prospectus – but, used confidentially, with the right people, it should be a powerful lever.

And Foraker, Mark said, was after all a great man to raise money. He 'inspired confidence'. And now – after suffering, admittedly, a grave shock – he was 'as good as new'. Right back in form. No reason at all why he should not raise the money, buy out Halm's interest, and get to work. No reason at all.

It would take, naturally, said Mark, a little time.

It began by taking the last days of February, March, and April.

Watching and listening to Foraker, accompanying him sometimes on familiar train journeys to Marseilles, I was at first surprised to find that, following the grim setback, and that hour of collapse at the café on the Beauvais road, he seemed as elated – more elated even – than he had been when he first read Rosen's report. Once, in the train, watching central France go by the window, he made a comment – apropos of nothing in particular – which seemed to give a clue to this attitude.

'The pity of it, Ned,' he said. 'Think of those unhappy wretches of the Military Commission. Dealing with things they can't hope to understand. And that unhappy fellow Halm – blind, you see. And the lawyers and the courts. All of them thinking they could stop me, beat me. They couldn't, naturally. Because.'

'Because what?' I said.

He smiled a gentle, infinitely superior smile, and in his big hands crushed together and twisted the newspaper he had been reading. 'Because,' he said, 'I can deal with things – just like *that*.'

At the end of April, Paulhan won the £10,000 *Daily Mail* prize with his London–Manchester flight. Foraker read the news, smiling and twisting imaginary materials in his hands. Then we had a May full of conferences, private colloquies with financiers. From some of these, in cases, that is to say, where the financier in question spoke adequate English, I was excluded. It seemed to me that I had less and less to do, and Mark Crane seemed to have less to do, too.

'Grant,' he would say, when I found him doodling in his office, 'is handling what has to be handled just at present.'

'Things are going well?'

'Very well, as I understand it,' Mark said happily. 'Of course, there is always a new War Scare. That makes these financial people pretty cautious – makes them nervous of anything in the way of a new venture. To hear some of them talk, you'd think the Germans were going to invade France any day now.'

'But apart from that? Things, you say, are going well?'

'Very well indeed, so far as I know,' Mark said.

That was on 8 June, and on 9 June, on a hot evening when Foraker was out on some private engagement, and Martha and I had dined with Delia, and Henriette-Louise-Marie had gone away to the kitchen, Delia, sitting on the sofa by the open window, looking away from us at the city, said:

'I think it's time you two realized that' – she turned her head slowly and looked at us one after the other out of her wonderful eyes – 'that the game's up. It's all no good.'

Her voice was hard until she came to the last two words, and then it broke a little, and she stared straight ahead, holding herself perfectly still.

17

Martha made no sound. I took one look at her and then I could not bear to look at her stricken face again.

Delia's voice, with no break in it now, went on and on, saying, it seemed to me, the same thing over and over: that it was all up, the end of the tether. From what seemed a long distance, like a voice on a telephone, I heard Martha say 'Why? But what's *happened* really? What's happened?'

I have no idea how long it took Delia to tell us the answers to those questions. However long it was, there was no answer to the answers. As she talked, and I looked back over that recent time when things had seemed to be going so well, I kept hearing the phrase, 'Fool's Paradise', playing itself repeatedly in my head.

For quite a long while, it appeared, Delia herself had lived in a Fool's Paradise, too. It was weeks before she began dimly to realize that none of the things that were supposed to be happening were really happening: they were only supposed to be going well because Foraker said they were going well. In reality, apart from the results of the two sets of legal proceedings, Foraker was getting nowhere at all. He was blocked at every turn. Every hopeful financial street he walked along turned out a blind alley.

An accident, a literally childish accident, first alerted her. Jephthah one day had stood moodily about the room when he was alone with her, and acted in such a way that she thought he was sickening for some illness, and when he suddenly burst into tears, she was sure of it. But it was worse than that. When he could talk, he said he was frightened. His father had frightened him and he sobbed again at the strange recollection. Frightened him one evening when they were alone in the flat, and Grant Foraker had come in and slumped down in a chair; when Jephthah came in to talk with him in the way they always talked together, Foraker had acted and talked strangely – talking as though he were talking to himself, or as though he had to talk to someone and Jephthah would do. And then, Delia made out, it seemed as though Foraker were talking to Jephthah because he was his son and he wanted to warn him about something – about life, apparently. That part seemed not very clear, but it was clear that, from there, Foraker had gone on to talk of more specific dangers, threatening not Jephthah, but himself. He had talked, Jephthah said, about Intelligence Service, and enemies trying to close in. And then he had jumped out of the chair and begun to laugh and boast, Jephthah said, of how no one could stop him.

'He didn't seem like him at all,' Jephthah said miserably. 'And that frightened me. And I was frightened about his enemies, too.'

Delia stopped and put her hand to her mouth, remembering visibly the fear she had had when Jephthah told her those things. A double fear, as his had been: fear of such enemies as might be closing in, of news of them that Foraker had had and had kept hidden, and the worst fear – of Foraker not 'seeming like him at all'.

'Are you trying to tell us,' Martha said with despair and fury in her voice, 'that Grant's out of his mind?'

'No, no,' Delia said. 'It's not like that at all. For all I know, he may be saner than anyone else. I mean, perhaps things really are the way he says they have to be. All I know is, he can't go on this way. He has to be got away.'

She went on talking, and I had a clear vision of the way things had really been with Foraker during that spring and early summer when we had thought things were going well.

The report of the Military Commission was naturally responsible for most – perhaps for all – the reluctance of potential backers to put up their money. But Foraker, at any rate, believed that there were other elements at work, too. How else account for the number of occasions upon which a negotiation would reach the very verge of success, appear to be almost entirely 'in the bag', and at the last moment the financier concerned would turn suddenly, totally, and quite unexplainedly cold?

In my mind's eye, as Delia talked, I could see Foraker

brooding gloomily upon all the individuals and groups and organizations that he had, in the course of his career, offended, insulted, thwarted, and, perhaps, ruined. Now he was aware of them, of people everywhere, crowding in upon him revengefully.

'He started to talk quite a lot,' she said 'about his father, and what they did to him in Indiana that time, after it wasn't the end of the world.'

Against these dark forces, Foraker, it seemed, had built for himself a barrier, or perhaps it was a battering ram, of faith – faith in himself, in his star, or his destiny or mission or however he thought of it to himself. He had looked back over his life and seen it as a continuous triumph of Foraker over the 'enemy'. When he crushed the newspaper in his hands, when he talked crazily to Jephthah, when he talked, more lengthily and coherently to Delia, he was expressing a faith which now was entirely and obsessively sincere.

Just once, talking with Delia, he had seemed to look at himself from the outside, and see a man obsessed by a faith that might be exaggerated, crazy, not corresponding to reality.

'But I have to believe that,' he had said. 'I have to.' And when she looked at him doubtfully, he said in a matter-of-fact manner, 'Obviously I do. Otherwise I might not be able to win, to bring it off.'

As he failed to raise money by ordinary means he thought of extraordinary ones. Delia had no idea of the details, and to this day I have only a somewhat vague idea of the real character of the complex network of shady and shadier transactions in which he involved himself. Delia did, however, find out that, unknown to Mark Crane, he had organized, or tried to organize, some kind of new company.

She had become alarmed, and questioned him about it. What kind of assets did it have? Where was the money coming from? How was he persuading people to invest? And Foraker had burst out in angry sneers. What he had said amounted to a statement that if people called him a swindler that was their own stupid business – they would see what they would see, when he won. And as for its being dangerous – he wasn't afraid, and nobody else need be, either.

It occurred to me that I had read often enough of financiers, statesmen, generals, riding furiously to ruin on just that road. The thought that this was a common thing to happen made it no easier to bear when it was happening to Foraker.

With a painful effort Delia controlled a spasm of the muscles of her face, and said, 'I've told you all this, because there's only one way out now. I'm sure of it.'

She had it in her head that if Foraker were at least to go credibly through the motions of 'pulling out', of abandoning the fight, and the Principle, then the 'enemy' – at any rate the main enemy – would be satisfied.

Her plan, worked out in heaven knows how many hours of agonized thought about a situation full of factors she barely understood, was that as a very first step Foraker must 'liquidate' his whole establishment in Paris. In any case, very soon there would be no money to pay for the office or the staff. She was going to make a supreme effort to persuade Foraker that that was the thing to do – she would tell him it was a way of deluding the enemy.

Although she had not discussed this plan with Lenoir she had certainly been talking to him, for she said, 'You see this isn't a personal matter, a feud between individuals. It may have started that way, but it isn't any longer. It's part of history. Maybe it was that horrible little Robinson that started it all. But it's got far beyond him. It's the British Intelligence Service and, I suppose, what they call the Old Guard in the Ministry of War that are after him now. If he proves to them he's not dangerous any more . . . that he's giving up . . . they won't want any more than that. Will they?' she asked, suddenly doubting her own statement.

Shovelling words into the abyss, I asked Delia whether she had any idea who were the people associated with Foraker in the 'new company'.

'Not much,' she said. 'One of them's a man called Paca. I had to talk to him on the telephone once when Foraker was out and there was something urgent that had come up.'

I said nothing, thinking vividly of that frenzied trio, grotesque in their greed, as I had seen them long ago on the platform of the station at Marseilles. I was conscious of being, so to speak, surprised at not being surprised by this disclosure of Delia's, which ought to have been astounding. I remember that, for a moment, I was preoccupied simply by the question whether it was by Paca or by Foraker that the first move had been made.

I could easily imagine Foraker himself, in a state of mind that was both exalted and terribly sensitive to the hidden doings of the 'enemy', grasping violently at the possibility of coming face to face with 'enemy' agents, smoking them out into the open, and, in that moment, dominating and converting them into instruments of his own. And it was true that, if one wanted to raise money by shady means in Paris, Paca was a likely enough instrument – the sort of person that would come readily to mind. Or, Paca could have made the approach; Paca and his friends who through all those months and years had been, distantly yet intimately, tenuously yet in the most practical possible manner, involved with the phenomenon of Foraker.

All that time, Foraker had been one of the fixed elements in their greedy dream, a part of the occult alchemy by which Robinson and his gift were to be set to work turning the future into cash. For Paca and company to get into direct contact with Foraker could seem to them a move assured of success, one way or the other. If things went well with the mystery man, Foraker, they might make something out of that. Or, more likely, they might make something – considering the kind of enemies he had – out of helping to bring him finally down.

Whoever made that first approach, it probably appeared to the other party as nothing startling or outrageous, but rather natural – and it seemed natural to me, too; their association, although in the capacity of enemies, had been a long one.

To my question about the origin of this bizarre partnership I never got a complete answer. It was too late. Too late, also, for Delia's careful, desperate plan. Too late, it seemed, for anything. For on the following day, 10 June, Foraker was arrested, charged with a long string of criminal offences which, in non-technical terms, all seemed to be variants of the crime of attempting to obtain, or obtaining, money under false pretences. Ironically, there was also a charge of attempted blackmail. It appeared that Foraker, by way of bringing pressure to bear on Halm – 'getting the poor fellow to see some sense' was no doubt how he phrased it to himself – had suggested that it might be awkward for Halm if Foraker were to disclose certain things he had learned about Halm's business through Mark Crane, during the period of their close association.

Bail – or whatever the French equivalent is – was refused.

I remember in some shame that I had heard with actual relief the news that – whether by normal procedure or as a result of special orders in this case – the number of visits Foraker was entitled to receive in the *maison d'arrêt* was strictly limited, except in so far as his counsel, provided by Mark Crane, was concerned. Perhaps, after all, I have no reason to be ashamed. The notion of seeing Foraker under those circumstances was, for the moment, entirely and naturally appalling.

But six days after his arrest, I had a letter from him, brought out by the lawyer. It was a longish document, entirely devoted to an astonishing request: he wished me to visit Mr Robinson.

Foraker's explanation of this strange mission did, however, have a kind of wild intelligibility. He declared, to begin with, that he had been thinking a great deal about Robinson, his 'countryman and former school-fellow'. He had intended, he said, some time to seek out Robinson and talk with him. 'It would have been interesting,' Foraker remarked, badly. As this was now impossible, he desired me to do it for him; to ascertain what Robinson was now doing; and, in particular, to make it perfectly clear to Robinson that Foraker 'understood' Robinson's behaviour and 'bore him no personal ill-will'. This statement stood out sharply on the page, as though in writing it Foraker had tried to express, or perhaps strengthen, the force of his own benevolence by actually grinding the pen-nib into the paper.

It was conceivable that Foraker, in this moment of disaster, could feel some general impulse towards an all-round forgiveness. Perhaps, too, I thought, to convince himself that he really did have no ill-will towards Robinson, was necessary as a final proof of his own superiority, assuring his ultimate victory. He referred – oddly in the circumstances – to 'our long connection'. And, finally, mentioned 'his own, and his father's, intense interest in the story of my own father, and in my own career.'

He wrote of this as though the Robinsons had spent their lives in the capacity of a kind of hereditary Boswell to the Forakers' Johnson. Or his attitude resembled that of opposing generals in a long series of campaigns who sometimes, by war's end, feel themselves actually closer to one another, more truly intimate with one another, more 'at home' together, than with the changing members of their own staffs.

The bond existing between Foraker and Robinson was so old and durable that just now it was viewed by Foraker as a link – his only link – with the past, with his father, with the continuity of his own existence from childhood until now.

With extreme repugnance I set out to call upon the Robinsons. I decided against a preliminary letter announcing the object of my visit. Remembering Mrs Robinson's last letter to me, I thought an abrupt appearance at the door would at least gain me admittance. Beside the front door of the apartment there was a considerable pile of newly delivered newspapers, but there was no answer to my repeated ringing, and the distant whirring of the bell somewhere at the back of the apartment seemed to emphasize emptiness.

I went down to the concierge's lodge to make inquiries. She said the Robinsons had left. About a fortnight ago.

Bribed to tell me where they had gone, she said she had no idea, and was obviously telling the truth, for she held this to be a grievance; supposing letters or other communications came for them, what was she supposed to do? What was she supposed to tell inquirers like myself? It was exasperating; caused waste of time.

There was a further grievance – they had not cancelled their order for the delivery of periodicals, and as these had been paid for a month in advance, the postman brought them by the dozen. And what was she to do with them? She waved an angry arm towards the back of her *loge*, where I could see, piled neatly in a corner, the papers which Mr Robinson had used to study so meticulously for indications of enemy movements.

'But why?' I said. 'Why should they have left so suddenly, with no address?' I felt a strange sense of deprivation, as at the disappearance of old friends. Like Foraker, I was aware of a bond between myself and that outrageous family Robinson.

The concierge, having taken her time to study me, became abruptly frank and confidential, sharing her burden.

'In my opinion,' she said, 'she took him off to a looney house somewhere in the country; or something as near a looney house as makes no difference. And obviously all those papers were what were part of his going off his head, and that's why she didn't want them sent after them.'

Very sudden, it had been, she said, and I must believe her when she said that the day of the departure had been frightful, just frightful. Did I remember, she asked, the map which Mr Robinson had on the wall of his study? With all the coloured pins in it? She had seen it several times. Of course that was part of his looniness, too, and for that reason, of course, Mrs Robinson had evidently planned to leave it behind when they went off – she meant to have it collected later and stored with the furniture.

Well then, on the day they left, the two of them had been getting into the cab with all the luggage, Mr Robinson looking like a person walking in his sleep. The concierge did an imitation of him. And there on the kerbstone he had suddenly cried out to know where the map was, and, when Mrs Robinson said it must be in one of the bags, he had actually rushed at the cab and started to drag the luggage out, so as to open it and make certain.

So in the end, Mrs Robinson had been forced to admit that perhaps it was still up in the apartment, and she went and brought it down, loosely rolled up, and there on the pavement some of the multi-coloured pins fell out, and Robinson down on his knees picking them up and cursing and whimpering like a maniac.

I wrote to Foraker telling him simply that the Robinsons had left Paris, and that I was trying to find their address.

The preliminary proceedings before the *juge d'instruction* were, of course, conducted in *camera*, but this did not prevent numerous, vaguely alarming, paragraphs on the subject of *l'affaire Foraker* appearing in the newspapers. It was a period of fright. The elections had been conducted in an atmosphere of violence. The strike wave was continually mounting. It was said that in a couple of months there would be a general railway strike, chaos, and at that moment the Germans would make a pretext for war and march in. Into this pattern of fearful thinking *l'affaire Foraker* was somehow fitted. The suggestion was made that there was more in the case of this foreign inventor and adventurer than met the eye; that it might not be unconnected with an affair of espionage. Spies everywhere.

It was on 23 or 24 June that, as I was passing in front of a café on the Boulevard des Italiens, I heard my name called, and, a moment later, felt my sleeve being gently pawed by a little man whom, after a moment's bewilderment, I recognized as the Dr Thaypi I had so abortively interviewed on my first arrival in Paris.

He was shy but determined. He knew, he said, that I had been connected with Foraker. Evidently he had boasted to his geological colleagues of his association with a person connected with dangerous characters. He had recalled how I had, at the very moment of my appearance in the capital, been dogged by the police – an affair of American criminals and confidence men. Now he wanted me to give him, briefly and confidentially, something of the inside story of *l'affaire Foraker*. His passion for the sensational, for the *roman policier* come to life, overcame his natural timidity. He virtually demanded information from me.

I told him roughly that I knew nothing, adding that in my opinion the whole thing was probably a mare's-nest. He looked at me with bitter reproach. 'You are making fun of me,' he said. 'Everyone knows this is going to be a *cause célèbre*. With vast ramifications. A colleague of mine has a friend high in the police. He says it will be tremendous.'

I found this absurd incident strangely disturbing – more so than the newspaper paragraphs. Also, my own examination by the *juge d'instruction* had been brief and perfunctory, and after it I had been informed by the police that I was not regarded as material to the case. I found this alarming, too. It seemed to imply that they were after big game, chasing something that I was unlikely to know anything about.

Cautiously, I made contact with Henri Lenoir, who made a rendezvous in a quiet café on the Left Bank. He listened to me gloomily, but without surprise, as though everything I said merely confirmed his own information.

He said, 'The best thing for you to do would be to go away for a while. There's nothing you can do here. And if it's a frame-up they may still pick you up and question you and, perhaps, involve you in some damaging admission. To go away now can't do harm, but may do good. Besides, it looks better, I think, if Foraker liquidates his establishment. Besides – who is to pay you here? How are you to live?'

I could see that he cared very little how I was to live, and that his real fear was that I might, under cunning examination, give something away – possibly the extent of his own connection with Foraker. But from every point of view it seemed that he was right. I made up my mind on the spot, and before we parted told him that what I was going to do was to visit my uncle in Barcelona.

'Good,' said Lenoir. 'But go quickly. This is a dangerous city. Things happen suddenly.'

'I could go tomorrow morning,' I said.

'There is a train tonight,' said Lenoir.

I saw that, if I was going at all, it was sensible to go at once. I telephoned to Martha, told her of my decision. I must see her, I said, to say good-bye. She said she could come to the Gare d'Orléans an hour before the train left – she would be there at a quarter past six that evening.

Lenoir, now obsessed with his notion of myself as a potential danger to his own position, had urged me not to visit the Foraker apartment before leaving – and indeed I had been quite glad to make my farewells over the telephone. But so far as Martha was concerned, things were different. Waiting for her in the café of the Gare d'Orléans I found myself thinking of her as I had months ago. All at once, it seemed to me intolerable and foolish to have given her up as I had. And it seemed, too, that it was not too late. She would arrive, I would tell her all that I felt, and she would feel the same way.

A little after half past six, Mark Crane arrived, sweating and mopping his face. He brought a message to say that at the last moment there had come word from Foraker's lawyer to the effect that he possibly could get permission to take an English secretary with him when he went to see Foraker late this afternoon, and would Miss Dukes be available? She was waiting in the office by the telephone for a summons to the *maison d'arrêt,* and could not come to the station for fear of missing it.

Mark, who at the first news of Foraker's arrest, had been thrown into a frenzy, was now quite calm, and talked of the affair with a kind of matter-of-fact gloom that you might expect of a man whose game of lawn tennis had been spoiled by rain.

'Things,' said Mark as we parted, 'haven't turned out quite the way I expected, I must say. However . . .'

My only hesitation in going to Barcelona had been due to a fear lest my uncle should treat the course of events as proof that my flight from the insurance business had been a failure, and I should be confronted with a string of I-told-you-so's. The fear was baseless. Almost to my embarrassment, my uncle treated me with really respectful admiration. In his eyes, my career to date had been a surprising, but complete, success.

'I am proud to think,' he kept saying, 'that you were able to impress favourably a man like Mr Foraker, and to show yourself – as you obviously must have – fully qualified to work with him.'

At Foraker's arrest he was bitterly indignant. 'Great men of that type,' he said, 'can always be victimized by lesser men. I've no doubt he will turn the tables on them before very long. I was sorry,' he added, 'that I couldn't do more in response to his financial proposal. I was very much flattered that he should have taken the trouble to consider me in that connection.'

With a sinking heart I asked him what he meant, and he showed me a letter he had received from Foraker about two months previously. It was a horrifying piece of work – a typical share-pusher's letter, in which Foraker made play with the fact of his meeting with my uncle as a preliminary to 'interesting' him in an 'undertaking which, though the general public might fail to appreciate its possibilities, could readily be seen by anyone in touch with modern developments in the technical field, to offer opportunities,' etc., etc., etc.

My uncle had 'invested' the equivalent of £100.

For the next fortnight, I spent my time trying to amuse myself in Barcelona, and trying deliberately to push Foraker and all that concerned him into some sort of calm perspective – some place where I could contemplate him without distress. Despite this effort, I caught myself eagerly reading the papers arriving twenty-four hours late from Paris.

On a morning in the third week of July, two things happened. In yesterday's copy of *Le Matin* I read a paragraph to the effect that, in connection with *l'affaire Foraker* a former associate of his, a Mr Robinson, had been arrested. Mr Robinson was stated to have been 'living in concealment at a farmhouse near Tours'. Owing to his 'state of mental health', he had been permitted, at the request of his wife, to remain at his home, under surveillance, while awaiting his preliminary examination.

While I was still digesting this news, a telegram was brought to me. 'Imperatively urgent meet me Hotel Portugal Toulouse three o'clock tomorrow afternoon Tuesday.' There followed some instructions about trains. The telegram was signed, 'Henri'.

I told my uncle, truthfully, that I had to go urgently to France on some business of Foraker's which I was not at liberty to divulge.

I still had a little money left, but my uncle insisted on

making me a present, too. 'It gives me great pleasure,' he said, 'to assist a man like that. I don't know when I have met anyone who impressed me more favourably.'

Twenty minutes before three o'clock on the following day I was seated on the terrace of the Hotel Portugal in Toulouse, uncertain whether I was supposed to inquire for Henri Lenoir, or simply be met by him. At a few minutes past the hour, just as I had made up my mind to ask for him at the hotel desk, I was approached by a man in civilian clothes who, nevertheless, had the almost unmistakable look of an elderly non-commissioned officer. I felt that it was with difficulty that he did not salute as he approached me, and handed me an envelope.

Inside was a single sheet of paper, with the words, 'Bearer will conduct you to meet me. H.L.'

In silence, the grizzled messenger led me out of the hotel and round the corner to where a small touring car was standing by the kerb, saw me settled in the front seat, got in beside me, took the wheel and drove off, leaving Toulouse on the Montauban road, and presently taking a fork leading north-westwards. We had been travelling for a little over an hour when we turned into a narrower, country road, passed through a long, straggling village, and at the very end of it stopped at a fair-sized inn, with no houses beyond it and part of a large garden visible behind it.

The messenger conducted me through the inn to the garden. On a bench by an iron table under an ancient apple tree, Henri Lenoir was sitting.

He stood up, shook hands, said, 'Good!', sat down, said, 'What will you drink?', gave an order to the messenger, and before I was seated on the bench myself said, 'Now, the situation. Point one . . .'

He spoke like an officer reporting the points of a tactical situation, fiddling with a nail file, from time to time making a long, firm scratch with it on the table-top. I think I have never heard so much told in so few words.

'Point One: Immediately after your departure from Paris the situation deteriorated. Information available showed two lines of policy being considered by the authorities. There was a move to concentrate on the financial charges against our friend. Objective: to deport him. Another move to subordinate the financial charges to charges of attempted espionage. Objective: to give him a long jail sentence. Both, from our standpoint, inadmissible. In the one case, he is either immobilized, or, in the end, works for another Power. In the other, he is immobilized for years, and in the meantime comes the war. Naturally, in the end, we would have been able to proceed without him. But how much time have we? Perhaps only eight months. Good.'

He ground the nail file across the table.

'Point Two: Objectives of necessary counter-action. To release Foraker. To release his machine. To work intensively on the machine so as to make it capable of flight in a shorter time than that envisaged at the moment of Halm's intervention at Christmas.

'These objectives,' he said, tapping the table with the file, 'have been achieved.'

The messenger returned bringing cognac, and I sat simply gaping at Lenoir until the man withdrew again.

'Yes, yes,' Lenoir said. 'You remember, surely, that I told you in Paris that our group in the Ministry and in other technical branches of the service is highly organized. Besides,' he said, flashing a haughty eye at me, 'in France there are always patriots ready for action when a real emergency occurs.'

I gasped out some question.

'Quite so. There was a raid at Beauvais. In quite considerable force. Skilled men, who knew what they were looking for and what to take. The not-quite-complete machine, partially disassembled, was taken away on lorries, the fuel, etcetera. It is now a mile away from where we are sitting. It has been reassembled by technicians of our group. Successfully, I hope.'

'I saw nothing about a raid like that. I should have thought the newspapers . . .'

'Naturally the news was suppressed. People don't like to be made to look as careless and idiotic as they are. Of course, they are hunting for it. From some hints that have been conveyed to them they are almost certain it has been taken across the Belgian frontier.'

'And Foraker?'

'That was more difficult. Also, it had to be left almost to the last moment. A falsified order to release our friend was served upon the governor of the *maison d'arrêt* late yesterday evening. The order was of the highest authority, and by keeping his telephone continuously blocked with outside calls, we prevented his making any inquiries he might have otherwise made. A useful tactic in such cases. The forgery was not discovered until a few hours ago. In the meantime, Foraker was removed from Paris. Roundabout, naturally. All being well, by late this evening, he will be here.'

Before I could interrupt with a question, he rapped the table again and said, 'Point Three: The flight. Objective: to demonstrate in an unmistakable fashion the significance of Foraker's Principle. Such demonstration will have as its immediate consequence the overthrow of those in the Ministry of War who have treated it with disdain. No government of France will dare to refuse the most serious consideration to an instrument which can alter the whole balance of power in Europe. They will listen to the advice of myself and my friends. Foraker will be cleared of all charges, immediately released. He and Rosen will put themselves at the disposition of the military authorities, will become technical advisers of the Ministry of War upon this phase of activity. Method of demonstration:' – the file scored a long mark right across the table – 'Trial flight at dawn tomorrow.'

I believe I just sat with my head on my hand, staring at him dully, as though he had told me a bit of gossip or a fairy story.

He looked at me sharply. 'Point Four:' he said, and took a sip of his drink. 'Possible unwillingness of Foraker to conduct this necessary test.'

'I don't understand.'

'Obviously there has been no opportunity to explain the plan to him. The final work on the machine has had to be carried out hurriedly, without benefit of his supervision. Under these circumstances the flight will be, I imagine, extraordinarily dangerous. The chances of disaster are very large. He may hesitate before such an undertaking. That is why I have sent for you. He likes and trusts you. You may be able to persuade him that it is essential.'

I looked around at the garden and the back of the inn – instinctively looking, I suppose, for some kind of escape from this appalling situation. Lenoir misunderstood my movement.

'We're perfectly secure here for the time being,' he said. 'First of all, the man who drove you owns the place. He is an old *sous-officier,* a comrade in arms of my own. Also, a patriot. Also, there is nothing unusual, in our being here. The field where the demonstration will take place is a place we use quite officially for various tests of other kinds – ballistic tests, etc., etc. And nobody, yet, connects us with Foraker. Not at least professionally. As you know, my only known connection with him is that I am supposed to have been the lover of his wife.'

I thought of Delia and Jephthah.

'What really are,' I said carefully, 'the chances? Foraker's chances in the machine?'

Lenoir shrugged irritably.

'I haven't,' he said, 'sufficient data to answer that question. Rosen might be able to tell you, if you think it important. Unfortunately, he will not be here, or rather at the field, until after midnight. It is dangerous to bring him earlier, he is so conspicuous. On the other hand, he is necessary – as an expert witness.'

His 'if you think it important' infuriated me. I said, 'As you've got Foraker this far, you could get him out of the country.'

'That,' said Lenoir, 'would be disadvantageous. At the best, time would be lost. After all, the machine is here. Besides, once he was abroad, who knows what might happen? In my view, he will appreciate the necessities of the situation.'

I said, bitterly, 'I always thought you were a friend of Foraker.'

Lenoir grasped his glass in both his hands and looked at me wide-eyed.

'Certainly I am his friend,' he said in a tone of astonishment. 'I consider myself among his closest friends. I don't think he likes me as well as I like him. But then, naturally, not being a Frenchman he does not always see the necessities of the European historical situation so clearly as I do. That is where I feel your influence may be decisive.'

I felt an overwhelming desire to get away from Lenoir and be by myself. I told Lenoir I wanted to rest. He said there was a room ready for me in the inn. I went there and lay down on the bed, intending to pass the whole terrible posture of affairs clearly and relentlessly in review. My mind, exhausted by a sleepless night of travel and a day of almost unbearable tension, fled from the task. I fell almost instantly into a sleep as deep as though I had been given knockout drops.

When I awoke it was almost dark in the room. Someone had come in. I turned my head sleepily and saw that it was Foraker. He moved over to the bed, standing with his hat on the back of his head and his hands linked behind him, looking down at me.

I got my feet on to the floor, and sat miserably on the edge of the bed, rubbing my face with my hands.

'Good,' Foraker said, as though resuming a conversation recently interrupted. 'The fact is that as a psychologist, a judge of men, our poor friend Henri Lenoir is frankly pitiable. Perhaps the French in general have that failing. A child could guess, from his conversation with me, that he imagines I may refuse to make this flight, and that you have been brought here to persuade me. A very, very unfair position to put you in, Ned.

'However,' he began to pace darkly about the small room, 'there's of course no need of persuasion. Obviously not. Unless, of course, those damned technicians and mechanics that work with Henri have absolutely wrecked the machine. Otherwise – take-off at dawn.'

I said, 'But – ' and he held up his hand to check me.

'It is important,' he said, 'to move in consonance and conformity with the pace of events.' He quickened his pace a little and repeated the phrase with satisfaction. 'I always have.' He spread out his arms so that he seemed to fill the entire room, and his voice was rich and vibrant. 'Past, present, and future,' he said. 'The whole damn situation. All of it.'

He dropped his arms and turned, making for the door. 'Time to eat,' he said over his shoulder.

Throughout dinner with Lenoir, the brother-officer who had conducted Foraker on the last stage of the journey from Paris, and myself, Foraker talked cheerfully and continuously, analysing the French judicial system, remarking upon certain weaknesses in the character and intelligence of the 'unfortunate' *juge d'instruction*.

Towards the end of dinner, Lenoir mentioned the arrest of Mr Robinson, of which Foraker had not heard.

'He is accused of using his contacts in the textile business to relay significant information about supplies of uniforms to the "agents of a foreign power",' Lenoir said. 'But, of course, if he had not been connected with you nothing would have happened.'

Foraker looked sadly at the backs of his hands. 'Poor fellow,' he said.

Lenoir shrugged.

'You see,' said Foraker, 'he has been connected with me all my life.'

'If you had stayed in prison,' Lenoir said, 'you would no doubt have been confronted with him before the judge.'

'Yes,' Foraker said, and brooded silently for a moment. 'Under happier circumstances,' he said gravely, 'I should have been glad to meet him again. There were several things I should like to have said to him.'

In a darkness lit by half-clouded stars we walked to the testing-field, which lay beyond a gentle slope of ridge behind the inn garden. In the obscurity I could make out the shapes of a number of hutments and sheds of a familiar French military type. In one of them, where a shaded light was burning, we were greeted by one of Lenoir's mechanics. From a bench in a dark corner of the hut, another figure rose and quietly came across to us – Dr Rosen, looking as though he had been kept waiting for the beginning of a committee meeting, but now it had begun, and the thing to do was to move briskly.

The mechanic led the way across the parched grass to another shed, or small hangar, where the assembled machine was under cover. Foraker said abruptly, 'I don't want a lot of people breathing down the back of my neck while I look this over. It'll take a couple of hours. I want the fellows that worked on it, and you, Rosie, of course.'

The rest of us wandered back to the shed we had started from.

There was nothing to do, nothing to be said.

For long periods together it seemed that time had simply stopped, and the night was going on for ever. And at other moments one had the impression that time was racing wildly towards dawn.

At the moment when Foraker and Rosen actually did return together, I was dozing. I came awake to see Lenoir clasping Foraker round the body with his arms, and kissing him on one cheek and the other. And then, as I had seen him do long ago in the hotel at Lyons, Foraker caught Lenoir under the shoulders and tossed him in the air, caught him, and held him there, shaking him and laughing.

He dropped him suddenly and strode across to me, still laughing. He took both of my hands in his and shook them.

'It's on, Ned,' he said. 'They've not made a very good job of it. I've done better work in the last three hours than they did in days, poor fellows. But it's good enough for a try.'

For an hour, again, nothing to do, nothing to be said. Foraker lay flat on his back on a bench and appeared to be sleeping. Lenoir and his brother officer walked up and down in silence. Rosen sat on a chair with his expression of a biblical prophet waiting in utter patience for God to make the next move.

A moment had to come, and it came. The stars, still quite bright when we went across to help trundle the machine out of the hangar, were going out by the time it had at last been got on to a little launching ramp which – as could now be seen in the very faint first light – had been erected almost in the centre of the level field.

At the last moment, tears sparkled suddenly in Lenoir's eyes. He embraced Foraker again, and then, standing back from him and holding him solemnly by the hand, said, 'It is a decisive blow for France that you are about to strike.'

'Listen,' Foraker said, in the tone of a man who has plenty of time to finish a discussion on the station platform before the train goes, 'I don't give a damn about France. I'm doing this because . . .'

The other officer, who had understood only the words about France, interrupted to call out in a low, choked voice, '*Vive la France.*'

Foraker looked at him with a smile at once kindly and derisive.

'All right,' he said. '*Vive la France*. But what's really going to *vive*, my friend,' he added with a curiously coarse chuckle, 'is Foraker's Principle. *Vive le Principe* Foraker,' he said in his frightful accent.

He turned his back on us and stood looking at the machine. Then he jerked his head over his shoulder, and looked at us as though surprised and annoyed to see us still standing there. 'All right,' he said. 'Everyone out of my way now. Get moving.'

His tone was such that we actually started to run back to the hangar. I looked back once, and Foraker was still standing looking at the machine. At the safe distance of the hangar we stopped, and now he was on the landing ramp, and starting to climb into the single driving seat.

Out there on the field he looked quite small. I remember that what struck me then and held my attention was the thought that I had never seen Foraker look little before.

We waited for a further period of minutes; perhaps, in fact, a quarter of an hour. During this period we could see nothing of Foraker, now inside the machine.

I had supposed that at the moment when he put the launching gear and what he called the 'boost' into action, there would be something earsplitting and searing in the way of noise and flame. And then, as I was thinking, 'Something has gone wrong, he can't start,' it happened, and there was just a rather loud series of explosions, and some bright flashes, and then the thing for which nothing had prepared me – the fact of the machine's unimagined speed of getaway, so that I saw it clearly only for a second or two as it rushed upwards and forwards, and then there was nothing to be seen but a white trail streaking into the clear morning sky.

When I became aware of other things besides that fast-fading trail in the sky, I saw that Rosen was writing carefully in a notebook. It was reassuring, giving an air of matter of factness to the whole enterprise. I saw his pencil jerk away suddenly from the paper, and in the same instant I heard the noise, too – a perfectly clear distant thud in the sky.

Lenoir and the other officer, who had stared after the machine all the time, said they saw flame in the sky, too.

Rosen stared into the sky, and for a moment his face was actually distorted, nearly unrecognizable as a violent spasm of emotion twisted it. Then he looked at his watch, made a further note in his book, and put the book back in his pocket.

Lenoir, in a strange voice, said, 'We have to calculate where...' He and the other officers walked stiffly back into the shed and started to make calculations, estimating where the debris could have fallen. With Rosen and the mechanics, I stood and watched them, without interest, but because it was the only thing to do.

They reached some conclusion, and now they could go back to the inn and take the car and drive out to that part of the country and make inquiries.

'There will be the question,' Lenoir said, just before they drove off, 'of Delia and the boy. Of telling them what has happened. You,' he said to me, 'can't very well go back to Paris, in all the circumstances.'

Rosen nodded. 'I will undertake it,' he said.

He was silent as the two of us went into the inn and sat waiting for hot coffee in the dim dining-room.

When he spoke it was as though he had been thinking aloud all the time and was simply passing to a new point in his deliberations.

'With the boy,' he said, 'it will not be so difficult. I shall explain to him, quite simply, the essential matters involved.'

I stared at him. 'You will?' I said, my mind bewildered by recollections of all that had been involved.

'Certainly,' Rosen said. 'I shall explain to him the essential nature and objective of the entire experiment carried out by Grant Foraker. He will be glad to realize that the experiment was, essentially, successful. Obviously, there was a defect somewhere – almost certainly due to extraneous circumstances – probably the haste with which the final preparations were made. The successful demonstration of the Principle is not affected. My notes on the launching,' he tapped the book in his pocket, 'the angle, speed, and stability of the machine after the take-off, its rate of travel, sufficiently indicate that. Naturally, the accident and consequent failure to complete the schedule, will mean that, for the time being, there will be no further interest in this line of development.

'In fifty years or so, however,' he said firmly, 'as I shall explain to Jephthah, I consider that the Principle will be generally accepted – perhaps even in less time if there are wars on a large scale. The essential thing is, as I shall be able to tell him, that it does work.'

The soldierly innkeeper came with coffee, and I sat in silence with a clear vision before my eyes of how Jephthah would clutch his subscription to the new *Encyclopaedia*, his father's last present, and listen while Rosen explained these things.

More about Penguins

Penguinews, which appears every month, contains details of all the new books issued by Penguins as they are published. From time to time it is supplemented by *Penguins in Print*, which is a complete list of all books published by Penguins which are in print. (There are well over three thousand of these.)

A specimen copy of *Penguinews* will be sent to you free on request, and you can become a subscriber for the price of the postage. For a year's issues (including the complete lists) please send 30p if you live in the United Kingdom, or 60p if you live elsewhere. Just write to Dept EP, Penguin Books Ltd, Harmondsworth, Middlesex, enclosing a cheque or postal order, and your name will be added to the mailing list.

Some other books published by Penguins are described on the following pages.

Note: *Penguinews* and *Penguins in Print* are not available in the U.S.A. or Canada

Beat the Devil

Claud Cockburn

Waiting in a seedy port for the broken-down S.S. *Nyanga* to ship them to Africa: an international group of wheeler-dealers on the brink of a million-pound deal; a diamond king and a clean-cut English couple en route for a coffee plantation.

But nothing goes right. And nobody's quite what they seem. Except the English who blow the gang's plans sky high. One with obtuse honesty; the other, with lies 'truer than true'.

The book of the famous John Huston film, Claud Cockburn's *Beat the Devil* is rich entertainment: deft, gripping, and mined with surprises.

I, Claud . . .

Claud Cockburn

In the 20s and early 30s Claud Cockburn was correspondent in Berlin, New York and Washington for *The Times*. But the windows of appeasement were frosting over and he quit *The Times* to found *The Week*, a mimeographed newsletter which the Nazi Government described as 'the source of all anti-Nazi lies in Britain'. He fought in Spain and became diplomatic correspondent and Foreign Editor of the *Daily Worker*. During the post-war decades he wrote regularly for *Punch* (in its Muggeridge hey-day), the *Sunday Telegraph* and today, with undiminished brilliance, he contributes a regular column to *Private Eye*.

I Claude . . . is not only Claud Cockburn's personal distillation of his *In Time of Trouble*, *Crossing the Line* and *View from the West*. It contains an extensive – some may think slightly startling – amount of new material.